STRANGERS & PILGRIMS

CROSSWAY BOOKS BY STEPHEN BLY

THE STUART BRANNON WESTERN SERIES
Hard Winter at Broken Arrow Crossing
False Claims at the Little Stephen Mine
Last Hanging at Paradise Meadow
Standoff at Sunrise Creek
Final Justice at Adobe Wells
Son of an Arizona Legend

THE NATHAN T. RIGGINS
WESTERN ADVENTURE SERIES (AGES 9-14)
The Dog Who Would Not Smile
Coyote True
You Can Always Trust a Spotted Horse
The Last Stubborn Buffalo in Nevada
Never Dance with a Bobcat
Hawks Don't Say Good-bye

THE CODE OF THE WEST
It's Your Misfortune & None of My Own
One Went to Denver & the Other Went Wrong
Where the Deer & the Antelope Play
Stay Away from That City . . . They Call It Cheyenne
My Foot's in the Stirrup . . . My Pony Won't Stand
I'm Off to Montana for to Throw the Hoolihan

THE AUSTIN-STONER FILES
The Lost Manuscript of Martin Taylor Harrison
The Final Chapter of Chance McCall ✦ *The Kill Fee of Cindy LaCoste*

LEWIS & CLARK SQUAD ADVENTURE SERIES (AGES 9-14)
Intrigue at the Rafter B Ranch ✦ *The Secret of the Old Rifle*
Treachery at the River Canyon ✦ *Revenge on Eagle Island*
Danger at Deception Pass ✦ *Hazards of the Half-Court Press*

HEROINES OF THE GOLDEN WEST
Sweet Carolina ✦ *The Marquesa* ✦ *Miss Fontenot*

OLD CALIFORNIA
Red Dove of Monterey ✦ *The Last Swan in Sacramento*
Proud Quail of the San Joaquin

THE SKINNERS OF GOLDFIELD
Fool's Gold ✦ *Hidden Treasure* ✦ *Picture Rock*

THE BELLES OF LORDSBURG
The Senator's Other Daughter ✦ *The General's Notorious Widow*
The Outlaw's Twin Sister

RETTA BARRE'S OREGON TRAIL
The Lost Wagon Train ✦ *The Buffalo's Last Stand* ✦ *The Plain Prarie Princess*

HOMESTEAD SERIES
BOOK ONE

STRANGERS
&PILGRIMS

STEPHEN BLY

CROSSWAY BOOKS

A DIVISION OF
GOOD NEWS PUBLISHERS
WHEATON, ILLINOIS

Strangers and Pilgrims

Copyright © 2002 by Stephen Bly

Published by Crossway Books
    A division of Good News Publishers
    1300 Crescent Street
    Wheaton, Illinois 60187

Cover design: Cindy Kiple

Cover illustration: Dan Brown

First printing, 2002

Printed in the United States of America

Library of Congress Cataloging-in-Publication Data
Bly, Stephen A., 1944–
 Strangers and pilgrims / Stephen Bly.
  p. cm. — (Homestead series ; Bk. 1)
 ISBN 1-58134-426-0 (TPB : alk. paper)
 1. Rural families—Fiction. 2. Nebraska—Fiction. I. Title.
PS3552.L93 S78 2002
813'.54—dc21   2002003728
                 CIP

15	14	13	12	11	10	09	08	07	06	05	04	03	02
15	14	13	12	11	10	9	8	7	6	5	4	3	2	1

For
Ebeth

These all died in faith,

not having received the promises,

but having seen them afar off,

and were persuaded of them,

and embraced them,

and confessed that they were

strangers and pilgrims

on the earth.

HEBREWS 11:13 (KJV)

One

"Someone ought to shoot them two before an old lady or a kid gets run over!" The voice cracked, whiskey-rough, yet sober. "Ol' Wallace's team done broke loose again!"

At the clamorous conversation auburn-haired Jolie Bowers wheeled around from the grocery store shelf she had been scanning. She looked at the two men huddled by the multiple-paned window staring out into the hot dirt street of Scottsbluff.

"It won't be the new deputy. Did you see that? They plum near bolted over the top of him." The second man's voice twanged of dry Nebraska dust.

Jolie pulled an embroidered linen handkerchief from the cuff of her long green cotton dress and patted the perspiration on her forehead and neck. She glanced down at the grime-streaked hankie and then neatly folded it into a clean square before shoving it back up her sleeve. She strolled toward the men, a basket on one arm and a small black leather purse on the other. "Excuse me, I can't seem to find any canned prunes." Her voice sounded tight and high but confident. "Do either of you gentlemen know which shelf has prunes?"

The shorter man rubbed his extremely pointed, unshaven chin, pulled out a wad of tobacco, and bit off a chew. "Did you see that, Raymond? I ain't never seen nothin' like that."

He handed the taller man the tobacco. Raymond scratched

under his arm and then gnawed off a bite and pitched it back. "Luke, that little lady ain't a dog's hair over five feet tall."

Jolie waited for either man to notice her.

"I bet she don't weigh as much as a sack of field-dug potatoes in October," Luke observed.

Raymond scratched his chin. "How in blazes did she corral that team?"

Jolie cleared her throat and stepped between the men. Her high-top, lace-up boot pounded the gritty wooden floor. "Excuse me, I need a little help."

"She captured Stranger's head, Raymond, and hauled him to the left and then wrenched his ear. My first wife did that to me one time."

Raymond puckered his lips and eyed the floor. Jolie pointed to a brass spittoon at the base of the window. He nodded at her and spat. "That one ain't Stranger. That's Pilgrim. The other horse is Stranger. But you're right. I ain't never seen any gal who could do that."

"I ain't never seen a man that could do that." Luke pressed his face against the glass and ogled the street. "She's got her hair in a braid. Maybe she's younger than I thought."

"Excuse me." Jolie raised her voice. "Can either of you help me?"

"Who do you reckon she is?" Raymond asked.

Jolie pointed Luke toward the spittoon. The force of the stream of tobacco spun the heavy brass container. "I ain't never seen her before. She looks Texas-tough to me," Luke replied. "Them west Texas women are like tornadoes."

Jolie pinched her lips together. "I have a question," she blurted out.

Raymond kneaded his unshaved chin. Crumbs plummeted to his shirt. "I say she's a widow lady, Luke. I predict she arrived here with a passel of kids and is tryin' her luck with a homestead. Them home-steaders are a different breed of folk."

"The town is filled with new people wantin' to homestead. Course, she ain't bad-lookin' if you like 'em small." Luke launched another tobacco bomb toward the spittoon.

Jolie flipped her auburn bangs off her forehead. "If I could interrupt you for just a moment!"

"You prospectin' for a grass widow, Luke?" Raymond snorted. "I thought you pledged off women. Or was that whiskey you pledged off?"

Luke plunged his hand past the unbuttoned collar of his shirt and scratched his shoulder. "I ain't swearin' off of nothin', but a woman who can stop a runaway team has got to have other talents. That's all I'm sayin'."

The heel of Jolie's black boot cracked the toe of the manure-crusted brown boot.

"Oooouch!" Luke hopped around holding his boot.

"Please excuse me," Jolie said. "I wonder if either of you gentlemen could steer me to the canned prunes? I can't seem to locate them."

"What do you take us for, missy? Store clerks?" the one with thinning gray hair huffed.

"No, to be honest, you look like unemployed drovers who got to town days ago and still haven't had a bath. You've consumed most of your leisure downing whiskey. Rye whiskey, by the fragrance of it. You have a square jaw and commanding chin. I certainly don't know why you don't shave off that woebegone beard."

"She's got you pegged, Luke!" Raymond hooted.

Jolie spun around. "And you, sir, must have spent this morning feeding hogs. No smell as rank as a hog pen. I've always thought it strange that most people who work around hogs lose offense at the aroma and have no idea what they pack with them."

Raymond looped his thumbs in his leather suspenders. "You're a nosy thing for a little girl."

"I'm seventeen, not at all nosy, and only wish to find some help in this store. Neither of you favor store clerks, that is true. But you both look like men who have purchased canned prunes."

Luke laughed. "Young lady, I don't reckon I ever run across a gal as pointed as you. Sort of use them words like nails on a stick, don't ya?"

"First, a small woman who stops runaway teams, and now a seventeen-year-old who cuffs us with conversation. This is quite a day, Luke McKay."

Luke motioned back down the aisle. "You'll discover them canned prunes on the floor right by that barrel of rolled oats."

Jolie nodded her narrow chin. "Thank you. Now would you happen to know where a clerk is?"

"Jeremiah should be in the backroom. I think Saddler went to the bank over in Gering," Luke reported.

"Say," asked Raymond, looping his thumbs in his bullet belt, "are you new to Scottsbluff? Don't think I've seen you before."

Jolie switched the basket of goods to her other arm. "We just arrived this morning."

"We?" He gaped at the groceries in her basket. "Are you married?"

"No, but I'll take that as a compliment." She wheeled back to the aisle of groceries and then paused and looked back. "By the way, the 'little woman with the braid' that you've scrutinized is Melissa Pritchett Bowers. She is not a widow. Her husband is over at the barbershop. He's the six-foot-two, broad-shouldered, handsome man with the mustache. And she's not from Texas, but originally from Michigan, then California, Nevada, New Mexico, Arizona, and Montana. She's four-foot-eleven and has weighed 109 pounds for the past ten years."

Luke attempted to brush a tobacco stain off his vest. "Are you her sister?"

Jolie squatted down next to the barrel of oats and fingered the airtight cans. "No, I'm her daughter, the oldest of four children."

Raymond wiped tobacco off his chin with the back of his hand. "I'll be a starvin' polecat."

Jolie bit her tongue as she placed two dusty cans in her basket and then scurried down the aisle. *Lord, thank You for helping me not to reply to that! We are indeed strangers and pilgrims here, and I would rather not offend them any more on my first day in town.*

With a full basket she advanced to a clerkless counter near the front door. While most everything in the store was covered with yellow-brown dust, the unpainted counters and shelves still reeked of newly sawed pine. Jolie stacked her items in front of her with precision.

I would think someone would be here to solicit my money. I do not like to tarry. Lord, I've never enjoyed lingering. I have much to do. I need to organize my kitchen, stock the cupboards, and hang out the linens. There will be beds to make, windows to wash, rooms to sweep.

She tapped her fingers on the counter.

Besides, Lord, You and I both know that something dreadful always happens when I have to wait.

Jolie spied a small brass bell. She seized it and chimed five times. After a moment a tall, muscular young man meandered out of the backroom. His white shirt was sweat-stained under the arms and around the collar. His black tie hung loose. His cotton apron was wrinkled but clean.

"Excuse me, miss. I didn't know you were here. I thought Raymond and Luke were makin' the noise. Hope you ain't been waitin' long."

"No, not really." Jolie leaned over and stared behind the counter. "I just finished. I will also need twenty pounds of cracked wheat flour and five pounds of sugar. Do you have coarse brown sugar?"

When she stood up straight, he was staring at her. He jerked back and blushed. "Yes, ma'am."

He eyed her as he scooped the sugar. When he was finished, he tallied up the bill. "You new in town?" he muttered as he wrote down several figures.

Jolie glanced around. Luke and Raymond still gawked out the front window. A woman with a toddler on her hip strolled into the store and ambled to the other side. "Yes, we just got here."

The clerk added up the column on the bill of sale and glanced up. "You just passin' through, or do you plan on stayin'?"

Jolie studied his yellow drooping mustache and then analyzed what he had written down. "Are you talking about passing through life in general or just Nebraska?"

"I was thinkin' only of Nebraska," he sputtered.

Jolie crossed her arms. "My family and I have just relocated here. We purchased a homestead."

"Lots of new folks movin' in ever since the railroad opened up." He shoved the pencil behind his ear. "The whole town is full of strangers. I've been here six months, and I'm an old-timer. That will be $8.22, miss. By the way, my name is Jeremiah Cain." He tugged his tie even looser.

"Mr. Cain, it's nice to meet you." She reached out for his hand. He had a strong, eager grip. Jolie tugged her hand free. "However, your tally is wrong." She pointed at the statement. "This adds up to $7.97, not $8.22. Twenty-five cents might be a minor oversight to you, but to me it represents needed cash." She looked up into his stunned blue eyes. "By the way, my name is Jolie Lorita Bowers."

"Miss Bowers, my pleasure." He forced a smile. She noticed a gap between his front teeth. "But my tally stands as it is. I don't make mistakes addin'," he snapped. Then his tense eyes softened. "And I might add, that's a very purdy straw hat."

Jolie nodded her head and caught a whiff of spice tonic. "Thank you very much, Mr. Cain. I bought this hat in Cantrell City from Carolina Parke. She's quite well-known up in Montana. Have you ever been to Cantrell?" She glanced around, half-expecting to see her father standing there. *Mr. Cain, your shaving tonic is commendable even if your math is not.* "But you did err. I would ask you to redo your tally."

He slumped over the counter and traced each number with his pencil. The back of his neck reddened through the shaggy blond hair. "No, ma'am, I ain't ever been up to Montana, but I did meet Tap Andrews one time in Denver. He lives up there near Cantrell, I hear." He shoved the paper toward her. "And your bill is still $8.22. I don't make addin' mistakes. Never have. If you don't have the funds, there ain't no reason to be embarrassed. It happens all the time. I can set one of them cans of blackberries back."

Jolie ran her fingertips along the smooth grain of the pine countertop. "I believe Mr. Andrews is a friend of Stuart Brannon's. My mother bought two horses from Mr. Brannon. She claims they were the fastest horses in Arizona, but my mother always buys fast horses. Does your mother buy fast horses?"

His chin dropped. He glanced around the room. "Eh, no . . . my mama and daddy are dead."

"I'm sorry to hear that." She brushed her auburn bangs back off her eyes and then pointed to the airtight cans. "And those are not blackberries, Mr. Cain. They are prunes. I believe you overcharged me. You're the one who should be embarrassed. I have sufficient funds to buy blackberries, had I so chosen."

His face froze. Only his lips moved in monotone dialog as his eyes searched the counter. "No foolin'? Stuart Brannon is still alive? I figured all the famous ones were gone except Andrews." He let out his breath, and his shoulders slumped. "I reckon you're right, Miss Jolie. Those are prunes. I surmised them was blackberries. I didn't think a young lady like yourself would be buyin' prunes." He cleared his throat. "Let me refigure this. Looks like you owe me $7.97."

Jolie pulled a small deer-hide coin purse from her bag and snapped the coins down on the crowded wooden counter. "I never make miscalculations in addition either, Mr. Cain."

He hesitated, coins in his hand, and then placed them in a cash box behind the counter. "I've got a produce crate in the back." He slipped the pencil into the vest pocket of his apron and flipped his blond hair behind his ear. "Would you like these goods boxed?"

Jolie dropped the coin purse back into her bag and slipped it on her arm. "Yes, thank you very much."

He seemed to be inspecting the stitches on her green dress. "I can carry them out to your rig if you like."

Jolie gathered her arms across her chest. Her nostrils flared. Her jaws tightened. "Do I look incapable of carrying my own groceries?"

Jeremiah glanced around the room as if to see if any others heard her reply. "Eh, no, ma'am . . . eh, Miss Jolie. That's what Mr. Saddler tells us to say to all ladies."

The crash of boot heels on the wooden floor prompted both to turn around. A girl with waist-length brown hair, brown eyes, and a long yellow calico dress scampered down the aisle. She bent over and rested her hands on her knees as she caught her breath. "Jolie, Jolie, guess what?" she blurted out.

Jolie rested her hand on the girl's shoulder. "What happened?"

"Mama bought us a team and a wagon. She got 'em cheap, too. Real cheap." The girl's animated face was perfectly smooth.

"That's nice." Jolie stood up straight, a foot taller than the girl. "Mr. Cain, this is my sister Estelle."

Estelle rubbed her upturned nose with the palm of her hand. "Everyone calls me Essie, and I'm twelve years old, but I'm rather mature for my age."

The clerk grinned and scooted around next to Essie.

Jolie studied him. *Jeremiah Cain, you have a very handsome smile when you aren't trying to impress someone.*

He reached out his hand. "Hello, Miss Essie. I'm Jeremiah Cain, and I'm twenty years old, but I don't think age should interfere with friendship, do you?"

Essie shook her head. "No. Jolie's my best friend in the whole world, and she's almost eighteen."

He smiled at Jolie. "As I said, I realize you're quite capable of packin' all them items, but I wonder if you would accept my assistance anyway? It's a store courtesy, with no judgment intended."

"You express yourself very well, Mr. Cain." Jolie allowed her hands to swing to her side. "Yes, I'll accept your offer. Thank you very much."

Jeremiah winked at Essie and then vanished into the backroom.

"He's very polite, Jolie."

"I believe you're right." Jolie put her arm around Essie's shoulder as they strolled to the front door.

"And he's quite strong."

"And you didn't mention the disarming wink," Jolie chided.

"That wink was for me," Essie insisted.

"I think he's a little old for you."

"I like older men."

"Since when?"

"Daddy is my favorite, but Lawson and Gibs are older too."

"Yes," Jolie laughed, "I see your point."

Outside the door the sun blazed brightly on the wide dirt street. Dust swirled in the air.

"You'll never guess what the new horses' names are," Essie squealed.

"The wheel horse is called Stranger, and the off horse is Pilgrim."

Essie licked something from the back of her hand. "How did you know that?"

Jolie looked back into the room and spotted Raymond and Luke at the front window. She lowered her voice. "I overheard those men talking."

When they reached the boardwalk, a tiny dust devil swirled in their faces. Essie clapped her hands over her eyes. "This is like Wyoming."

Jolie blinked her eyes open when the dust passed. "Where's Mama and that new team?"

When Essie pointed east, Jolie noticed that her yellow dress had a black stain on the sleeve. "She drove it down to the station. Lawson's helping her load up our goods."

Jolie studied her sister's dress. *I'll put lye paste on that stain, soak it in cold water all afternoon, and then brush it good before it dries—perhaps while the custard is baking and before I cook the biscuits. Lord, I really hope we have a large stove because you know how I like to cook.*

A large insect rattled across the boardwalk and perched in front of them.

"Is that a locust?" Essie asked.

"It looks like a grasshopper."

"Can I catch him?"

"No, you may not," Jolie replied. "What do you want with it anyway?"

"Gibs likes using them for bait when he fishes. He said he wanted to go fishing as soon as we get to our homestead. Doesn't that sound wonderful, Jolie? *Our* homestead."

"Anything would be better than living in the city. Helena was too hectic and noisy. It was hard to get organized. I do like to be organized, you know."

Essie stared at her sister.

"What? What is it?"

"Everyone in the state of Montana knows how organized you are."

"Nonsense." Jolie frowned. "Besides, we're in Nebraska now. They will all have to learn also." She looked across the street. "Where's Daddy?"

"He's still at the barbershop, I reckon. You know how he likes to look neat." She pulled her long hair around and covered her face with it like a veil.

"Yes, and I know how he likes to talk and argue."

"He's very good at arguing."

"Yes, he is," Jolie replied.

"Miss Bowers, where would you like these goods?"

Essie grinned. "We'd like them in our wagon, please."

"Eh, and how about you, Miss Jolie—where would you like these?"

"Deposit them on that bench, please. It looks like we have to wait a little. Mother drove the team to the depot. She'll be back by. Thank you very much."

He positioned the groceries on the pine bench. "Did your mama really purchase ol' man Wallace's team?"

"Yes, but I haven't seen them yet." Jolie tried to study the clerk's soft blue eyes. "Is that a problem?"

"They're just very, eh, spirited." Jeremiah wiped his hands on his apron. "Nobody can handle them much, especially ol' man

Wallace. I heard he acquired them on a bet. He must've been the one who lost."

"Our mama doesn't buy any horses that aren't spirited," Essie declared.

Jeremiah towered between the sisters and watched as two cowboys trotted down the street. "Your mama has bought other horses?"

"Mama is always buying and trading horses," Essie said.

"Have you ever seen them two drovers before?" Jeremiah asked.

"There's no one in this town I've seen before, excluding my own family," Jolie replied.

"I think I've seen 'em down in Colorado." He rubbed his thick, drooping mustache. "Anyway, as I was sayin', around here men buy most of the horses."

"I wonder why that is?" Jolie challenged.

His face flushed as he stroked the sweat off his forehead. Two ox-driven freight wagons rolled in front of them. "Say, where's your homestead? Is it on this side of the river or over on the south?"

Jolie bit her lip to keep from grinning. *You're changing the subject in defeat, Mr. Jeremiah Cain.* "We're not too sure. We haven't been out there yet. It's east of here a few miles, I understand."

"It's in sight of Chimney Rock," Essie called out.

"There're a lot of places where you can see Chimney Rock. You can see it from the top of Fleister's Hardware Store."

Jolie gazed down the dirt street. Several dusty men rode toward them. "We haven't seen it yet. It's supposed to be near the river."

"There are bench homesteads and riverside homesteads. How close is it to the Avery place?" he asked.

"It *is* the Avery place," Jolie declared. "Do you know where that is?"

"You bought the Avery place?"

"We bought it from Mr. Avery sight unseen," Jolie responded.

"I can't believe you bought the Avery place!" he gasped.

Three men on horseback tipped their hats to her. She nodded their way. "Jeremiah, is there something wrong with the Avery place?"

"I reckon ever' place has its advantages and disadvantages," he mumbled.

Essie curtsied to the three men on horseback. "What does that mean?"

"Some say them places are too close to the river, but that's all in the eye of the beholder, I surmise."

"We wanted a river-view estate," Essie blurted out.

"That's exactly what you got. Good luck, Miss Jolie and Miss Essie. I better get back to work. If you need any help, you just holler at me."

"I will," Essie said.

"Thank you, Mr. Cain." Jolie watched him disappear into the store. She turned as a woman in a blue-flowered dress drove up in a razor-wheel carriage pulled by a cream-colored mule. The mule stopped in front of the store and refused to take another step.

Jolie eased onto the bench next to the groceries and brushed down her green skirt. Essie plopped down on the other side.

"That was a very nice curtsey you made to three complete strangers," Jolie remarked.

"Thank you," Essie replied. "I wanted to be friendly."

"But we don't know them."

"We don't know anyone. You said so yourself."

"That's true."

"I think that funny-looking lady is having trouble with her mule." Essie pointed to the street.

"She just needs to whack him one on the rump. I believe she's too timid or kindhearted to do it," Jolie observed.

"Look, there's Gibs!" Essie jumped up and waved. "Hi, Gibs, we're over here!"

Fourteen-year-old Gibson Hunter Bowers loped across the street toward his sisters, carrying a Winchester 1890 pump rifle across his shoulder.

The woman in the carriage said something to him. He stepped up, slapped the cream-colored mule on the rump, and the animal trotted down the street. Gibs trooped on over to them.

"What did that lady ask you?" Jolie questioned.

"She asked me if I knew what was the matter with her mule."

"What did you tell her?"

"I said he was lazy, and I cuffed him on the rump."

"Yes, I saw that. Where have you been?" Jolie asked.

"Down at the sheriff's office." Gibson's brown eyes widened. "Did you know they have a $1,000 reward posted for Mysterious Dave Mather? He was seen across the river in Gering in April. Why, he could be livin' around here anywhere. I could surely use that reward."

Jolie stared at her brother. *Lord, I've never seen anyone who wanted to be a lawman more than Gibs. I truly hope he lives to see the day.* "Right now, Mama and Lawson could use your help loading our baggage down at the depot."

Gibs shoved his felt flop hat back. "Did she buy us a team and rig?"

"Yes," Essie called out, "and they are named Stranger and Pilgrim. They are both quite naughty horses but very big and strong. Mama said she could plow with them and teach them some manners."

"Are they broke to ride?" Gibs asked.

"I seriously doubt if they're even broke to drive," Jolie responded. "But you know Mama and her horses."

Gibs scratched his brown head and looped both arms over the rifle stretched across his shoulders. "I reckon I'll mosey down and help 'em load."

"That's a good idea," Jolie replied.

Gibs flashed a dimpled grin. "Sheriff Riley promised that as soon as I turn twenty, he'll employ me as a deputy."

Jolie studied the brown eyes of her youngest brother. "That's just six years away."

"Five years, seven months, and fourteen days," Gibson reported. "I told him we bought the claim on the Avery place." He put the rifle to his shoulder and followed a grasshopper with the gun sights as it vaulted along the sidewalk.

"Is there anything unusual about it?" Jolie asked.

"The grasshopper?"

"No, our homestead."

"The sheriff said it was a river-view place and that we wouldn't need special irrigation."

Jolie was relieved when Gibs let the hammer down with his thumb and pulled his finger off the trigger. "Mother will irrigate her flowers and her garden, I'm sure."

"She cried when she left her garden in Helena," Gibs mumbled. "Mama don't cry very much . . . for a girl."

"Jolie, can I go to the depot with Gibs?" Essie asked.

"Yes, tell Mama I stayed here with the groceries."

"Have either of you seen Daddy?" Gibs asked.

Jolie nodded her head up the street. "He's still at the barbershop, I think."

"Are you goin' to be all right by yourself, sis?" Gibs asked.

Jolie studied the men and women who meandered along the street. "Yes, thank you, Gibson Hunter Bowers. I always feel safer with you around, but I'll be fine. This seems like a nice town."

He kicked the grasshopper out into the middle of the street with the toe of his boot. "Ever'thin' is new here. New railroad. New people. New town. I think it'll be nice to have a new start, don't you?" Gibs added.

Jolie nodded. "It sounds very peaceful to homestead in Nebraska. I think we'll all like it. I look forward to a quiet country life, just the six of us settling down on our own place."

She leaned back on the bench as her brother and sister walked on down the wooden sidewalk. She rested her hands in her lap. *We'll stop by the butcher's on the way out of town and pick up a roast. Mr. Avery said there was a nice-sized stove. We'll have roast and beets and, if I have time, raisin-walnut pie. I won't have time to make bread, but I could . . .*

"Excuse me, miss."

Jolie was startled to see that two men had ridden their horses over to the sidewalk in front of her. She looked past their unshaven faces and studied their eyes. "Yes?"

The one with thick, black hair tipped his brown felt hat. Hair sprayed out in all directions. "We're sort of new in this town, and Chug wanted to know if—"

"It wasn't my idea!" the man blurted out and then dropped his chin into his soiled bandanna.

She looked at Chug. His shirt was stained with dried blood.

The other man nodded. "Ma'am, I'm Leppy Verdue. Don't believe ever'thin' you've heard about me."

"I've never heard of you."

The other man guffawed.

"This old boy is Charles Quintin LaPage, but most folks call him Chug. He's a little shy."

"I can see that." She stared into Leppy's blue eyes. "What exactly was the question?"

"We just rode into town and was thinkin' of restin' up a day or two before we ride down to Cheyenne. And ol' Chug said—"

"It wasn't me!" the other man interrupted.

"Mr. Verdue, get to the point. And please don't ask me if all the girls in Scottsbluff are as 'purdy' as me."

Chug looked up.

Leppy's mouth dropped open. He glanced over at his partner. "They're all purdy, and wise to us, Chug. I reckon we should ride on."

Jolie noticed two deep dimples in the unshaven face when he smiled. "That combination sort of scares you, does it?"

"Yes, ma'am. Throw in virtuous, and we become plumb terrified," Leppy hooted.

Jolie laughed out loud. "Oh, my, honest drifters."

"We ain't exactly penniless drifters," Leppy boasted. "We do have money."

"As soon as we get the rest that's due us," Chug mumbled.

"Yes, I can see you're drovers."

"How do you reckon that?" Leppy asked.

"Bashful Charles Quintin LaPage has blood on his shirt. That either means he's clumsy and cut himself, that you're gunfighters, or that you've been on a spring gather and have been cutting and branding calves."

A voice boomed out behind her, "Miss Jolie, are these two pesterin' you?"

Jeremiah Cain loomed beside her, his arms folded. He filled the doorway.

"No, Jeremiah, we were merely visiting."

"What business is it of yours?" Leppy growled.

Cain dropped his hands to his side and stepped toward the drover. "I'm makin' it my business right now."

Jolie folded her arms across her chest. "I would appreciate it if you men would just calm down and . . ."

"You're actin' mighty brave for a man wearin' an apron," Leppy snarled.

Cain threw his shoulders back and squared his jaw. "And your arrogance comes from hidin' behind a gun. I heard all about you, Leppy Verdue. I come up from Colorado, too."

Jolie's neck tensed. She gripped her hands tight. "Now, listen, this has gone far enough. I think it's time for all three of you to go about your business."

Leppy's right hand rested on the walnut grip of his holstered Colt .45. "You think I can't take you on with my fists?"

Jeremiah stepped out to the middle of the boardwalk. "I think you're afraid to get off your horse."

Jolie stood up. "I've really had enough of this. Now stop it!"

Leppy rode his horse up on the wooden sidewalk. "Mister, you have no idea what you're talkin' about."

"And you're still on the horse, Verdue!" Jeremiah snarled.

Jolie grabbed the horse's nose and pushed him back off the sidewalk. "I expect better behavior from all of you!"

"Chug, hold my reins," Leppy ordered. "I reckon we'll only stay in Scottsbluff long enough to pound some reason into this grocery store clerk."

Jeremiah Cain yanked off his apron and tossed it back into the store. "I'm glad your partner is here. He can throw you over the saddle and haul your sorry bones out of town."

Jolie stamped her feet. "I'm serious. I demand that you stop this right now."

"Kind of a strange town where the girls are smarter than a whip, and the boys are dirt dumb." Leppy climbed down off his brown horse and handed the reins to Chug, slumped in his saddle, his hand on the grip of his revolver.

"Get rid of the gun, too," Jeremiah demanded. "I ain't fist-fightin' someone who's goin' to shoot me in the back."

"Mr. Cain, I believe you have a store to run. Would you kindly return to your chores," Jolie fumed.

"I'm afraid I cain't do that, Miss Jolie."

Leppy unbuckled his holster and looped it over his saddle horn.

"How do I know you ain't carryin' a sneak gun?" Jeremiah challenged.

"How do I know *you* ain't?" Leppy growled.

"I don't need no gun to whip you."

"You have two to whip, store clerk," Chug informed him. "You came out here insultin' us both."

"This is ridiculous!" Jolie shouted. "I want you to stop it immediately."

"The clerk's right about one thing, Miss Jolie. It's too late to back down. Unless, of course, he wants to turn tail and run."

The grocery store hangers-on appeared in the doorway.

"Raymond, you and Luke have to make them stop this," she pleaded.

Leppy threw a punch that missed Jeremiah by a foot. The return punch was wide as well.

Luke chomped on a wad of tobacco. "Miss, it ain't right to jump into a fight when we don't know why they're fightin'."

Several men paused on the boardwalk to watch.

"They're fightin' over her," Chug announced from the saddle.

"They most certainly are not," she huffed. "They're fighting because they're bullheaded, thoughtless, foolish men who think somehow this will impress me."

Leppy's blow landed with a thud in Jeremiah's stomach. The clerk cracked his fist into the drover's jaw.

"Does that impress you, ma'am?" Raymond called out.

Luke spat a stream of tobacco out into the dirt street. "That was a purdy good blow right there, missy. Don't you reckon that hurt?"

She marched over to the two combatants. "I said, stop it right now!"

Jeremiah lunged at Leppy and brushed against Jolie. She tried to leap back out of the way, lost her footing, and crashed down on the bench next to the crate of groceries. Neither young man paid any attention to her.

Several rigs in the street stopped to watch the commotion.

Lord, I will not be a part of this. They will stop, and they'll stop right now! You and Sam Colt will just have to help me.

While the two men wrestled to the ground, Jolie stomped over to Leppy's horse and yanked his gun out of the holster. She cocked the hammer with both thumbs. The two men rolled to their feet.

She stepped between them and waved the gun back and forth. "I said, I want this stopped right now," Jolie shouted.

"What do you think you're doin'?" Leppy called out.

"I'm getting idiots off the street of Scottsbluff, Nebraska."

"Go sit over there on the bench," Jeremiah shouted.

She spun around and jammed the gun in the tall clerk's ribs. "Mr. Cain, get in that store right now."

"Are you sidin' with them?"

"I'm insulted that you would even say that. Now get in the store." This time the gun barrel dug deeper into his ribcage. He staggered back. He tried to say something, but Luke and Raymond dragged him inside the store.

Leppy retrieved his dirty hat. "You done chose the right side."

She could see blood on his lip. "I certainly did not choose sides. Now get on your horse."

"Why, you surely are a spunky gal." He grinned. "I like 'em spunky, don't I, Chug?"

She shoved the cocked revolver into his temple.

He stopped smiling.

"Not that spunky. Come on, Leppy, I think she means it," Chug called as he rode through the crowd leading the other drover's horse.

Leppy mounted the horse. "That's my revolver you got, miss."

Jolie pointed the gun to the sky, eased the hammer down one notch, flipped open the cartridge door, and spun the cylinder with her thumb until all the bullets dropped to the dirt. The gun still in her right hand, she spun it around and handed it up to him, grip first.

"I would appreciate it if you rode on down the street," she insisted.

"I suppose this means you don't want me to come callin'?" Leppy holstered the gun and stared down at the bullets in the street.

Her voice was loud, firm. "I would appreciate it if I never saw you again this side of heaven."

"What if you do see us in heaven?" Chug called out.

"Then it would be a wonderful demonstration of the mysteries of God's grace. Good day to both of you."

Leppy opened his mouth and pointed his finger, but Chug slapped the rump of Leppy's horse, and both men rode west. Most of the two dozen people standing or in wagons applauded.

Jolie glanced up to see two large draft horses dancing in front of a heavy wagon.

The woman at the reins was not applauding.

"Mama! How long have you been there?" Jolie called out.

"We saw them throw the first punch," Lawson told her as he loaded the grocery crate into the back of the wagon.

"I presume they were fighting over you," Mrs. Bowers said.

Jolie ambled over to the wagon. "I don't know why they do that, Mama."

Mrs. Bowers sighed. "I do."

"Can you teach me to empty the cylinder one-handed like that?" Gibs hollered from on top of a wooden box in the back of the wagon, his .22 across his lap. "I wanted to shoot 'em, but Mama said you had ever'thin' under control."

"Mother, I begged and pleaded for them to stop."

"I know Jeremiah Cain," Essie said, "but who were those other two?"

"Just drovers . . . cowboys, I suppose. They just rode into town."

"Lawson, help your sister into the wagon."

"She don't need no help."

"No, but you need to learn to be courteous."

Her sixteen-year-old brother held out his hand. Jolie climbed into the wagon, adjusted her hat, and sat down on the front seat. Lawson climbed up next to his brother.

"Did you get everything?" her mother asked.

"Except the meat. You said we'll get that on the way out of town."

"Yes, well, it's time to get it," Mrs. Bowers declared. "I suggest we leave town before you cause another riot in the streets."

"Mama, I didn't cause it. I was just sitting there."

"I know. Let's go find Daddy."

"Hang on, Jolie," Gibs called down.

She glanced at her brother. "Why?"

"'Cause Stranger and Pilgrim like to race."

"I don't have the 'want to' run out of them, but they'll make wonderful driving horses once I get them trained," Lissa Bowers said.

When she slapped the reins on the rump of the big horse, the team bolted forward at a gallop. Jolie grabbed her hat with her left hand and the iron rail of the wagon with her right.

"Oh, my," she called out.

"Isn't this fun?" Essie shouted.

They thundered down the street and reined up in front of a meat market. A fog of dust surrounded them.

"My, that really clears the street in front of us," Jolie gasped.

Lissa winked. "That's the part I like best. Jolie, do you need any help with the meat order?"

Jolie climbed down from the heavy wagon. "I can get it, Mother."

Mrs. Bowers kept a tight grip on the lead lines. "I'd better stay with the team."

Gibs held his .22 out in front of him. "Do you want me to go with Jolie in case she needs protectin'?"

"Ha!" Lawson scoffed. "Jolie Lorita can take care of herself. She done proved that."

Mrs. Bowers never took her eyes off the team. "It would be nice of one of you boys to go help Jolie carry the meat."

"I'll go," Lawson offered.

"Mama," Essie asked, "do you think the boys will ever fight over me?"

Lissa Bowers kept both hands white-knuckle-tight on the lead lines. "I'm sure they will."

"If they don't," Essie declared, "I'll punch them in the nose."

"Yes," Mrs. Bowers countered, "that should persuade them."

Lawson and Jolie entered the store and strolled over to a butcher's block in the middle of the room.

A man with a black bow tie and a bloody white apron dragged a hacksaw across the carcass that hung from the ceiling hook.

"Can I help you?" he called.

"We want to purchase some meat," Lawson said.

The man laid the saw down. "I sort of figured that."

Jolie pulled a small scrap of brown paper out of her purse. "We will need three pounds of cured bacon, a ten-pound roast, and six beef chops one inch thick. I would like fresh meat."

The man rubbed his sweaty forehead and left a small streak of blood. "All of our meat is fresh," he retorted.

Jolie studied the beef hanging in the middle of the room. "The carcass you are sawing is not fresh, as you are well aware. I'd like my meat from the one over there."

The big man folded his hairy arms. "Oh, you would?"

"Yes, please." Jolie straightened her straw hat. "And I'd like to see the bacon before you wrap it up."

He looked her up and down. "Yep, I kind of figured you would. Young man, you have a very demanding girlfriend. Or is she your wife?"

"Wife!" Lawson gasped. "Jolie's my sister!"

Jolie nodded after looking at the bacon. They waited for the man to cut and wrap the meat. He handed the packages to Lawson. "That will be $2.86."

"That seems a little high." Jolie pulled coins out of her purse. "How much were the chops?"

"Twenty cents apiece for a one-inch chop."

Jolie shook her head. "Those were not one inch."

"That's what you ordered. That's what you got. The meat was cut as per your instruction," he insisted.

"Open that package," Jolie demanded.

"What?"

"I want to make sure of my goods before I spend my money."

He unwrapped the brown paper. "There. Are you satisfied?"

"I most certainly am not!"

"That there is the freshest meat I have."

"That might be, but those chops are three-quarters of an inch thick, not one inch. I expect a price reduction."

Lawson stared at his boot tops.

"Miss, those are my one-inch chops."

"They are not one inch."

"Well, I ain't cuttin' you any more."

"Then I suggest you reduce the bill by one nickel per chop."

"I'll do no such thing."

"Then we'll have to take our business to an honest butcher."

"Not on this side of the river. I'm the only butcher for fifty miles in either direction."

"Do you have a ruler?"

"Why? Do you want to measure them steaks?"

"Yes, please."

"I told ya, those are approximately one-inch steaks."

Jolie counted out $2.56.

Lawson nudged her with his elbow. "You're thirty cents short, Jolie."

She stared straight at the butcher. "I believe that is approximately $2.86, is it not?"

The big man roared. "I reckon it is, miss. Say, would you like to come to work for me in the meat market?"

"No, thank you. I'll be quite busy." She folded her coin purse and dropped it back in her bag and then jotted down the sum on the brown envelope. "My family just bought the old Avery homestead east of town. We'll have to work hard to make it succeed."

"The Avery place? Well, I'll be."

"Why are you surprised?" Lawson asked.

"You like to fish, son?"

Lawson clutched the packages in both arms. "Yes, but my brother is the best fisherman."

"That's mighty good," the butcher boomed, "'cause the Avery place is—"

"Next to the North Platte River?" Lawson interrupted. "Yes, that's why we wanted to buy it. Mother has some ideas on how we can irrigate the farm."

"She does, does she?" The butcher walked with them to the door. "I should have known ol' Avery would sell it to a widow."

"Mother is not a widow. Why do people keep assuming that?" Jolie asked. "Our father is over getting a haircut."

"Well, good luck on the farmin'. And the offer still holds on the job. My name is B. E. Bengsten."

"And mine is J. L. Bowers," Jolie replied.

"Did you get us some beef?" Gibs called down as the two approached.

Lawson helped Jolie up on the wagon and crawled up behind. "Jolie jacked him down on his price, and he offered her a job."

Gibs plucked a grasshopper off Lawson's shoulder and dropped it in his own shirt pocket. "I ain't never heard of a lady butcher."

Jolie settled in next to her mother. "He tried to sell me three-quarter-inch chops as if they were one-inch ones."

Lissa Bowers grinned. "I'm afraid that was a fatal mistake for Mr. Butcher. No one can slip anything by Jolie Lorita Bowers. Hang on, everyone. Let's go find Daddy."

Mrs. Bowers circled the wagon on a gallop. All of the children grabbed their hats. A stagecoach and two freight wagons skidded to a stop and let them thunder by. In a fog of dust the team rumbled up to the barbershop and slid to a prancing stop.

"Can I go get Daddy?" Essie begged.

"I will not have my daughter go into a barbershop alone. It's not an appropriate place for a young girl," Mrs. Bowers insisted. "Lawson, go with Essie and retrieve your father."

Jolie pulled her straw hat down in front to block the sun and scooted to the middle of the wagon seat. "Mother, how do you like Nebraska so far?"

"I think I'll like it. Whatever it brings, this is home. We aren't moving again," Lissa Bowers announced. "I told your father this is my last move."

"Ever?"

"Yes. We wouldn't have left Helena except for Daddy's grain mill going broke. And we had to leave California when the bookstore burned down. Then we left Nevada after that fracas with the livery stable."

"I thought you left Nevada when Daddy got into an argument with the governor," Jolie pressed.

"Yes, that was part of it. Arizona was not kind to us either."

"Of course, I remember leaving New Mexico. Daddy had to go when he wouldn't take that bribe."

Lissa tightened her grip on the lead lines. "You remember that, do you?"

"It was right after Essie was born, and we packed up in the middle of the night." Jolie reached over and plucked a gray hair off her mother's dark blue blouse. "At least when we left Helena, we could take the train in the daylight."

Mrs. Bowers licked her lip. "Daddy is a good man, Jolie Lorita."

"I know, Mama."

"But we aren't moving again. We'll make it on the farm. I just know we will."

"I think you're right," Jolie agreed. "We're all looking forward to it. What do you think a sod house will be like?"

"A 'modest' sod house," Lissa corrected her.

Jolie brushed the wrinkles out of her skirt. "Will it be like our adobe house in Santa Fe?"

"I suppose, but it won't have a red tile roof."

Jolie tried to look through the barbershop window. "The butcher told us the fishing was good at the Avery place."

Lissa glanced back at her youngest son. "Gibson will be quite happy."

Essie and Lawson strolled out of the barbershop on each side of a tall, strong-shouldered man wearing a dark suit, vest, and tie. His hat was tilted a little to the left. His dark brown hair and thick mustache were neatly trimmed. His brown eyes danced.

"Doesn't Daddy look handsome?" Jolie whispered.

"The sight of him makes my heart race," Lissa admitted. "Even after almost twenty years."

Matthew Bowers surveyed the team of horses and wagon full of goods and ambled over to look up at his wife.

"Rice," he said. "The answer is rice."

Two

This is a fine-looking team, Mother," Matthew Bowers said.

"They're naughty horses, Daddy," Essie informed him.

"Their naughty days are nearly over," he laughed. "Lissa Bowers has a way of eradicating naughtiness out of man and beast."

"How 'bout girls?" Essie giggled as she squeezed in next to her father.

Matthew surrounded his youngest daughter with strong, gentle arms. "Why, darlin', didn't you know—girls don't have an ounce of naughtiness in them."

Jolie enjoyed the smell of spice tonic on her father's clean-shaven face. She studied his infectious grin. *Lord, I do believe Daddy is a very handsome man.*

"Hah!" Mrs. Bowers said. She tossed her long braid over her shoulder and retied her straw hat. "Hang on, everyone, because this could be a little testy for a while."

Jolie reclined against her father's shoulder. It was like leaning against a rock. "What did you mean by 'rice'?"

Matthew yanked his felt hat down to his ears. "The Young Farmers' Alliance believes it's the crop of the . . ."

Melissa Bowers slapped the lead lines on the rump of the horse, and the team bolted into a full gallop. Mr. Bowers clutched the railing with his right hand and Essie with his left.

Hooves pounded. Dirt flew. People and rigs scurried.

"My word, Lissa," he shouted, "perhaps you should drive more slowly through town."

"This is slow," she hollered back.

"I told you they're very naughty horses," Essie yelled.

People froze in place and stared at them as they thundered out of Scottsbluff. When the road narrowed, rigs pulled off and waited for them to roll by.

Jolie coughed, but she didn't dare loosen her grip on her father's arm or the back of the wagon seat. The constant noise of hooves and wheels kept them all silent until they reached Telegraph Road east of town.

Lord, sometimes people say we have a very peculiar family, but I don't think so. All of us know that Mama likes fast horses. There's nothing peculiar about that. She glanced at the back of the wagon. Lawson and Gibs gripped tight to the sideboard, laughing.

Jolie couldn't see another rig on the road. "Daddy, what did you mean when you came out of the barbershop and said 'rice'?"

Mr. Bowers leaned so close she could smell peppermint on his breath. "They say it's the crop of the future for the farms along the river in the North Platte Valley," he declared.

Jolie picked a short string off her father's suit coat sleeve. "How do you grow rice, Daddy?"

"I have no idea in the world," he hooted. "But I read an article in an Omaha paper while in the barbershop about a professor who's going to give a series of lectures at the university about the future of rice-growing along the Missouri River basin."

Jolie watched 160-acre homesteads appear and disappear beside the road. "I thought we were going to grow corn, melons, beans, and maybe wheat."

Mr. Bowers rubbed the dust out of his thick mustache. "Everyone will be growing them, darlin'. What we want is to grow somethin' no one else is growing."

Jolie turned back to her mother who held the lines taut on the bolting horses. "Daddy wants to grow rice, Mama," she called out.

"Yes, I heard," Lissa shouted.

"What do you think?" Jolie replied.

"I intend to plant corn, melons, and beans as soon as we get the ground plowed. And then some winter wheat. But Daddy is right. We do have to think about the future. I know nothing about rice."

"Neither does anyone else," Matthew said. "If it were closer, I'd take the train down to the university and listen to those lectures."

Essie leaned against her father's shoulder. "Daddy, I thought you knew everything!"

"You must have me mixed up with Jolie Lorita Bowers," he laughed.

"Daddy, two boys got in a fight over Jolie," Essie blurted out.

"Again?"

Jolie stiffened. "I had nothing to do with it! I told them to stop it."

"They weren't exactly boys," Mrs. Bowers added. "Both were quite handsome men, as I recall."

Matthew reached across and patted Jolie's knee. "My sweet, darlin' Jolie, at least the men in Nebraska have good taste even if they do lack decorum."

The team took the dip in the road at a full gallop. Jolie felt her stomach rise up and drop. Gibs and Lawson laughed and shouted. She caught her breath. "Daddy, I wish they would stop doing that. It doesn't impress me one bit."

He glanced over at Mrs. Bowers. "Maybe we ought to just leave big sis out at the homestead and never take her to town. That way she won't be so tormented."

Jolie brushed her wavy auburn hair back off her ear. "Oh, Daddy, I don't hate it that much."

The road veered north and up the slope of the rolling prairie. Wild sunflowers bloomed among the yucca and sage. The Nebraska sky reflected a sun-bleached blue. Hot dust fogged behind them. Lissa slowed the team as they approached the first homestead. Chickens scattered across the bare dirt yard. Two horses watched from a small rock corral behind the house.

"Look, Mama, they have a sod house," Gibs called out from the crates in the back of the wagon.

Jolie studied the dirt-colored structure set back off the road in a treeless spot. It was about fourteen feet wide and twenty feet long with small windows on each side of the front door and a stone chimney in the middle of one wall. A small basket hung by the front door. Multicolored petunias sprayed out over the edge. Lace curtains adorned the tiny windows.

"Their house looks very neat from the outside," Jolie observed.

"Yes, but it's small."

"Mr. Avery claims our sod house is quite roomy," Jolie reminded her.

Mrs. Bowers kept her eyes on the road ahead. "Mr. Avery wasn't married with four children."

"Are the boys really going to sleep in the barn?" Essie asked.

"Maybe, darlin', if we have to build onto the house." Mr. Bowers struggled to pull a gold watch from his pocket.

The south sloping prairie was broken up by occasional homesteads. About two miles east of town the horses settled down to a very fast trot.

"How much farther, Daddy?" Essie prodded.

He pulled a folded piece of paper from his vest pocket "Mr. Avery told me it was just five miles or so beyond Scottsbluff. He says this road will cross the railroad tracks and run on the south side of the tracks for a couple of miles, and then it will swing back north. Just as it crosses back to the north, there will be a modest dirt road leading to the river, and that road dead-ends right at his house."

"*Our* house, Daddy," Jolie corrected.

He patted her knee. "Yep, our house."

Essie's waist-length hair flagged back into her father's face. "I like Nebraska," she declared.

He ran his fingers through her hair and then grabbed the railing as they hit a pothole. "That's good, darlin'."

"That was a good one, Mama!" Gibs shouted from the back. "Lawson almost fell out of the wagon."

"I did not! I was just grabbin' my hat."

Jolie took out her handkerchief and wiped dust from her fore-head. "As soon as we get to our homestead, I think we should all hike around the boundary together. We can dedicate it to the Lord."

"That's a mighty good suggestion, darlin'," Mr. Bowers agreed. "How about you being in charge of the dedication ceremony."

"We should have lemonade," she replied. "Ceremonies always have lemonade."

"The first thing I need to do is turn these horses out into a stout corral. They will want to run back to town," Lissa shouted. "But I do like the idea of circling the place and praying over it."

"We can each carry four stones and place them on the four cor-ners," Jolie added. "Me and Essie can pray at one corner, the boys at the next, Mama at the third, and Daddy at the last."

"It's not exactly Sunday dinner," Mrs. Bowers laughed.

"Can we have cookies and lemonade?" Essie pressed.

"I haven't finished planning the menu yet," Jolie replied.

Essie clasped her father's neck. "Where are we going to church, Daddy?"

"Either Scottsbluff or Minatare. We'll have to see which is most convenient. I hear we are about halfway between the two. The Lord will lead us."

"Are you going to sing in church, Daddy?" Essie quizzed.

"Only if they ask me. Maybe Jolie and I can sing a duet some-time."

Jolie stared ahead. *Lord, I get too nervous to sing unless it's with Daddy. Mama says he's the best church tenor west of Chicago. Lead us to a church where he can sing, and I can be quiet.* "Look, Daddy, there's another sod house."

"It looks rather modest," Mrs. Bowers remarked.

A woman in a long black dress ran across the dirt yard followed by two yapping black and white dogs.

"She's waving at us," Essie hollered.

Lissa stood up, yanked back on the lines, and shouted, "Whoa!" so loudly that Jolie could feel the concussion of sound on her eardrums. The big, loaded wagon slid to a halt at the driveway to the sod house.

"You've got to help me," the woman cried out, her voice shrill, her eyes panicked. Dark hair that had been pinned behind her head now streamed down.

Matthew leaped off the wagon. "What happened, ma'am?"

"Alfonso's in back, and he's hurt. The head flew off the axe and cut his foot. I can't get the bleeding stopped. You have to help me." She tugged on Mr. Bowers's arm.

"I'll go with you," Jolie offered. "Is Alfonso your husband?"

"I'm a widow. He's my son, my only son. We're workin' to make this homestead pay, and now this! Why?" she cried out.

Lawson and Gibs jumped off the wagon. Mr. Bowers helped Jolie climb down.

"I need to stay with this team," Mrs. Bowers called. The big horses danced back and forth. "They're too hot to leave standing."

"Lawson, stay and help Mama," Mr. Bowers ordered. "Essie darlin', you wait with Mama, too."

"Why can't I go see?"

"It might be bloody," he replied.

"I ain't afraid of blood."

A stern glance at Essie ended the discussion.

Mr. Bowers, Jolie, and Gibs, still carrying his rifle, trooped behind the frightened woman.

Plows, empty barrels, dried stacks of sod, and a broken barrel with the word "Idaho" on it in faded white paint littered the yard. Behind the house, two chickens pecked at the bare, packed dirt. A hog slept in the shade of the outhouse. At the woman's holler, the two dogs retreated and crouched next to the hog.

A tall, young man sat in the dirt clutching his bloody right boot. The dirt was dark red all around his foot. "Who are you?" he cried out.

"They came to help," the woman replied.

Jolie marched up to him and stared at the foot.

"I don't want you staring at me," he cried out.

Jolie squatted down. "Then close your eyes. Gibs, roll his pant leg up to his knee. We need to wash this wound and see how bad it is. Mrs. . . . ."

"Mrs. DeMarco. Sheridan DeMarco. Folks call me Sherry. This is Alfonso."

Mr. Bowers knelt down in the dirt beside his daughter. "I'm Matthew Bowers. This is my son Gibs, the best shot in Montana, and my daughter Jolie. She's thirty."

"Thirty!" Mrs. DeMarco choked. "She looks so young."

"I'm only seventeen, almost eighteen. Daddy teases me."

Mr. Bowers pulled out a large folding knife and opened it up. Gibs propped his rifle against the woodpile.

Alfonso tried to crawl away. "Mama, what're they goin' to do?"

Mrs. DeMarco jammed her hand on his head. "Hold still."

He tried to shove Jolie away. "I don't want her to touch me when I look like this," he pleaded.

Jolie huffed, then shook her head. "On second thought, just jerk off the boot, Daddy."

Mr. Bowers paused. "Won't that hurt him?"

"Not for long. He's about to faint."

"I ain't the faintin' type."

Mr. Bowers grabbed the heel of the shredded boot and yanked it off.

Alfonso slumped unconscious to the ground.

"How did you know he was goin' to faint?" Sherry DeMarco asked.

"I could see it in his eyes." Jolie pressed her fingers hard against the bloodiest part of the wound.

Mrs. DeMarco sucked in big, deep breaths. "Did you ever work for a doctor?"

"No, she hasn't," Gibs reported as he bent low to inspect the wound, "but our grandfather was a doctor, and he showed Jolie how to treat some things. And Jolie's just been around quite a few boys who fainted."

"I think I'm goin' to be sick," Sherry DeMarco mumbled.

"You might need to walk it off," Mr. Bowers suggested.

"Gibs, make a tourniquet of your belt and tie it halfway between his knee and hip." Jolie searched around. "Mrs. DeMarco, you need to go into the house and put your head between your knees. When you feel better, bring out some clean water and towels to wash this wound."

"What else do you need?" Mrs. DeMarco asked.

Jolie peeled back the bloody sock. "Some rubbing alcohol, a needle, and some thread."

"What color thread?"

"It really doesn't matter." Jolie studied the gaping wound. "Dirt color might be good. Daddy, press your hand right here. Gibs, go get my handbag from the wagon. I know I have a needle and thread there. I'll go with Mrs. DeMarco and get what else I need."

Jolie scrambled back into the yard with a handful of towels and a white-enameled tin pitcher of water. When Gibs returned from the front of the house with Lawson, she heard the wagon roar down the road.

"Where's Mama going?" she asked.

"Those horses wouldn't stand any longer; so she's lettin' 'em run," Lawson replied.

"How's Mrs. DeMarco?" Mr. Bowers asked.

"She has her head in a bucket. I think she's going to vomit," Jolie reported.

"You goin' to sew him up now?" Gibs asked.

"As soon as I get the wound clean. Keep pressing there, Daddy. Lawson, rip this rag up into two-inch strips," Jolie ordered.

Mrs. DeMarco shuffled up to them, a sewing basket looped on her arm.

Gibs studied Alfonso's face. "What if he wakes up?"

Jolie washed red blood off the foot. "Then hit him over the head with the barrel of your Winchester."

Gibs grabbed the pump rifle. "You're joshin' me, ain't you, Jolie?"

"Yes. I'll hurry."

With the foot washed and now resting on a clean towel, Jolie glanced back at the sewing basket.

Sherry DeMarco handed her a needle with bright yellow thread. "It's the quickest thing I had," she said.

Jolie began to stitch the loose skin back to the foot with straight, evenly separated stitches. "Mrs. DeMarco, is there a doctor in Scottsbluff?"

Sherry DeMarco stared out across a field of corn about two inches high. "There's a doc on a homestead right down the road in Minatare. Dr. Fix."

"Dr. Fix?" Gibs hooted. "I like that. I went to a doctor in Montana whose name was Dr. Paine. I reckon you have to consider your name before choosing a profession. Now, me, I'm Gibson Hunter Bowers. With a name like that a fella has to be a lawman, don't you reckon?"

"Eh, I suppose," Mrs. DeMarco murmured. "Do you think I ought to send for Dr. Fix?"

"Either that or take Alfonso to see the doctor today. This is a serious wound, and he's lost a lot of blood. What I'm doing is temporary. The doctor can take care of things better, and he can do a more thorough job."

"She."

"You have a lady doctor?" Jolie asked.

"Dr. Georgia Arbuckle Fix."

"That's wonderful!" Jolie tied off the thread and handed the needle back to the woman. "Please take him to the doctor right away. Today." Jolie began to wrap the foot with the narrow strips of white cotton rag.

"I can bind up that wound now. You've done enough," Mrs.

DeMarco offered. "I don't know how you did that without getting a drop of blood on your dress."

"I like to be neat," she murmured. Matthew helped Jolie stand up. Gibs retrieved his belt tourniquet. Jolie held out her hands as her father poured water over them to wash off the blood. "Mrs. DeMarco, don't bind it too tight. My grandfather, who was a doctor in the war, says to give it room to swell. And don't raise his foot up in the air."

Mrs. DeMarco looked up from wrapping her son's foot. "You surely know a lot for a young lady."

"I read a lot. I never forget what I read."

"Never?"

"No, never." Jolie dried her hands on a towel.

"You ought to be a schoolteacher," Mrs. DeMarco suggested.

"Jolie teaches us sometimes," Gibs told her.

Sherry wiped her son's forehead with a rag. "Can I give him some smelling salts?"

"Certainly." Jolie looked around. "Gibs, go out and see if you can signal Mama to come back and pick us up. Mrs. DeMarco, would you like Lawson to hitch up your rig so you can take Alfonso to the doctor now?"

"I've hitched my own team for fifteen months . . . ever since my husband died. So I reckon I can do it, but thanks for offering."

"You will get him to the doctor today?"

"Yes, as soon as we both are able." Mrs. DeMarco cradled her son's head and waved the small bottle under his nose.

With sweat dripping off his forehead onto his already wet shirt, Alfonso DeMarco blinked his eyes open and tried to sit up. "Don't let her touch me. I don't need no girl's help."

Jolie folded the towel and placed it on the woodpile. "I'm sorry, Mrs. DeMarco. There's nothing more I can do for him."

"Who wrapped up my foot?" Alfonso asked.

"Your mama did, of course," Jolie replied.

He grabbed his mother's hand. "I'd feel better if she was gone."

Jolie picked up her bag. "Do you need help getting him inside?"

Alfonso struggled to sit up. "She don't need no help from you."

"I was going to suggest that my father help you."

"I reckon that's okay."

Matthew Bowers and Sheridan DeMarco helped Alfonso to his feet and half carried him around to the front door of the sod house. Jolie waited with Gibs and Lawson out near the road until her father emerged from the sod house. "Mrs. DeMarco wanted us to have these." He held up a cotton bag.

"What's in there?" Lawson asked.

"She called them cornmeal biscuits."

"Can I have one?" Gibs requested.

Mr. Bowers tossed him a yellow biscuit.

"It's hard as a rock," Gibs groaned. "I can't even bite it."

Mr. Bowers reached for it and dropped it back into the sack. "Mrs. DeMarco said you have to soak them first."

"What does that mean?" Jolie asked.

"I don't have any idea. I thought you'd know." He grinned.

"I'll have to read up on it. Perhaps you soak them in milk."

"She said her husband liked to soak them in whiskey."

"Yes, and he's dead," Jolie said.

Mr. Bowers stared back toward the river. "I believe this is good rice country. With the right canals and channels, this land could be flooded."

"Here comes Mama," Gibson hollered.

They were all lined up next to the road as Lissa pulled the horses to a stop.

"Did you settle them down, Mama?" Lawson called out.

"That rise to the north helped. I made them run uphill until they got tired. I just don't think these boys have been run good in years, and they are just lazy."

Essie pointed to the house. "Did what's his name die? Gibs told us he was hurt bad."

"No, but it's a serious wound. It was very bloody."

"Jolie sewed him up with yellow thread," Gibs reported.

Essie put her hands over her ears. "Ahhhhhh! I'm not listening."

Jolie settled in next to her mother. "I cleaned the wound and sewed him up, Mama, just like Grandpa taught me. But he needs a doctor." She spotted several drops of dried blood on her skirt. *So I wasn't as careful as I thought. Cold water will bring those out, but I need to soak it soon.*

Lissa reached over and brushed Jolie's auburn bangs. "Is there a doctor around?"

"They have a lady doctor," Jolie reported.

"I suppose she'll give you competition," Mrs. Bowers commented.

"I don't doctor anyone except in emergencies."

Lissa held the lead lines taut. Matthew and the boys climbed into the wagon.

Mr. Bowers plopped down, straightened his black tie, and slipped his arm around Essie. "Did you go down by the river? What's it like down there?"

"Mama said it's a mile wide and a foot deep," Essie replied.

"Wider in places," Lissa added. "But the shoreline is receding, and so the high water has passed." She glanced back at Lawson and Gibs. "You two hold on now."

"We could see Chimney Rock," Essie said. "It's just like the drawing in Jolie's book."

"I think it's time to go find that homestead," Lissa announced.

Matthew and the children grabbed onto the wagon.

The road paralleled the south side of the railroad tracks and then jogged north. Lissa yanked the team to a prancing stop.

Jolie stared at the paper in her hand. "According to Daddy's map, there is supposed to be a road going straight toward the river."

"Avery said it was an unassuming road," Matthew declared.

"What's an unassuming road, Daddy?" Essie asked.

"One that isn't used much, I reckon," he replied.

"Mama, I think that's a road over there." Lawson pointed south.

"That's a game track down to the river," Gibs insisted. "It ain't nothing but a deer and antelope trail."

Lawson stood on top of the crates. "No, there are parallel trails. Game goes single file to the river, not side by side. I say a wagon has been down there sometime."

"Is it an unassuming road, Daddy?" Essie asked.

"I reckon we'll find out, darlin'." Mr. Bowers motioned for Lawson to sit down. "I suppose it's our best guess. Avery said he hadn't been here since January 1."

Lissa turned the horses down the faint wagon ruts. Everyone except her clutched the wagon with both hands.

"I think Mama is tryin' to lighten the load," Matthew hollered.

"If this is our road," she yelled back, "we need to scrape it smooth. It's a little rough. But we're almost home."

After a teeth-jarring jolt, Mrs. Bowers turned the team out toward the prairie.

"What're you doin', Mama?" Essie asked.

"I need to make them pull down a little. They're still too energetic." She started to circle the wagon round and round in the sagebrush.

"Do you reckon this corner place is a homestead?" Jolie asked.

"I suppose so." Mr. Bowers held onto his hat. "But it doesn't look like anyone's on it."

"It ain't a bad-lookin' place," Lawson shouted.

Lissa cut the wagon in such a tight corner that they all slid to the outside edge of the wagon seat.

"You can't see the river or Chimney Rock from here," Essie declared. "You can from our homestead."

"Yes, and this one doesn't even have a house," Jolie added.

Lissa slowed the horses to a trot and reentered the unassuming trail south. "If he hasn't been here since January, our house will be musty, I suppose."

"Mama, don't worry, I'll clean it up," Jolie assured her.

"Li'l sis can help you," Mrs. Bowers said.

"Lawson and I will unload the wagon," Mr. Bowers put in.

"Can I go huntin', Daddy?" Gibs pressed. "I want to see what kind of game is on our place. Maybe I can shoot us some supper."

"No hunting until we settle in," Mrs. Bowers insisted.

The trail followed the contour of the gently sloping bottomland. The dirt was dry, the grasses thinly scattered. Pale green yucca and prickly pear cactus were dispersed as if thrown down from heaven in clumps.

"I can see a house and a fence . . . or corrals . . . and a barn . . . an unassuming barn!" Lawson yelped from the top of a crate.

Jolie stood and braced herself against her father's shoulder. "Where?"

"Look, there's Chimney Rock," Gibs shouted. "Just a little bit to the southwest."

Mr. Bowers hugged Essie. "Mr. Avery was right, darlin'. We'll be able to look across the river at Chimney Rock."

The wagon lurched over the ruts and swells. Jolie sat back down and clutched the wagon seat with both hands. *Lord, this is the place You have been leading us to for all these weeks. You said You would show us the place You have prepared for us, and I believe this is it. Father, help us to accept Your leading and be grateful for Your goodness.*

"This road goes right down into the river," Gibs hollered. "I can walk down there to fish. I'll have to dig for worms. All I have now is one dead grasshopper."

"Perhaps we're on the wrong road," Mr. Bowers announced. "I don't see Avery's sod house."

"It's right over there, Daddy." Lawson pointed.

"No, no, that's just a shed."

"Stop, Lissa darlin', there's a sign down in those weeds," Mr. Bowers requested. "Let me see what it says."

They rumbled to a halt.

"Gibs, retrieve that sign," Mr. Bowers ordered.

Gibs leaped down, still toting his .22 rifle. He lifted the sign up, turned it toward the others, and shouted the words: "Avery Place. For sale or trade. Cheap!"

"You mean, this is our homestead?" Essie groaned.

Jolie pointed to the structure. "That's our 'modest' sod house?"

"It don't even have a door!" Lawson called out.

Mr. Bowers stood up and surveyed the landscape. "Oh, I'm sure it's around here somewhere."

"The house ain't two hundred yards from the river," Gibs shouted. "That makes it easy to fish."

Jolie stood up beside her father. "I thought a homestead was half a mile square."

"It's 160 acres, but I don't think it has to be square," he replied.

"The big rock corral is busted down," Lawson said. "The little one is okay. There's a woodshed, but I don't know where they get wood. We haven't seen a tree in miles. There's another little building without an east wall and a sod privy. We got a sod privy!"

"I can't believe this!" Mr. Bowers climbed down off the wagon. He studied the hand-drawn map. "He said river view, not underwater."

Lissa Bowers parked the rig in front of the house. The children jumped down and sprinted toward the sod building.

"Mama," Lawton hollered, "the house is full of dirt."

"It will sweep," she replied.

Jolie stared in at the dark front room. "It will have to be shoveled. There's a foot of dirt in places on top of a wooden floor."

"And not only that, but someone's built a fire in the front room," Gibs observed.

Lissa held the team in place. "There's a fireplace, isn't there?"

"Yep," Gibs answered, "but someone built a fire right smack dab in the middle of the floor."

Matthew surveyed the front room and then brushed off his hands and turned toward the wagon. "Get back in the wagon, children. We're not staying."

"What do you mean, Daddy?" Jolie untied her straw hat and fanned herself.

He pulled off his hat and ran his fingers through his hair. "I will not put my family in a place like this."

"Where will we go?" Jolie asked. "We don't have much money left. I spent most of what you gave me for groceries."

He glanced back at the sod house. "We could camp out next to the wagon. We'd be better off than in that hovel."

Lissa tossed her hat into the back of the wagon and lifted up her braid to cool her neck. "Then why not camp out next to the wagon right here. I think we need to survey the possibilities. This is our homestead."

"It stinks in that house. The possibilities for what?" Essie probed.

"That this is where the Lord has led us," Lissa replied. "That is what we want to know more than anything. Wait here. Let me park Pilgrim and Stranger."

She snubbed the team to a rock wall of the corral and hiked back across the bare dirt yard. Jolie, Lawson, Gibs, and Essie sat on the front step. Matthew stood out front, his suit coat over his arm, his tie loosened.

"It has a nice river view," Lissa offered.

"It's flooded," Matthew replied.

She slipped her arm in his and gripped it tight. "I'm sure it's not this way all year."

"Avery deceived us."

"We all felt the Lord calling us here."

"The river will destroy half our crops every year," he said.

"I thought rice needed to be flooded. I want to stay."

His brown eyes perked up. "Lissa, you're a jewel."

"We can at least find out what we have."

"I'm goin' to start right now. I'll step it off and try to find the corner markers."

"It'll be a little muddy," she observed.

"I'll pull off my boots and roll up my pant legs. I don't think it's more than six inches deep." He hiked over to the wagon and laid his suit coat on the tailgate.

Essie stood up. "What's Daddy doing?"

"He's going to walk off the homestead," Jolie declared.

"Daddy, can I walk in the mud with you?" Essie begged.

He glanced at his wife.

"Go on, take her, but make sure your clothes don't get ruined," Lissa instructed. "Pull your shoes off and tuck your skirt in your bloomers, Essie Cinnia."

Jolie took off her hat and fanned herself. "Mama, the house isn't that bad—just two or three inches of silt over most of it. The fire never got to the wooden floor. I think the house just got flooded—that's all. The walls are sturdy, almost two feet thick. The rooms are large once you go into them."

"Can you and Gibs shovel it out?"

"We'll try."

"What do you want me to do?" Lawson asked.

"Come help me rebuild this corral. We need to turn out the horses. Stranger and Pilgrim need a place to stretch."

"That's what we are, Mama," Jolie mused. "Strangers and pilgrims."

"Someday they'll call us pioneers," Gibs remarked.

"Not unless we stick it out," Lissa reminded him.

Jolie stood in the doorway. "There isn't any furniture in the house, Mama."

"We'll make some things out of crates. Is there a stove?"

"No, but there's a rock fireplace, sort of."

"But you can't see daylight through the chimney. I done looked. I think someone has camped in here during a storm," Gibs declared.

Her sleeves rolled up to her elbows and braid draped down her back, a hatless Lissa Bowers and Lawson rebuilt the broken stone fence and turned the horses out in the corral. Then they shoveled silt out of the barn that turned out to have only three sides.

The sun had slumped to just above the distant western shadow of Scott's Bluff when Matthew and Essie waded back to the house.

Jolie met them in the yard. "Daddy, Gibs and I have the house cleaned down to the floor, but there's still fine silt that I can't sweep up."

Mr. Bowers stuck his head through the open doorway. "Darlin', it surely looks a whole lot better than it did."

"There's no use to sweep anymore until all the dust settles," she replied. "I read in *Prairie Homemaker* that you can soak some newspaper strips in diluted vinegar and sweep up with those."

He winked at Essie. "I reckon big sis will be writing the second edition of that book, don't you?"

"I could teach them a thing or two. The man who wrote it lives in Pittsburgh, Pennsylvania. Whoever heard of a prairie expert living there?"

"Perhaps you should write to him," Mr. Bowers suggested.

"You remember what happened last time I wrote a critical letter to an author."

"What?" Essie asked.

"The author sued Jolie." Her father scowled.

"But the judge threw out the case," Jolie declared. "It's too bad because I know I would have won." She waved toward the barn. "Mama says we'll make camp out by the wagon and cook over an open fire."

Essie tried to brush dried mud from between her fingers. "Jolie, how are you going to cook a roast on a campfire?"

"We'll slice it into strips and broil them on a skewer. The same with the potatoes. I don't think I'll be baking a prune pie though."

"Every adversity has value if one searches for it."

"What does that mean, Daddy?" Essie queried.

"It means he doesn't like my prune pie. But that's okay. I read that it's quite the rage in Baltimore," Jolie laughed.

Gibs sprinted up. "Guess what me and Mama found behind the shed?"

"The outhouse?" Mr. Bowers roared.

"No, the privy is next to the shed. It's made out of sod, too," Gibs reported.

Essie curled her lip. "Does it have a door?"

"Of course it does."

"Nothing else around here has a door," Essie grumbled.

"What did Mother find?" Matthew asked.

"The well," Gibs announced.

"Does it have clean water?" Jolie asked.

"Yes! And it has a screen sieve."

Jolie glanced down at her father's mud-covered feet. "Good, because Daddy and Essie need to wash up."

Jolie could not find wood suitable for skewers, so she sliced the meat up and fried a few pieces at a time in the big iron skillet over the campfire near the wagon. She boiled the beets, mashed the potatoes, and soaked the cornmeal biscuits in apple juice. Gibs and Lawson unloaded the wagon and stacked the goods in the dirt front yard, except for a few crates they scattered around the fire to use as chairs.

The sun slid down across the Wyoming line as they finished supper.

"These biscuits taste like apple pie," Gibs mumbled with his mouth full.

"The meat was tough," Essie complained.

"Jolie did the best she could," Mrs. Bowers explained. "It's difficult to cook thick meat tender in an iron skillet."

Jolie stabbed a piece of meat on her tin plate. "Essie's right. It is tough. I shall speak to that butcher next time we're in town."

"Gibs can go to the butcher shop with you next time," Lawson mumbled as he pulled a bite of meat out of his mouth.

"Daddy, I was wonderin' if we could trade this homestead for another one," Gibs remarked. "I like that one on the corner where we turned off Telegraph Road."

"I wonder that same thing myself. Perhaps I should go back to Gering tomorrow and check at the land office."

Lissa unbuttoned the high collar of her formerly white blouse and rubbed her neck. Her long braid now dangled down in front. "Do all of you remember gathering around the kitchen table in Helena and praying over this homestead deed?"

"Yep, we prayed over it ever' night for six whole weeks," Lawson said.

"And what conclusion did we come to?" his mother challenged.

"That the Lord wanted us to come to Nebraska and homestead this very ground," Jolie admitted.

"How many of us felt that way?"

"We all agreed, Mama," Gibs declared.

Lissa picked up a piece of meat with her fingers and popped it in her mouth. "So the Lord must have a purpose in this."

Jolie waved a fork. "And we can't leave until the Lord accomplishes His purpose."

Matthew Bowers stared down at his plate.

"Daddy," Jolie prodded, "are you all right?"

"Just a little melancholy, I reckon. Children, look over there at Melissa Pritchett Bowers. What do you see?"

"It's Mama!" Essie giggled.

He tilted his head to the side and sighed. "I see Judge Pritchett's oldest daughter, a lovely young lady living in a two-story white house on the eastern shore of Lake Michigan. A girl with a crown of flowers on her head and wearing a beautiful white dress and a veil that hid those wonderful brown eyes."

"That was your wedding day, Daddy," Jolie said. "We've seen the picture a hundred times."

"Children, I told that young lady that I didn't know what the future would bring, but I'd certainly try to take care of her in the way to which she was accustomed. So I dragged her to California, Nevada, New Mexico, and Montana . . ."

"You forgot Arizona," Jolie corrected him.

"And Arizona. And after twenty years of marriage, this is what I have to present to her." He waved his hand toward the doorless sod house.

Lissa Bowers walked over and stood behind him as he sat on a crate. She began rubbing his neck and shoulders. "The truth is, I fell in love with Mr. Matthew Allis Bowers because he was nothing like my father. Your daddy is willing to live life to the fullest. He takes a risk and tries things that scare timid souls."

"And fails," he mumbled.

"There are four wonderful examples of success sitting all around, Mr. Bowers."

He glanced at the children, one at a time.

"Taking risks is the second best thing he does."

"Lissa!" Matthew protested.

"What's the best thing that Daddy does, Mama?" Essie asked.

"His kisses, darlin'."

"Mother!" Jolie scolded.

"Darling, this man promised to love and adore me every day of my life. And for almost twenty years he has kept that promise every moment of every day. There are lots of ladies in big two-story, white, lake-view houses who can't say that. And I wouldn't trade places with a one of them. So I say let's stay right here until the Lord has accomplished His purpose."

"We have sixty acres underwater," he reminded her.

"That means we have a hundred that are dry."

"We've got a dirt house with two tiny rooms and no furniture."

She glanced at the quilts airing on the wagon. "I'm so tired I could fall asleep on a blanket on the dirt."

"We don't have a decent barn."

"But we have a good well," she countered.

"And a very nice sod outhouse," Essie contributed.

"I bet we don't have fifty cash dollars left," he said. "No telling how long that will have to last."

"But we have the strongest two horses in the panhandle of Nebraska," Mrs. Bowers said.

Mr. Bowers studied his children's faces. "Winters can get severe out here."

"They were severe in Montana, and we survived," Lawson declared.

"There isn't a tree for miles in either direction."

"There's firewood in the shed," Gibs responded.

"I understand there's cedar and scrub pine up on the rim south of Scottsbluff. We certainly have the rig to haul it down," Lissa added. "We'll all stay warm, I'm sure. Small houses are easier to heat."

"Besides, we have five nice buffalo robes," Jolie said.

"And there are six of us," Mr. Bowers reminded her.

"You and Mama have to share," Essie declared.

Lissa laughed. "Which proves my point about staying warm, doesn't it, Matthew Bowers?"

He covered his mouth and coughed. "Eh, yep, I reckon it does, Mama."

She waved her braid in her hand like a pointer. "Then we're going to stay?"

He pulled her around to sit on his knee. "If you put it that way, I reckon we will."

"How're we going to live in two rooms?" Lawson asked.

Gibs stabbed a piece of meat with his pocket knife. "Two *tiny* rooms."

Jolie took a stick and drew in the dirt. "Here's the way I've decided we should arrange the house. The front room is the biggest and has the stone fireplace. So that will be the kitchen, if we can get the chimney unstopped, and dining room, and where Mama and Daddy sleep."

"Who gets the backroom?" Essie asked.

She continued to sketch in the dirt. "I'll hang a blanket divider, and the boys will be on one side and the girls on the other." Jolie turned to her parents. "How does that sound?"

Mrs. Bowers slipped her arm around her husband's neck. "I think Jolie Lorita is getting our house organized, Daddy."

"What're we going to do tomorrow?" Lawson asked.

Mr. Bowers patted his wife's knee. "I'm going back to the courthouse to post papers on this place to make the transfer official."

Lissa slipped her fingers into her husband's hand and kept it on her knee. "Lawson and I will see if we can plow the dry land. It's late, but with a good fall, we can still bring in some crops."

"How're you goin' to plow if Daddy needs to drive the team back to town?" Jolie asked.

"And how is Daddy goin' to drive that team?" Gibs hooted.

Mr. Bowers stared at the campfire. "Yes, those are problems, but I hate for all of us to go back to town. Possession is nine-tenths of the law. I want someone here on the land."

"I'll stay, Daddy," Jolie offered. "I have a lot of work to do to get everything organized."

Gibs nodded toward his gun that rested against the wagon wheel. "And I can stay and protect Jolie."

"Why don't I just send Mama to file the papers?" Mr. Bowers suggested. "Maybe I can salvage enough lumber from the crates to make us some furniture."

"But don't you have to present yourself and sign in front of the land agent?" Jolie asked.

"I don't have to. An adult over twenty has to sign. Mama can do it."

"Then the homestead would be in her name," Lawson noted.

"What difference does that make?" With a dramatic sweep of the hand he pointed toward the river. "Just think, Melissa Pritchett Bowers, this can all be yours."

She kissed his cheek. "Thank you, Matthew, but are you sure you aren't trying to get out of having your name on the deed to the Avery place?"

"That thought did cross my mind," he laughed, then brushed a soft kiss across her lips.

"How long would a round trip to town take?"

"I think she could be back by one or two in the afternoon," he declared.

"We should both go," Lissa maintained.

He raised his dark brown eyebrows. "And leave the children?"

She got up and paced around the glowing fire. "I believe Jolie Lorita can take care of things quite nicely here."

He grabbed her arm and pulled her back to his knee. "You mean, just you and me go to town?"

She walked her fingers up his arm and over to his lips. "Do you have trouble being alone with me in a wagon?"

"Mother, you're embarrassing me," Jolie protested.

"What did she say?" Essie called out. "I didn't get that. Oh, rats. I never understand those in-your-windows."

"Innuendos," Jolie corrected.

Mr. Bowers winked at Jolie. "Would you like to go with us and chaperone?"

"No, she wouldn't, but I would," Essie insisted.

"No, you can't," Jolie objected. "I need you here. We have cleaning to do. We'll get the house all fixed up for Mama and Daddy. The boys can help us, too."

"I've never in my life seen a daughter so identical in spirit to her mama," Matthew said.

Lissa pulled her braid across her face like a mustache. "Nor one who looks so different."

"Mama, I think you're very pretty anyway," Essie said.

"Thank you, honey. I believe that's a compliment."

"What time will you go to town?" Jolie asked.

"Right after breakfast," Mr. Bowers replied. "Boys, I'll need you up early to make sure the corner posts are set. We'll use rock. I haven't seen a stick of wood over a foot long."

"I wonder why there aren't any trees around here?" Gibs asked. "Most rivers have trees along them."

"One of the men at the barbershop said he figured it was the constant crossing of the big buffalo herds that stomped the banks flat and made it impossible for trees to grow."

"But those buffalo herds have been gone for ten years," Lawson said.

"We'll plant some trees," Lissa announced.

"Shade trees?" Gibs asked.

"And windbreak trees."

Jolie glanced around at the barren yard. "It would be nice to have trees here."

Essie slapped her neck. "Oh!" she squealed.

"What was it?" Gibs called out.

"A mosquito!"

Jolie rubbed her own neck. "I'll dig around in the crates and find the citron salve."

"While you're looking, find our large silver tray," Mrs. Bowers requested. "I want to take it to town."

Matthew stood up and followed his wife around the campfire. "Lissa, you are not selling off that silver. That's a wedding present from your Aunt Cinnia."

She spun around and faced him. "Matthew Bowers, how many times in the last nineteen years have we used that tray?"

He rubbed his chin. "Once. The week after we got married."

"That was when my Aunt Cinnia came to visit. She died twelve years ago, just before Essie was born. I'm tired of packing it around."

"But it's the principle. What will we use for company when we build a big house with a formal dining room? Besides, we can't sell wedding presents."

"No, but we can trade them," she insisted.

Lawson squatted by the fire and piled on a couple more thin logs. "What do you mean, trade them?"

"If a couple received a wedding present that was a duplicate of something they already had, what would happen?" Lissa challenged.

"You'd trade it in for something you need, I reckon."

"We have other platters, and so I don't need that one. I'm trading the gift for something I really need."

"What's that, Mama?" Essie asked.

"A milk cow."

"A cow?" Gibson hooted. "What kind of wedding present is that?"

Mrs. Bowers began to pull her braid loose with her fingers. "A very tasty one if you like fresh milk, butter, and cheese. What about it, Matthew Bowers? Shall big sis look for that useless old silver platter?"

He turned his back to the campfire. "You deserve better than this."

"Do you hear me complaining?"

"Mama, you never complain about anything," Jolie said.

Lissa swatted the back of her hand. "I'm going to complain about these mosquitoes if we don't find the citron salve soon."

Essie scooted under the wagon on a quilt pallet next to her sister. "Jolie, it's too hot to sleep under the covers, but I'm afraid of mosquito bites."

Jolie held the quilt open for her sister. "Mama said she would try to bring home some mosquito netting, too."

"What do you think Mama and Daddy are talking about over there by the fire?" Essie whispered.

"About husband and wife stuff."

"Do you want to get married, Jolie?"

"Of course. Don't you?"

"No."

"You're only twelve. That will change someday."

"Did you think about what it would be like to be married when you were twelve?"

"I thought about it when I was seven," Jolie admitted.

"Really?"

"Oh, I didn't think about boys, but I thought about taking care of a house, cooking meals, sewing clothes, and about going to church on Sunday with my husband and my children and filling up a whole pew."

"You thought about that when you were seven?"

"We were in Santa Fe, and Daddy found us a little Methodist church on the east side of town, and it was tiny. We would go to church and sit in the second row on the south side of the sanctuary. Daddy would sit on the aisle because he would help take up the offering. And Mama would sit next to him, holding you in her arms.

Then we laid that little pink and yellow quilt of yours folded up like a pallet in the pew so Mama could lay you down if she needed to. I sat next to you, then Gibs—he was only three—and then Lawson. We filled up the whole pew."

Essie snuggled up next to her sister. "I never heard that story before."

"I guess that's when I got to wondering what it would be like to have my own family—my husband sitting next to me and my children on the other side of me," Jolie admitted.

"And a cute baby in your arms?"

"Yes. I suppose that sounds kind of silly for being only seven at the time."

"It sounds okay for you," Essie announced. "But I think I'll just live with Mama and Daddy a long, long time."

Jolie ran her hand through Essie's long hair. "Good night, sweet Estelle."

"Good night, Jolie. Welcome to our first night in Nebraska."

Jolie rolled over on her back and peeked out from under the wagon bed at the stars. *Lord, everything seems to be swirling in my mind. I can close my eyes, and it feels like I'm in Montana or even New Mexico. Sometimes I lose track of the days and weeks and places. I have a wonderful family, Lord. They always make me feel special. Now I want a place where I'm at ease, where people know who I am without my having to introduce myself. I want to feel settled. I want to watch the world pass by instead of being the one on the journey.*

She watched the silhouette of her mother resting her head on her father's shoulder.

Lord, I know this is killing Daddy. He always feels like he has failed Mama and us. And I don't know what to do about it. It's like he's never quite sure what it is You want him to do with his life. Lord, this homestead just has to work. I don't think he has the heart to fail again.

Mr. and Mrs. Bowers crawled under the wagon with the children. Soon Jolie could hear her mother's rhythmic breathing. Jolie stretched her arm above her head and ran it off the edge of the blanket. The packed dirt felt cool. She pulled her hand back and felt something on her finger.

I'm too sleepy to even swat mosquitoes. Maybe I should have used more salve.

She brushed off her hand. Something crawled up her arm.

"Get off me!" she hollered.

"It's on me!" Essie screamed.

Jolie heard Gibs pump a bullet into the chamber of his .22.

"What is it, darlin'?" her father called out.

"Get it off me!" Essie cried.

Lissa rolled over and lit a sulfur match. "It's just a grasshopper, baby." She grabbed it and tossed it out from under the wagon.

"It was on me," Essie whimpered, "and I didn't know what it was."

"The unknown is always the scariest, darlin'," Mr. Bowers said.

"I flipped it off me. I guess it landed on you. I'm sorry, Essie," Jolie said.

"Mama, can me and Jolie sleep up in the wagon bed?" Essie begged.

"Sure."

"Can I sleep in the wagon, too?" Gibs called out. "I'll protect the girls."

"That's nice of you. How about Lawson? Does he need to protect the girls, too?" Mr. Bowers laughed.

"He's asleep, of course."

It took several minutes for them to rearrange the quilts and change places. Jolie had just dozed off when Essie poked her in the ribs. "What is it now?"

"Jolie, how high do you think grasshoppers can jump?"

Three

"Do you think it's goin' to rain today, Jolie?" A wide yellow ribbon held Essie's waist-length brown hair behind her ears.

Jolie splashed water on her face, reached her hand out, and waited for her sister to hand her a towel. "I've read that the summer clouds over the prairie are often empty. According to the *Prairie Homemaker*, this should be a dry month. I think it will just rumble awhile and then blow over."

Essie handed her a towel and then yawned. "Is that the book Lawson gave you for Christmas?"

"Yes. I just love it."

"How do they know what the weather is going to be like in June?"

"They keep records over the years."

"But nobody lived out here until a few years ago."

"Essie, it's in the book—it must be right," Jolie insisted.

"Not everything in the book I'm writing is true. I make some of it up."

Jolie folded the towel and wiped her face again. "I still say it isn't going to rain."

"Jolie, do you like sleeping on the ground?"

The clean towel felt soothing on Jolie's smooth face. "No. Do you?"

"Nope. Daddy says tonight we'll sleep inside. I wish we had a mattress. We don't even have straw. He said we have to save what hay we have for Stranger and Pilgrim."

Jolie picked at her short auburn bangs with the long-tined comb. "We have those big buffalo robes. They'll be soft on the wood floor."

"What about winter, Jolie? Are we goin' to sleep on the floor all winter? We had beds in Montana."

Jolie scrunched up the towel and wiped the small window of the backroom. Sunlight streaked across the bare dirt yard. "Winter is a long time away."

Matthew Bowers stepped to the open doorway as he fastened the top button on his shirt. "I still can't believe that less than twenty-four hours after arriving in Nebraska, we're driving off and leaving you."

Jolie scooted over to him and straightened his tie. "Daddy, you're leaving us at home."

He stared around at the dark, dusty, empty room. "It doesn't feel like home."

"That's my job, Daddy. I'll try to make it feel like home. You'll see. It'll be quite snug."

He smiled. "Yep, I reckon you will, darlin'."

Lissa Bowers stood on the front step and pinned a brooch on the high collar of her white blouse.

"Mama, you look pretty!" Essie called out.

"Thank you, darlin'. It does feel good to put on nice clothes every once in a while." She stepped over to Jolie. "How does my hair look in the back?"

"You pinned it up nice, Mama. Let me fix a couple of strands."

"I've almost forgotten how to set my hair in combs. It makes me look a little more mature, but, my, how I miss my braid."

"Lissa Bowers, you've never been accused of being immature in your whole life." Mr. Bowers slipped his arm around his wife's tiny waist. "Unless it was your decision to marry me."

She held tightly to his arm. "My decision to marry you is the smartest thing I ever did in my life, and you know it."

Jolie watched her father shake his head and rub the corners of his eyes. He stared out across the partially flooded homestead. "Now it seems to me Judge Pritchett told you marrying me was an 'injudicious decision with potential long-term grievances that will more than negate any short-term benefits.'"

Mrs. Bowers began to laugh. "Ah, but my father never kissed those sweet lips of yours, Matthew Bowers." She stood on the toes of her lace-up black boots, closed her eyes, and puckered her lips.

"Mama, are you going to embarrass us again?" Jolie asked.

"You can embarrass me, Mama," Essie said. "'Cause I never know what you're talkin' about anyway. Not unless I ask Jolie, and she always says to wait until I'm older. I think when I'm older, she'll have to talk for two weeks solid just tellin' me all those things I'm not old enough to know now."

Mrs. Bowers opened one eye. "That sounds like a delightful plan. Are you going to kiss me, Mr. Bowers?" She closed her eye again and puckered.

He kissed her.

Firmly.

On the lips.

Lissa eased back down on her heels and grinned at her daughters. "Now, Estelle, go round up your brothers while I drive the team around."

Jolie stepped over by her father and picked a small yellow string off his coat sleeve. "Daddy, you just might be the most handsome man in Nebraska."

He hugged her. "Darlin', the Lord spoils a man rotten by givin' him daughters. Thank you for saying that, and I believe you because I assume you've been eyeing the Nebraska men."

"I have studied a few, but their behavior isn't much different from Montana men." She pointed to the door lying in the dirt yard. "Daddy, can we hang that door today?"

He brushed back his thick mustache. "It won't be dry yet."

Jolie walked her father out into the yard. "I know, but Lawson said that if we hung it, we could nail turn-latches in the corners to keep it from warping as it dries out."

Mr. Bowers glanced back at the open doorway. "Lawson said that? It's a great idea. We should hang it someplace where it has a chance of drying straight. There aren't any hinges."

Jolie laced her fingers into her father's callused hand. "Gibs said we could cut up his old boots for leather hinges."

He kissed her forehead. "I see someone has been makin' plans already."

Jolie wrinkled her nose. "Just a few. Is it okay?"

"Darlin', this is your place to fix up. We told you that. Me and Mama will be workin' night and day to get a crop in."

"And the water out," she added.

Lissa Bowers drove the wagon around to the front of the house. The children lined up next to her side of the wagon while their father climbed up on the other side. Lissa glanced down the line of four children. "Now we'll be back right after noon. You remember, Jolie's in charge while we're gone."

"You don't have to tell us that, Mama." When Lawson grinned, his large ears wiggled.

"No, I suppose not."

"Jolie's in charge even when you *are* here . . . most times," Gibs laughed and then covered his mouth with a dirty hand when Jolie scowled at him.

"Don't worry, Mama, we'll all take care of each other," Jolie assured her. "We always do."

Lawson leaned against the sideboard, his eyes level with the top edge. "I'm going to try to spade up a garden on the south side of the corral. There's plenty of manure over there already. I think the ground is ready to turn."

"I'm goin' to go huntin'," Gibs announced. "We'll have fresh meat for supper. Why, I might find an antelope or deer."

Mrs. Bowers pointed to the gun over his shoulder. "With that .22

perhaps you should limit your hunt to rabbits or prairie hens. You'd only torment a deer."

"If I got close enough, I bet I could bring him down," Gibs mumbled.

"If anyone in Nebraska could, it would be you, son," Mr. Bowers said.

Essie tugged at the tiny gold locket hanging from her neck. "I'm goin' to pick some wild sunflowers for our table—eh, if we had a table."

Mrs. Bowers shook her head. "My, you are a busy family. How did you all learn to be such good workers?"

Mr. Bowers laughed. "Lissa darlin', those kids have a 'tornado of work' for a mother. What do you expect?"

"I don't believe I've ever been called a 'tornado of work' before. I think you're exaggerating, Matthew Bowers."

"Tell your mama the truth, kids—is she a tornado?"

Jolie glanced down the line at the others and winked. Then in unison they all nodded their heads.

"Oh, my." Lissa laughed. "Then it must be true because, like their daddy, my children never lie. We'll be home as soon as we can."

Lissa Bowers slapped the lead lines on the team. The horses bolted to an instant gallop. Standing in the cloud of dust, Jolie watched her father clutch his hat and the iron handrail.

She thought she heard her mother laugh.

Jolie swept the two-room sod house with vinegar-soaked newspaper strips and had the boys tote in the heavier crates by midmorning. Then Lawson, with the sleeves of his white shirt rolled up to his elbows, spaded the dark black soil on the south side of the stone wall.

The backroom had a small four-pane window about two feet square on the south side of the house. The double row of sod was two feet thick and allowed a deep shelf for the windowsill. Essie bunched a bouquet of sunflowers, jammed them in an empty tin can, and set them in the window.

Jolie dug out a white pillow case embroidered with pansies. She tacked a string across the top sill of the window and pinned the pillowcase to the string with clothespins to make a curtain. Then she had Lawson come in and stretch a rope along the cedar rafters, dividing the backroom. She cut strips of canvas from a worn-out tarp and sewed them to Grandma Bowers's orange quilt, making a row of loops. Jolie slid the quilt onto the rope and tied the end to a rafter, making two tiny rooms.

"We get the room by the window," Essie announced.

Jolie stepped into the empty room. "Yes, we do."

"The quilt doesn't go clear to the wall."

"We'll call that the doorway," Jolie said.

Essie skipped through to the other side and back. "But we don't have a door. How can we keep people out?"

"We'll just have to become very hospitable." Jolie rearranged the sunflowers in the tin can.

Essie studied the hanging quilt. "And it doesn't hang to the floor." She got on her hands and knees and pressed her cheek to the floor. "If the boys get down here, they could spy on us."

Jolie rubbed her hands and was surprised that they felt callused. "Yes, but we could spy on them, too."

Essie stood up. "So no one will spy 'cause they know that if they spy on us, we could spy on them."

"That's the idea."

Essie paced the room. "Can I sleep by the quilt?"

Jolie put her arm on her sister's shoulder. "Certainly, but won't you be worried about the boys spying on you?"

Essie folded her arms and peered out at the yard. "Not as worried as having someone spy on me through the window."

"Sis, we live at the end of the road. No one wants to come down here and peek at us. And, besides, we'll close the curtain at night. One of the joys of this place is its privacy. If I went out to milk the cow in my bloomers, no one would care."

"We don't have a cow."

"I think Mama is going to buy one."

"Someone comes back here. They built a fire in our front room."

"They were probably lost and cold. Now help me scoot the crates in here."

"All of them?"

"No, not all. But we can make dressers and benches."

"Ohhhhhhhhhhh, noooooooooooooo!" Gibs shouted from the front room.

The girls rushed to the doorway just in time to see him pull his soot-covered head from the rock fireplace. "I got the chimney clean," he mumbled.

"Yes, we can see that. Did you use your head for a chimney brush?" Essie teased.

"I used a broom. I think a tumbleweed was in it with a bird's nest on top and soot on the bottom."

Jolie handed him a bar of lye soap. "You wash up. I'll clean this up."

"Can I go hunting when I'm clean?"

"Yes, but not more than a mile or two away."

"Maybe I ought to leave my face covered with soot. That way the deer won't see me coming."

"Gibson!"

"Yes, Mama." He grinned, showing straight white teeth in the middle of a darkened face.

Jolie cleaned up the soot, and she and Essie had just finished arranging things in the backroom when Lawson stepped to the open front doorway. "I'm goin' to get a drink. Do you want me to fetch you some water from the well?"

Jolie walked back around to the front room. "Toss out what's in that basin and bring us some fresh, please."

"You want to hand it to me, Jolie? My boots are kind of muddy. I don't want to track in on your floor."

Jolie ambled over and picked up the white-enameled tin basin and carried it to the open doorway. "Isn't it strange that yesterday this house was full of dirt, and now you're worried about getting it dirty?"

Lawson stared down at his muddy brown boots. "We surely got good dirt, Jolie. I bet we can grow any crop we want to. No clay or hardpan—just occasional river rocks, and they are easy to push out with a pry bar."

"What are you doing with the rocks?" she asked.

He nodded toward the barn. "Tossin' them up against the corral wall."

"Maybe we could tote them over to the house," Jolie suggested. "I'd like to make a border around the yard or something. Since we don't have a bush or tree, a rock outline might be nice. When I save enough money, I'll send for a mail-order rosebush."

"Wouldn't that be somethin', Jolie? Havin' our own rosebush." Lawson took the basin and tossed the water out into the yard. "You and little sis have surely slicked up the house nice. Yesterday I figured it was good for nothing but a lair for wild animals."

"It will stay cleaner once we hang this door."

Lawson grabbed the door and with great effort turned it over, wet side up. "You want me to help you with it now?"

"Maybe we should let it dry some more. We do need to move the rest of the crates and trunks inside."

"I'll help you after I get some water."

Essie grabbed Lawson's arm. "Did you see the flowers in our window? I arranged them myself. Well, Jolie fussed over them a little, of course."

Lawson hiked toward the side of the house. "I'll look right now."

"Let me show you." Essie skipped beside her brother. "I want to see how the curtain looks from the outside."

Jolie stood at the open doorway and watched Lawson and Essie admire the flowers and then move on out toward the well.

To the south, the lower acres still stood underwater. The wide, muddy river crept slowly to the east. Beyond the river, she saw more sloping valley land, then the rim of mountains. In the southeast, the tall spire of Chimney Rock almost touched the heavy gray clouds.

Lord, this could be a very pretty place. All it needs is a way to keep the water back, some trees planted around the house, some flowers in planter beds, a nice big barn, crops in straight rows, a little picket fence, and a gray cat stretched out on the front step. A swing. We need a swing and a clothesline and a wood-frame house. Oh, yes, a wood-frame white house with two stories and a great room with a piano. And a covered veranda with a big white chair and a glass of lemonade.

Jolie glanced at the corrals. She could no longer see Lawson or Essie.

I suppose a sip of clean, fresh water will do. Lord, do You look at a place and see what it could become? Do You look at people and see what they could become? Mother says I have a very active imagination. Do You have a good imagination? Today is always easier to bear if we have a tomorrow to look forward to.

She stepped around to the east side of the house.

And there's one other thing, Lord. We need a decent road to get into our place. How can we ever entertain company in that big two-story white house if no one can drive down here to it?

Jolie gazed up the trail that led toward the railroad track. Two men on horseback ambled slowly down the trail. "Someone's coming?" she mumbled. "They can't come yet; the house is a mess."

She scurried back toward the front of the house. *I don't want company. Not now. The yard is littered with crates. I'm a mess. I've been working in this dress for two days. I want them to turn around and go away.*

"Yo, the house!" a man's voice hollered. "Can we ride into the yard?"

She stepped around the corner. Even though it was cloudy, Jolie shaded her eyes.

"I suppose so. What is the nature of your visit?"

"My-o-my, sweet Kansas, we didn't expect to find a purdy girl back here."

The man on the black horse had a full beard and sunken eyes. His hat was set crooked, and his eyes creased into a scowl. "This ain't good, Maxwell—this ain't good."

The clean-shaven, blond-headed man stood in the stirrups and surveyed the yard. "Now, Shakey, that's where I disagree with you. It's my humble opinion that being in the presence of a fair, young lady is always a good situation . . . a very good situation." He plopped back down. When he pulled off his hat, shoulder-length hair tumbled out. "Excuse me for askin', ma'am, but we've been down this road before, and there's never been anyone livin' back here except a conniving ol' man named Avery, who would cheat his grandmother out of her baptismal certificate if he could."

Jolie felt the eyes of both men inspecting her. "We bought this homestead."

Shakey gazed at the flooded ground. His dark beard was flecked with red hair or red dust—Jolie couldn't determine which. "That's hogwash. It might sound good at the land office in town, but you can't homestead this. I've seen bayous with more dry land. What're you really up to back here?"

Maxwell held up his hand to silence his partner. "Now, Shakey, don't question the lady's word. When folks in Bayard asked our occupation, we said we was line inspectors for the telegraph company, and they had the decency not to press it. So we can do the same. Obviously, she ain't the homesteadin' type, but it ain't no business of ours why she's here." He jammed his hat back on his head. "You alone, ma'am?"

Jolie refused to glance back toward the well. "Now that would be absurd, wouldn't it? There is no way I would be out here alone." There was a rumble of thunder so distant it took her a moment to identify the sound.

The blond man studied the clouds. "Yes, ma'am, I reckon it would. My name's Maxwell Dix, and this scruffy one is Shakey Torrington."

"You may call me Jolie."

"That's a peach of a name," he replied. "Miss Jolie, since you're standin' out here by yourself, I reckon you're waitin' for someone."

"That's true." Jolie folded her arms and rocked back and forth on her heels. "I suppose they'll be roaring back fairly soon."

Maxwell stared up the trail. "They?"

"I'm waiting for more than one, as you'll find out when you hear their horses gallop up. I told you I'm not out here alone."

Shakey stood in the stirrups and surveyed the narrow trail that led back to the railroad tracks. "I don't see no one else."

Jolie rubbed her chin. It felt slightly gritty. "And you don't see anyone here at the house but me. That means you have no idea how many guns could be trained on you right now."

Shakey's hand went to his gun. "I could find out."

"Shakey," Maxwell cautioned, "that's something we don't need to know. We ain't plannin' on no trouble, and we aren't goin' to start any."

She arched her eyebrows. "I surmise you had something else planned when you rode down this trail."

"Yep, Miss Jolie, we was just passin' through lookin' for an old acquaintance."

"He ain't all that old," Shakey contradicted him.

Maxwell patted his gray horse's neck. "But we aren't in a hurry."

Shakey let fly a big wad of tobacco. "Yes, we are!"

The wad landed close to the abandoned door.

"Now, Shakey, we can sit with this lady and keep her company until her people return. Our intentions are honorable."

"Thank you, but I'm quite self-sufficient. I don't need any company," she insisted.

He pulled his hat off again and flashed a dimpled grin. "But it ain't right to leave a purdy girl alone in the wilderness. My mama brought me up better than that. We'll stay with you and protect you. Why, if I'd known Nebraska girls are so lovely, I would have thought about settlin' down myself."

"You're beginning to sound like Leppy Verdue," Jolie said.

Both men yanked their revolvers out of their holsters.

"You know Leppy?" Shakey growled.

Jolie bit her lip and took a step back. She could feel her heart race. "My, I didn't know a name could get such a reaction. I take it you have a disagreement with Leppy?"

Maxwell relaxed and shoved his gun back in his holster. His dimpled grin returned. "No, we just were a little set back when you mentioned his name. Actually we were lookin' for him. He's an ol' partner of ours in a business venture."

Jolie felt a drift of air cool her sweaty forehead. "You were in the cattle business with him?"

"Leppy told you?" Shakey pressed.

"Of course he told her," Maxwell laughed. "Look at her. Leppy always gets the purdiest girlfriends—you know that."

Shakey Torrington shoved his gun in his holster and wiped his full lips across his dusty white shirtsleeve. "You and Leppy is close, huh, Miss Jolie?"

"That ain't polite to ask a lady." Maxwell again tipped his hat. "Miss Jolie, your private business is none of ours. But if you don't mind, where did you last see Leppy, and when do you expect him back? We really need to find him. Trust me, we mean him no harm."

"He and Chug were in Scottsbluff when I—"

"Chug's dead," Shakey blurted out. "He was shot in a saloon two weeks ago in Magdalena, New Mexico."

Lord, I really don't want to be talking to these men. Now would be a good time for them to ride off. "This Chug is one Charles Quintin LaPage. He's very shy, very grimy, and very much alive."

"That's him, all right," Maxwell said. "I'll be. That's good news. It's a good thing we didn't take condolences to his sister. Do you reckon they're still in Scottsbluff?"

Jolie glanced around the yard, but she still couldn't spot Lawson, Gibs, or Essie. "No, there was an altercation. They left town in a hurry."

"They got in a fight, and someone chased them out of town?" Shakey pushed his hat back. "I ain't never met a man tough enough to do that to Leppy Verdue."

I didn't say a man chased him out of town. "I wouldn't say he was chased. But when his gun was empty, he decided he didn't want to stick around anymore."

"I reckon I underestimated Nebraska," Maxwell mumbled. "Where did he and Chug go?"

"They told me Cheyenne."

"Cheyenne?" Shakey pulled off his grimy red bandanna and wiped his neck. "What in tarnation are they doin' goin' to Cheyenne?"

The breeze accelerated. The clouds to the east thickened.

"Leppy always did like a challenge." Maxwell shrugged.

"He's crazy!" Shakey turned his chestnut horse toward the trail back out to the road. "I ain't goin' to Cheyenne. I reckon I made that mighty plain last time. That Colorado sheriff will have spies in Cheyenne."

"We got a delivery to make," Maxwell insisted.

"You make it. I ain't goin' to Cheyenne again until all of this blows over," Shakey declared.

Maxwell glanced down at her. "He's right, Miss Jolie. It would not be judicious for us to go to Cheyenne at the present time."

This sounds like a Stuart Brannon novel. "No wonder you're riding the high line."

Maxwell raised his sloping blond eyebrows. "You and Leppy being, eh . . . pals, I reckon you know all about it."

"I know you were hoping to meet Leppy here instead of in town. I wonder why you're afraid of Scottsbluff?"

"We'd probably jist get chased out of town for the same reason Leppy was." Shakey spat tobacco on the edge of the door that sprawled in the yard.

Maxwell might get chased out for the same reason, but you never would, Mr. Torrington. "If you aren't going to town nor to Cheyenne, you aren't going to find Leppy and Chug."

"I've been ponderin' that very fact. Ain't that the truth. Listen, Miss Jolie, I got a big favor to ask of you. We're headin' west into Wyoming and then up toward Montany. Can I leave a, eh, package with you for Leppy?"

"You cain't leave it with her," Shakey protested.

"Are you an honest lady, Miss Jolie?"

"Yes, I am."

"See there, Shakey. She's honest."

"You're a fool for purdy women, Maxwell."

"Yep, and I can think of many things a whole lot worse to be a fool over." Maxwell reached back in the saddlebag.

Jolie wrung her hands. "I don't know if I will ever see him again."

Maxwell rode the gray horse over to her. "Darlin', I know Leppy, and I can guarantee he'll come back to *you.*"

"Unless he's dead," Shakey added.

Maxwell turned in the saddle. "If he's dead, he won't be missin' his share, will he?"

"Nope. I don't reckon so."

Jolie stared at the thick brown envelope in his hand. "What're you asking me to do?"

Maxwell held the envelope down toward her. "Just keep this in a safe place, and when he shows, hand it to him. Tell him it's from Shakey and Maxwell. We'd be obliged, Miss Jolie. If he and Chug have already painted Scottsbluff, we need to get to Wyoming today."

Jolie hesitated. "You just want me to hold it until Leppy comes calling?"

"Yes, Miss Jolie. That's it."

She brushed her auburn hair back over her ear. "And if I promise to do that, you'll ride off right now for Wyoming?"

Maxwell showed deep dimples. "Yep."

"Then give me the envelope." She reached out her hand.

"I cain't figure how you can trust her," Shakey repeated.

"Leppy must trust her. That's good enough for me."

"Let's get out of here then. I never did feel safe in a place like this where there's only one way in and out," Shakey said.

"Perhaps now is a good time for you two to leave."

"Say," Maxwell drawled, "just how many guns do you figure are trained on us right now?"

Jolie glanced back toward the house. "You didn't call my bluff, and so you don't see my cards."

"Whoa! Maxwell, she done pinned you there. Say, do you have any sisters?" Shakey asked.

"Just one," Jolie replied.

"Is she as purdy as you?" Maxwell asked.

"She's as purdy as she can be."

Maxwell tipped his felt hat. "I hope to see you on down the trail."

Shakey rode up next to her as they headed out of the yard. "Miss Jolie, did you ever work at April's at Pingree Hill?"

She scowled.

"Them was the purdiest women in Colorado until the place burned down."

"Shakey don't see many women except in the dancehalls," Maxwell explained.

"Good-bye," she snapped.

"Come on, Shakey, let's ride."

"Somethin' don't seem right."

"Well, it seems right to me."

With a kick of their spurs, they galloped north.

Jolie strolled back into the house and meandered through the crates to the backroom. She knelt down by the buffalo robe next to the window and shoved the envelope out of sight. *Lord, I tried to do the right thing. I tried to protect myself, to be smart and not to lie. I tried to get rid of them in a hurry, without angering them. But now I feel guilty. I just don't know why. I agreed to hold this and give it to*

Leppy if he calls. I'll do just that. And I will not look at what's inside it. At least, I hope I won't.

"Jolie, come here and see what we found!" The voice was deep enough to be a man's voice. Almost.

She hurried out to the yard. Lawson and Essie stood with muddy bare feet and an eight-foot log between them.

"Lawson, where did you get that?"

"There's twenty-three of them down in the tall grass at the end of our place. Each one's exactly eight feet, and each has two sides squared off and two sides rounded."

"That's a very stout timber. What were you doin' down there? I thought you went for water."

"I just mentioned to Essie that I bet deer were hidin' down there in the long grass, and she said, 'Let's go look.'"

Essie stared down at her filthy legs. "But it was too muddy, and so we pulled off our shoes and stockings."

Lawson ran his fingers through his brownish-blond hair. "I think they were cut for railroad ties, but floated down the river and washed up on our place like driftwood before they could be used."

"Do they belong to anyone?"

"Driftwood is driftwood. They belong to us now. The top ones are bleached almost white, which means they were down there a long time. Shoot, Jolie, I reckon they might have been left over from when they built the railroad."

Jolie knelt down and patted the beam. "This is a wonderful find!"

"But we felt a sprinkle or two. I figure we ought to drag as many out as we can before it rains and gets too boggy. We can use them for fence posts or corner posts."

"Or bedposts," she added.

"With twenty-three of 'em we could build a lean-to on the side of the house and add a room."

"Let me get the rest of the goods inside the house, and I'll come help you."

"Where's Gibs?"

"Still hunting, I guess."

"Here he comes!" Essie shouted. "Look, he shot something." She took off running toward her brother. "We found twenty-three big logs!"

"Who were those two men?" Gibs called out.

"What men?" Lawson asked.

"We had visitors while you were gone," Jolie informed him. "Two men drifted by looking for a friend, but they left."

Lawson stared back down the long drive. "I didn't see any men."

Jolie studied the dark clouds. "They didn't stay long."

Thunder rumbled across the river on the distant ridge.

"Did they fight over you?" Essie asked.

"No, of course not."

"That's different," Gibs teased. "Don't reckon two men have ever been around you that didn't fight."

"You and Lawson don't fight."

"Yeah, but we aren't . . . I mean, you're our sis. That's different."

"I suppose so. I do believe we will get a rain."

Gibs held up his game. "I've got two prairie chickens and a woodchuck," he bragged.

"You shot a prairie dog?" Essie gasped.

He stared at the limp brown carcass. "Is that what this is?"

"I reckon," Lawson replied.

Gibs held it up higher. "I wonder if you can eat one?"

"I'm not going to eat it," Essie declared.

"Then we'll jist eat the chickens."

"I'll dress the chickens," Jolie offered. "You help Lawson and Essie drag those logs up here from the tall grass."

Gibs studied the beam. "If we had enough of these, we could build a fort."

"What do we need a fort for?" Lawson asked.

"I don't know. It just seems fun to think about." Gibs glanced at his sister. "Jolie, did you ever think about livin' out here in the old days?"

"I suppose we all live in someone's past and another's future."

Gibs turned to his brother. "What does that mean?"

"Beats me." Lawson shrugged. "Let's drag those logs up here."

"Can we build a fort?"

"Maybe."

It took two hours to retrieve the remaining muddy timbers. Jolie helped drag up the final two beams. She insisted that they be neatly stacked, but allowed the boys to make a small corral out of them next to the stone corral wall.

"It ain't even started to rain," Gibson observed. "Maybe these Nebraska summer storms is all bluff and no kick. I was thinkin' of callin' this Ft. Gibson. What do you think?"

"Perhaps Ft. Bowers would be more judicial," Jolie suggested.

"Yeah, and it would be more fair, too," Essie added.

"We need to clean up. Mama and Daddy will be home in an hour or two. We don't want to look like mud dogs."

"Let's bring a couple of buckets of fresh water out in the yard to wash our feet, legs, and hands. I left a towel for us on the door over there."

"And we can let our dresses back down where they belong. My dress is all muddy even though I tucked it in my bloomers," complained Essie.

"Jolie's isn't," Gibs observed.

"Mama said mud is afraid of Jolie. It won't come near her," Essie replied.

"I might keep my clothes a little cleaner, but look at my feet. They're so muddy you can't tell I have skin."

"It's a new style." Essie strutted around the yard. "Mud shoes—it's the latest fashion in San Francisco."

Gibs stared up the driveway and shouted, "Hey, here come Mama and Daddy!"

"Oh, no, look at how messy we are," Jolie moaned. "Maybe we can hurry and get cleaned up. I haven't even got the prairie chickens boiling yet."

Lawson stared down the driveway. "I don't think it's Mama and Daddy. It's a farm wagon all right, but they're movin' at a slow trot. Mama don't drive nothin' at a slow trot."

"Do you think we have company?" Essie asked.

"It can't be company," Jolie fumed. She stared at her mud-covered feet. "We live at the end of a desolate trail. We moved in yesterday, and no one knows we're here. Besides, we already had two unexpected visitors today. We simply can't have more company."

"Whoever it is, they have kids in the back," Essie shouted. "I wonder if they have any girls my age."

"I wonder if they have any girls my age?" Lawson mumbled.

"I can't have them see me like this," Jolie hollered. "Essie, go get my shoes and stockings and meet me by the well. I'll get the towel."

"I can't go into the house all muddy."

"Well . . . well, at least I can meet them with clean feet and my skirt down."

"What about us?" Lawson asked.

"You're boys. You're supposed to be muddy. Visit with them until we get back," she ordered.

"Me?" Lawson gulped. "I never know what to say to strangers."

"Have Gibs tell them about his hunting trip or something. Please, Lawson."

Jolie and Essie ran to the well and drew a bucket of water.

"Ewwww, look!" Essie pointed to the bucket. "There's a grasshopper in the water."

"Scoop it out."

"Me? It's still alive and kicking."

Jolie scooped out the grasshopper in a handful of water and flung it away. "There. Now hurry."

She heard the rig pull into the yard. Kids yelled. A dog

barked. Horses whinnied. A woman with a high-pitched voice gave commands.

Jolie dried her feet and brushed down her dress. "How do I look?"

"Why, you look plum purdy, Miss Jolie," Essie drawled. "I think I musta died and gone to heaven."

"Estelle Cinnia!"

"That's how all the boys talk around you."

"I don't trust all the boys, but I trust my Essie. How do I look?"

"You look fine," Essie giggled. "Why, that smudge on your nose makes a nice beauty mark."

"Smudge!" Jolie gasped. "Where?"

"Over there on the left."

Jolie wiped the beige towel across her nose. "Did I get it?"

"Now you made it big."

"Oh, no! The towel is filthy. What am I going to do?" Jolie moaned.

"Bend down here," Essie instructed.

Essie lifted up her own dress to a clean spot and used it as a rag. "You can wipe your hands on my dress, too. It doesn't bother me. Daddy always says little girls just look cute when they're messy."

"Thanks, sis, you're my pal. But you aren't that little anymore."

"Your barefoot pal."

Jolie glanced at her own white toes. "We're all barefoot. Come on, let's go see the company."

As they rounded the sod house, Jolie spied three girls, a tall slender man, and a woman.

A very large woman.

She marched straight over to them. "You must be Jolie and Essie. Your brother told us about you. I'm Mrs. Vockery." She held out a massive, callused hand.

Jolie felt her whole body vibrate as the woman shook her hand. "Gibs is quite a talker."

"No, no, it was Lawson that was so talkative."

Essie's eyes widened. "Really?"

"I'm proud of him. He's sometimes shy with strangers," Jolie explained.

"He certainly wasn't shy with April. He took her down to show her the driftwood ties he salvaged. He's such a courteous young man." The large woman laced her ringless fingers. "How old is he?"

"Sixteen," Essie reported.

"My April will be fifteen in a few weeks. Isn't that nice?" she mumbled. "Isn't that nice?" she repeated.

Jolie tried to survey the corral and still face the woman. *Lawson with a girl? Showing her the woodpile? Lord, You are doing amazing things.*

As they walked back to the yard, Jolie noticed the man hanging a door on their house, using brass hinges. The big woman led the way over to two young girls. "This is May and June. May's fourteen, and June is thirteen."

Both girls wore long dark blue dresses and starched white aprons. Both were barefoot.

"Is your youngest daughter named July?" Jolie asked.

"No, it's funny how many people assume that. This little blonde-haired princess is Mary."

"Hi," the short, stocky girl called out. "I'm not that little. I'm twelve."

"Really? I'm twelve too," Essie said. "Do you want to go pick some sunflowers with me?"

The barefoot blonde grinned. "Sure." She took Essie's hand.

Gibs helped the man with the door.

"This is Mr. Vockery. We homestead along the river just past the schoolhouse. Earnest, this is Jolie, the one Lawson called his second mama."

Mr. Vockery, with screws between his lips, nodded at her.

Jolie spied tiny splatters of mud on her sleeve and brushed them off. "Did you say there's a schoolhouse out here, Mrs. Vockery?"

"Oh, yes, just down Telegraph Road about three miles from here. There aren't any homesteads between us. Most folks think this is too close to the river. But I say it has its charm. Isn't that right, Ernie?"

He plucked the brass screws out of his mouth. "You surely do, dear."

"Mr. Vockery, thank you for hanging our door. We were just about to do it ourselves. We were waiting for it to dry out a little more."

"This ain't that door." Gibs pointed out to the yard.

Jolie glanced back and saw the door still lying in the yard. "Where did the door you're hanging come from?"

Mr. Vockery finished tightening a screw. "In April we got flooded out, like you did, and we lost our door. We thought it washed down the river. We needed a door right away and didn't have the funds. So knowin' that Avery had this place for sale and figurin' no one would buy it, I appropriated the door, at least till someone came along. I heard this mornin' that you folks had moved in, and I hurried down before the rain to install your door. Sorry for the inconvenience."

"It's wonderful of you to hang it for us."

"Guess what?" Gibs called out. "That door we're trying to dry belongs to the Vockerys."

"Really?"

"Yep," Mr. Vockery said. "This one never fit our doorway too good. We had to stuff rags under it. We'll be haulin' that one off." He screwed in the hinge and stood up and swung the door back and forth. "I looked downstream for that door for several days, but I didn't think of lookin' upstream. I have no idea how it got up here."

"I set a pie in the front room on one of them crates," Mrs. Vockery said. "I hope you like walnut and raisin pie."

"Oh, how wonderful! Thank you, Mrs. Vockery."

"Darlin', those of us along the river take care of each other. We're mighty happy to help. Isn't that right, Ernie?"

"Yes, dear," he replied.

"I gave Mrs. Vockery my prairie dog," Gibs announced.

Jolie felt her face blush. "You should give her one of the prairie chickens."

"Nope!" Mrs. Vockery exclaimed. "I'm boilin' up a pot of stew today. I'll just slice him right in with the rest."

"So they *are* edible." Jolie rubbed her cheek. It felt sticky.

Mrs. Vockery picked at her ear with her small finger. "You wouldn't want a steady diet of them, but with potatoes and turnips they cook up quite tasty."

"They taste better than porcupines," May announced.

Mrs. Vockery tugged on the front of her dress and fanned herself with her hand. "Gibs here tells me your Daddy is an educated man."

"He and Mama both took some college courses in Michigan. That's where they met."

"Do you think either of them would consider teachin' at Riverbend School this fall? We're havin' a tough time gettin' a teacher out here. If the mosquitoes don't chase them off, the slick roads do. We're beginnin' to think only one of the locals will stick it out."

"Slick roads?" Jolie asked.

"Oh, my, yes. Anytime it rains, the roads south between the railroad tracks and the river slime up, and you can't bring a wagon in for days."

"You mean, like our drive?"

"Yep. Mr. Avery claimed he was stuck back here for six weeks last winter and couldn't get out. Course, you have to take his word with a grain of salt. I didn't find him to be the most truthful man I met." She glanced up at the clouds. "As soon as this rain hits, that road will be impassable."

Mr. Vockery swung the door open and closed.

"Oh, dear, Mama and Daddy are in town and won't come home for a while," Jolie worried.

"If they hurry, they can probably make it home. You might be stuck here for a while. But then we're all homesteaders. We'll do all right. Say, did you ever live in a sod house before?"

"We had an adobe house in Santa Fe when I was younger," Jolie reported.

"Sod is different from adobe. Adobe is a dirt brick. Sod is just dirt. Did you have a tile roof in New Mexico?"

"Yes."

"Here you have a mud roof. They have a tendency to melt."

Mr. Vockery studied the thick, weedy sod on top of the house. "You got any oiled canvas tarps?"

"I don't think so. We have rubber tarps."

"Rubber? I didn't know they made rubber tarps."

"Daddy was running a store and ordered some in. He was sure they would become real popular, but they stretch and melt too much in the summer heat. So we got stuck with them. They work good in the rain, but sort of freeze up and become brittle in the winter."

"If I was you, I'd take them rubber tarps and stretch them over as much of the roof as you can," Mr. Vockery said. "Your roof is a little worse for wear, and the rain will drip through right onto your goods inside."

Essie's eyes grew wide. "Really?"

"Yep," Mrs. Vockery added. "And it's muddy water to boot. Sometimes if it leaks too bad, I'll carry an umbrella in the house. Especially over the stove. Don't like mud in the prairie dog stew, if you know what I mean. Do you have an umbrella?"

"Yes, ma'am. Somewhere in these crates," Jolie replied.

"May and Junie, you go fetch your sisters. We need to scoot." Mrs. Vockery strolled to the wagon while Gibs and Mr. Vockery loaded the door from out of the yard. "Hate to rush off, but we want to stay ahead of the slick roads."

Jolie reached out for the woman's hand. "I understand. Thanks so much for the pie. And the visit. It doesn't seem nearly so isolated when we know our neighbors."

The big woman swung up into the wagon with seasoned ease. "Jolie, tell your mama I'll be back to see her after the roads harden."

A red-faced Lawson Bowers strolled back to the house alongside a blonde-haired April Vockery. His hat was pushed back, and her calico bonnet was untied, with the strings hanging down the front of her dress.

Jolie stared at him, but he avoided her eyes. *Lawson Pritchett Bowers, you are growing up real fast today!*

Mrs. Vockery settled in next to her husband. "And don't forget to tell your daddy and mama about the need for a schoolteacher."

All four Bowers children watched as the wagon rolled north.

"I like the Vockerys," Essie declared. "Mary is very funny!"

"I ain't never known a girl so easy to talk to as April Ann," Lawson mumbled.

"Oh, her name is April Ann?" Jolie smirked.

"That's a purdy name, ain't it?"

"Hmmmm," Essie teased, "you've never said three words to any purdy girl in your life."

"That's not true. I talk to you and Jolie all the time," Lawson huffed.

"Yeah, me too," Gibs added.

Jolie winked at Essie. "Did you know those Bowers boys are smooth talkers?"

"I just thought they were telling the truth," Essie giggled.

Thunder exploded near them. "Mr. Vockery has a rowboat," Gibs reported. "He said he'd take me fishin' on the river after the storm breaks and the water recedes."

"You boys go wash the mud off your legs and feet and then let's cover the roof with the rubber sheets. Mr. Vockery said that our roof would probably not hold. I do think it will rain. The Almanac must be wrong. I shall write to them and point that out."

Gibs studied the sod house. "We ain't got nothin' to tie the tarps to."

"I got plenty of big rocks in the garden," Lawson reported. "We can tie to them and use them like anchors."

With rocks and ropes in place around the house and a sporadic drizzle falling, Lawson stood on a crate and hoisted Gibs to the sod roof.

"Spread out them rubber sheets, and then I'll help you down," he ordered.

Jolie and Essie, now both wearing shoes, watched from the front yard.

"You ought to see this roof," Gibs shouted down to them.

"What do you see?" Jolie asked.

"Grasshoppers. Hundreds of them."

Essie wrinkled her nose. "Are they dead?"

"Yep. What shall I do with them?"

"Just cover them up for now," Jolie instructed. "We need to get the house covered before it rains hard. Be careful."

"I can see Scott's Bluff and Chimney Rock from up here," Gibs shouted.

"Perhaps we'll have a two-story house someday, and we'll see them both from the balcony. Hurry." Jolie tugged on one of the rubber tarps. "This west one is caught on something, Gibs. Can you free it?"

"It's a stick . . . no, it's an old rifle barrel!" Gibs shouted. "It's a Henry! There's a rusted Henry rifle up here!"

"Toss it down," Lawson called out.

Gibs hesitated. "It's mine. I found it!"

"Yes." Jolie motioned with her hand. "It's yours. But hurry; it does smell like rain."

By the time the rain hit hard, the boys had washed their feet and legs, and all four huddled in the crowded front room in the midst of crates and boxes. They found some candles and soon had the room aglow. They left the new front door standing open.

Jolie stood by a crate preparing the two prairie chickens. "I hope Mama and Daddy don't have trouble with Stranger and Pilgrim on the muddy roads."

Lawson sat on the floor barefoot, leaning against a black trunk and reading a seed catalog. "April Ann said squash really grows well along the river. Did you know this catalog has fourteen different kinds of squash?"

Essie sat on a bucket combing her long brown hair. "The rain is comin' down the chimney. I think I heard something out there." She scurried to the door. "Did you hear anything?"

"Just thunder and rain." Gibs scraped dirt and rust off the old Henry into a bucket. "Hey, look at this! Someone carved notches in this butt stock. I wonder if this was used in the Indian wars?"

"On which side?" Jolie asked.

Essie came over and stood next to her sister. "What did Mrs. Vockery say about school?"

"There's a schoolhouse down the road a few miles. I think it's called Riverbend School. Mrs. Vockery wanted to know if Mama or Daddy would teach. I don't believe Mama will want to teach. She likes to be outdoors too much."

"There is summer squash and winter squash," Lawson reported. "April Ann said that her daddy has some squash that he has to cut open with an axe, but the fillin' cooks up tender like pumpkin. I ain't never sliced open a squash with an axe."

"Do you remember the time lightning hit the tree behind our house in Helena? Montana has trees. I wish we had some trees here," Essie said.

"Looks like initials on this butt stock, too," Gibs announced. "N.D.M."

"Daddy, on the other hand, would make an excellent teacher. He knows something about everything." Jolie placed the prairie chicken next to the other one in a large pot of water. "But I don't think he would want to be tied down for months. He always finds a new cause, a new invention, a new crop to investigate."

Lawson thumbed through the catalog. "Mama said what we need is a cash crop, something we could plant this month and sell for cash in the fall. But it seems to me to make any money, we would need to grow something others don't grow. I wish I had this year's catalog."

"They said the tree in our Montana backyard was over one hundred years old. If we planted a pine tree here at our house, it wouldn't be that big until 1991. I'd be 112 years old," Essie mused. "I once met a lady who was 101 years old. She was shriveled up like a prune, but she could sing all of the words to 'Farewell at the Door.'"

Gibs ran his fingertips across the butt stock of the gun. "Must be the initials of the person who owned it."

Jolie carried the pot over to the fireplace. "I wonder how many students they have at Riverbend School? I wonder if the North Platte River actually bends there?"

"Maybe we should try Flannigan's Jumbo Watermelons. Look at this illustration," Lawson hooted. "It says here a man from South Carolina grew one that weighed 102 pounds. I wonder who would buy watermelons that big?"

"Compared to a woman 101 years old, Daddy is a young man," Essie mused. "Sometimes he says he's getting old and hasn't accomplished much in life, but I don't think so."

"I bet it was Dave Mather's gun! The last initials are D. M. Wow, I wonder how many men he killed with this?" Gibs rubbed the rusty relic. "None lately, I presume."

Jolie stirred spices into the pot hanging over the fire. "Did you know that in some places they let sixteen-year-olds teach? I'm almost eighteen, but, of course, I need to help here. Who would cook and clean house if I were teaching?"

"Everyone likes watermelons," Lawson rambled on. "April Ann said watermelon was just about her favorite food, next to pecan caramel fudge."

"I don't know why Daddy talks that way," Essie murmured. "He has accomplished some things in life. He accomplished all four of us. You know, it smells musty in here. Do you think we should boil some vanilla?"

"But that doesn't explain how to get Mysterious out of an N," Gibs puzzled. "Maybe Dave is his middle name."

Jolie wiped her hand on a towel and stepped to the open doorway. She stared out at the rain. "I suppose one of the good things about having slick roads is that we won't have any visitors. I can't believe the company we had this morning."

Lawson folded his arms and closed his eyes. "I ain't never had pecan caramel fudge, but it surely sounds tasty. April Ann said her daddy thinks pecans will grow along the river, but it takes seven years to make a payin' crop out of them. Still, we could plant a few just to see."

"Oh . . . look! There's some water dripping down here by the chimney," Essie cried. "You missed a spot."

"Jolie said not to put the rubber sheet too close to the chimney or it would melt," Gibs said. "Perhaps his Christian name starts with an N. I wonder if he'll be back for his gun? I'd surely like that thousand dollar reward."

Jolie paced around the crates in the flickering candlelight. "I like company most of the time, but not until we have some furniture and everything unpacked and tidy. I like a tidy house."

"They have four kinds of eggplant in here," Lawson continued. "I surely hope we don't plant eggplant. If it didn't sell, we'd be eatin' it all winter."

"I'll just turn this bucket up and catch the water. Ewwwww! The water is really muddy. Kind of like the river." Essie adjusted the bucket, sat on a tall wooden box, and continued to comb her hair.

"If I can make this Henry shootable, I'm goin' huntin' with it." Gibs held the old gun up to his shoulder and pointed it at the ceiling. "A .44-caliber rim-fire ain't much of a bullet, but it's better than a .22. I could shoot deer and antelope and buffalo . . . well, maybe not buffalo."

Jolie wiped her fingers across the dust on one of the crates. "I imagine a sod house is hard to keep tidy. I hope I don't have to use wet newspaper to get the dirt off the floor every day. We'll soon be out of newspaper."

Lawson tossed down the seed catalog. "April Ann said the winters here can be hurtin' cold, but the snow don't get very deep except in the drifts."

Essie held her hair out in front of her. "Did you see how wavy May Vockery's hair is? I wish mine was wavy. Jolie, maybe on

Saturday we could heat the irons and curl our hair. I think I'd look more mature with wavy hair, don't you?"

"Of course, I don't have any bullets. I wonder where I could get some .44 rim-fire cartridges. Was there a gunsmith in Scottsbluff? I should have asked the sheriff," Gibs went on.

"Daddy said that where they have electricity, a person could run a fan backwards and suck up the dust, but he never could figure out what to do with the dust once it was back in the air." Jolie scooted a bucket by the fire to catch two muddy drips from the ceiling.

"April Ann told me she wore a buffalo robe coat inside the house sometimes in the winter just to stay warm." Lawson leaned his head back on a rolled-up corner of the buffalo robe. "Don't you reckon she looks fine in a buffalo robe coat?"

"Did I tell you Mary Vockery and me decided to be best friends for the rest of our lives?" Essie said.

"This barrel is full of mud and won't swivel. I can't get into the magazine," Gibs complained. "I need a cleanin' rod."

Jolie scooped up all the chicken feathers into a shallow bowl. "Daddy thought maybe he could suck up the dust with a reverse fan, and then have it stick to flypaper or something like that. But it seems to me it would take a lot of flypaper to catch all the dust and dirt from a Nebraska sod house."

Lawson continued to lay back with his eyes closed. "Jolie, I've been meanin' to ask you something. How does a person know if they're in love with someone?"

Essie clapped her hand over her mouth and giggled.

The Henry rifle clattered to the floor.

Jolie coughed and sprayed prairie chicken feathers across the room.

Lawson Pritchett Bowers sat up, turned bright red, and gulped. "I didn't think anyone was listenin'."

four

Two prairie hens simmered in a blackened pot over a smoldering sage and cedar fire in the river-rock fireplace that separated the two rooms of the sod house.

Lawson stared into the dark yard. "It don't look like it's goin' to stop rainin'."

Jolie quartered the small peeled potatoes. "Leave the door open. We need the draft for the fireplace."

"When do you think Mama and Daddy will be home?" Essie asked.

"If anyone could get through, it would be Mama," Gibs ventured.

"They may have to wait until morning." Jolie glanced at the pan in front of her. "But I'll cook plenty just in case they come rolling in."

Essie meandered toward the fire. "I thought our house was supposed to have a stove."

Jolie took a deep breath and began slicing a big yellow onion. "It was supposed to have lots of things."

Lawson slicked his brownish-blond hair behind his large ears. "I reckon when I'm old enough, I won't buy me a homestead sight unseen."

"You goin' to homestead?" Gibs waltzed by the table and grabbed for a piece of raw carrot. Jolie's raised eyebrow caused him to change his mind.

"Yep, unless I save up the money to buy it outright." Lawson walked over to the others. "There's still a lot of land around that a man can buy from the government for $1.25 per acre. I'd surely like to own my own section someday."

"A whole 640 acres?" Essie asked. "How much would that cost?"

"That's $800 plus $24 for filin' the patent deed," he replied.

"That's a lot of money," Gibs declared. "I don't reckon I've seen that much money in my life. Did you ever see that much money, Jolie?"

"Only in a bank vault."

"You been in a bank vault?" Essie asked.

"Don't you remember that time Jolie got accidentally locked in the bank vault with the banker's son?" Lawson asked.

"The banker's son?" Essie squealed.

"It wasn't an accident," Jolie fumed.

"How come no one tells me anything?" Essie complained. "What happened?"

"Nothing happened. I just saw a lot of money, that's all."

Lawson leaned over the table. "Here's how I figure it—if a man took a city job at $50 a month, he could save back $20, and in just four years he could save enough to have the land. Providin' the cow don't die, of course."

"No boy ever locked me in a bank vault," Essie complained.

"The cow die?" Gibs asked.

"You know, some unforeseen emergency. Of course, a man would need some start-up money, and that would take another year of scrimpin' and savin'. But it seems to me, a thrifty man could have a fine place in five or six years."

"No boy ever locked me in the woodshed, or the barn, or the school closet with him either." Essie paced around the table. "How come boys always get locked somewhere with Jolie?"

"You're only twelve," Jolie said.

Gibs laid his Henry rifle across his lap. "But you wouldn't have a house."

Lawson reached inside his boiled cotton shirt and scratched his shoulder. "A house ain't important at first. A person can sleep in the barn."

"How old were you when the banker's son locked you in the vault?" Essie asked.

"Eh, eleven, but that's not the point." Jolie stopped cutting the onion and wiped her eyes with a towel. "Lawson, if you don't have a house," she sniffed, "I take it you plan on living on your place alone?"

Lawson blushed. "I did until this mornin'. Now I reckon there could be a change of plans. Anyway, I can build a sod house for $12. If I got a job in town when I was eighteen, I figure I could have enough saved to have my own place by the time I'm twenty-three or so. I reckon that ain't too bad."

"Eleven?" Essie groaned. "You were eleven?"

"Yes, so you can see the whole thing is silly." Jolie dug through a crate for some bowls and pans. "Lawson, it sounds like a wonderful plan to me."

Lawson looped his thumbs in the pockets of his ducking trousers. "How about you, Jolie? You got plans for the future?"

"Oh, I have dreams, Lawson, but you have a plan. There's a lot of difference between dreams and a plan."

Gibs snatched a piece of carrot when Jolie wasn't looking. "Of all the places we've lived, Jolie, where would you want to live with your family someday?"

"To tell you the truth, it doesn't matter. I guess moving around so much keeps me from getting attached to a place. I'd like to be wherever all of you and Mama and Daddy settle down."

"Mama said she wasn't goin' to move again," Essie said.

"That was before she saw this place." Gibs moseyed to the open door.

"If it weren't for the river floodin', this would be a nice place," Lawson declared.

Gibs stared out at the rain. "I wonder if the river will flood again?"

"If it does, will it flood out our house?" Essie asked.

"Oh, I trust not." Jolie scooped all the vegetables into a big bowl. "I think I made too much. I hope we're all hungry."

"You know, if we had a two-foot high levee around the house, I bet the water would never get to the door," Gibs called out.

"Lawson, what kind of a levee would we need to surround our place?" Jolie asked.

"You mean all 160 acres?"

"No, just the part that floods."

Lawson rubbed his smooth, narrow chin and stepped to the door next to Gibs. "I bet three feet thick at the bottom and sloped up two-thirds of the way ought to do it."

"How would you go about building such a levee?" Jolie quizzed.

"Are you serious?"

"Curious."

"Let me ponder it. A flood-control levee? Hmmmm . . ." Lawson dug a stubby pencil from the pocket of his trousers and began to draw on top of a crate.

Essie plopped down next to the green trunk and opened a worn brown leather book. She chewed on a wooden pencil and then looked up. "Jolie, how do you spell limb-ped?"

"L-I-M-P-I-D," Jolie replied. "Why are you asking? What are you writing?"

"My book. I found my journal from the gray house in Helena where I started to write a book. I think I'll be a writer someday. Either that or a train engineer."

Gibs pointed his rusty Henry rifle at imaginary targets in the storm. "You can't be a train engineer. You're a girl."

Essie wiggled her nose and curled her bottom lip. "In that case, I'm goin' to write a story about a girl named Sierra Nevada who becomes a railroad engineer and saves the entire town of Durango, Colorado, from a runaway train."

"The Sierra Nevadas are mountains," Gibs protested.

"Yes, isn't that a coincidence?" Essie giggled. "Perhaps they were named after her."

Jolie spooned the vegetables into the pot with the boiling chicken. "You didn't tell me why you wanted to spell *limpid*."

"I think the rain stopped," Gibs called from the doorway.

"I want to write about Sierra Nevada having 'lovely auburn hair and limpid gray-green eyes.'"

"What?" Jolie spun around. "Where did you get that line? You're too young to use language like that."

"I'm not all that young."

"You are too. Where did you come up with that?"

Essie shot a quick glance at Gibs and then stared down at her journal. "I heard it once."

Jolie stalked over to her sister. "What do you mean, you heard it? Where did you hear it?"

"Eh, in Helena."

"Where in Helena?"

Essie gulped. "Behind the brown sofa next to the wall when Caleb Watters came to call on you."

"You were spying on me?"

"No, I wasn't spying. I was just listening. Gibs was the one spying."

"What? My own brother?"

Gibs lowered the Henry to his side. "Eh, I was just making sure you were okay, sis."

Jolie folded her arms across her green dress. "I can't believe my own family spying on me!"

"How am I ever going to learn anything? Nobody locks me in a bank vault. Nobody ever tells me anything. Caleb said you had limpid gray-green eyes, and I figured that was something nice because you said, 'Thank you, Caleb, my sweetie.'"

"I absolutely did not say, 'Caleb, my sweetie!'"

"Maybe I made that part up. What does limpid mean, Jolie?"

"It means clear or lucid, transparent. I still can't believe you were—"

"There's Daddy!" Gibs shouted from the doorway. "He's leading a cow and carrying a calf across his shoulders."

All four children ran out onto the front steps.

"Is that our cow?" Gibs called.

Jolie held a lantern up.

"Yep," Matthew Bowers said. He let the lead rope drop to the mud. "And our calf."

"You want me to put them in the barn?" Lawson asked.

"I'd appreciate that, son. I'm a little cold and muddy."

"Come in, Daddy," Jolie urged. "The fire's warm."

Essie plowed through the mud out to him. "Where's Mama?"

"That's a long story. Let me come inside and get some dry clothes, and I'll tell you. You've got the rubber tarps stone-anchored to the roof and a front door that wasn't the one in our yard."

"That's a long story, too."

"And we didn't even mention the part about my two prairie chickens."

"Or the twenty-three railroad ties that drifted into our weeds."

"Or the Vockery family that paid us a visit and left a very nice pie."

"Or the two men visitors that Jolie had, and they didn't even fight over her."

Mr. Bowers set the calf down in the yard. "Well, you tell me your long story, and then I'll tell you mine."

By the time Lawson returned to the house, Mr. Bowers had pulled off his suit and changed into ducking trousers and a long-sleeved wool shirt. He parted his damp brown hair in the middle and perched his spectacles on his nose.

The children explained their day as their father stirred the fire.

"That surely is a fine cow!" Lawson exclaimed. "I was afraid you'd run her to death if you tied her behind Mama's wagon."

"What's the cow's name, Daddy?" Essie asked.

Matthew slipped his arm around his youngest daughter. "I don't believe the cow has a name, darlin'."

She licked her lips. Her brown eyes sparkled. "Milk cows are supposed to have names."

He tilted his head toward the fireplace and winked at her. "Miss Estelle Cinnia, why don't you name her?"

"Okay." Essie bit her tongue and rolled her eyes. "The cow's name shall be Margaret."

"And the calf?"

"Is it a boy calf or a girl calf?" she asked.

Mr. Bowers laughed. "Well, it's sort of a boy calf, I reckon."

"Oh!" Essie giggled. "In that case, his name is Francis."

"That's a nice name, but you do realize that when Francis grows up, we will eat him?"

"Daddy, of course I know that. But I don't have to think about it now, do I?"

"I reckon not." Mr. Bowers added a short log to the fire.

Jolie stirred the pot of stew. "You haven't told us where Mama is."

He stood with his back to the fire. Two lanterns and the glow of the fire illuminated the room. "We got the papers filed at the courthouse. Then we sold some of Mama's silver and some gold buttons of mine that I haven't used in eighteen years. We bought the cow and calf from a Mr. Upriche. We purchased boards for bed frames and shelves and got some mosquito netting. By the time we left town, it had been raining awhile. Folks said there was no way to make it back here."

"But where's Mama?" Essie insisted.

He held up his hand. "I'm coming to that. It seems that Stranger and Pilgrim are just big, strong, and ornery enough to pull in this mud. It slows them down, but they kept on pulling. When we reached the DeMarco home, she flagged us down. Mrs. DeMarco said Alfonso was in bad shape, and her team couldn't pull when it slicked up."

"He's in bad shape?" Jolie interjected.

"Yes. And Mama had met Dr. Fix in Scottsbluff. So she loaded up the DeMarcos and sloshed her way back to town. I hiked on home with Margaret the cow and totin' little . . . eh . . ."

"Francis," Essie squealed.

"There's a shortcut across a couple of unimproved homesteads."

Jolie pressed her fingers against her chin. "What was wrong with Alfonso? What did the doctor do yesterday?"

Mr. Bowers combed his wet hair with his fingers. "She didn't take him to the doctor yesterday."

"What?" Jolie choked.

"Darlin', what she did was let him bind his foot tight and rest it up on a pillow."

"Oh, no!" Jolie burst out "Why, his foot could get gangrene . . . and . . . he could lose it . . . or his leg . . . or his life! Daddy, I can't believe they did that. I tried so hard to do it right. Why didn't they listen and do what I said?"

Mr. Bowers shook his head slowly. "I don't understand it either, darlin'. I reckon that's how the preacher feels every Sunday, don't you?"

"Will Mama be home tonight?" Essie asked.

"She's plannin' on it. It might depend on this rain. She said she would stay at the DeMarcos' house if she can't get all the way back." Mr. Bowers put his arm around Jolie's shoulder.

With kerosene lamps flicking shadows on the walls, Jolie gathered them all around the two boxes that served as a table. "You can thank Gibs for the prairie chickens. They're a little bit stringy, but that's my fault. I wasn't able to cook them in an oven. The good news is, there's plenty of stew. I sort of got carried away with the potatoes."

"I bet it tastes better than prairie dog," Lawson teased.

Jolie carried over a napkin-covered dish. "Mrs. Vockery made the pie. I don't know how good it is, but someone at this table stuck a finger in it already."

"It's very tasty," Gibs admitted.

"Mr. Gibson Hunter Bowers, it's Thursday, and so it's your turn to say the blessing." Mr. Bowers dropped his head.

Gibs cleared his throat. "Lord, this is Gibson. Bless our food even though the chicken is a little tough, and keep Mama safe and out of the storm, and if You're needin' to thin out the deer, You might send some our way. Thank You. In Jesus' name, amen."

When the plates had been scraped clean, Jolie poured her father and herself a cup of coffee. "Did you see Lawson's idea for wrapping a levee around our place?"

"Yes, it's a very good idea." Mr. Bowers held the coffee in front of him and let it steam his face. "The important thing will be to construct it in some fashion so that it won't wash away."

"Daddy thinks we ought to build it out of river rock and cement mortar, like the rock corral," Lawson told the others.

"There's a rumor of a cement company starting in Scottsbluff. Perhaps they will have fair prices. I'd like our house to have rock foundations, too, perhaps even some rock walls."

"A stone house?" Lawson asked.

"Just the first floor, I'm thinkin'."

"Will you make gun slots?" Gibs queried. "Then it will be like a rock fort. That ought to protect us when attacked."

All the others in the room stared at him.

"Eh, maybe I was just daydreamin'," he admitted.

"I figure the only enemies we have here are the river at flood stage and the weather," Mr. Bowers said. "I heard that every once in a while a tornado blows through."

"I didn't see any other stone houses around here," Jolie remarked.

"Then we'll be trendsetters," Mr. Bowers answered. "It would be good protection to have a solid lower level, and we wouldn't need to use up so much stick lumber. But who would do all that stonework?"

Lawson jumped to his feet. "How about you and me learning, Daddy?"

"I was hopin' you'd say that, son. I could study up on it, and we could build a little at a time as we have the rocks. It might take us a while, but I'm sure we'd learn."

"We have plenty of rocks in our fields," Lawson said.

Matthew Bowers grinned. "There you have it. You and I will build the big house."

"Daddy, do we have to have our own rooms in the big house?" Essie asked. "I like being with Jolie."

"What if I built your rooms right next to each other with your own private door between the two?"

"Oh, yes!" Essie said. "Would that be all right with you, Jolie?"

"Only if you promise to come slip in my bed when there's a lightning storm outside."

Essie grinned from ear to ear. "I promise."

Jolie cut pieces of pie and passed them around.

"Hey, why did I get the one with the hole in it?" Gibs protested.

Essie giggled. "Because it's your hole."

Jolie stuck her fork into the pie. "What do you think about that schoolteaching job, Daddy?"

He chewed for a moment and then waved a fork at her. "I think it sounds perfect, darlin'."

"Really? You do?" she gasped. "I'm surprised."

"Yep." He forked another bite of raisin-walnut pie. "You ought to take that job, darlin'."

"Me?" Jolie dropped her fork. "I'm only seventeen."

"You'll be eighteen in August," Essie mumbled through her napkin.

"Why don't *you* take the job, Daddy?" Jolie asked. "You would be such an excellent teacher."

"Oh, no, darlin'. I have way too much to do." He tapped Lawson on the arm. "Did I tell you about my idea for a drain well?"

Jolie studied her father as she gathered up the dirty dishes and stacked them in a large tin basin. *Lord, Daddy is such a wonderful dreamer. His plans are so glorious.*

"I say, when the place dries off, we dig a well down on our property line. We could stretch that rock wall levee out from both sides of the well."

Jolie poured hot water over the dishes and added cold water and lye soap shavings. *But somehow his plans never quite come together. There was the hacienda hotel planned for Arizona and the vineyards in New Mexico and the rooftop reservoir for fire protection in Montana. They all sounded so grand.*

"We'll dig down below the water line, which can't be more than six to ten feet. There should be a strata of river sand," Mr. Bowers explained.

With hands in sudsy water and sleeves rolled up to her elbows, Jolie scrubbed on the enameled tin dishes. "Essie, come rinse and dry for me." *Lord, just once I want Daddy to be able to complete one of his dreams. I want to be there and see his eyes dance when he shows it to Mama. Every man deserves to succeed at something, doesn't he?*

"Then we fill the hole with those big river boulders so that any water that flows into it will just drain right out of our place."

Essie dipped the dishes into a basin of cold water and dried them with a thin white cotton towel as she rocked back and forth and chewed on a strand of hair.

Jolie stared at her own shriveled fingertips. *They've been in the water too much. Maybe a person's spirit kind of shrivels, too. Daddy always had such a wonderful big spirit, but I think it's starting to shrivel. I can see it in his eyes. He and Mama never talk about it much, not in front of us. He needs this homestead to work. He needs it real bad.*

"But on top we would have a square weir about four feet tall. On this side there would be a steel gate to raise up and down to allow the water to drain off the field."

A sharp pain struck low in Jolie's back, and she tried to rub it out with a damp hand. *Lord, if Daddy only gets one success in life, please allow him to build his dream house for Mama. I don't think he will ever feel like he's achieved anything until he can present her with a nice home. He has pined to do that since the day they got married. He has aimed for it in every place they ever lived.*

Mr. Bowers's brown eyes danced as he waved his hands. "And on the far side would be another gate. We'll use that one to turn the water back to the river if the water level rises up and floods out of the well."

"Daddy surely has wonderful plans, doesn't he?" Essie whispered.

Jolie nodded as she scrubbed on the blackened pot. *Lord, I love my daddy dearly, but I don't know if I could marry a dreamer. I need more control. I don't mean I have to control. He can control, but there has to be some pattern, some consistency, some . . . some direction. But on the other hand, Mama just grins and says, "Darlin', all those scoffers have never tasted your daddy's sweet kisses." But surely there's some young man for me who is practical and . . . very good at kissing.*

"Jolie, are you blushing?" Essie challenged.

"I think I got too close to the fire."

"Daddy, wouldn't it be simpler to abandon this place and find one that isn't so close to the river?" Lawson suggested.

"Son, when I promised your mama this was the last move, I meant it. And your mama likes this place."

"But the fire is dying down," Essie whispered. "How did that make you blush?"

"Gibs, if it's not raining too bad, run out to the shed and get us another armload of wood," Jolie instructed.

"Can I carry a lamp? I don't want to step in a bog hole."

"Certainly."

"Can I have another piece of that pie when I get back?"

"Yes, you may."

"Thank you, Mama!" Gibs grabbed up the little kerosene lamp, swung open the front door, and let out a yelp. "Oh! We got company!"

A deep male voice replied, "Sorry. Didn't mean to startle you."

Mr. Bowers ambled to the doorway.

Jolie peered over his shoulder to see a tall, broad-shouldered man in ducking trousers, suspenders, and a white shirt with the collar turned up against the storm. His hat dripped water and covered his eyes, but his square chin accented an apologetic mouth. She thought he needed to shave.

"Can I help you?" Mr. Bowers asked.

"Sorry to intrude, sir. We have a loaded wagon about a mile north of here that got stuck on the slick road next to the tracks. We had some protection under a railroad bridge but couldn't get a fire started. I was goin' to hike for some help and saw a light flicker way down here. I hate to ask you this, but do you have a team that could help pull us out?"

"Come in." Mr. Bowers motioned. "Scoot over by the fire. Jolie, do you have something to feed this young man?"

The man stared around the sod house.

"I'm Matthew Bowers, and these are my children—Jolie, Lawson, Gibson, and Estelle."

"Everyone calls me Essie," she corrected.

"Daddy, I can fry up a beef chop," Jolie offered.

The man pulled off his hat, and his wet hair stuck out like tent awnings over his ears. "My name is Tanner Wells. I'll pass on the chop, at least for now. Mama ain't feelin' too good, and I'd like to get her out of the cold as quick as I can."

"I understand." Mr. Bowers motioned toward the fireplace. "Warm yourself for a minute. You'll be of better help to your family."

"I'll go get some more firewood." Gibs bolted out the front door.

Jolie handed Tanner a cup of coffee. He stared into her eyes. "Thank you, Miss Essie."

"I'm Essie! She's Jolie."

He nodded his head and took a sip. "Then I apologize to both of you."

"How many in your family?" Mr. Bowers asked.

"Mama, Daddy, me, and the boys."

"Boys?" Essie asked.

Tanner took a long sip of coffee and then glanced around the room. "Gregory, Theo, and Bullet."

"You have a brother named Bullet?" Essie marveled.

"His Christian name is Chester, but everyone calls him Bullet. He's about your size, I reckon."

"He is?" Essie glanced over at Jolie and grinned.

"Tanner, let me tell you what we can do. We don't have a team here right now. Mrs. Bowers had to run a sick neighbor to town, and the team is gone."

Wells held the coffee cup with both hands. "On these slick roads?"

"She's got a strong team that goes along pretty good. If they were here, they could probably pull you out. But I don't think you would get a quarter of a mile without getting stuck again."

"Maybe we could borrow some firewood, and we'll camp under the bridge."

"Is it still raining?" Mr. Bowers asked.

"It stopped, but it's chillin' down, and everyone is wet."

"Can they make it here?" Jolie blurted out. "We'll put you up for the night."

"I don't want to impose."

"We just moved in yesterday, as you can see. But we do have a fire and a dry spot, as long as the rubber tarps hold." Jolie tossed instructions with her hands. "We can shove the crates aside, and you can have the floor, can't we, Daddy?"

"Of course we can."

"What about our team and wagon?" Tanner quizzed.

"Bring the horses down here," Mr. Bowers instructed. "I think they can make it. I walked a cow in earlier this evenin'. And just leave the goods by the tracks. I can't imagine anyone out to steal in a storm like this. No one can go down that road in a rig."

Gibs burst back in with an armful of wood and shoved a couple of sticks on the fire.

"I'm a gunsmith and have all my tools on the wagon. I reckon I'll stay with the rig. My whole future is in that wagon."

"The boys and I'll go with you. We'll carry some firewood down and help guide the family back."

"That's mighty kind, Mr. Bowers. I don't know what to say. Daddy bought a homestead sight unseen in Denver, and we've been pushin' for three weeks to get here."

"You plan on farming, do you?"

"Daddy's a wheelwright, but business was slowin' down with all the iron wheels, so he wanted to try farmin'. I was hoping to set up a gunsmith shop in Scottsbluff. Do you know if they have any armories there?"

"They have two in Gering and one in Scottsbluff. I heard that the man in Scottsbluff is a thousand years old and wants to retire," Gibs piped up.

Mr. Bowers nodded to his youngest son. "Gibs is our gun and hunting expert."

"I've got me a Winchester 1890 pump .22, and I found a Henry up on the roof. Maybe you could show me how to make it usable," Gibs suggested.

Mr. Bowers held up his hand. "First, we're goin' to go get the Wells family out of the storm."

"Tanner, are you really goin' to camp down at the railroad bridge even if your family comes here to the house?" Gibs asked.

"Yep."

"You need some company? I could camp with you, and we could talk guns. Did you ever meet John Browning?"

"Yes, I did. I worked for him for a while. He's a great man, but we had some theological differences."

"Are you a believer, Mr. Wells?" Jolie asked.

He tipped his soggy hat and grinned. "Yes, ma'am. I surely am."

"If a bore is rusty, do you have to rebore to another caliber, or can you just clean it up and use it anyway?" Gibs asked.

"Gibson Hunter," Mr. Bowers warned, "no questions now. We need to help him."

"Can I spend the night at the track with Tanner?" Gibs asked.

"You're welcome to stay, but it might be cold," Tanner reported.

"Sounds neighborly as long as you don't pester him to death," Mr. Bowers said.

"Essie and I will scoot the crates back while you're gone. Daddy, you can sleep in the boys' room with Lawson. I'll cook a meal for the Tanners. I've got plenty of stew, and I'll fry up some ham."

"We've got bread and eggs in the wagon," Tanner said.

"That's good. There's a little pie left, I think. And I'll soak some corn muffins. Essie, let's dig out every quilt and blanket we can find. We'll need to make five pallets. The roof leaks near the fireplace, so we can't put you too close. I'm sorry it smells musty in here. I'll boil some vanilla if I can find it. Now you men hurry and get Mrs. Wells out of the storm."

Tanner stared at Jolie and then at Mr. Bowers. "You said your wife was out in the night drivin' a team in this storm?"

"Yes."

"And your daughter . . ." He gawked at Jolie.

"Yes, well, Bowers ladies are extremely decisive."

"And cute," Essie blurted.

"Yes, Miss Essie." Tanner tipped his hat. "I can see that."

It helped that the rain had stopped, but the road into the homestead was still so slick and boggy that it took over an hour to bring the Wells family down to the house. They left the wagon and team with Tanner and a talkative Gibson Bowers.

Mrs. Wells was about the size of Lissa, but Jolie decided she was even thinner. The woman didn't say much. She sat by the fireplace sipping coffee and saying, "Thank you," over and over, especially when Jolie pulled one of the buffalo robes out and draped it over the woman's shoulders.

After supper Gregory and Theo crowded into the corner with Lawson and a small lantern, searching the seed catalogs and laughing.

Bullet Wells stood on a crate, declared that he was a mountain lion, and pounced at Essie. She met his leap with a clenched fist in the nose, and he sulked over to the corner and stared at the wall.

Jolie washed the new batch of dishes while Mr. Wells and Matthew Bowers sat at the table, drinking coffee and talking about wagon wheels.

Essie scooted up to her. "Jolie, I think Bullet is very, very strange," she whispered.

Jolie's hands were once again shriveled. "He's just a little active."

"Did you see him pick his nose and belch at the same time?"

"No, fortunately I missed that. Was that before or after you busted him in the nose?"

"Before. But I was only defending myself."

"I don't think he intended to do any more than scare you."

"Well, I didn't think it was funny," Essie said.

"Perhaps you should tell him you're sorry for clobbering him."

"But I'm not sorry."

"Not even a little bit?"

"Nope. He deserved it. That's justice, and the Bible says we're to 'love justice.'"

"It also says to turn the other cheek."

"If he had done that, I would have clobbered it, too," Essie added.

"I don't think that's quite what the verse means."

Essie pointed to the backroom. "Can I take the vanilla candle into our room and read?"

"Yes, but let's make sure Bullet is all right." Jolie glanced at the boy hunkered in the corner.

"You make sure," Essie said. "I don't want to talk to him."

Jolie dried her hands on her apron and squeezed around the others in the crowded room. "Bullet, wouldn't you like to join the boys?"

He kept facing the dark, empty corner of the sod house. "Not until she apologizes for breaking my nose."

Jolie stepped up behind him, Essie at her side now. "Not until who apologizes?"

He pointed over his shoulder without looking. "That girl."

"She has a name, and you know it," Jolie said.

"Not until *Estelle* apologizes," he drawled.

"I'm not going to apologize until that boy says he's sorry for jumping off a box and scaring me."

Jolie scowled at her sister. "He has a name, too."

"Not until Chester says he's sorry."

Still seated on the floor, he spun around toward them. "Don't call me Chester," he snapped.

"Then don't call me Estelle."

He began to smile.

"I'm sorry for hitting you so hard, Bullet."

"I'm sorry for scaring you, Essie."

"There," Jolie asserted, "isn't that better?"

Bullet stood up, picked his nose, and then pranced on one foot and then the other. "Where's the privy?"

When the dishes were finished, Jolie stepped into the backroom and rubbed the lower part of her back. She spotted Essie stretched out on the buffalo robe. "Are you all right, little sis?"

"This is not the way I thought it was going to be."

Jolie sat down on the buffalo robe on the floor next to her sister. "Rub my shoulders, Essie, and tell me why you're disappointed. I'm sore all over."

Essie kneaded Jolie's shoulders with her thumbs and fingers. "For months we had to live in Mrs. Letbetter's basement in Helena. It was cramped, but we knew Daddy had to settle matters after the grain mill burned. Then we decided to homestead and talked about wide-open Nebraska. I knew the house wouldn't be very big at first, but I thought it wouldn't be too bad because it would be just the six of us out on our very own farm. And now this is the first night to be in our tiny little dirt house, and Mama isn't home, and there are five strangers in the other room—one of them an idiot."

"Maybe Bullet's just a little nervous about meeting new people," Jolie offered.

There was a noise outside the window.

"Maybe Mama made it home." Essie yanked back the pillowcase curtain.

Chester "Bullet" Wells mashed his face into a grotesque position against the glass and stuck out his tongue.

Essie dropped the curtain and screamed.

Jolie rubbed her temples and shook her head. "I believe you're right, sis. He *is* a strange little boy."

The front door squeaked open, and Essie ran to the doorway between the rooms and peered out. She stuck her tongue out and then strolled back over to Jolie. "I guess that wasn't a very mature thing to do."

Jolie hugged her. "Oh, I don't know. I was thinking of doing the same thing."

"Really?" Essie said.

"Yes."

"Jolie, can I ask you one question?"

"Certainly."

"And you won't get mad at me?"

"No, of course not."

"And you'll answer me and not just get up and leave?"

Jolie brushed the bangs back off her sister's forehead. "Oh, dear, what kind of question is it?"

"It's very secretive."

"Do you want to wait and ask Mama?"

"Only you know the answer."

"Okay, Estelle Cinnia Bowers, ask me."

Essie scooted up close and held her hand to Jolie's ear. "What is in that fat brown envelope under the buffalo robe?" she whispered.

Jolie's hands went to her cheeks. "Oh, dear, I had almost forgotten."

"And why are you hiding it?"

"You said you were just going to ask one question. Now you've asked two. Which one do you want an answer for?"

"Hmmmm. Okay, let me think." Essie chewed on her tongue. "Here's my question: What's in the envelope?"

"I have no idea. It doesn't belong to me," Jolie replied.

"That's no fair," Essie protested. "You didn't tell me anything about it."

"But I told you the truth."

"Who does it belong to, Jolie?"

"I can't tell you."

"Please, please, please, Jolie. I'll be your best friend if you tell me."

"Estelle Bowers, you already *are* my best friend."

"How can you have secrets from your best friend?"

Jolie hugged her. "Okay, best friend, I'm not sure what the Lord wants me to do about that envelope, and until I find that out, you can't tell anyone. Will you promise me?"

"Not even Mama and Daddy?"

"No. If they ask you about the envelope, tell them to ask me."

"I promise."

"The two men who stopped to visit yesterday, Maxwell Dix and Shakey Torrington, left it with me because it belongs to that cowboy named Leppy Verdue, who was in the fight with the store clerk, Jeremiah Cain."

Essie chewed her tongue. "Leppy was the one with cute dimples when he smiled."

"I see you looked them over. Yes, that was Leppy."

"Why did they leave it with you?"

"I think they thought this house was still abandoned. I believe it had been a rendezvous location for them. Anyway, I mentioned that I knew Leppy Verdue, and they assumed . . ."

Essie stacked her long hair on top of her head and held it there. "That you were his girlfriend?"

"I suppose. But I didn't tell them that. I just wanted them to leave. They handed me that envelope and said to give it to Leppy when I see him again."

"How come you didn't look inside?"

"Because that's like reading someone's mail."

"And it's sealed up."

"So you checked it?"

"Yes. And held it up to the lamp," Essie admitted.

"I did the same thing."

"Jolie, if it's just a letter you're holding for someone, why did you hide it under the buffalo robe?"

"That's the argument I'm having with myself. There's something in there besides a letter. It's way too fat."

"Will you tell me when you settle the argument with yourself?"

"Of course. You really are my best friend."

Essie threw her arm around her sister. "Jolie, I love you."

Jolie hugged her tight. "Why don't you get some sleep now? I'm sure when the storm lets up, and the road dries, everything will settle down, and the company will leave."

Essie flopped back on the buffalo robe. "What're you going to do?"

"I need to go out and be the hostess because Mama isn't here."

"I thought your back hurts."

"Yes, and so do my shoulders, legs, and feet. But poor Mrs. Wells doesn't look too happy. I should check on everyone. Besides that, there's a dolt named Bullet I need to stick my tongue out at."

Jolie slipped into the front room and poured coffee for the men who were now discussing growing rice. She took the pot over to Mrs. Wells and filled her cup and then sat down on a box next to the bucket that was under the leaking roof.

"Are you warming up some?" Jolie asked.

"Yes, thank you," Mrs. Wells replied. "Your family is very kind to us."

"It seems we're all in this homesteading together. I think our families are alike in that we're moving from the west to Nebraska to start something very different from what we've been doing."

Mrs. Wells scooted over to Jolie, the buffalo robe on her shoulders. Her voice was barely audible. "My husband knows nothing about farming."

"Daddy's never farmed much either, but my mother knows quite a bit."

"I've never lived out in the country. I don't know how to be a farm wife. I begged him not to move out here."

"We'll all just have to learn together."

Mrs. Wells sighed. "I don't even know how to milk a cow."

"It's easy. I can teach you."

"How did you learn?"

"My mother taught me when I was five."

"You see, I'm so out of place."

"Is your husband happy with this move?"

"I've never seen him happier. I suggested that we stay in Scottsbluff for the night, but he wouldn't hear of it. He wanted to spend the night on 'our' homestead."

"Mama says sometimes she feels like Sarah in the Bible. God told Abraham to 'go to a place He would show him,' and Sarah went with him, having no idea where they were headed or what they would be doing."

The deep creases around Mrs. Well's eyes dissolved. "I suppose it happens to lots of us."

"Mama said she would rather live with Daddy in a tent in Alaska than live without him in a palace in San Francisco."

Mrs. Wells nodded. "Yes, I do understand that."

"How far away is your homestead?"

"We have no idea. We got lost in the dark and the storm."

"Is it along the river or up on the shelf?"

"It's supposed to be on the river within view of Chimney Rock."

"We found out that most every place between Scottsbluff and

Camp Creek bridge can be in view of Chimney Rock. I hope we're neighbors."

"That would be nice. Jolie, you're very easy to talk to for a young woman. I suppose you're like your mother."

"Mother is very easy to talk to if you can catch up with her. But she and I are really nothing alike. You'll love her, but she'll tire you out."

Mrs. Wells smiled for the first time. "I'm already tired, honey, and I haven't even gotten to the farm."

"Can I get you anything to eat?"

"Please, just slow down."

"I'll go check on the men, and then I'll go to bed. This is your family's room for the night. Just make yourself at home with those blankets. And there is another buffalo robe."

"Bullet seems to have fallen asleep already. He's a very active boy," Mrs. Wells remarked.

"Yes, I noticed that."

"Quite the opposite of Gregory and Theo. And Tanner? Well, there's no one like my Tanner. How I wish he were staying on the farm. You're probably wondering about all the years between my oldest son and my second son?"

"Mrs. Wells, I was born on a mining claim near Virginia City, Nevada. I lived my entire life in the West. This house is the farthest east I have ever been in my life. And one thing about us Westerners—we don't ask a lot of personal questions. People get judged by what they are right now."

Mrs. Wells stared down into her coffee cup. "I married Lucian Tanner when I was sixteen. He was a young lieutenant assigned to Ft. Leavenworth. He went out on a campaign two weeks later. Six weeks after that, I found I was expecting. The day after that, I found I was a widow."

Jolie slipped her arm around Mrs. Wells's thin shoulders. "Oh, dear!"

"There were some very difficult years. We nearly starved to

death. For months on end, Tanner was the only thing that kept me wanting to live. But God was very gracious to me. I love Mr. Wells dearly, and he's such a good worker. I've never had a worry since we've been married—until now."

"Mrs. Wells, how is it that Tanner is your son's first name and last name?"

"Tanner immediately took a liking to Mr. Wells and was thrilled to be called a Wells. But he was worried about losin' his real daddy's name, and so it was Mr. Wells's idea just to call him Tanner."

"It's a nice name."

"Jolie is a very unique name also."

"Mama named me after a horse. Mama's an only child and grew up on a horse ranch in Michigan. My grandfather is a judge back there. She didn't have many friends close by. So her horse Jolie was her best friend. It was the most precious name she had, and she gave it to me. I used to get teased about being named after a horse, but I'm delighted with my name."

"May I be so bold as to ask you a personal question?" Mrs. Wells asked.

"Certainly."

The woman lowered her voice. "Are you pledged to a young man?"

Jolie grinned. "No, I'm not. Now may I ask you a personal question?"

Mrs. Wells laughed again. "Yes, you may. No, Tanner is not pledged to anyone either."

A few minutes later Jolie scooted a crate up next to where the men sat. "Are you two still talking wheels and wagons?"

"No, we've been discussing farming," Mr. Bowers said.

"And what have you decided?"

"That the North Platte River Valley has deep alluvial soil that should grow most anything and plenty of water if we could channel it to the right places."

"You mean, some canals?"

"That's what we were thinking. Next time I'm in town I'm going to check and see if anyone has any plans for canals."

"Of course, we haven't seen our place yet," Mr. Wells added. "But from the description, it's along the river similar to yours."

"Mr. Wells has been reading up on sugar beets," Mr. Bowers announced.

Jolie took a sip of just-right coffee—not too hot, not too luke-warm. She sat up perfectly straight and eased the pain in her back. "I thought sugar only grew in tropical areas."

"No, it's sugar cane that needs the warm, humid climate. Sugar beets grow like potatoes. But they need irrigation," Mr. Bowers reported.

"What do you do with them? How do you process them?" she asked.

"Send them to a refinery," Mr. Wells replied.

"They probably mash them, boil the sugar out, and evaporate off the water," Mr. Bowers speculated.

"Where's the nearest refinery?" she asked.

"Don't have any idea at all," Mr. Wells admitted.

"That would be a good thing to know," Jolie mused.

"It could be a better crop than rice," Mr. Bowers said.

"I suppose you could plant corn," she challenged.

Mr. Bowers rubbed his mustache. "Everyone plants corn, darlin'. You can't make much on a crop everyone has."

Jolie took another sip of coffee. "Lawson figures squash would be a good cash crop between now and the fall freeze."

"If we had gotten here earlier, we could plant beans. I think if we could guarantee delivery, we could get a government contract to deliver them to Ft. Mitchell and Ft. Robinson, maybe even Ft. Laramie," Mr. Bowers said. "I heard at the barbershop that the army is shipping out beans from Iowa."

"That's an intriguing idea," Mr. Wells pondered. "Someone

needs to organize the homesteaders, and we could sell as a block unit."

"You're just the one, Daddy," Jolie declared.

Matthew Bowers stretched his long legs out. "First, a man would have to know if the government would even consider such a deal. Next time I go to town, I could ride out to Ft. Mitchell and do some preliminary discussion. Perhaps the quartermaster there could put me in touch with army purchasing. It would take quite a quantity to supply them. We'd need lots of homesteaders growing beans."

Jolie patted the back of her father's hand. "You would have all winter to talk to the homesteaders."

"The whole farm wouldn't have to be in beans," he replied. "Just forty acres each."

"If we had a hundred homesteaders, that would be four thousand acres of beans," Mr. Wells said.

Jolie raised her auburn eyebrows. "A hundred sounds ambitious."

"That's true. We could start out with twenty-five. That would give us a thousand acres of beans."

Jolie glanced over to the fireplace. Mrs. Wells slept on the buffalo robe. "Beans, sugar beets, rice . . . you men have some ambitious plans."

Mr. Bowers watched a muddy drop of water fall into the bucket. "However, the first thing I need to do is levee and drain this homestead."

Mr. Wells unfastened the dirty collar of his white shirt. "And the first thing I need to do is to find my place."

"Where did you say it was?" Mr. Bowers asked.

Mr. Wells spread a hand-drawn map out on the box. "We were to drive east on Telegraph Road. Then the road was to jog over the tracks here . . . then back to the left here . . . and there is a road to the right. But the storm was so severe, I don't know if we have the right jog in the road at all. There's certainly no road to the right."

"Except our lane," Jolie added.

"At night I couldn't even see that."

"We had a difficult time in daylight," Mr. Bowers informed him.

Mr. Wells leaned forward and lowered his voice, glancing at his sleeping wife. "To tell you the truth, I don't expect too much. I bought the place very cheap."

Mr. Bowers pointed to the shadowy walls of the front room. "Yes, and this one isn't a place of luxury either."

Jolie set her coffee cup down and rubbed her shoulders.

Mr. Wells held his graying temples with his fingertips. "I do hope we have some furniture in ours. DeLila is despondent enough as it is. I don't believe she could handle too much more disappointment."

"She'll perk up once she has her own place," Jolie said.

"I know you folks are new here, too, but perhaps you know of this man's place," Mr. Wells probed.

"Probably not. We just got the papers filed on this one," Matthew said. "But I did glance at the names of our neighbors while I was in the land office yesterday. Whose homestead did you buy?"

"Avery's." Mr. Wells beamed. "We bought the Avery homestead."

five

When Lissa and Gibs Bowers charged the team into the yard the next morning, mud whipped off all four wagon wheels like pinwheels on the Fourth of July. The other children bounded out to greet them in the bright Nebraska sunshine.

Gibs hopped off the wagon, his Henry rifle over his shoulder.

Lawson took the lead lines. "I'll put up the horses, Mama. I have the corral and barn repaired."

Mrs. Bowers tugged up the hem of her long dress and climbed out of the wagon.

Jolie scooted over next to her. "Mama, how's Alfonso DeMarco?"

Mrs. Bowers glanced up at her daughter, who stood several inches taller. "It isn't good, darlin'. Dr. Fix pitched a fit at them for not listening to you. She gave them a what-for up one side and down the other." She hugged Jolie. "I think you'll like the doctor. She said she wanted to meet you soon."

"Another family thought they bought this same homestead," Jolie reported.

"So I hear." Lissa untied her straw hat. "I pulled the Wells wagon out and got them going. Daddy and Gibs introduced me to everyone."

"Me and Tanner talked almost all night," Gibs reported.

"Is Daddy going to the land office with them?" Jolie asked.

"Yes, since we had already filed, and our bill of sale was dated earlier, the place is ours. But he feels bad for the Wells family."

"I can hardly believe Avery sold this place once," Lawson mumbled, "let alone twice. He's not an honest man."

"Mrs. Wells broke down and cried, Mama," Jolie said.

Lissa Bowers led the way through the mud to the house. "She's just scared, honey. It's okay to be scared."

"What's going to happen to them?" Essie asked.

"Daddy said perhaps the land office will have another place they could homestead. He didn't know if there are any others unclaimed. If they have to buy another, it could be a hardship."

"How's Daddy going to get back?" Essie asked.

"He's going to pick up the DeMarco team and wagon and keep them here. Mrs. DeMarco was worried about her animals. Daddy said either he or Lawson would ride up there and feed the other animals every day. She's going to stay in town with Alfonso until he gets better or . . ."

Jolie squeezed her mother's arm. "Mama, no . . ."

Lissa Bowers patted her daughter's hand. "Anyway, we'll keep her team until she returns."

"We don't have a lot of feed," Jolie said.

"Mrs. DeMarco told me to have Daddy bring a load of hay from her place with him. So we'll do all right."

Essie laced her fingers in her mother's. "Mama, did you meet Chester Wells?"

"The one they call Bullet? Yes, I met him. He said you were lots of fun."

"Lots of fun? He mentioned me? Ahhhhh! This is horrible!" Essie groaned. "I can't believe that after I clobbered him."

"I take it you didn't get along too well."

"Mother, he's horrible! Isn't he, Jolie?"

Jolie stopped at the front step and scraped mud off her shoes with a small stick. "He's a very strange little boy."

"I did notice that he was wearing a canvas feedbag for a hat and had his shirt on backwards." Mrs. Bowers waited as Jolie scraped her shoes as well.

"Mama, can I fry you an egg and boil some coffee?"

"That would be delightful, honey. I'll change into my old dress. We have lots of work to do around here."

"Did Daddy mention my plans for a levee to keep the river out of our homestead?" Lawson shouted across the yard.

"No, but it sounds wonderful. You'll have to tell me about it while we work," Mrs. Bowers called out.

"The garden's too wet to work this mornin', Mama. I done tried it. And the field won't plow for a week, I reckon," Lawson informed her.

Mrs. Bowers pulled off her boots and stood next to Jolie, who towered over her. "Then we'll just have to make the beds."

"We ain't got no beds to make," Gibs reminded her.

"What I meant was, we'll build the beds. I have some lumber in the wagon. Gibs, help Lawson with the team. Then you two unload the wagon. Where are the railroad ties Daddy said you found?"

"Behind the shed," Lawson answered.

"Haul ten of them around by the front door. We'll saw them up and use them for bedposts, table legs, and benches. Find the carpenter tools. We're going to do some building." She marched through the doorway. "Nice door! Did anyone milk the cow?"

"Jolie milked her before breakfast," Essie declared. "Her name is Margaret. The calf is Francis. He's very friendly."

While Mrs. Bowers, Lawson, and Gibs built beds, Jolie and Essie wove, stretched, and tacked rawhide strips as bedsprings. The buffalo robes served as mattresses. Jolie stuffed several pillowcases with old rags and sewed the ends shut to make pillows. Soon a bed almost filled up the girls' side of the backroom.

Essie stretched out on it. "I like a high bed."

"We'll have room underneath to store things," Jolie noted.

"Mama said we can have the big mirror," Essie said. "She'll put the little one by the front door."

Essie stretched her arms out on the bed. "Daddy said he was going to get started on our big stone house when he gets back."

"That will take him a long time, of course."

"I know. Jolie, I sure like sleeping with you. Will we really sleep together in the big house?"

"You heard what Daddy said."

"But what if there isn't a thunderstorm? Can I sneak in sometimes anyway?"

"How could I giggle myself to sleep without my best friend under the covers with me?"

Essie sat up on the edge of the bed. "Sometimes I like bein' poor. Remember Katrina DeSmet in Helena? She lived in the big white Victorian house with two maids and a butler," Essie said.

"I never went to her house."

"I did. Her bedroom was way far away from her mama's and daddy's. She said when she had a bad dream and woke up scared, she had to pull a satin cord that rang a bell downstairs. One of the maids would get up and come see what was wrong. That sounds very, very lonely. All I have to do is roll over and hug my big sister. Or call out, and Mama, Daddy, and two brothers are just steps away. I like that."

"So do I, Estelle Cinnia."

Gibs appeared at the foot of the bed. "Hey, guess what?"

"This is the girls' room. You're supposed to knock before you come in," Essie scolded.

"You ain't got a door or even a wooden wall. I can't knock on the quilt or the sod wall."

"Next time whistle or something," Essie said.

"Really?"

"We would like a warning just in case, you know, we're indecent," Jolie explained.

His brown eyes widened. "But you two always look decent."

Jolie grinned. "Thank you, Mr. Gibson Hunter Bowers. Now what is the excitement?"

"Mama and Lawson are makin' us boys army beds."

"What do you mean, army beds?" Essie questioned.

"Two bunks stacked on top of each other. She said it would give more room to our side. That way we don't have to sleep in the same bed. Mama said she and Daddy could use your bed if you two wanted beds like ours."

Jolie looked at Essie. They replied, "NO!"

He looked startled.

"Gibs, what would be the fun of being sisters if we couldn't hide under the covers and tell secrets to each other?" Jolie said.

After Lawson and Lissa built the bunks, they hammered together another double bed for Mr. and Mrs. Bowers and shoved it into a corner of the front room to serve as a sofa as well. Jolie and Essie crammed crates and boxes under beds and into corners. Curtains were crafted for the small front windows.

With the sun drawing steam off the sod house, the boys pulled the rubber tarps off the roof. Then they dug worms, pulled off their shoes, rolled their pant legs to their knees, and sloshed off through the mud to go fishing.

Mrs. Bowers hammered together two four-foot benches out of one of the cleaner railroad ties. Jolie brought out coffee and rye crackers to the yard, and they sat on the benches to enjoy their snack.

Essie swatted her arm. "The mosquitoes aren't too bad until sunset."

Lissa unfastened the high collar of her sweat-stained old white blouse. "I hope the mosquito net and citron candles help some. I think once the water recedes off the place, the mosquitoes will thin out. Did I ever tell you girls about the tiny little gnats in Nevada?"

"Was that when Jolie was a baby?" Essie asked.

"Yes. I had her in a basket draped with mosquito cloth. Still those no-see-ums got in there and bit her precious little round face. She was crying, and I was crying because I couldn't do anything about it. It was the night we left Carson City. Not a happy memory."

"Which time was that?" Essie shoved an entire rye cracker into her mouth.

"Daddy bought the livery stable there so cheap and then found out the next week that the previous owner had bet the entire place on a horse race. Daddy had signed the deed assuming all liens."

"So we left town in the middle of the night?" Jolie asked.

"Oh, yes. The man who won the race insisted that we owed him more than the livery was worth. Judge Kingston refused to hear the case, but the man spread lies that Daddy welshed on his debt. Your daddy couldn't live with that. So he packed us up, and we drove and drove and drove until we got to Arizona. All the way those little bugs bit baby Jolie. I held you for a week under my blouse with just your head and red hair popping out. I constantly brushed your face to keep them from lighting on you. I prayed day and night for you, darlin'. But still the Lord allowed the bugs to bite you. By the time we got to Arizona, your little face was bright red, and mine was red from all the tears. Poor Daddy—he was beside himself, he was so helpless. Then we crossed the Colorado River on a ferry boat. The bugs disappeared just like that."

Lissa stared across the farm toward the river.

Jolie felt her face itch but refused to scratch. "Mama, do you ever regret all the moves?"

"No, darlin'." She sipped her coffee and then tilted her head back and closed her eyes. "Sometimes things happen outside your control. Most of our moves have been like that."

"But don't you ever get tired of moving?" Jolie asked.

Lissa opened her eyes. Her thin lips were tight. "Baby, I'm bone-tired most of the time. But the Lord never promised us an easy life. He promised to keep us in His hand and to be with us and to lead us home to heaven. I reckon that's good enough for me. How about you?"

Jolie felt a tear swell in her eye. "Oh, yes, Mama."

"I feel very, very lazy just sitting here. But it does seem good to relax in the sun with my girls. I hope you both have wonderful daughters of your own someday."

"Hmmmmm," Jolie sighed.

Mrs. Bowers raised her eyebrow. "Oh? I'm just guessing that was about a certain Mr. Tanner Wells."

"Did you meet him?" Jolie asked.

"Yes, I did. Daddy said he figured you were smitten by a gunsmith."

Jolie sat up and held her coffee cup in her lap. "I am not smitten."

"I was smitten once," Essie admitted.

"Oh? When was this?" Lissa asked.

"In Helena."

"And who was the boy?"

"Charles David Jordan."

"You hated Charles David Jordan," Jolie reminded her.

"Yes, that's because he smote me with a snowball."

Lissa grinned. "Oh, that kind of smitten."

"Yeah, but I smote him back. Real good, too. Gibs taught me how to make a cannonball."

"A cannonball?" Jolie queried.

"A cannonball snowball," Essie explained. "You pack them real tight, dip them in water, and let them set out in the freezing temperature overnight."

"That sounds like a dangerous weapon," Mrs. Bowers remarked.

"It kept Charles David Jordan from pestering me after that."

Lissa Bowers took another sip of coffee. "I imagine it did."

"Was that the little boy with dimples when he smiled?" Jolie asked.

"Yep."

"I do remember him smiling a lot when he came over to play," Mrs. Bowers added.

"Yeah, until I clobbered him with the cannonball. But any boy can smile nice, Mama. A girl should wait until she sees how he kisses."

Lissa's shoulders stiffened. "Who told you that, young lady?"

Essie hung her head. "Jolie."

"I most certainly did not," Jolie gasped.

Essie shrugged. "Then maybe it was Katrina DeSmet."

"I think maybe it's time to get to work." Mrs. Bowers finished her coffee. "I was going to build us a table."

At the sound of distant hooves, Essie ran to the side of the house. "There's a wagon coming!"

"Is it Daddy?" Jolie called out.

"I don't know . . . no . . . it's not Daddy."

Jolie stood. "Is it the Vockerys?"

Mrs. Bowers remained seated. "Is that the family with April, May, June, and Mary?"

"No, it's just two men," Essie shouted.

Mrs. Bowers tugged on Jolie's arm. "Sit down, big sis. We don't need to greet men standing. They should come to us. Never show that you're anxious to meet a man."

Jolie plopped back down as the farm wagon pulled around the corner and into the yard. The load in the back was covered with a brown canvas tarp. She watched her mother pretend to sip out of the empty coffee cup. Jolie did the same.

Far in the distance, the fresh air and bright sun made the Wildcat Mountains look close. *Lord, Mama is either the classiest pioneer lady or the hardest-working city lady you ever made. Let me be like her. Just a little bit anyway.*

Essie ran over and stood behind Mrs. Bowers, who had fastened the top button on her blouse.

A tall, barrel-chested, middle-aged man swung down to the ground. The other man held the reins of the team of black horses.

"Excuse us, ladies, for pullin' right up to the house. It just works better this way." The man yanked off his hat, revealing thick gray hair, neatly trimmed. "I'm Captain Richardson. I own the Double-

O Ranch way up on the bench to the north. This is my foreman, Jocko Martinez."

The Mexican tipped his wide-brimmed black felt hat with its silver concho hatband and grinned. His teeth were bright white but crooked.

Jolie fought the urge to stand. She thought she caught a whiff of garlic. She faked a sip of coffee from the empty cup.

Captain Richardson held his hat in front of him. "I reckon you three are sisters."

Lissa Bowers laughed. "Oh, Captain Richardson, what a delightful lie. Thank you very much for that." Mrs. Bowers held her coffee cup now with her left hand. Her gold wedding ring caught the bright sunlight. "Captain, I presume you're from Texas."

He rubbed the graying stubble of his three-day beard. "Yes, ma'am. Does it still show?"

Lissa glanced at her daughters. "Girls, there are no flatterers on earth better than Texas men. They can make a lady feel wonderful with their words."

He stuck his hat back on. "Thank you, ma'am."

A tiny smile curled Lissa's narrow lips. "As long as you don't start believing what they say, you'll get along fine."

Jocko Martinez hooted. "You got the ol' man figured out."

"I'm Lissa Bowers. These are my daughters—Jolie Lorita and Estelle Cinnia."

"You can call me Essie."

"What can we do for you, Captain Richardson?" Lissa asked.

"Actually, Mrs. Bowers, we was just returnin' somethin' that rightfully belongs to you." Richardson pointed to the back of the wagon.

"Oh?"

Jolie noticed that the captain was bowlegged and wore spurs even though riding in the wagon. He laid his arm on the sideboard. "Last winter in a big snow we had fifty head break off the bench and head down here toward the river. When we rode down to round them up, this soddy was abandoned. The boys found a nice cook-stove that they wanted for the cow camp. We figured no one was coming back, so I let them haul it off. Last night while chasin' cows in that storm, I ran across Ernie Vockery. He said folks had bought the Avery place. So as soon as the road dried, I wanted to return your cookstove. Jocko slicked it up for you."

Jolie jumped to her feet to get a better look, but Lissa remained seated. "That's very thoughtful, Captain Richardson."

The Mexican tugged the canvas tarp off to reveal a scrubbed-clean black iron and copper stove. "She cooks very nice. I will miss her. I call her Estefania."

"The stove has a name?" Essie asked.

"Cow camps can get very lonely, señorita."

"If Mr. Bowers is around, we'll get this installed for you. We even brought some stovepipe in case yours disappeared." The cap-tain surveyed the homestead. "Mr. Bowers is still . . . eh, with us, isn't he?"

Jolie studied her mother. "Yes, he is, Captain. He's in town at the land office."

Jolie thought she saw a sadness in the captain's eyes. "That's all right. I reckon Jocko and I can set it up for you."

Within thirty minutes, the stove had a small fire boiling in its belly, and the two men rattled out of the yard with several jellied crackers each.

Mrs. Bowers led the girls into the house. "The Lord is very good to us."

"The captain is a nice man," Essie said.

"He's a lonely man," Jolie observed.

Lissa glanced over at her. "You caught that, too?"

"Can I go tell the boys about the stove?" Essie asked.

"Can you hold your dress up above the mud?" Mrs. Bowers chal-lenged.

Essie pulled off her shoes and stockings and scooted out the front door.

Jolie settled in next to her mother. "Mama, for just a minute you made the captain's eyes sparkle."

"Darlin', we can never control how men look at us. There's nothin' to feel guilty about. But we can control how we look back."

Jolie brushed her mother's hair back behind her ear. "You're a pretty woman, Mama."

"Darlin', darlin', darlin' . . . I'm a plain, middle-aged farm wife with an unruly and uncharacteristic braid. Standing next to you, I feel like a very ordinary old lady."

"Mama!"

"Jolie Lorita, if you ever realized how beautiful you are, you'd know why all the young men act so foolish around you."

"Mama, you always make me feel good about myself."

"That's what mamas are for," Lissa said.

"Can I bake a pie in the new oven? And maybe some biscuits? I want to try it out."

Mrs. Bowers hugged her. "Jolie Lorita, one of these days the most blessed young man on earth is going to take you away and make you very happy. Then your mama will have to learn how to cook and sew and clean all over again. Sweetheart, will I ever miss you. But until then, this stove is yours, and you never have to ask me to use it."

Jolie opened the oven door and peeked inside. "I don't think I'll be going very soon. We have lots of work to do on the farm. I want to make this work as much as you and Daddy."

Lissa Bowers strolled over to the open front door and stared out at the bare, treeless yard. "It's a family project, isn't it?"

"I know the boys feel that way, too. This place belongs to all of us."

Lissa slipped her arm around her daughter's waist. "Jolie, when Daddy and I look at you four children, we know that we're the richest people in the world."

"I think maybe the value of money is overrated."

"That's true, darlin'." Lissa stepped out on the front step and stretched her arms. "Now you bake your pie. I have some hooves to clean."

Jolie shook her head and grinned.

"What's the matter?" Mrs. Bowers asked. "Why are you smiling?"

"The thought of you with your 109 pounds yanking up a hoof on a 1,200-pound horse and cleaning it. How do you do that?"

"There's almost nothing on earth more satisfying than to have a big, powerful horse completely under my control."

"Almost nothing?" Jolie quizzed.

Mrs. Bowers raised her eyebrows and then marched out.

Jolie had just pulled the pie from the oven and studied the golden brown crust when she heard the rattle of a wagon.

Essie shouted from the yard, "It's Daddy!"

Jolie hiked out to the stone corral where Mrs. Bowers pulled the rigging off the DeMarco team. Matthew Bowers spread his coat on the wagon seat and rolled up his shirt sleeves. His tie dangled around his neck. "Jolie, I can smell that apple pie clear out here."

She wrinkled her nose. "I know how you like it."

Lissa waved the hames like a pointing stick. "Matthew, what happened in town at the land office?"

Essie jumped into her father's strong arms.

"On the way over to pick up the DeMarco rig, the Wells boy leaped out of the wagon three times." He spun Essie around and plopped her down next to the wagon wheel.

"Chester?" Essie asked.

Matthew let the tailgate down. "The first time he claimed to fall by accident. But by the second and third times, it was kind of obvious he was pretending." Matthew plucked up a worn pitchfork.

Jolie folded her arms and tilted her head. "How was, eh . . ."

Matthew Bowers stabbed the tall stack of hay on the back of the wagon. "Tanner?"

"Yes."

"Oh, I hardly noticed him." Mr. Bowers tossed the hay inside the doorless barn. "Bullet was taking all my attention. Let's see, Tanner's the tall one, isn't he?"

"Daddy, you're teasing me."

He stabbed another bite of hay. "We didn't talk much, darlin'."

"That's okay, Daddy. I understand."

He tossed another fork load of hay into the barn. "Come to think of it, he did ask if I might allow him to come visit my daughter."

Jolie's chin dropped. "He did?" she gasped.

Mr. Bowers stabbed the hay again. "Yes, but he didn't say which daughter."

"I think he's too old for me, Daddy," Essie giggled.

"Hmmmm . . . I suppose young Bullet is about your age."

"No. NO!" Essie protested. "I like older ones than that!"

Jolie waited until he tossed the hay into the barn and then sidled up to him. "Did Tanner Wells really ask to call on me?"

Matthew Bowers leaned on the handle of the pitchfork. "Yes, he did, darlin'."

Jolie licked her narrow lips. They tasted like straw. "What did you tell him?"

"I told him I wasn't the one who needed to be convinced." He spiked another bite of hay.

"You told him he had to talk to Mama?"

"Not hardly, darlin'. I told him you are a very intelligent, decisive young lady who can make up her own mind. So he can call anytime he wants, but that you might just pitch him out on his ear." He tossed the hay into the barn.

"Really? That's what you said?"

"Something to that effect."

She tugged on his arm. "What were your exact words?"

"Oh, darlin', it doesn't matter—"

"Matthew Allis Bowers!" Lissa challenged.

He glanced at his wife. "Hmmm. I see it does matter. I did tell him about your intelligence and decisiveness and that who you visited with is your choice, not mine. I told him that he is always welcome to visit our home since this homestead was almost the Wells homestead."

Jolie bit her lips together. *Lord, I'm not sure whether it's Your Spirit leading or the silly heart of a seventeen-year-old girl, but I really, really want to get to know Tanner Wells better, and I'm not sure why. You know my heart, Lord, and sometimes I wish I did.*

Lissa Bowers led Pilgrim into the corral. "What did the land office tell you?" she called out.

Matthew continued to fork hay into the barn. "Like I thought, the property is officially ours. We did have an earlier dated bill of sale, but the most important thing was the fact that we had already filed."

"And what if someone else shows up holding a bill of sale?" Lissa asked.

"The land agent said the matter is closed." Mr. Bowers pulled his tie completely off and tossed it over his coat. "It's our place, and nothing could reverse that unless we abandon it."

"Poor Mrs. Wells," Jolie said. "She's so weak and anxious already." *If Mr. Tanner Wells is going to come visit, I need to keep my hair neat and wear a clean dress and always have on my earrings and necklace. I should be sitting by the fire reading Milton. And wear my burgundy dress. I need to clean my black shoes. I wonder if I can borrow Mama's ivory combs?*

Lissa closed the gate behind the horses and hiked back to the wagon.

"I think I got things taken care of for the Wells family," Matthew reported.

"What did you do?" Lissa moved over to her daughter and whispered, "Wear your burgundy dress when he comes over, darlin'."

Jolie nodded but kept her eyes on her father.

"I went by to see Mrs. DeMarco," he reported. "She has Alfonso at Mrs. Fuentes' boardinghouse. They were friends in Omaha and . . ."

"How is Alfonso?" Jolie asked.

"It doesn't look good. He refuses to let the doctor amputate the foot."

"Amputate? Then gangrene has set in?" She held on to her father's arm. "I can't believe it. Daddy, I just want to cry."

He hugged her, and she could smell his shaving tonic water. "Darlin', we all make a lot of choices in life—some smart, some foolish, some minor, some eternal. Then we have to live with the choices."

"But it's senseless," Jolie blurted out. "He's a young man. He has a whole life to live."

"Foolishness is always senseless, Jolie." He tossed more hay in the barn.

"What about the Wells family?" Lissa pressed. "How did you help them?"

"Sheridan DeMarco is up in the air about what to do with the homestead. First her husband, now Alfonso. She asked if I knew anyone who would look after her place. She even talked of selling."

"It's on higher ground than ours," Essie said.

"Yes, but this is our place, and we're goin' to make it right here. Besides, she isn't sure what she wants. It all depends on Alfonso, I think."

"So what's the solution?" Jolie pressed.

He paused. "The Wells family is going to move into the DeMarco house and look after the place."

"Really?" Jolie said. "They'll be our neighbors."

"Just a mile away from us if you cut across the other places. We will pass their place on Telegraph Road every time we go to town," he reported.

Jolie fingered her gold necklace. "Did, eh, Mr. Tanner Wells go to Scottsbluff to find a gunsmith job?"

Lissa grabbed a short-handled pitchfork to help her husband.

Mr. Bowers matched his wife, fork for fork. "No, Tanner said he wanted to get his folks situated first."

"Will Mrs. DeMarco let them take over her farm?"

"Or work it for the summer. I'm not sure what they arranged, but the Wellses are moving into the DeMarco homestead."

"A mile isn't very far," Jolie mused. *If he walked across the field, I could spy him coming and have time to straighten myself up a bit. Maybe I could meet him halfway and . . . no, Mama says wait for them to come to you.*

"A mile ain't nearly far enough," Essie sighed. "Daddy, what are these saddles doin' back here in the wagon?"

Mr. Bowers hiked around to the side of the wagon. Mrs. Bowers continued to toss out the hay. "They belong to the DeMarcos. They want us to ride their two horses as much as we can. She says they get cranky if they aren't ridden every day."

Jolie pressed her nose against her face. "Perhaps Essie and I should go for a ride this afternoon to settle them down."

"I think I'll stay with Daddy," Essie countered.

"I said, me and my very best friend in the whole world want to go for a ride this afternoon," Jolie puffed.

Essie's brown eyes widened. "Oh, yes, on second thought, I do want to go for a ride."

Mr. Bowers grabbed his wife by the waist and raised her up on the wagon. She tossed hay to the back of the wagon, and he tossed it into the barn. "Where are the boys?" he asked.

"Fishing," Jolie replied.

"I don't think they can catch anything until the river clears." He hurried to keep up with every forkful his wife tossed.

Lissa wiped sweat off her forehead with the sleeve of her blouse. "I believe the North Platte is muddy almost year round."

"In that case, if there are any fish, they're used to it. Perhaps the boys will do all right."

"What about Essie and me going for a ride, Daddy?" Jolie pressed.

"I think it would be nice for the girls to ride," Lissa suggested.

"There's only one sidesaddle."

"Estelle can ride in a regular saddle," Lissa replied.

"Or I could just stay home," Essie said. "I don't look forward to seeing Chester."

"Essie!" Jolie snapped.

She rolled her eyes. "Some days it's like having two mothers."

Lissa Bowers had both of the horses saddled by the time Jolie combed her hair, carefully pinned it up, and put on her straw hat.

Essie's hair hung to her waist, held behind her head by a crooked yellow ribbon.

They were just getting ready to mount the horses when they heard a shout from the far end of the property.

Essie waved her arm. "It's the boys."

"What in the world do they have?" Matthew asked.

Lissa shaded her eyes. "Where did they get that?"

They all watched as the boys came closer.

"Mama," Gibs shouted, "we found us a pig."

"Can we keep him?" Lawson hollered.

"He was runnin' wild along the river," Gibs explained.

"But he isn't wild now," Lawson said. "I reckon he must have belonged to someone."

"I think he got tired," Gibs reported. "It wears a pig out to run through mud."

"I'll remember that." Mrs. Bowers continued to fork the hay.

Suddenly the black and white pig veered to the north and made a dash for the open front door of the house.

"No, you don't, Mr. Pig! You stay out of the house," Lissa shouted. The pig immediately veered toward the shed.

Matthew scratched his head. "Even pigs are smart enough to mind your mama."

"Can we keep him, Daddy?" Gibs asked.

"Make a temporary pen out of those railroad ties and put him in there. But someone may come to collect him."

"He can eat our scraps," Jolie offered.

"Make the pen on the other side of the corral," Lissa instructed. "I don't want to smell pig every time I come out the front door."

Jolie and Essie mounted the horses.

"Where are you two goin'?" Gibs asked.

Jolie settled in on the sidesaddle, the flat horn tucked under her dress between her knees. "We're just goin' for a ride."

"To see Tanner Wells," Essie giggled.

"We most certainly are not," Jolie protested.

Essie leaned across the saddle horn and stroked the black mane of the bay horse. "We aren't?"

Jolie smoothed out her skirt across the horse. "Of course, while exercising these horses, we might stop by to see dear Mrs. Wells. You know her health isn't too good."

"Yeah, that's what I meant." Essie kicked the horse in the flanks.

The girls rode east of the house and then north toward the narrow lane.

Jolie reined up at the first gulch. "Let's cut across here."

Essie turned around and rode back to her. "You think we can cut across those gullies?"

"The horses seem quite surefooted. Besides, the gulch isn't very deep, and it's the shortest distance."

"I suppose we shouldn't waste any time going to see poor Mrs. Wells," Essie giggled.

"Quite so!"

Jolie led the way across a shallow gully and into a field that had been plowed at one time and then abandoned.

"Do you think these homesteads belong to anyone still?" Essie asked.

Jolie surveyed the land and could no longer see their sod house behind them. "I don't know. Daddy said there are no more available homesteads close to us. But sometimes the maps at the land office aren't up to date."

Essie bounced, hatless, on the worn basket-stamped saddle. "But no one lives on them."

"I don't think you need residency for the whole year to prove them up. Perhaps the owners know a way around those regulations."

Essie pulled a piece of foxtail grass from the horse's mane. "We didn't even ask what the horses' names are."

"Perhaps Daddy knows."

"It seems rather rude to ride a horse and not even know his name."

"You can give him a nickname."

Essie leaned over, her eye only inches from the horse's. "I'm going to call him Leppy."

"You're going to use Leppy Verdue's name for a horse?" Jolie quizzed.

"Yes, because he's strong and has a black mane and very determined eyes. Besides, you were named after a horse."

"That's true. So if that one is Leppy, how about this one?"

"You have to give him a nickname," Essie insisted.

"Then I'm going to call him Pullman."

"Why?" Essie asked.

"Because he's as smooth as a Pullman car on the railroad." Jolie stopped at the top of the rise. "It looks like someone planted a crop over there."

"But I don't see a house."

"Perhaps they'll build it this summer." Jolie cut across the plowed, unplanted portion of the homestead.

"Is it corn?" Essie asked.

"I think so."

"It's awful muddy here."

Jolie pointed west. "If we stay over there on the prairie grass, it might be a little better."

"This place is full of gullies and draws. I don't think a person could farm this too well."

Jolie urged her horse into the brush-lined gulch. "It does feel good to be riding again though, doesn't it?"

"This is a peaceful way to travel. Wait at the top for me."

Jolie turned her horse back and waited for Essie to catch up. "Look way over there, Essie. There's Chimney Rock. When we're down in the gully, we can't see any other person or farm."

"It's just like being on the Oregon Trail, rolling into empty land," Essie sighed.

"I think the Oregon Trail was on the south side of the North Platte River," Jolie corrected.

"I know, but I can pretend. What do you think it would have been like to make history? They all knew they were doing something that would be remembered. They kept journals and everything. Remember that book you read to me about Red Bear?"

"Retta Barre."

"Yeah. She had an exciting life every day."

"It was a novel."

"I wish I was in a novel. I'd change my name to Sierra Nevada," Essie declared.

The girls continued to ride northwest.

"You keep a journal, don't you?" Jolie asked.

"Yeah, but I never have anything exciting to put in it. Do you think that we missed all the history?"

Jolie clutched the saddle horn and kicked the horse up a rise and through low brush. "Every day is historic, but some include important events to record. I suppose that's a basic desire of all people, isn't it? To do something meaningful, something that lasts beyond themselves."

"Gibs wants to be a famous lawman like Pappy Divide or Stuart Brannon. Do you ever want to do something historic, Jolie?"

"I want to live my life in a way that good people remember me, but I don't know about historic. Working a homestead along the North Platte River in Nebraska doesn't sound very historic, but I like it."

"Do people always know they're doing something historic?" Essie asked.

"I don't think so, but some do. Lewis and Clark knew. The '49ers who went to California knew. The Pony Express riders knew. The first railroaders knew."

Essie rode up beside Jolie. "I know I haven't done anything historic yet."

"Time will tell. What if someone you met in the past couple of days turns out to be someone famous? Then that first meeting will become historic."

"Like who?"

"What if Bullet Wells becomes governor of Nebraska someday?"

Essie gagged. "Him? What if he becomes an outlaw like Mysterious Dave Mather?"

"Would they call him Mysterious Chester?"

"Peculiar Chester." Essie laughed.

"That would be historic, too."

"I'm going to write a book about our family," Essie declared.

"What about your book about Sierra Nevada?"

"I can write more than one book. If I write about us, we all become historic, don't we?"

Jolie laughed. "I reckon so. And what will you call the book?"

"Maybe I'll write three books. What's that called?" Essie asked.

"A trilogy." Jolie kicked the sorrel gelding with her heels. He broke into a trot.

Essie bounced along to keep up. "That's it. The first book will be called *Essie Bowers: The Early Years*."

"That does have a catchy sound to it. But I think your publisher will make you call it *Estelle Bowers: The Early Years*."

"Really?"

"I'm afraid so."

"In that case, I'll call it *Soggy Soddy and Other Tales from Western Nebraska*."

Jolie burst out laughing. "Oh my, that was quite a change."

"I'm good at book titles."

"I can see that."

"I'm not very good at the writing part yet, but I'm good at titles. Slow down, Jolie!" Essie called.

Jolie reined her horse back to a walk. "Is your backside getting sore?"

"No, you have something on your hat. I just wanted to see what it is."

"What is it?" Jolie demanded.

"Just a grasshopper, I think."

"Get it off of me."

"Me?" Essie gasped. "I don't want to touch it."

Jolie reached up to the brim of her straw hat. The grasshopper buzzed off across the field.

The girls rode across prairie and around a patch of prickly pear cactus.

"Jolie, what do grasshoppers eat?"

"Plants, I suppose."

"Like corn?"

"Like anything green." Jolie stared north. "I think that's a house way up there."

"Is this where the DeMarco place begins?" Essie asked.

"I presume so."

"Their corn is starting to come up."

"We'll have to hurry, I'm afraid, to make a crop this year."

"Is Daddy really going to plant sugar beets and rice?"

"I'm not sure. He will certainly study up on them. I don't think we should raise anything we can't eat without a refinery."

"That's the DeMarco house, isn't it?"

"Yes."

"Do you see the Wells family?" Essie asked.

Jolie scanned the back of the homestead. "I don't even see a wagon or team."

Essie pulled her long brown hair around so that it hung down the front of her dress. "Maybe they aren't there."

"You mean we rode all the way here for nothing?" Jolie felt pain in her lower back and scrunched around to find a different position. "This has not been a real comfortable ride."

"Your back hurts a lot?"

"I suppose, but this sidesaddle isn't all that comfortable."

"I thought we were just out for a sisterly excursion anyway." Essie grinned.

"Next time we have a sisterly excursion, remind me to take the wagon."

"Look, I see a horse," Essie called out.

"And there's a wagon," Jolie added. "Isn't that someone standing on top of . . ."

"He's standing on top of the privy. It's him. It's Chester. Oh, no. That's exactly why I wanted to stay home," Essie moaned.

"Remind me not to use their privy."

"I'm not getting off my horse," Essie announced.

"We'll have to stop and sit a spell," Jolie said. "It's the neighborly thing to do."

"Can I sit right next to you?"

"I believe so."

A blond-haired boy about thirteen years old jogged out toward them.

"Is that one Theo?" Jolie whispered.

"He's Gregory."

"I think that's Theo."

"Hi," the boy hollered.

"Hello, Theo," Jolie greeted him.

"I'm Greg," he replied.

Jolie glanced at Essie, who rolled her eyes.

"What're you doin' here?" He grinned.

"We just went for a ride and thought we'd see how you were settling in."

Mr. Wells burst out of the barn wearing an old leather apron and carrying a large square wooden mallet.

"This is a surprise." He motioned to the girls. "Please, come down and visit us. We're just unpacking a few things. It's difficult to know how much to settle in. Everything is so tentative with Mrs. DeMarco. She could show up tomorrow . . . or never come back."

Jolie rode over next to him. "I'm quite concerned about Alfonso DeMarco."

"The lady doctor said the next three days are crucial. So I believe we'll be here for at least three days." He held up his hand to Jolie.

Jolie brushed dust off her dress, grabbed his hand, and slid off the horse. "Perhaps that will give you time to discover the Lord's leading."

"I was thinking the very same thing." Mr. Wells nodded. When he pulled off his felt hat, sweat dribbled down his forehead. "Mrs. Wells is inside. She'll be delighted to see you." He offered his hand to Essie. "Bullet is around here somewhere, young lady."

"Thank you for warning me." She scowled and then leaped to the ground.

As Jolie walked toward the side of the sod house, she noticed blood on the woodpile and dirt where she had tended Alfonso's foot. *Lord, I pray that his foolishness has not cost him his life. Please teach him Your lessons and restore his health.*

Essie tugged on her arm. "Jolie, Mrs. Wells called to you."

She looked up to see the tiny woman, apron-clad, hunched beside the sod house.

"Excuse me, Mrs. Wells. I was just thinking of Alfonso DeMarco."

"Yes, poor boy. Please come in. I'm delighted you stopped by. Is your mother with you?"

"No, but she does look forward to a visit. She was cleaning the horses' hooves when we left."

A brown-haired boy about fourteen appeared in the doorway behind Mrs. DeMarco.

"Hi, Theo!" Jolie called out.

The boy grinned. "Hi, Miss Jolie. Thanks for rememberin' my name."

"I don't often forget a nice smile like that." Jolie glanced over at Essie, who held her hand over her mouth.

"I was just rearranging a few things. Come in." Mrs. Wells led the way.

"Theo, you go help Daddy repair that wagon wheel," Mrs. Wells ordered.

"Daddy don't need any help."

"Theo!"

"Greg is out there."

"Young man, the ladies and I are goin' to have tea, and you aren't invited," Mrs. Wells announced.

"Oh. I don't like tea."

"You see."

"Bye, Miss Jolie."

"Good-bye, Theo."

"Theo!" Mrs. Wells nodded toward Essie.

"Bye, Miss Estelle."

"Bye, Theodore."

They watched as Theo trudged across the yard. "I'm afraid you Bowers girls have completely won over the Wells boys."

"You have such nice bo—"

Essie poked Jolie in the ribs with her elbow.

"Eh, you have such a nice place here. Mrs. DeMarco kept it quite tidy."

"Yes. I cried for hours when we found out the Avery place belonged to you. Then, as if by divine miracle, this place became available. I just know the Lord led us here."

Essie plopped down. "I like this leather sofa."

"Can you imagine space for a sofa in a sod house? It's quite roomy for a two-room house."

"I believe it's wider than ours."

"Bullet sleeps on that couch."

Essie jumped up and scooted over by Jolie.

"Just sit at the table, girls. I really do have tea. I'm afraid the flatbread is a little stale, but the currant jelly makes it edible."

"Mrs. Wells, it was worth the ride clear over here just to see you at ease and settling in." Jolie glanced at the grotesque face pressed against the window pane. Then she looked over at her scowling sister. *Bullet is indeed a very strange little boy.*

"I'm afraid I was a mess last night. I just couldn't seem to control my emotions. You'll have to forgive me."

"Mrs. Wells, it was completely understandable."

"Your family helped me immensely. You're all so gracious."

"I'm glad we could get you out of the cold." Jolie was distracted when Bullet began licking the glass window pane in the wall behind his mother.

"I'm so grateful for that. But seeing all of you crowded into that little place of yours, so peaceful in the midst of a new beginning and uncertainty, I just realized that we're all in this together. We don't know how it will work out, but we will make it work. Anyway, it was a comfort." Mrs. Wells retrieved the teapot.

Bullet made faces at the window.

"I'm glad you're feeling better." Jolie tried to focus on Mrs. Wells.

"I do feel a bit guilty. This house is so cozy, with a shake roof, flowers in the planters, and furniture."

"Mrs. DeMarco seems like a very nice woman." Jolie glanced over at Essie, who stuck her tongue out at the boy in the window.

"And such a tragedy!"

"I don't understand that. I told her and Alfonso not to bind the foot tight or raise it up."

"Oh, yes, her son. That's tragedy upon tragedy. I meant her husband," Mrs. Wells offered.

"I didn't hear about her husband. What happened?"

Bullet appeared at the window with a sunflower in his hand.

"Mr. DeMarco was shot to death last year on his way home from town. The team came in on their own. When she and her son retraced his route, they found him dead."

"Oh, no. Who did such a thing?"

"No one ever found out. But he still had a $20 gold piece in his pocket. I trust such happenings are a thing of the past."

"Let's hope so, but I suppose we will always have the sinfulness of man with us."

Bullet Wells held the sunflower out in front of him as if to offer it to Essie.

"I suppose being out here on the road will mean more visitors than back at your place."

"That's probably true. Mrs. Wells, what arrangements did you make with Mrs. DeMarco?"

Essie shook her head at Bullet's offer.

"She's not coming back. So we'll get to stay here. Of course, the papers need to be signed first."

Jolie sipped her tea from a chipped china cup hand-painted with delicate purple violets near the rim. *Lord, Mr. Wells said they might have to leave any day. Mrs. Wells thinks they're going to stay forever. There's a potential fuse burning here.*

Once again the boy behind the window pane offered the flower to Essie.

"What did you think of Tanner's new plan?" Mrs. Wells asked.

Jolie glanced around the room. "His . . . eh . . . new plan?"

"His new plan to open his gun shop right out here along the highway rather than in town."

"That would keep him close . . . to all of you. Wouldn't that be nice? But I didn't see Tanner yet. Is he helping Mr. Wells in the barn?"

Essie shook her head again at Bullet Wells.

"Oh, my no." Mrs. Wells slapped her hands against the top of her head. "You mean, you didn't see him at all?"

Jolie glanced around the room. "Where is he?"

"He saddled one of the horses and went calling on you."

"Calling on me?"

"Didn't you meet him on the road?"

"We cut across the gulch and up through the field," Essie blurted out.

"Oh, dear," Mrs. Wells said.

"You mean Tanner went to see Jolie at the same time Jolie came to see Tanner, and they missed each other, and now they're stuck having to visit with each other's families?" Essie giggled.

Jolie straightened her back. "I came to check on Mrs. Wells."

"Children can be so brutally honest, can't they?" Mrs. Wells passed Jolie a cracker.

At that moment Chester "Bullet" Wells ate the sunflower.

Six

Thirty minutes later Jolie and Essie politely excused themselves and mounted up to return home. The formerly tight curls of Jolie's auburn hair sagged with sweat on the back of her neck. She settled on the saddle of the long-legged sorrel gelding and used her straw hat for a fan.

Mama likes the rush of wind in her face. I suppose I do, too. I know it's not too proper, but no one ever told me, Lord, who decides what's proper or not. Did You ever stand in a boat on the Sea of Galilee and let the wind whip Your hair dry just for the fun of it?

Jolie kicked her horse and trotted up Telegraph Road.

Essie pulled up beside her and then glanced back over her shoulder at the DeMarco sod house. "Wouldn't it be faster if we cut across those unoccupied homesteads again? I thought you'd be in a hurry to see Mr. Tanner Wells."

Jolie tugged down the lace sleeves on her burgundy dress. "A lady must never appear to be in a hurry to see a man."

"Even when she is?"

"Especially when she is."

"Then why did we cut across there in the first place?" Essie held all her hair on top of her head.

"To see poor Mrs. Wells, of course, and to give the ponies a good workout."

"Exercising the horses! I never even thought of that reason."

Essie pulled her hair across her lip like a mustache and spoke in a deep voice: "Well, howdy, Miss Essie! I surely am surprised to see you way up here!" "Hello, Captain Handsome. How nice to see you. I was just out exercising my horse." "But you're thirty miles from your homestead!" "And your point is . . .?" Essie finished with a coy smile.

Both girls burst out laughing.

"You really should be a writer!" Jolie exclaimed.

Essie grinned. "But the only exciting thing to write about is you, and everyone would think it's fiction. So we're really going to stay on the road and not cut across?"

"A gentleman should come to the lady, not the lady to the gentleman."

"Is that a rule?"

"Yes."

"There sure are a lot of rules to remember," Essie sighed.

"Oh, it's not too bad."

"Who wrote the rulebook, Jolie?"

"Henrietta Pritchett."

"Great-grandma?"

"All Pritchett women trace their ladylike manners back to Henrietta," Jolie explained. "But don't worry. Mama said we can adapt the rules to our present needs."

"Oh?"

"For instance, Mr. Tanner Wells left on this road, which means he will return on this road."

Essie rubbed her nose on the sleeve of her brown dress. "And you think we will meet him along the way?"

Dropping the reins across her lap, Jolie tied the straw hat on her head. "Unless Mama's employed him to build shelves and tables."

"Or Gibs has him talking gun repair."

"Or Daddy's discussing sweet potatoes, rice, or the Young Farmers' Alliance," Jolie added.

"Or Lawson is showing him a design for a levee. I guess our family is kind of hard to get away from."

"And we aren't even there."

"Jolie, did you ever notice how everyone in our family likes to talk?"

"Yes, I had noticed that. I think it's Daddy's fault, don't you?"

Essie bounced along in the saddle. "I suppose so. He always wants to know all of our opinions. Jolie, do you think we have the best family in the world?"

"I think we have the best family in the world for Matthew, Melissa, Jolie, Lawson, Gibson, and Estelle Bowers. I can't imagine any of us having a better one. But it might not be for everyone."

"Yeah, that's what I meant. Do we have any really strange members in our family?"

Their shadows stretched out ahead of them as they rode east.

"Like Bullet?" Jolie asked.

"Yes. He's so strange. Did you see him—"

"Eat that sunflower?" Jolie said. "Yes, I did."

"That wasn't the strangest thing he did."

"Oh?"

"Never mind," Essie sighed.

"What did Mr. Bullet Wells do?"

"I don't want to talk about it."

"That bad, huh?"

"If Gibs had done it, he would have gotten a whippin'."

"I'm glad I missed that." Jolie stared at the benchland to the north. "I think there are two men up on that rim."

Essie shaded her eyes with her hand. "Maybe it's a team plowing."

"That could be. Now are you going to tell me more about Bullet?"

"No. But I was thinking, we don't have anyone really strange in our family, do we?"

Jolie smiled. She felt the sun warm the back of her neck, and so she pushed her hat back. "I'm not sure any family can recognize what makes them different. I suppose you would need to ask someone outside the family."

Essie jammed her thumbs into her temples and circled them around and around. "What if each one of us were really strange, and we didn't know it? And everyone just shook their heads at us?"

"As long as we didn't know, we'd be happy and have no reason to change." Jolie brushed a ladybug off her sleeve.

"Someone should tell Chester that he's peculiar. Maybe he just doesn't know," Essie maintained.

"I think one should do it judiciously."

"What does that mean?"

"Don't just blurt it out," Jolie explained.

"Okay. Pretend that I'm Chester. How would you tell me I'm strange?" Essie probed.

"I might use a word like *bizarre*."

"He'd think that was a compliment."

"You may be right."

"Go ahead, Jolie, pretend like I'm Chester. How would you tell me?"

Jolie cleared her throat and slowed the horse to a walk. "Chester, I'm a little confused by your behavior."

Essie puffed out her cheeks, stuck her fingers in her ears, hummed loud, then rolled her eyes.

Jolie's shoulders slumped. "What're you doing?"

"I'm pretending like I'm Chester."

"You saw him do all of that?"

"I saw him do more than that."

Jolie stiffened her shoulders and back. "Chester, before you make any more of those comic faces, may I have a serious word with you?"

"How come your eyebrows are crooked?" Essie hollered.

"What?" Jolie reached up and brushed her eyebrows with her fingertips. "Is that better?"

Essie shook her head. "They really weren't crooked. I was just trying to be Chester."

"Are you sure my eyebrows are all right?"

"Yes!"

Jolie cleared her throat. "Mr. Chester Wells, I don't know why a strong, healthy boy like yourself keeps doing dumb things to get attention. It seems rather sad."

Essie stuck her finger up her nose.

"Don't do that," Jolie snapped.

"Chester does that."

"It's unbecoming even in jest."

"Is that in Great-grandma's book?"

"I'm sure it is."

Essie leaned forward until her head rested on her horse's mane. "That's all you'd say to him?"

Jolie wiped the sweat from her neck with her handkerchief. "No, I'd say, 'Chester, I don't want to be around you if you continue such behavior. Do you understand? You're not welcome in my presence until you act better.'"

Essie hugged her bay horse's neck. "You'd really tell him that?"

"Yes, I would." *I should have brought that little vial of perfume. Not that Tanner Wells will get close enough, but one should always be prepared. I wonder if that's in Great-grandmother's book of manners?*

Essie sat up. "I can't wait to hear you tell Chester that."

"Me? No, if he were pestering me, that's what I'd tell him. But he's not. It's you who has to confront him. Do you think you can?"

"I guess." Essie leaned back in the saddle and rested her hand on the horse's rump. "I was hopin' just to hide up on the roof of the house and drop a muskmelon on his head."

"That does sound ladylike."

"I'm not old like you. I don't have to follow all the rules yet."

"Is that what Mama tells you?"

"Mama and you were born ladylike. You don't know how big a struggle it is for someone like me."

"Essie, you're learning quickly. Within a year I'll bet you'll be turning boys' heads."

"Maybe, but I'm saving a large muskmelon just in case."

"Considering Chester, that might be prudent."

"I do believe there are two men riding this way." Essie sat up and brushed her hair back over her shoulders. She swung her right leg over the saddle horn, next to her left, and smoothed down her dress. "How do I look?"

"Very mature."

Essie grinned. "Do you know who they are?"

"No."

"What do we say?"

"Nothing unless they speak first."

"Are they Indians?"

"I think perhaps Mexican. Captain Richardson employs Mexican vaqueros, I believe," Jolie said.

"The one on the right looks young," Essie whispered.

As they approached, the taller man tipped his wide-brimmed felt hat. "Buenas tardes, Senoritas Roja Bonita y Mirasol Bella."

The younger man pulled off his hat, and his black hair curled out. He smiled at Essie, revealing two gleaming gold front teeth.

"Buenas tardes, señors," Jolie replied as she rode past them. "Vaya con Dios!"

"Y ustedes tambien," the man called back.

The girls rode along the track for a few moments without saying anything.

"Don't stop and look back," Jolie whispered.

"Is it against the rules?" Essie giggled.

"Yes."

"What did that man say?"

"He said, 'Good afternoon, Miss Pretty Red Hair and Miss Beautiful Sunflower.'"

"He called me a beautiful sunflower?" Essie squealed.

"Yes, he did."

"And he didn't call me little sister?"

"No, I think young Mr. Gold Teeth was quite taken with you."

"Is that okay? I didn't do anything wrong, did I?"

"No."

"That's the first time ever."

"That a man has said something nice to you?"

"No, it's the first time I've ever been with you when they treated me . . . you know . . ."

"Like a lady?"

"Yes!" Essie slung her right leg back over the saddle horn and straddled the horse, her dress well above her knees, revealing her bloomers.

When they reached the second jog in the tracks, they paused at the two ruts through the weeds that served as a lane to their homestead.

"I can't see any rider coming this way, can you, Jolie? I guess Tanner will be waiting for you at our house."

"That's why we will take our time getting home."

"Are you going to make him wait even longer?"

"It won't be too much longer."

"But what if he has nothing to do and . . . and finds that fat envelope under our bed?" Essie asked.

Jolie laughed. "Estelle Cinnia, he will not be going into our room, and under no circumstances will he be looking under our bed."

They rode on toward the house.

Jolie glanced at her sister. "Besides, what makes you think the envelope is still under our bed?"

Essie fanned her dress up and down. "You moved it and didn't tell me where?"

"Yes, I did."

"But I'm your best friend," Essie complained.

Jolie watched her sister. "There are some things you do not even tell your super-best friend." *Oh, how I'd love to fan my dress up and down. Don't grow up too quickly, little sis. Some days will never come back again.*

"Like what?"

"Like the worst thing you ever saw Chester Wells do."

"Oh, you're right," Essie gasped. "We don't have to tell each other everything, do we?"

The sun cast long shadows as they rode south toward the distant sod house. The slight breeze up from the river smelled of silt, horse sweat, and sage. *Lord, I felt so boxed in at Helena. This is what I missed—wide-open fields and prairies and riding along with Essie or the boys or . . . Mr. Tanner Wells. I wonder why I'm so fond of thinking of him? It's not like he's the only man around. But before, it seemed like I would just sit there, and the boys came to me. This time . . . hmmmm . . . Lord, am I chasing Mr. Tanner Wells? I don't think I've ever done that before. I'm not chasing him, of course. I only met him once and know hardly anything about him. Besides the strong shoulders, square chin, soft drawl, and pretty blue-gray eyes. Oh, my . . . my heart is even racing.*

"Jolie, what're you thinking about?"

"Eh . . . racing."

"You want to race to the house?"

"No, it wouldn't be very ladylike to go racing up to the house while Mr. Tanner Wells is there."

"Why? What's unladylike about riding a horse fast? You have a sidesaddle."

"I might get sweatier."

"Ladies aren't allowed to sweat?"

"Only when company is gone," Jolie said. "Besides, I might get my hair messed up."

"It's already messed up."

"Oh, dear." Jolie reined up the sorrel and tugged off her hat. She plopped it over the saddle horn and pulled the combs out of her hair.

Essie stopped beside her. "What're you doing?"

"Just freshening up a bit."

"Do you think I need to freshen up a bit?"

"You look fine, Essie."

"Chester teased me about my long hair."

"What did he say?"

"He said it looked like a horse's tail."

"That wasn't very nice." Jolie set her hair in her combs and then tied the straw hat back in place. "Now does that look better?"

"Yep, except you have a smudge on your chin."

"Oh, dear, how long have I had that?"

"Since before we got to the Wellses'."

Jolie's mouth dropped open. "You mean, I sat over there with a smudge on my face?"

"It's not that bad. Kind of looks like a birthmark or some freckles. I bet those two vaqueros hardly noticed it."

Jolie pulled out her handkerchief and wiped her chin. "How's that?"

"Now you have a large smear."

Jolie licked the handkerchief and wiped again. "Better?"

"It's clean now. Jolie, did you ever notice that people are very much like animals?"

"What do you mean?"

"We clean ourselves with our own spit." Essie shrugged.

"I just wet my handkerchief."

"That's what I mean."

As they approached the backside of the sod house, Essie stood in the stirrups and surveyed the yard. "I don't see Tanner's horse."

"He's probably out in the corral with Stranger and Pilgrim."

Gibs jogged up to them. His dingy white cotton shirt was buttoned at the collar, his sleeves rolled up. He held up the battered rifle. "Hey, Tanner got the lever workin' on my Henry rifle. He surely does know a lot about guns."

Jolie straightened the bodice of her dress and adjusted the gold locket and chain. "Is he, eh, is Mama in the house?"

"Mama's out there linin' out her vegetable garden," Gibs reported as he walked alongside the girls.

"I thought it was too wet," Jolie said.

"The ground is too wet to spade, but she was twining out the rows. You know how Mama is—she just can't sit still."

"Is anyone helping her?"

"I was, sort of." Gibs scratched his neck. "But I wanted to visit a spell with Tanner."

Jolie slid down off the horse. "Where's Daddy?"

"He's using some of them railroad ties to build a hog pen for Mudball," Gibs replied.

Essie climbed off the bay horse and dropped the reins to the dirt. "You named that pig Mudball?"

"Yep."

Jolie led the sorrel gelding toward the small barn. "Is Tanner helping Daddy?"

"Tanner?" Gibs replied. "He ain't here, Jolie."

She spun around. "What do you mean he isn't here? His mother said he was . . ."

"Oh, he was here. But he left about ten minutes ago."

Jolie folded her arms. "He most certainly did not. We came all the way around the place on the road. We didn't see him."

"He cut across the gulch and the open land," Gibs informed them. "He said, 'Miss Jolie and Miss Essie might have trouble crossin' the barranca. So I reckon I'll take the shortcut and help them across.'"

"He actually mentioned me?" Essie asked.

"Yep. He called you Miss Essie."

Jolie stormed in circles around the yard. "I can't believe this."

Essie giggled.

Jolie stopped in front of her. "I don't see anything funny."

Essie curtsied and then mimicked, "Mama says it's ladylike to sit still and let the boys come to you."

Jolie could feel her heartbeat in her temples. "Well . . . well . . . I have half a mind to ride right back there and tell Mr. Tanner Wells what I think."

Essie stared across the scattered sagebrush and yucca. "If you cut across the fields, and he came around on the road to see you like last time, you could miss each other again. Wouldn't that be funny?"

Gibs looped the rifle over his shoulder. "We could just hold up a cup of water and biscuits as you rode by, and you could keep going around and around all day."

Essie stacked all of her hair on top of her head and held it there. "It would get dark after a while. I suppose they would have to stop then."

"What if they had lanterns?" Gibs suggested.

Essie let her hair drop and clapped her hands. "Oh, yes, that might work."

"Perhaps they could catch a glimpse of each other's distant lantern," Gibs hooted.

Essie chewed on her tongue. "I don't have to ride with her, do I?"

"Nope," Gibs said. "She don't need a chaperon if she can't catch him."

Jolie glared at them. "Are you two quite finished?"

Gibs meandered over next to her. "I really like Tanner, Jolie. I think you'd like him if you ever happened to run into each other."

"That's it," Jolie shouted. "I don't want to hear another word."

Gibs rocked back on his heels and stared down at the dirt. "You want me to put up your horse?"

"Yes," she snapped.

"Jolie, you ain't mad at us for funnin' you, are you?"

She rubbed her forehead and then put her hand on his shoulder. "No, not really. I'd be laughing myself if it had happened to someone else. The Lord has ways of keeping us humble."

"Do you feel humble?" Essie asked.

"Yes. And foolish. From now on Mr. Tanner Wells is just going to have to come see me if he wants to."

Jolie hiked out behind the woodshed where her mother was driving small stakes into the soft, muddy earth.

"Hi, darlin', how were Mr. and Mrs. Wells?"

"Fine, Mama. They seem right at home in the DeMarco place."

Mrs. Bowers stood up and rubbed the small of her back. "Did you get to see Tanner?"

Jolie dropped her chin to her chest. "No, I guess we missed each other."

Her mother strolled over to her. "He and I had a long visit, honey."

Jolie peered into her mother's penetrating brown eyes. "What about?"

"You mainly." Lissa Bowers lifted her skirt to her knees and fanned herself. "It's hot today."

"What did he say? Mama, your bloomers show when you do that."

"That's why I do it." Lissa continued to fan herself. "It wasn't what he said. It was the way his eyes lit up every time he drawled, 'Miss Jolie.'"

"Really, Mama? Really?"

"Yes, and he has big plans for a gunsmith business and building a stick frame two-story house in town with a second-floor veranda facing Scott's Bluff." Mrs. Bowers stared at the distant western horizon. The declining sun erased any trace of Scott's Bluff.

"He told you all of that?" Jolie watched her mother continue to fan her skirt. "Mama, you aren't being very discreet."

"We talked about lots of things, darlin'. And as for bein' discreet, the main reason I wanted a homestead was so I could fan my bloomers any time I wanted."

"Mother!"

Lissa Bowers dropped her skirt. "Sometimes I wonder who the real mother is."

"Why didn't Tanner tell me all those things he told you?"

Lissa bent over and tied a loose end of brown twine around a small peg driven in the soft mud. "I think it has something to do with the fact that you weren't here."

"Did he talk about coming back?"

"Hand me that ball of twine," Mrs. Bowers commanded. "He said he might stop by again in the next few days."

Jolie handed the grapefruit-sized ball of twine to her mother. "Next few days? What kind of promise is that?"

Mrs. Bowers stepped off twenty paces. "Oh, I don't think it was a promise."

"Mother, this is very, very frustrating."

"Bring me that shovel, darlin'. I think I might be able to spade this half of the garden. The soil looks a little more sandy over here."

Jolie handed her mother the shovel. "I'm going to go start supper."

Lissa Bowers glanced at the declining sun. "It's a little early, isn't it? We'll probably want to work until almost dark."

"Then I'll go see if I can do some mending. Mother, I have to do something. I'm not going to sit around and pine for someone I hardly know."

Lissa circled Jolie's waist with her arm. "Jolie Lorita, are you pining for Mr. Tanner Wells?"

"Yes, Mama, I am. And for the life of me, I don't know why."

"I think you know, darlin', I think you know."

For three straight days the Bowers homestead had no visitors. Mrs. Bowers and Lawson spaded the garden and planted seeds in straight rows running north and south.

When Gibs wasn't hunting, he helped his father carry rocks out of the dry part of the field by hitching a sledge behind one of the DeMarco horses.

Every evening Mr. Bowers lined the rocks up in the dirt yard in front of the sod house, in an outline of the future stone foundation for their house.

Essie assisted Jolie with household chores and so befriended the calf that Francis followed her around like a puppy.

Jolie cooked, washed clothes, and then unpacked all of their household goods. From time to time she glanced north up the rutted driveway.

But he didn't come back to see her.

Jolie had just finished washing dishes in a pan on a bench in the front yard when Essie meandered up with Francis tagging along behind. "The ground is dry enough to plow at the north end," Essie announced.

Jolie dried a plate with a flour sack towel. "How's Mama doing at teaching Daddy how to plow?"

"It's very slow, but they're both in a good mood." Essie rubbed the calf's ear. "If a boy ever wants to teach me how to plow, I think I'll turn him down."

Jolie dried another plate. "Why?"

Essie wrapped her arms around herself. "'Cause there's a lot of huggin' when you teach someone to plow."

Jolie raised her eyebrows. "I didn't know that."

"Francis was embarrassed."

Jolie looked at the moon-eyed calf. "He doesn't like hugging?"

"Only when it's me hugging him," Essie answered.

"Ah, there's the basic problem. We all like to be hugged. It's other people hugging that makes us a little nervous."

"Maybe that's it." Essie wandered toward the barn with the calf trailing her.

"Where are you going?" Jolie called out.

"To learn more about plowing."

Jolie had Gibs tie a rope between the woodshed and the barn. She and Essie hung out wet sheets as Mrs. Bowers came their way.

"How's the plowing student, Mama?" Jolie asked.

Mrs. Bowers grinned. "He's a little slow at learning some things, and he can't plow straight. But he tries hard, and so I reckon he'll do."

Jolie pinned up another sheet. "Essie tells me there's been a lot of hugging going on out there."

"Jolie!" Essie squealed.

Mrs. Bowers hugged her youngest daughter. "Oh, she did? Some students require a lot of supervision and encouragement."

"Mama, I like the way you love Daddy," Jolie said.

"That's good, darlin', because I just can't seem to help myself."

"Think about it, Mama. You and Daddy are different that way. Some children never see their parents touch at all," Jolie added.

"Let alone smooch!" Essie squealed as she handed Jolie a clothespin.

Lissa laughed. "Girls, I'm crazy about your daddy. I always have been. So you'll just have to put up with me. Now are you about through with the wash?"

Jolie flung a pair of faded ducking trousers over the rope. "This is the last piece."

Mrs. Bowers gathered up the empty clothes basket. "Good, because we ladies are going to town."

Jolie glanced over at Essie. "When?"

"Right now."

"What about dinner for Daddy and the boys?"

"They can take care of that themselves. We need a few things, and I want to run Pilgrim and Stranger. They're still a little too hot for your Daddy to plow with," Mrs. Bowers explained.

"Can I wear this dress?" Jolie asked.

"You look fine. I'll harness the team and wash up. We'll leave in about half an hour."

"Can I wear this brown dress?" Essie asked.

"Surely."

"Essie, I think your pale blue dress makes you look more mature," Jolie offered.

"I'll change!" Essie sprinted to the sod house.

"She's pursuing mature," Jolie commented.

"Yes, I see that."

Lissa and Jolie Bowers plodded to the house.

"We'll go right by the DeMarco place," Jolie said.

Lissa slipped her arm into her daughter's. "Did you want to stop and see Tanner?"

"No, I do not."

Mrs. Bowers squeezed Jolie's hand. "If I wanted to see Mrs. Wells, I reckon you could be sociable, couldn't you?"

Jolie couldn't hold back the wide grin. "I'll try, Mother."

The team jolted up the rutted drive northward as Jolie and Essie clung to each other and the iron railing. When the heavy wagon rounded the corner to the west and turned onto Telegraph Road, the massive outside wheels of the freight wagon lifted off the dirt. With wide eyes, Jolie and Essie shook their heads at each other while Mrs. Bowers whipped the team on to a faster speed.

The thunder of the team made conversation useless. Jolie clamped her hand on top of her hat. *Lord, Mama loves her horses and driving fast. I like it, too, but sometimes I worry that it's sinful. I don't know why I think that. Maybe it's the rush of air, and the rattle of the wagon, and the roar of hooves. It's the excitement, I guess. I wonder, Lord, while You were here on earth, did You ever feel that excitement?*

The big horses' hooves slid in the dried mud when Lissa brought the team to a stop in front of the DeMarco home. A barefoot boy ran out to meet them.

"Hi, Miss Jolie."

"Hi, Theo. You've met my mother and sister."

He jerked off his hat. His brown hair was parted in the middle and neatly slicked down. "Howdy, Mrs. Bowers. Howdy, Miss Essie."

"How are you today, Theo?" Jolie asked.

He tugged at the collar of his shirt. "Sweaty. Me, Gregory, and Daddy are hoein' the corn. It's hot today."

"We don't even have ours planted yet," Mrs. Bowers said.

"It's Mrs. DeMarco's corn, but we like to call it ours. I ran up to the house for some water. Mama's takin' a nap. Do you want I should wake her?"

"Heavens, no!" Mrs. Bowers exclaimed. "We'll be back this way this evening. I'll say hello to her then. Tell her I stopped by."

"Yes, ma'am, I surely will." He hiked around to the other side of the wagon. "Miss Jolie, if you came callin' on Tanner, he isn't here. He want to work in town, you know."

"I didn't come calling on Tanner. Mama wanted to check on Mrs. Wells. He went to work in town? I thought he was opening a gun shop out here."

"I reckon his plans changed. A couple days ago, Mr. Betters—he has the Platte River Armory in Scottsbluff—well, he's laid up with a busted leg and wanted to hire Tanner to come in and run the shop for a while. Tanner moved to town three days ago. He's staying in a room at the back of the gun shop. Didn't Bullet tell you?"

Essie stood up and looked around. "We haven't seen Chester."

Theo rubbed his chin. "Tanner sent him over three days ago with the message."

"Bullet didn't come," Jolie insisted.

"That's odd. He said Miss Essie looked quite purdy in her light blue dress."

"How did he know what I wore?"

Theo slipped his brown leather suspenders off his narrow shoulders. "Maybe he forgot the message."

"Maybe he forgot to say hello," Essie mumbled.

"Tanner's worked in town for three days. Don't know when he'll be home."

Lissa Bowers retied her hat. "Tell your mother and father we called."

"Yes, ma'am, I will."

Essie sat back down between her mother and Jolie. "Theo, where is Chester?" she asked.

Theo stared across the prairie. "Last I seen of him he was all costumed up as a sagebrush."

Jolie stared north across the road at the unturned prairie. "A sagebrush?"

Theo pointed out across the field. "He said he wanted to hide along the edge of the road and shoot rabbits when they crossed."

"Chester has a gun?" Essie gulped.

"No, Daddy won't let him have one until he's fourteen." Theo shoved his thin hands into the back pockets of his ducking trousers. "He's got a slingshot."

"Good-bye, Theo," Mrs. Bowers said. "You and Gregory should come visit the boys sometime."

"Thank you, ma'am, we'd like that." He jammed his floppy hat back on his head. "Good-bye, Miss Jolie . . . eh, and Mrs. Bowers . . . and Miss Essie."

A slap of the reins, a shout, and the thundering hooves once again plumed dust high into the warm Nebraska sky.

"I do believe Theo is heartsick for Jolie Lorita," Mrs. Bowers shouted above the roar.

Jolie held her hat down. "He's three or four years younger than me."

"That's about right for being truly heartsick."

Jolie leaned across Essie's lap and shouted, "Mama, I think you're exaggerating."

Lissa whipped the team faster. "Darlin', I've seen heartsick boys stare at you like that since you were five."

Essie clutched Jolie's arm as they bounced up and down on the wagon seat.

"Mama, am I doing something wrong?" Jolie asked.

Mrs. Bowers wrapped the lead lines around her wrists and stood up to drive. "Oh, darlin' . . . you're doin' something very right," she called out. "You're being exactly the way the Lord created you. You keep making Him happy, and don't worry about the boys. I guarantee you, you're making them happy with just your smile."

"Did you see that sagebrush move?" Essie shouted.

Jolie sat back. "Little sis, when Mama is driving, all the sagebrush move."

With her knees cocked and taking the impact of every jolt, Mrs.

Bowers continued to stand. "Now you two like fast horses, too," she called out.

"And we'd like to have a long life," Essie added.

"Okay, I'll try to slow down on the corners," Mrs. Bowers called out. Then she slapped the lines on the horses' rumps. "But we aren't at a corner now!"

They hit the edge of Scottsbluff twenty feet ahead of the dust cloud they generated. Chickens scurried. Dogs hid. Men on the sidewalk pulled off their hats and stared. The dust caught up to them when Lissa reined up at the water trough in front of Snyder's Livery.

Both horses were sweating and breathing hard.

Fifteen-year-old Andrew Snyder sauntered up to them, coughed at the dust, and took the lead lines. "You got Stranger and Pilgrim tuckered out, Mrs. Bowers." He reached up to help her down.

She took his hand. "Yes, I did, Andy. Aren't you glad?" When she reached the ground, she stood a foot shorter than the boy.

"Yes, ma'am, I'm mighty grateful. I ain't never seen 'em tired before. You want me to turn 'em out and grain 'em?"

Mrs. Bowers brushed off her green gingham dress. "No, leave them hitched. Give them water and a little hay. Dry them down with a brush and sack them, but absolutely no grain. I barely got their morning oats run out of them."

Jolie and Essie climbed down from the other side of the wagon and slapped the dust off their dresses. The three marched to the boardwalk on the south side of the street.

Jolie brushed her curls with her fingers and retied her straw hat. "Where are we headed first, Mama?"

"I want to go to a furniture store."

"Can we afford furniture?"

"No." Lissa Bowers clutched her purse. "But perhaps they give credit."

They had just walked into the front of the Colorado Furniture Emporium when a man with receding gray hair ambled over to them.

"Three beautiful ladies in my store in the same moment. This is a fortunate day for Ephraim Mendez!"

"Thank you, Mr. Mendez," Lissa said. "I like a man with a discerning eye. I'm Lissa Bowers, and these are my daughters." She reached out her hand. "I presume a man with such a commanding presence is the owner of the store?"

He stood tall and threw out his chest. "Yes, ma'am, I am. Very pleased to meet you."

Jolie bit her lip and noticed that Essie had covered her giggle with her hand. He seemed to be looking at Jolie while he shook hands with her mother.

Lissa Bowers's voice was melodic. "Ephraim, I would like to know if I could purchase two full-size feather mattresses and two bunk mattresses, if you have such an item, and six feather pillows."

The man's gray eyes widened. He almost danced down the aisle. "Yes, Mrs. Bowers . . . eh, Lissa, you came to the right store. This is probably the only store in a hundred miles to carry all of that in stock."

She walked beside him. The girls trailed behind. "Now, Ephraim, here is a more important question. We're homesteading out east of here and won't have the funds until the crops come in this fall." She reached over and patted his arm. "I presume you'll hold the bill for us until then."

"Whoa, Mrs. Bowers, let's back up a minute." He pulled his arm back. "Normally all sales are on a cash basis. That's why I'm able to offer such reasonable prices."

"I'm aware that is a good business policy, but I thought perhaps you'd make some exceptions. I don't believe I've introduced my daughters, Jolie and Estelle."

"You can call me Essie."

"Nice to make your acquaintance. Just where is your homestead? You must be new in town, but then again everyone on this side of the river is fairly new."

Lissa stopped to examine a curved glass and oak secretariat.

"We've only been here a couple of weeks. We've purchased a homestead north of the river."

Mr. Mendez pulled his thinning hair down over his balding forehead. "There can be no liens against homesteads, of course, but I suppose if there were items of personal property, they would serve as collateral. I'd certainly like to be able to help, eh . . . Lissa." He looked at the wall while he talked to her. "Which homestead did you buy?"

"The Avery place," she replied.

The man's face turned pale. His eyes seemed to be examining the ceiling. "Old Avery's place? Why that place is a—it's a swamp and mosquito nest. What do you have for collateral?"

Jolie watched as the man looked at her mother from foot to hair. *Lord, I don't think I like the way that man is looking at my mother. Is that the way the boys look at me?*

Lissa motioned for him to lean down closer to her. When he did so, she spoke in a loud voice. "Mr. Mendez, that look insulted me. I trust you're a businessman of virtue and integrity."

He jumped back and blushed. "Eh, yes, ma'am. You misunderstood." Again he stared at the ceiling. "But . . . but that homestead is worthless. You can't possibly make it. So you would move on, as would my collateral. There's not another person in Colorado, Wyoming, or Nebraska who would even buy the place, let alone put up money on it. Do you have any animals to trade?"

"We need the ones we have," Mrs. Bowers mused. "We could use our team as collateral, I suppose."

"Stranger and Pilgrim are very strong horses," Essie declared.

"You're the one that bought Tal Wallace's team? I wouldn't come within a block of those two horses."

"Mama can handle them," Jolie insisted.

"She might be the only one north of Hades who can."

"How about Mudball?" Essie offered. "He's a three-hundred-pound pig."

"Pigs are hardly collateral," he said.

"Your family does eat bacon, don't they?" Jolie pressed.

"No, as a matter of fact, we don't," he replied.

Lissa Bowers grabbed her daughters by the arms. "Never mind, girls. We don't have to do business here. Mr. Mendez doesn't have the only store in town."

He shuffled along behind them. "No, ma'am, but I'm the only one with ready-made mattresses in stock."

She was almost to the front door when she paused and glanced back. "I'm afraid we'll just have to save up our money and order them from the Sears and Roebuck catalog."

"Why would you do that?"

"Because they don't look me over from head to toe like I was a hog ready for market," she snapped.

Jolie gasped.

Essie giggled.

Mr. Mendez's mouth dropped open. "Eh, well, Mrs. Bowers, Lissa . . . ma'am, I—I trust you understand that was not intentional. I'll tell you what I will do to try to make it up to you. I'll make an exception just for you. If your husband comes in and signs for the goods, I'll let you wait until fall to pay. I'll take the team as collateral. That includes the wagon, of course."

"My husband has to sign?" Lissa questioned. "Are you saying that my word isn't good enough for Ephraim Mendez?"

"That's just the way business is done around here. It isn't anything personal."

"My honesty and integrity are very personal to me," she replied.

"It's strictly a legal decision," he tried to explain. "I'm sure you understand that the person's name that's on the homestead has to be the one who signs for the goods."

Jolie stepped between them. "And how do you know that my mother's name isn't on the papers?"

"She's a married lady. Husbands always sign. Only widows get the homesteads in their name."

"Is that a law, Mama?" Essie asked.

"No, I don't believe it is," Mrs. Bowers said. Then she turned to the store owner. "Is it, Mr. Mendez?"

He loosened his black tie. Sweat beaded on his high forehead. "Are you telling me that your name is on that claim?"

"It might be," Lissa said. "But most of all, I'm telling you that my word is good. I pay my debts."

Jolie thought she saw his eyes relax. She could tell her mother's were dancing.

"I don't doubt your intentions, but that would be a whole different way of doing business. Besides, the Avery place is not a—how shall I say this? It's not a prime homestead. It's very unlikely that you'll last through the winter."

Jolie watched her mother's neck stiffen. She took her mother's arm. "Come on, Mama. I don't like this man's mattresses. They're probably lumpy. We can do fine without trading at this store."

A family with six children tramped into the store and circled a huge oak table. "If you ladies will excuse me for a moment," Mr. Mendez said, "I'll check on these other customers."

"Please go ahead," Mrs. Bowers replied in a loud voice. "I wouldn't want to do business with anyone who treats women with such disdain."

He motioned with his hand for her to lower her voice.

"Mr. Mendez," Jolie said in a voice that matched her mother's, "I know we'll be on our homestead come spring, but how can you stay in business that long when all the homesteading women find out how you treat them?"

"Please, not so loud."

The couple rounded up their six children and marched back outside the store.

"Mama, I could stand outside on the sidewalk while you and Essie shop and warn women of the business practices of Mr. Mendez," Jolie offered.

"You can't slander me," he puffed.

Jolie smiled softly. "I have no intention of saying anything but the truth. You refused to do business with Mother because she's a woman."

"Is this blackmail?" he boomed.

"Another accusation? You look us over and then accuse us of crimes. What kind of store is this? Come along, girls."

Mr. Mendez trailed after them. "Wait . . . okay, Mrs. Bowers. You sign the papers. Then have your husband drive Stranger and Pilgrim to the alley. I'll personally load the mattresses."

"Does he think you can't drive a rig, Mama?" Essie asked.

"Rather shallow of him, wasn't it, darlin'? Ephraim, I'll be around for the mattresses and six pillows when we conclude our other shopping. I'll sign the papers then. And thank you very much. I'll be shopping here again in the future."

"That would be a nice thing for you to tell the family that just stalked out of here. I think you scared off my customers."

"Yes, I'll tell them I was mistaken."

"Thank you, Lissa."

"And thank you, Ephraim." She held out her hand, which he promptly shook. "Excuse me if I sounded a little testy."

He walked her to the door. "I suppose we were both testing."

Jolie was surprised to see the man, woman, and six children lounging on a new wooden bench in front of the furniture store.

Mrs. Bowers strolled up to them. "I'm truly sorry for how that sounded inside. I was trying to prove a point to Mr. Mendez. He's not a bad person to do business with. I'd encourage you to shop there."

The thin man pushed a dusty hat back. "That's all right, Mrs. Bowers. We didn't come to buy furniture. We wanted to talk to you."

"Me? But I don't even know your name."

The man stood, and when he did, the two boys stood up also. "Sorry about that. I'm Cart Mecker. This is my wife, Emma, and the boys—Champ and Skeet, and the girls are Prissy, Pammie, Patsy, and Peteluma."

"They call me Pet," the five-year-old blonde announced.

"And these are my daughters, Jolie and Estelle."

"I'm Essie!"

Both boys tugged off their hats. "Hi, Miss Jolie," they mumbled.

Lissa Bowers adjusted her purse on her arm. "What did you want to see me about?"

Mrs. Mecker stood. "We just got to town."

"We've been on the road almost a month from Prescott, Arizona," Mr. Mecker added, rubbing a two-week beard.

"That's where Stuart Brannon is from!" Essie blurted out.

"Do you know Pop Brannon?" Mrs. Mecker asked.

"Oh, no." Essie shook her head. "But my brothers read every one of those books about him. Do you know him for real?"

"The boys often played with his son Littlefoot," Mr. Mecker replied. "Anyway, we came up from Arizona. We purchased a homestead east of here. When we pulled into the livery stable to ask for directions to the place, the Snyder boy said we should talk to Mrs. Bowers because she would know right where it is."

"Perhaps it's one of the places between Mrs. DeMarco's and ours," Jolie suggested. "There are two that have absentee owners, at least for now."

"Is the land good?" Mr. Mecker asked.

"One is a little rougher than the other, but it's on the tableland next to the river. I believe crops will do well," Lissa explained.

"Oh, that's wonderful," Mrs. Mecker said. "We tried renting a place in Arizona, but it was so dry we couldn't do much more than graze some sheep and goats. We finally sold the stock and just drove off."

"Might I recommend you go over to Gering and do the paperwork at the land office before going on out? It could save you a trip," Lissa suggested.

Mrs. Mecker took her husband's arm. "We're all very anxious to look at it first."

"I understand. The land office does have the places marked. We haven't been here long and don't know too many people yet."

"It's the Avery place," Cart Mecker offered. "Have you heard of it?"

Jolie heaved a big sigh.

"Cart," Mrs. Bowers began, "I believe you and Emma should sit down while I tell you something."

Lissa shook her head as they walked west along the shaded boardwalk. "I can't believe a man like Mr. Avery. How could he sell that place over and over? The distraught look on the Meckers' faces . . ."

"It isn't even a very good place," Jolie said.

"But it's ours, darlin', and nothing in the land office will change that."

"I hope they can find another homestead," Jolie said.

"I like the Mecker family," Essie maintained. "Did you notice how the boys talked to Jolie, and the girls talked to me?"

"That's your imagination," Jolie replied.

"Nope."

Lissa Bowers paused in front of an unpainted cafe. "Let's divide up the chores. I need to go across the street to the hardware to get a plow scraper. Jolie, you need to pick us up some whole pepper and baking powder with the food money. Let's meet back at the livery in about an hour. That will give you enough time, won't it?"

"For the groceries?" Essie asked.

"For your sister to meander up and down the boardwalk in front of the Armory," Lissa replied with a tight, sly grin.

Jolie straightened her lace collar. "Do you know where the gun shop is?"

Mrs. Bowers reached over and brushed Jolie's bangs off her forehead. "No, but I'm sure you'll find it."

"Can I go with Jolie, Mama?" Essie asked.

"Oh, yes, I insist. One of us needs to watch out for her."

"You mean I have to baby-sit?" Essie giggled.

"You know how our Jolie is."

"Mother!" Jolie protested.

Mrs. Bowers hiked up her long, dark dress to her ankles and jogged across the street

"Jolie, did you ever see Mama move slow?" Essie asked. "She runs everywhere."

Jolie took her hand as they strolled west. "Mama's in a hurry. Every moment is an exciting adventure for her. There's so much she wants to see and do and experience. I think she doesn't want to miss any part of it."

"Daddy said she ran down the aisle when they got married. Do you think she ran down the aisle?"

"No, because Grandpa Pritchett would never have allowed it. But I do believe she was in a hurry to marry Daddy. They probably ran out of the church."

"Maybe she wanted to give him plowing lessons." Essie winked.

"Hmmm. How old did you say you were?"

Essie laced her fingers and plopped them on top of her head. "Some days we seem close in age, don't we?"

"I was thinking the very same thing." Jolie smiled.

They continued to stroll, stopping to peek in several windows. *Lord, sometimes my mother seems like such a difficult person to keep up with. She tires me out just watching her. Does she really need to be in such a hurry? It's like there's something missing in her life, and she's running to try to find it. Daddy notices it, too. I know he does. He is so opposite. He loves to just sit in one place and study the world that comes to him. I'd like to be someplace in the middle.*

I think.

Essie tugged on her arm. "Look, Jolie, there's the grocery, and there's . . . eh, what's his name?"

"Jeremiah Cain."

The tall, blond clerk, wearing a white apron, stood at the door. His black tie hung loose at the open collar of his white shirt.

"Howdy, Miss Jolie." He grinned as they approached.

"Hello, Mr. Jeremiah Cain. How are you?"

"Seein' you walk down the boardwalk sure picks up my day." He stepped out onto the sidewalk and towered above them. "Are you comin' to the store?"

"Yes, we are," Essie informed him.

"Oh, hi, eh . . . little sis."

"My name is Essie."

"That's right. I remember. I never forget a purdy girl. It's short for Esther, isn't it?" he said.

"Estelle."

"Yes, that's what I meant." He stepped aside and allowed Jolie to enter. He started to follow, but Essie moved in ahead of him.

"How can I help you?" he asked.

"I need one-half pound of whole uncracked pepper and a box of baking powder," Jolie said.

"That's all?"

"Yes, thank you very much." She picked up a long, narrow china plate. "What are these, Jeremiah?"

"Them's asparagus plates, Miss Jolie. Mrs. Krausmeyer ordered them all the way from New Orleans."

Jolie set the plate down but counted the stack while Jeremiah retrieved the pepper. *Why would anyone in western Nebraska need twelve asparagus plates? I must meet this Mrs. Krausmeyer someday.*

Jeremiah placed the bag of pepper on the counter. "When I spotted you out on the sidewalk, I surmised you was comin' by to thank me for rescuin' you the other day."

She stared at him for a minute. *He doesn't believe that surely. My goodness, I think he does.*

"Jeremiah, as a matter of fact, I was thinking of you recently."

"I've been thinkin' about you a lot," he mumbled. "What were you thinking?"

"That you never apologized to me for that mortifying scene in front of the store. I was very embarrassed."

"Embarrassed? You mean you like that no-account Leppy Verdue?"

"He has a cute smile," Essie interjected.

"It was my first day in town, and there you were fighting over me. What kind of reputation does that give me? It's no business of yours or Leppy's who I talk to. In the future, would you please not offer your assistance until I ask for it?"

A big grin broke across his face. "Yes, Miss Jolie. I understand. You're thinkin' about our future, ain't you?"

Jolie glanced down at Essie, who rolled her eyes.

"Just find my baking powder, please."

"Sort of makes me glad I'm me," he said as he strolled across the store.

"Dumb," Essie muttered. "You bawled him out, and he thought it was a compliment."

"Some men don't listen very well, do they?"

Jolie strolled over to the two men who sat in oak chairs by the window. "Raymond and Luke, you two look handsome all scrubbed up."

Both men stood up quick, scooting the chairs back on the polished floor.

"Howdy, Miss Jolie." Luke tipped his hat.

"And little Miss Bowers," Raymond added.

"Essie."

Raymond rubbed his neatly trimmed beard. "That's right . . . Miss Bessie."

Essie just shook her head and stared out the window as a stagecoach rumbled down the street.

Jolie stood in front of the men. "Now what caused you to clean up?"

"Why, you did, of course," Luke replied.

"Me? But I only saw you that one time."

Raymond scratched the back of his neck. "You kind of gave us the what-for because we was dirty. So we figured if we was goin' to hang out in public, we ought to be more presentable."

"That's commendable."

"We seen your mother runnin' across the street. Is she all right?" Luke asked.

"Mother always runs," Jolie said.

Raymond let fly a wad of tobacco that rang in the brass spittoon. "How's that homestead of yours?"

"We're getting it livable," she reported.

"Has the river gone down off your place?" he asked.

"Do you have a handkerchief, Raymond?"

"Yes, ma'am!" He jerked a red bandanna from his back pocket. "Here you go."

She folded it and wiped the corner of his chin. "If you're going to chew that foul stuff, you should keep it off your nice-looking chin." She handed back the bandanna. "About a third of our land is still under shallow water. We have plans to levee it, but we're starting to plow the high side."

Jeremiah Cain called out from across the room. "Your goods is ready, Miss Jolie."

She and Essie walked back to the counter. Essie grabbed the two items.

"How much do I owe you?" Jolie asked.

"Forty-three cents."

"That much?"

"I added them three times."

"Then it must be correct." Jolie opened her purse and pulled out some coins. She counted out the change in his hand and then pulled her hand back when he clutched her fingers. He walked them to the open front door.

"Jeremiah, why did you put my money in your pocket instead of in the cash box?"

"Oh, did I? I'll be." He pulled the coins out of his pocket. "I reckon I was plumb distracted."

"That's strange," Essie mumbled.

"Jolie can be very distracting," he replied.

"No, I mean those drovers. One looked just like Leppy Verdue."

Cain stepped up beside her. "Where?"

"Riding west."

Jolie glanced around the room. "Jeremiah, do you have a back door?"

"Sure, Miss Jolie. Through the storeroom and into the alley."

"We'll let ourselves out that way."

"You don't need to be afraid, Miss Jolie. I can protect you from the likes of Leppy Verdue. I'll stop him if he tries anything."

"Now that, Mr. Jeremiah Cain, is exactly what I'm afraid of."

Seven

The path was narrow, winding, and weedy, but Scottsbluff was a new enough town that the clutter, garbage, horse manure, and trash of most older western towns had not yet collected. Essie toted the small sack of groceries and held onto Jolie's arm as they hurried east.

"Where are we going?" she asked.

Jolie tugged her sister forward. "That's what I'm trying to decide."

Essie pulled her arm loose. "If we don't know where we're going, why are we in such a hurry?"

Jolie slowed her pace. "That's a very good question, Estelle Cinnia Bowers."

"What if I hadn't seen Leppy Verdue? Then where would we be going?"

"I do need to see Leppy and tell him about Maxwell and Shakey leaving that envelope. But I wasn't going to flag him down with Jeremiah Cain at our side."

"*Our* side? He wasn't pantin' like a thirsty dog after me."

"I didn't want another confrontation." Jolie paused behind a brick building with a doorway covered only by a canvas drop cloth. "If you hadn't seen Leppy, we might be strolling by a certain gun shop."

The girls continued down the muddy alley.

"What if a certain tall, broad-shouldered gunsmith didn't see us walk by?" Essie asked.

Jolie tilted her head. "Then we would have to walk by again."

Essie snatched a long-stemmed weed and chewed on it. "What happened to the idea of waiting on the boy to come to you?"

"There are exceptions to the rule. Sometimes you have to prime the pump."

"You're good at priming, Jolie."

"Thank you."

"You're welcome," Essie giggled. "So are we going back to the livery now? Because if we are, we're headed the wrong direction."

Jolie waved her arms. "I thought this might be a good time to tour the alleys of Scottsbluff."

"There isn't much to see. Why don't we go out to the street? I wouldn't mind visiting with Leppy, even if you don't want to."

"Is my little sis developing an eye for older men?"

"The only boy I've met in Nebraska that's my age is Chester Wells. What choice do I have?"

"A very good point." Jolie stopped at an unpainted, clapboard-sided building. "Look, someone has left the back door open."

"For fresh air, I suppose. What kind of store is it?"

Without stepping closer, Jolie peered in through the open doorway. "I can't tell. The store's up front. The backroom is dark."

"I wonder why they don't put the name of the store on the alley door?"

"I suppose they expect customers to enter by the front door." Jolie pointed to a long, empty wooden box. "What does it say on that box?"

"'Winchester Repeating Arms Company, New Haven, Connecticut,'" Essie read.

"It must be a gun crate."

"But how do we know for sure?"

Jolie peered again into the backroom. "Looks like a cot. I think it's a small apartment."

"Theo said Tanner was living in the back of the Armory. Do you reckon this is the gun shop?"

"It might be." Jolie motioned to her sister. "Why don't you go in and look?"

"Me?" Essie gasped. "He's not my beau!"

"He's not mine either."

"Jolie Lorita!"

"Well, not yet anyway. I mean, he doesn't know it yet." Jolie tugged Essie to the open back door. "Go on. Just see if anyone is at home."

"What if someone is?"

"Ask them if it's the gun shop."

"What if it isn't?"

"Excuse yourself and come back out."

Essie pulled her arm back. "I can't, Jolie. I'd die of embarrassment if it's the wrong place. Really, I can't do it."

Jolie looked up and down the alley. "Then I'll just have to do it myself."

"Are you really going in?"

"Yes. And you?"

"I'll come in behind you."

Jolie stole to the open doorway and knocked lightly. Essie wrinkled her nose and peeked in. "Maybe no one's here."

"Of course someone's here. The door is open." Jolie marched into the dark storeroom. When her eyes adjusted, she saw a bed piled with crumpled quilts and a pillow. *He really should make his bed and try to be tidy. A tidy person lives a quiet life. Anyway, that's what Grandma Pritchett always told us.*

"This place is a mess," Essie whispered.

"Perhaps I should make the bed and sweep."

"That's silly," Essie complained. "You don't even know whose room it is."

"It's Tanner's."

"How do you know?"

Jolie took a deep breath. "I can smell him."

Essie smashed her nose flat with her finger. "You mean, he stinks?"

"Of course not. He has a certain aroma." Jolie's lace-up shoes made little noise as she crept across the room.

Essie stomped behind her, paused by a shelf, and stared into an open cigar box. "But you only met him once."

"There are some things a girl doesn't forget."

"Chester stinks," Essie declared.

"Yes, I agree."

Jolie hesitated by the doorway to the store. "I think I hear voices. Perhaps he has a customer."

"Are we just goin' to barge into the store?"

A knock on the doorjamb behind her caused the hair on the back of Jolie's neck to stand out. She spun around. A blonde woman carried a napkin-covered wooden tray into the room.

"Who are you?" Jolie blurted out.

"Oh, I didn't know he had company. I'm Bailey Wagner from the cafe next door. I deliver Tanner's lunch every day. He didn't tell me he had company."

"We aren't really company," Jolie explained. "We're merely on our way to the gun shop."

Bailey surveyed the room. "We? I don't see anyone else."

"My sister and I were merely . . ."

"I don't see anyone."

"Essie?" Jolie called out.

"It ain't none of my business, I reckon. Tanner can have all the gals he wants in his bedroom." She shoved the tray onto the small table near the bed. "Maybe I was hoping the competition wouldn't be so stiff. Tell Tanner I'll put the lunch on his tab, and if he wants me to bring two meals ever' day, just to whistle." Bailey turned to leave. "You movin' in?"

Jolie folded her arms and glared. "That's insulting, and I will not reply."

"Honey, you don't have to convince me. I've been in a man's

room a time or two myself. Are you an actress? Are you Abby O'Neill from Omaha?"

"She's Jolie Lorita Bowers, recently from Helena," Essie piped up from across the room.

"Oh, so there *are* two of you. Anyway, that's Tanner's business. I heard about Miss Jolie Bowers, but to tell the truth, you don't live up to the reports."

"What did Tanner say about me?" Jolie asked.

"I didn't say it was Tanner." Bailey Wagner ducked back out into the bright sunlight of the alley.

Jolie prowled the stacks of crates. "Why did you run and hide?"

Essie stepped out from behind the boxes. "I didn't want to get in trouble."

Jolie wiped her finger along the dust on the shelf. "But you did manage to tell the girl from the cafe my name."

"She already knew about you."

Jolie examined the dirt on her fingertip. "I wonder who talked to her about me? I really should spend some time cleaning this room. It's simply horrid." She reached out for the door leading to the store. The brass handle felt cold, hard, slick. "Come on. It's time to make our entrance."

"You make an entrance. I'll slink in behind you."

Jolie burst into the gun shop, her purse on her arm. She squinted in the bright light of the oil lanterns.

"What are you doin' back there?" a deep voice boomed.

"Eh . . . your lunch is ready," she muttered, trying to focus on the men by the front counter of the cluttered gun shop.

"Ain't that somethin', Chug?" It was another man's voice. "Now we know where she's been hidin' out."

Tanner Wells overshadowed the two drovers who stood across from him examining revolvers.

Leppy Verdue shoved his hat back, revealing twin dimples. "Chug, I do believe it's the famous Miss Jolie Bowers."

Jolie felt the stares of all three men. "Eh, the gal from the cafe just brought your lunch."

"The blonde one named Bailey Wagner," Essie added.

"You mean there's a whole passel of purdy women in the store-room?" Chug chuckled.

"It's more like a bedroom," Essie blurted out. "But it's very messy. Hi, Leppy. My name is Essie."

"I didn't know Miss Jolie had a twin sister."

"I'm a little younger than she is." Essie grinned. "But I'm quite mature for my age. We were just cutting through the alley."

Jolie noticed that the back of the room was full of shop tools and benches. The front was mainly glass display cases.

"You don't have to explain to me," Leppy said. "I've been known to enter buildings by the alley door."

Tanner loosened his tie. "Well, she has to explain to me."

"We thought this was a back entrance to the store," Jolie said. "Since the door was open, we assumed it welcomed customers."

"You buyin' a gun, Miss Jolie?" Chug asked.

"No, I was merely—"

"Our brother Gibs needs .44 rim-fire bullets for his Henry rifle," Essie interrupted.

"I used to have a Henry. Lost it out near the soddy during that big flood," Chug said.

Tanner reached up into a cigar box on the shelf behind him and picked up a couple of small copper-cased cartridges. "I told Gibs the Henry isn't safe to fire yet."

Jolie tugged on her gold necklace. "I know, but I think having a few bullets will motivate him to continue to clean it up. But please go ahead with Leppy and Chug."

Tanner's face angled to the window. Sweat dropped off his square jaw as he talked. "You seem to know these two."

"Yes, we met once briefly last week."

"Leppy got in a fight with a backwater store clerk over her," Chug hooted.

Jolie stormed past a glass case of lever-action rifles. "That's ludicrous. They were not fighting over me. I insisted that they stop. They refused to listen."

Tanner wiped a blue bandanna across his forehead. "You don't have to explain to me."

"I most certainly do," she snapped.

Leppy scratched the back of his neck. "Before you two get in a lovers' spat, how about we buy those two used Colts with the seven-and-a-half-inch barrels?"

"A lovers' spat!" Jolie exclaimed. "I only met the man once in my life."

Essie scooted up next to Leppy Verdue. "But she did try to go see him, and he wasn't home 'cause he went to see her, and they missed each other. She was very, very disappointed."

"Estelle!"

Leppy slapped Essie on the back. "Now that tells a story, don't it?"

"I'm leaving," Jolie fumed.

Tanner held out the cartridges. "Without your bullets for Gibs?"

"I'll get them another time."

"Leppy, how old do you think a girl should be before she gets married?" Essie asked.

He jerked his hand back. "What kind of question is that for a little girl?"

"Jolie and me was having a debate."

"Does she talk about marriage a lot?"

Essie grinned and wiggled her nose. Jolie stomped toward the front door. "Estelle!"

"Aren't you going to tell Leppy and Chug about the brown envelope?" Essie called out.

"What envelope?" Chug asked.

Jolie turned around and tried to control herself. "Your friends Maxwell and Shakey left an envelope with me and asked me to give it to you."

Chug glanced at Leppy. "You know Maxwell and Shakey?"

Essie trailed over to Jolie. "My sister knows lots of men."

"Estelle, that's enough."

Essie rolled her eyes. "Well, you do."

Jolie grabbed Essie's shoulder. "A Mr. Maxwell Dix and Shakey Torrington stopped by our homestead and left a letter for you."

"It's a very fat letter," Essie added.

"And you didn't bring it with you?" Chug pressed.

"I didn't know you were in town."

"Why didn't Maxwell bring it to us as planned?" Leppy asked.

"I suppose because he thought you went to Cheyenne. He said he didn't want to go there," Jolie reported.

Chug twisted his thick, drooping mustache. "We didn't go to Cheyenne."

Jolie caught a drift of spice tonic water but couldn't determine which man was wearing it. "I heard you say the other day you were goin' to Cheyenne."

"That was just in case a certain Colorado sheriff came lookin' for us," Leppy said.

"Why would a Colorado sheriff be looking for you?" Essie asked.

"I said, just in case, Miss Essie. Anyway, we've been waitin' for days for Maxwell and Shakey to show up."

"I told them you went to Cheyenne," Jolie explained.

"And so they just up and left the envelope with you?" Leppy queried. "Why did they do that? They didn't know you from Lola Montez."

Essie stood on her tiptoes and edged away from Jolie's reach. "They thought Jolie was your girlfriend," she told Leppy.

"Why did they think that?" Tanner asked.

"It was a mix-up," Jolie replied.

"Men are always thinking Jolie's their girlfriend," Essie said. "That don't mean nothing."

"It doesn't?" Tanner said. "You seem to be in the center of several mix-ups."

Jolie's green-gray eyes narrowed. "What did you mean by that, Tanner Wells?"

Leppy stalked over to the tall, muscled gunsmith. "Yeah, are you impugnin' my girl's honor?"

"Your girl?" Jolie cried out. "I am nobody's girl, especially not yours."

Leppy looked down at Essie. "She said I was special, didn't she?"

"I'm really sorry, Leppy, but she likes Tanner best," Essie declared.

"All they do is argue," Chug guffawed.

Jolie rushed to the doorway. "Come on, Essie!"

Leppy trailed along. "Does your sister get into jams like this often?"

"All the time, but it's never her fault."

"Estelle Cinnia!"

Jolie stomped out to the boardwalk, yanking Essie along by the hand.

"Where are we goin'?" Essie asked.

"To the livery."

"Are we goin' to shop anymore?"

"No. Never!"

"Never?"

"I will never come to Scottsbluff again in my life, especially with you."

"You want me to go tell Mama you pitched a fit and want to leave town now?"

"I did not pitch a fit. I'm merely upset. You didn't help at all in there."

"Why are you so mad at me? I thought I was just telling the truth," Essie protested. "I didn't want to go into the gun shop in the first place. Remember?"

Jolie took a deep breath and let out a sigh. "You're right. I'm not mad. Not at you anyway. Go on and tell Mama I'll be waiting at the livery, but there's no hurry. I just need to clear my head."

"How about your heart? Do you need to clear it, too?"

Jolie offered a faint smile. "No, Essie, my heart knows what it's doing. That much I'm sure of."

Jolie had stalked to the corner of the boardwalk when she heard spurs jingle behind her. She spun around to face Leppy and Chug. "Why are you following me?"

"Just calm down. We ain't goin' to follow you."

"You can follow *me* if you want to," Essie offered.

"Why, thank you." Leppy's dimples flashed when he smiled. "You're a very kind young lady."

Chug stepped a little closer. "Do you really have that letter from Maxwell?"

"Yes, I do."

"You homesteadin' Avery's old swamp farm?" Chug asked.

"That's not what we call it, but, yes, that's our place now."

Leppy pulled off his hat. "Can we stop by before sundown and pick it up? You don't even have to come out and greet us. Just send Essie-girl out with it."

"That will be fine."

He tipped his hat. "Thank you, Miss Jolie. And I'll see you later, Estelle."

Jolie waited for Essie to correct him but glanced down to see a big grin on her sister's face.

Someone behind them shouted, "Verdue!"

A red-faced Jeremiah Cain stomped out the doorway of the grocery store and pulled off his apron. "Are you harassin' Miss Jolie again?"

Jolie Bowers folded her arms. "Jeremiah, get back in the store and shut up!"

"What?"

"If you come out here, I'll personally break your nose. Is that clear enough?" she fumed.

"But I thought—"

"You haven't thought right yet, Jeremiah. Leppy and Chug were just leaving. That is, if they intend to get a certain letter."

Leppy shoved his hat on. "Yep, Miss Jolie, we're leavin'."

"You see, Mr. Cain, I did not need your help at all. In the future I would enjoy the privilege of asking for help before you offer it. Is that clear?"

"Yes, ma'am." Cain slipped on his apron. "You're makin' plans for our future. That's good."

Jolie had stomped away only ten feet when Leppy called out, "I'll come visit you before dark, darlin'!"

She glanced over her shoulder. "Yes, that's fine." Then she saw Jeremiah Cain stare out the window at her.

Lord, there's no way to explain all of this. It's like a bad dream. I must endure it all and wake up safe in my bed. That is, if I had a mattress. "The mattresses! We still have to load up the mattresses before we leave town."

When Jolie reached the livery, Andy Snyder lounged in the shade on a stump with a tall glass in his hand. "I didn't expect you back yet."

"Mother's still shopping. I thought I'd wait here. Is that all right?" Jolie asked.

When the fifteen-year-old grinned, his ears wiggled. He scooted over. "You can share a seat with me here, Miss Jolie."

"Thank you, Andy." She plopped down next to him and pulled off her hat to fan herself.

"Would you like some lemonade?" he asked.

"Yes, please, I'd love some."

He handed her his tall glass.

Jolie stared at it.

"Sorry, I don't have any ice."

Jolie licked her lips and chugged a big gulp. Her lip instantly curled.

"I was a little short of sugar," he admitted. "But them lemons was straight from San Bernardino, California. Makes your tongue dance and sing, don't it?"

She handed him back the glass. "I think that's a good way to put it."

"You got through early, Miss Jolie."

"Yes, but we have to pick up some bedding at the furniture store."

He slurped a swig and grimaced. "You buy from ol' Mendez?"

"Yes."

"He's a funny guy, ain't he?" He handed her the lemonade glass again.

"What do you mean?" Jolie drew a deep breath, took another big swallow, and immediately gritted her teeth.

"With those eyes of his off-center, he can be starin' out the front window, and you'd swear he's givin' you a spy. It bothered my mama till she learned that he wasn't lookin' at her at all."

"That does explain a few things." Jolie took a sip and handed the glass back to the boy. *Lord, we misjudged the man and pressured him into business practices he doesn't normally follow. Why did we assume he was lecherous?*

"Stranger and Pilgrim were as calm as I've ever seen. Your mama sure does know her horses."

"She says it's because she knows how to talk horse." Jolie jumped up. "I should drive them over to the store."

"I didn't say they were that tame," he cautioned.

"I can drive them. I could go get those mattresses loaded before Mama and Essie get back. We can get home sooner that way."

Andrew rose to his feet. "Are you sure you want to try it?"

"Look at them parked over there, half-asleep. I can drive them the few blocks to the store."

"I'll go check the riggin'."

Jolie hiked across the livery yard and climbed up into the big farm wagon.

"They only have a fast and a stop, you know," he warned.

"I can do it, Andy."

"Okay, Miss Jolie. May the Lord have mercy on your soul."

"Indeed He already has."

When the lead line slapped Stranger's rump, the two horses bolted forward. Jolie fell back into the wagon, but she clutched the leather lines. This brought the horses to a trot. She was surprised when she sat up that they maintained that moderate speed.

"See, I knew I could do it." With her right hand, she clamped down her flat straw hat. Jolie rounded the corner behind the furniture store. She was pleased that no wheels left the ground when she made the turn. She pulled the hand brake, tied the lines, and climbed off the rig. The horses stood.

Several knocks on the back door brought Mr. Mendez.

"I'm here to pick up the bedding," she announced.

He seemed to stare her up and down. "Where's your mother?"

"Still buyin' a new plow, I believe." *I think he's looking at the wagon, not me.*

"She hasn't signed the invoice yet."

"I'll sign it."

Mendez stared at the team of horses that danced in the alley. *Now I wonder what he's really looking at? He could be looking at me.*

"I suppose you'll put up an argument if I refuse."

"Yes, I'm quite good at it. But Mama might be by before we finish loading. Mr. Mendez, you've been kind to us, and I'm sorry if we were rude."

Mendez disappeared into the store. When he returned to the alley, he and a clerk toted a feather mattress. Jolie stood by the horses as the four mattresses and a crate with six pillows were loaded.

"This is a big wagon," Mendez commented as he wiped sweat onto his handkerchief. "I forgot how big Wallace's wagon was. He never did calm those two horses enough to actually use it. Did you ever consider hauling cedar shingles with it?"

"What do you mean?"

He stared at her as he patted Stranger's rump. "I need shingles for my house, but I have to go up to Carter Canyon to buy them off old Finnegan. Then I would have to make a dozen trips in my buckboard. I could rent a big wagon like this, but I've never been much of a driver. Tell you what I'll do—if your daddy hauls me down two loads of shingles, I'll buy a third load, and he can keep it for pay."

Jolie tried to look him in the eyes but never succeeded. "Thank you, Mr. Mendez. I'll tell Mama and Daddy about the offer. They might want to take you up on that."

"And tell them I sent you six new pillowcases for free."

Jolie reached into the back of the wagon for a rope. "Thank you. That's very generous of you." She turned to the clerk. "Would you please tie the load down with this rope?"

"They ain't goin' to shift or move," the grinning clerk argued. "We packed them in tighter than an olive pit in July."

"When my mother drives a team, everything, including one's toenails, shift and move. Please tie them all down."

Jolie noticed the clerk staring at her. *I can see there's nothing wrong with your eyes.*

With the load secured, she climbed up on the wagon and plopped down. Mr. Mendez handed her up an invoice. "I reckon this is one of the more foolish things I've ever done. You aren't even of legal age to sign."

"Mr. Mendez, you're a pioneer businessman." Jolie signed the bill of lading and handed the paper and pencil back down to him. "Someday all businesses will recognize women as good credit risks."

"I'll be happy to have my mattress money come fall."

"You'll get it, and thank you for putting up with novice home-steaders."

He glanced at the invoice and scratched his head. "You know, Miss Bowers, I believe you. But I can't figure out why."

Jolie carefully wrapped a lead line around each wrist.

"What're you doin' that for?" the clerk asked.

"I'm teaching Stranger and Pilgrim to trot. Just watch."

Jolie jammed her heels against the floorboard, leaned back in the wagon seat, let off the hand brake, and slapped the lead lines. The horses bolted forward. Jolie tumbled back, but the lines held tight on her wrists. The team slowed to a trot. She drove down the alley and west onto Main Street. As they rolled up to the hardware store, she jammed her heels on the floor rail, threw her shoulders back, and yanked the lines back. The horses came to a sliding stop.

A tall, dark-haired clerk in a white apron stood in the doorway. "That was a nice stop, miss."

"Thank you. Is Lissa Bowers in your store?"

He slicked down his hair with his hands. "No, ma'am. She left a few minutes ago to go get a wagon for her goods."

"I'm her daughter, and this is her wagon. Could you load things up for me?"

"I reckon I could. Say, you aren't married, too, are you?" There was a slight blush in his cheek.

"Did you ask my mother if she were married?"

"No, not me. Mr. Fleister done asked her."

Mother, Mother, Mother . . . did you have a hardware man pining over you? She flashed the clerk a slight smile. "I'm not married."

"Me neither. My name's Harvey."

"And I'm Jolie, but I don't imagine you'll keep your job long if you don't get to work and load up our goods."

"Yes, ma'am . . . Miss Jolie."

She gazed down a nearly empty Main Street as several items were loaded on the back of the wagon.

"Tie them down, please," she called back.

"Miss Jolie, there ain't no way that heavy plow is goin' anywhere."

Her glare silenced the clerk. He tied down the plow and crate.

Jolie rewrapped the lead lines around her wrists. She jammed her lace-up boots against the floorboard and talked to the horses: "Well, boys, you might as well run down to the livery. We'll give Main Street another show." She leaned forward, locked her legs around the wagon seat, and slapped the lead lines.

This time there was no yank on the lines. The horses galloped, and Jolie felt on the verge of losing control. Her heart pounded, and her hat slipped off, attached by the ribbon around her neck. The hooves thundered. The wagon rattled. The wind blasted her face, and the lead lines surged with power.

Oh, my . . . oh, my . . . this is why Mama loves it so. Oh, my . . . I hope this isn't sinful.

Men rushed out of stores and saloons to watch her roar down Main Street. As she approached the east end of town, a rider appeared to the left of the wagon.

"Leppy, what do you think you're doing?" she hollered.

He doesn't hear me. Is he trying to outrun me?

She slapped the lines, and the team lurched ahead of the rider. *This is absurd. What is he doing?*

"Don't worry, Miss Jolie," he screamed. "I'll save you!"

As he pulled aside Stranger, Leppy looped his rein on the saddle horn and kicked his boot out of the stirrup.

I'm in control, Mr. Leppy Verdue, and I do not need to be rescued.

When they were in front of the livery, Jolie flung her shoulders back, and the lead lines snapped taut against the harnessed horses.

Stranger and Pilgrim slid to a stop.

And Leppy leaped.

He tumbled face-first into the dirt street in front of the panting horses and somersaulted several times. He ended up on his back in the dirt and with his boots in the water trough.

Essie ran up, and Lissa Bowers walked behind her.

"Why did he do that?" Essie called out.

"I believe he was rescuing me."

Leppy sat up in the street, dirt plastered to his face and hair.

"Rescuing you from what?" Essie asked.

"You'll have to ask him."

Essie meandered over to the cowboy. "Leppy, thanks for saving my sister."

He tried to spit dirt out of his mouth. "Hmmpth, bpthee."

"Very good driving, dear," Lissa called out as she approached.

"Thanks, Mama. I can get them to trot, too."

"You can? Splendid. You'll have to show me how."

"Would you like me to drive home?" Jolie asked.

"Did you think the team was a runaway?" Essie asked.

Leppy picked pebbles out of his hair. "Ain't never seen a gal drive like that."

"I see you loaded our goods." Mrs. Bowers crawled up in the wagon beside her daughter. "Did you sign for the mattresses?"

"Yes, Mama."

"I'm surprised Mr. Mendez agreed to that."

Jolie grinned.

"No." Lissa nodded. "I'm not all that surprised."

"Mama is the real driver." Essie held out her hand to help Leppy up.

He took her hand. "Miss Estelle, is your whole family so unpredictable?" He staggered as he stood.

Essie grabbed his arm and steadied him. "Yeah, I suppose we are."

"I ain't never seen a family quite like yours then."

"Thank you!" Essie retrieved his hat, and when she handed it to him, he jammed it on her head.

"I believe horses run either because they're afraid or because they just plain like to run," Lissa declared.

Jolie clutched the lead lines taut. "These two just love to run, don't they?"

Her mother sat down beside her. "Yes, they do."

Leppy retrieved his hat from Essie's head. "Thanks, Miss Estelle. Are you sure you ain't twenty-one?" he laughed.

"I'm twelve and two-thirds," she reported.

Leppy slapped the dirt off his ducking trousers. "You tell your sis that next time I'll let the team stampede."

"I'll tell her," Essie said.

Jolie kept her eyes focused on the horses' ears. "Mama, are we goin' to stop to see Mrs. DeMarco?"

"I think we should."

"May I wait in the wagon? I'm not having a very good day, and I don't think I could face them without getting upset."

Lissa Bowers tugged her long brown braid around and let it drape down the front of her dress. "Estelle told me you got a little steamed at Tanner."

Leppy limped to the side of the wagon, still leaning on Essie's shoulder. "And when I come out to the homestead, I'd rather see you than her come out and greet me. You get my drift?"

Essie grinned. "I think you acted very brave."

"Thank you, ma'am."

"You're quite welcome."

Jolie glanced down at the two and then at her mother. "I wasn't steamed at Tanner. It was a very confusing scene. He jumped to conclusions without giving me a chance to explain, and so I marched out."

"And slammed the door?"

"I didn't realize it would make such a racket."

"But you weren't steamed?"

"Perhaps just a little."

Essie poked Leppy in the ribs. "Men are always jumping to conclusions around Jolie."

"And most times they fall on their faces?" he asked.

"Well, not as dramatically as you did."

Leppy drew alongside the wagon. "Good day, Miss Jolie."

She glanced down. "I do hope you're not seriously hurt."

"Thank you for carin'. I was beginnin' to surmise that you hadn't noticed."

"I don't believe you've met my mother, Lissa Bowers."

He yanked off his hat, revealing dirty hair. "Your mother? I figured she was another sister." Leppy tipped his hat. "Howdy, Mrs. Bowers."

"Thank you for your heroics, even though they weren't needed," Mrs. Bowers replied. "Did I hear you say you are coming out to our homestead?"

"Yes, ma'am. A friend left somethin' of mine with Miss Jolie that I need to pick up."

Mrs. Bowers glanced at her eldest daughter. "I believe I missed hearing about that, dear."

"I'll tell you about it on our way home, Mama."

Mrs. Bowers turned to Leppy. "You'll stay for supper tonight, I trust?"

Leppy glanced down at his boots. "Mrs. Bowers, I've been around your daughter twice, and both times I got hurt. I reckon it would be judicious for me just to pass on supper. Don't want to press my luck."

Lissa Bowers roared. "That seems to be a wise decision."

Leppy lifted Essie up into the wagon. "Now I'd be happy to have supper with you and sweet Miss Estelle. She's a darlin'."

"Perhaps that could be arranged sometime—in a few years."

"Mother!" Essie giggled.

He tipped his hat again. "Good day, ladies. I believe I'll go wrestle a grizzly bear or some other activity safer than hanging around Miss Jolie Bowers."

Mrs. Bowers patted Jolie's knee as the cowboy walked away. "He seems like a pleasant enough man."

"He's bowlegged and quick-tempered," Jolie whispered.

"He called me a darlin'. I like him!" Essie countered.

"That's obvious," Mrs. Bowers laughed. "Now, Jolie, take us to Mrs. Fuentes's boardinghouse to see the DeMarcos."

"Hang on."

Jolie yanked Pilgrim and Stranger to a trot when they rounded Fourth Street. When they stopped at the two-story boardinghouse, they didn't even skid.

Lissa held her chest and took a deep breath. "I'm quite impressed."

"I like driving them, Mama."

Mrs. Bowers flipped her long braid behind her back. "I can see that."

Essie squinted her eyes closed, waiting for the cloud of dust to drift past them. "Can I wait out here with Jolie?"

"Yes, but if he's up to company, I think Jolie should come see Alfonso."

"I can't believe he didn't go to the doctor. It distresses me to tears," Jolie sighed. "I don't think I can look either of them in the eyes without getting angry."

"Let me check on them." Mrs. Bowers climbed down and tramped to the front steps.

Essie scooted next to her sister. "Jolie, did you notice that Leppy has a very cute smile?"

"He is also ten years older than you."

"You didn't answer my question."

"Well, yes, his smile is pleasant enough."

"Pleasant? It's very cute. He has dimples."

"I really didn't pay that much attention."

"Why not?"

"Okay, I did notice the dimples. But you shouldn't be sizing up older men."

"I wasn't sizing him up. I don't even think I know how to size up a boy. I was just thinking that someday I'll be as old as you. I won't be as pretty, but I'll need to look at boys. I wanted to think about what kind I would look for."

Jolie tightened the lead lines and kept the horses still. She leaned her shoulder against Essie's. "You'll look for a boy like Leppy when you're my age?"

"No. I'll probably look for a boy like Lawson and Gibs, but they're hard to find."

Jolie watched as two men crossed the street about a block away. "Yes, you're right about that."

Essie paused, then murmured, "I don't think I'll look for a suit-and-tie man."

"You don't like men who wear nobby clothes?"

"Here come two suit-and-tie men. They look sort of weak-eyed. You know what I mean?" Essie whispered.

The men shied clear of the horses and walked straight up to the wagon.

"Is this the Bowers wagon?" the younger man called out.

Jolie studied the man's wire-framed spectacles and narrow nose. "Yes. May I help you?"

He tipped his hat. "Mrs. Bowers, we'd like to talk to your husband. Is he inside the boardinghouse?"

"That's not Mrs. Bowers," Essie informed him. "That's my sister Jolie. Mama is inside."

He glanced at his stocky partner. "Excuse me, Miss Jolie, is your father in town? We'd like to speak to Mr. Bowers."

"No, he's plowing."

"Could you take a message to him? My name is Hubert Monroe, and this is Case Eller. We visited with Mr. Bowers last week in the barbershop. Tell him that Congressman William Jennings Bryan is holding a meeting in Lincoln in two weeks. He wants to meet with Young Farmers' Alliance members from all over the state. We want your daddy to be part of the delegation from the Nebraska panhandle."

"But Daddy just moved to Nebraska last week."

"Yes, ma'am, but all of us are pilgrims and strangers."

Case Eller unfastened the top button on his shirt. "Your daddy surely has a way with words. He would make a fine representative."

"The Alliance would pay his expenses, of course," Monroe added.

"Just what matter does he need to discuss with Mr. . . ."

"Congressman Bryan."

"Your daddy will remember," Hubert Monroe insisted.

Jolie felt her neck and shoulders tense. "Are you thinking I wouldn't have the brains to understand the issue?"

"No, miss. It's nothing to worry your pretty, little head over."

Still clutching the lead lines, Jolie nodded her head at the two men. "Essie, do you see these men?"

"Yes."

"Several years from now when you're looking around for a man to marry, avoid this kind."

"What way is that to talk?" Hubert Monroe asked.

"I'll tell my father that two rather patronizing men in tight suits asked me to pass along a cryptic message about him going to Lincoln to meet with the congressman."

Monroe tipped his hat and grinned. "Thank you, Miss Bowers. That's all we was askin'."

The Bowers girls watched as the two men retreated across the street.

"They want Daddy to go to Lincoln? What was that all about?" Essie asked.

"I don't know. I suppose Daddy will."

"I thought you insulted the men, but they just said, 'Thank you.'"

"So I noticed. But my tongue is too sharp sometimes. I get angry when people treat me as if I couldn't grasp what they're talking about. The Lord has been trying to change me."

"Jolie, how does the Lord do that? Mama and Daddy are always talking about how the Lord is changing them, but I don't think He's changing me."

"Does it bother you?"

Essie wound her long hair around her neck like a scarf. "I get to thinking I'm doing something wrong."

"Sometimes He changes us, and we don't even notice. It helps if we have a goal in mind."

"What do you mean?"

"I need the Lord to make me more gracious to men who belittle me."

"So what do you do?"

"I'll pray about it. And next time I see those men, I'll be able to tell if the Lord has been changing me. If I'm able to converse with them for five minutes without snapping at them, well, that would be a change."

"Maybe I need a goal, too," Essie mused.

"Yes, that would give you a measurement."

"But I hardly know anyone in Nebraska yet, except for Mary Vockery and Leppy Verdue. I reckon I don't have many faults around them."

Jolie started to chuckle. "How about Bullet Wells?"

"Oh, no, not Chester. I don't want to change the way I treat Chester."

Jolie winked at her sister. "It would be a test."

"You mean, I have to want the Lord to change me until I like Chester?" Essie gasped.

"I think you could ask the Lord to change you so you can be pleasant to him."

Essie folded her hands across her chest. "I don't want to be pleasant to him."

"Then the Lord has a lot of work to do in your life."

"Jolie, that's not what I had in mind!"

"You want to go through the rest of your life despising Bullet Wells?"

"Why not? If he continues to act like a jerk, I'll treat him that way."

"It would be a good test, wouldn't it?"

"But don't you understand?" Essie protested. "I don't want it to happen. The Lord wouldn't change me just to spite me, would He?"

"No, but I have a feeling He could hound you until you want to change."

"I think we should talk about something else."

"What?"

"Anything. . . . Look, here comes Mama!" Essie pointed.

Jolie frowned at the look on her mother's face. "What's wrong, Mama?"

Mrs. Bowers climbed into the wagon. She took a deep breath and stared out over the horses.

"What is it, Mama?" Essie echoed.

"Oh, no!" Jolie gasped. "Dear Lord, no!"

Mrs. Bowers bit her lip and nodded.

"What is it?" Essie pleaded.

Jolie tried to hold her breath, but the tears burst out. "Is he . . ."

Her mother nodded.

Jolie could barely breathe. *Lord, I don't understand. How could he neglect his own life like that? How could he play around with such an injury? What makes a person so stubborn as to risk dying from the slip of an axe?*

Mrs. Bowers put her head against Jolie's, and they wept.

"What is it?" Essie demanded. "Why are you both crying?"

Jolie gasped and then held her breath. *Lord, I didn't even know him, but he didn't need to die. Why, Lord? Why didn't he listen to me? What did I do wrong?*

Mrs. Bowers put her arm around Essie. "Alfonso DeMarco died this morning."

"Died? But he just hurt his foot—that's all. Jolie doctored him and everything."

I should never play doctor. I should have put him in the wagon and driven him to the doctor. Maybe he didn't hear me. Did they misunderstand? Oh, sweet Jesus, did they think I fixed it up so well they didn't need a doctor?

"He got gangrene and then wouldn't let Dr. Fix remove his leg."

"But—but people don't die when they cut themselves, do they?"

Jolie leaned forward, elbows on her knees, her face in her hands. *Lord, is this what it feels like when someone rejects Your salvation and dies under Your just wrath? When they're too stubborn to take Your cure for sin?*

"Sometimes deep cuts are very dangerous," Mrs. Bowers replied.

"Why is Jolie crying? She only met him once."

Jolie sat up and retrieved her handkerchief to wipe her cheeks. *Essie's right. I didn't know him. Lord, I sincerely thought I was helping him.*

Mrs. Bowers slipped her arms around both her daughters.

"Because Alfonso would be alive if either he or his mother had listened to Jolie."

"Mama, do you think Alfonso is in heaven?" Essie asked. "Can a person go to heaven even if they do dumb things?"

"Oh, my, yes, baby. Heaven will be filled with people who did dumb things. It's what a person accepts about Jesus that makes the difference."

"Then he could be in a place much, much better than a Nebraska homestead."

Mrs. Bowers hugged her youngest daughter. "You're right about that, darlin'."

Jolie tucked her handkerchief up her sleeve and took a deep breath. "I'm sorry for crying so."

Mrs. Bowers patted her knee. "Jolie Lorita Bowers, there are some things in life worth crying over."

"Mama, I know everyone is responsible for their own decisions, but I could have actually saved a life. I've never had that opportunity before. I don't know if I ever will again. But I just couldn't convince them. Do you think they would have listened to me if I were a man?"

"Darlin', the 'what ifs' of life will kill you. 'What if' we had moved to Michigan after we got married? 'What if' the bookstore in Stockton had been a great success? 'What if' that railroad bridge had washed out one day later? 'What if' someone else had owned our homestead when we got to Nebraska?" Lissa tugged Jolie's handkerchief from her sleeve and patted her own eyes dry. "Forget the 'what if, Lord?' Let me live in the 'what now, Lord?'"

Jolie slipped her arm around her mother's waist. "Thanks, Mama."

"Would you like me to drive home, big sis?"

Jolie shook her head. "I need to drive. I really need to do it. Do you understand, Mama?"

Lissa Bowers gave her daughter a hug. "Jolie Lorita, there's no one on this earth who understands that need better than me." She turned to her youngest daughter and held her tightly. "Hang on, Estelle Cinnia. Big sis is going to race us home."

The lead lines popped like Gib's .22, and the team exploded down Main Street at a full gallop. The inside wheels were a foot off the ground when they turned onto Telegraph Road and thundered east.

Mrs. Bowers reached over and untied Jolie's hat ribbon.

"What're you doing?" Jolie called out.

"Trust me, darlin'," Mrs. Bowers shouted. She handed the hat to Essie and then reached over and pulled the combs out of Jolie's hair. The auburn hair flagged out straight behind her.

"Oh, Mama, that feels good," Jolie shouted.

"Can I take off my hat?" Essie hollered.

"Yes, we all will. Shove them under the seat."

Lissa untied the ribbon at the bottom of her braid. With her fingers, she combed the three strands out until her hair sailed west like her daughters'.

"Mama, I like fast horses," Jolie shouted.

Lissa reached over to her daughter's dress and unfastened the three top tiny buttons on the lace collar.

Jolie never took her eyes off the horses. "What're you doing now?"

"Isn't that better?"

"Oh, Mama, it feels so good!"

"I know, Jolie," Mrs. Bowers hollered. "There are some days you just have to let the horses run."

"You let Stranger and Pilgrim run almost every day," Essie bellowed.

Lissa bounced along with the rhythm of the jostling wagon. "I mean, the horses in our hearts, baby."

Eight

Jolie didn't slow the wagon at the railroad crossing.

Nor at Wildhorse Creek.

Nor at Three Corners.

But she did wrap the lead lines around her wrists and throw herself straight back to bring the team to a sliding stop in front of the DeMarco homestead.

Theo Wells trotted out to meet them. "Miss Jolie, I figured by the dust that it was your mama drivin'."

Jolie maintained the tension on the flat brown leather lead lines. "She's letting me practice."

Theo pulled off his hat and wiped his forehead on his shirtsleeve. "You all comin' in to sit a spell?"

Mrs. Wells scurried out to them, wearing a white canvas apron over her dark blue serge dress. "Yes, by all means, please come in."

Lissa Bowers climbed down. "We can only stay a minute, but I did want to talk to you and your husband."

"Mama, I'll stay here with the team. I don't think they'll stand," Jolie offered.

"Yes, I believe that would be good."

"Mama, can I stay with Jolie?" Essie asked.

Mrs. Wells shaded her eyes and surveyed the dirt yard. "Bullet is around here somewhere. Estelle, I'm sure he'd be pleased to play with you."

"Sis and I have some girl-talk to do," Jolie intervened.

Essie nodded her head.

A smile crept across Mrs. Wells's thin face. "Yes, my sisters and I used to do that. Having only boys makes me forget about girl-talk."

Jolie grabbed her hat from under the wagon seat and tied it on.

"Miss Jolie, would you like me to wipe down your horses?"

"That would be very kind of you, Theo."

"Shoot, that's just the way I am."

Jolie watched her mother and Mrs. Wells stroll arm in arm into the house. *Lord, we've only known them a few days, but there's a bond among homesteaders. None of us know if we'll make it, but we all hope the best for each other. I like that.*

Essie scooted next to her sister. "What're you looking at?"

"Mama, I guess. She looks so young when she walks away with that bounce in her step."

"Everyone thinks you and she are sisters."

"I don't think we look like each other."

"No, but you look like sisters. That's because she looks young, and you look . . ."

"Old?" Jolie supplied.

"Mature," Essie said.

Jolie hugged her sister. "That was very quick thinking."

Essie leaned against her. "Thanks for letting me stay in the wagon with you," she whispered.

"You didn't want to see if the Lord is changing your attitude toward Bullet?"

"'Thou shalt not test the Lord thy God.'"

Jolie clapped her hands. "Is it too much to expect from Him so soon?"

"It's too much to expect from me so soon."

"There you go, Miss Jolie," Theo said.

"Thank you so much, Theo."

"Did you see Tanner in town?" he asked.

"Yes, we did."

"Ain't that about the best gun shop you ever saw?"

"I didn't get to look at it much," Jolie admitted.

"Did you see that thirty-six-inch Sharps rifle with an extra-heavy barrel? I'll bet it weighs fifteen pounds."

"I think we missed that one."

"He had a Winchester 1886 carbine that's never been used."

"I'm afraid I didn't pay attention to the firearms."

"Surely you saw them Colts with the ivory handles."

"I think perhaps Leppy and Chug were looking at them."

"Leppy Verdue and Chug LaPage?" Theo asked.

"Yes," Essie replied.

Theo rubbed his dirt-smeared chin. "I thought they was dead."

"Do you know them?" Jolie asked.

"I ain't never met them, but Tanner told me the story about them pullin' down that town. And he heard it from a former U.S. deputy marshal."

"They pulled down an entire town?" Essie gasped.

"It was a real small town," Theo explained.

"How did they pull down the town?" Essie asked.

"They drove a herd from northern New Mexico up to Colorado. Purtneer died crossin' the desert and the river. They settled the herd on the edge of town, and then Leppy, Chug, and some others went to town to let the wolf howl."

"What?" Essie asked.

"I'll explain later," Jolie told her.

"All the stores and saloons was closed because the mayor was givin' a speech at a picnic down at the river," Theo continued. "It was a new mining town. Most of the buildings were tent tops. The boys rode up and asked to join the picnic, but the mayor said they weren't properly attired."

"What do you have to wear to a picnic?" Jolie asked.

"Clean clothes, I reckon. When they asked the townspeople to open the stores so they could buy some good clothes, the mayor told them they should ride down the trail to Bonner, which was more their type of town."

"What did they do?" Essie asked.

"The deputy told Tanner that they looped the center posts of most of the buildings and jerked them down like dominos. Then they went back out, rounded up the herd, and drove them right over the top of the busted buildings. Ain't no town there anymore. I reckon the mayor was out of a job."

"What was the name of the town?"

"Placid City, Colorado."

Jolie clapped her hands and burst out laughing.

"What's so funny?" Theo asked.

"I wonder if the former deputy ever read the Stuart Brannon book *Up from the Rio Grande*?" Jolie mused.

"Ol' Brannon did the same thing?" Theo asked.

"Yes, but the name of the town was Placid Valley, Utah."

"Ain't that a coincidence? Maybe ol' Leppy read the same book and was inspired."

Jolie glanced at Essie and winked. "Perhaps."

Essie stood to stare across the road. "Did I just see that sagebrush move?"

"I don't see anything," Jolie said.

"Hand me the shotgun," Essie shouted. "I believe there's a prairie chicken over there. As soon as that sage moves again, I'll blast it."

A short, thick sagebrush leaped to its feet and scampered down the draw across from the house.

"My, it's a sagebrush with legs," Jolie laughed.

"It's just Bullet," Theo said.

Jolie leaned over toward her sister. "You aren't exactly letting the Lord change you."

"Sure I am. I didn't shoot him, did I?"

"We don't even have the shotgun."

"See? I thought I was very mature about it."

Greg Wells stuck his head around the corner of the building. "Theo, Daddy says to get back here and help me."

"I was just takin' care of Miss Jolie's team."

"You was sportin' up to her—that's what you was doin'."

"I was not."

"Yes, you were."

"I bet you a fine shinley I wasn't," Theo declared.

"It's a bet."

Theo took off running after his brother.

Essie looked at Jolie. "What's a fine shinley?"

"I have no idea. Do you know what 'sportin' up' means?"

"No. Don't you?" Essie asked.

"No."

"Boys can be very annoying," Essie declared.

"They aren't calm and logical like us girls."

"You mean like you in Tanner's gun shop?" Essie giggled.

"Estelle Cinnia! I expect you to go to your grave never telling anyone about that."

Essie scrunched her nose up. "I'm not planning on going to my grave for a long, long time."

Jolie scowled. "Plans change."

When they reached home, Lissa took the team to the barn while Jolie and Essie dusted off the mattresses. Lawson and Gibs helped haul the bedding in and then disappeared outside. Essie traipsed out to the barn and back.

"Can Francis come in and see the new beds?"

Jolie frowned. "Absolutely not."

"That's what I told him, but he wanted me to ask."

Essie watched Jolie sort through the big black trunk. "Can I go try the bed now?" she asked.

"I just got the covers tucked in."

"I'll lay on top."

"Kick off your shoes," Jolie instructed.

"Yes, Mama!"

"Do I really mother you?"

"Most of the time, but it's okay. It's like havin' two mamas. Prudy Collier in Helena didn't even have one mama."

Essie disappeared into the backroom.

Jolie straightened a comforter over the bed in the front room and then peeked into the backroom.

"It's really, really comfortable," Essie called out as she stretched out on her back. "Do you want to test it out with me?"

"I need to start supper."

"Supper will wait five minutes."

"Okay, li'l sis, scoot over."

"You have to pull off your shoes. It's a rule."

Jolie sat on the edge of the bed and untied her high-top, lace-up shoes. "And I'm pulling off my stockings."

"Can I pull mine off, too?"

"Of course." Jolie lay down beside Essie. "It feels good to wiggle our toes, doesn't it."

"Oh, yes, I don't know why Mama wears stockings to bed."

"Her feet get cold."

"She says all she needs is stockings, and she's quite warm," Essie remarked.

Jolie closed her eyes. *Lord, Mama seems to enjoy life more than any woman I know. Help me to do the same.*

"Do you think Mama's too skinny?" Essie asked.

"I never thought about it much. Mothers aren't really skinny or fat. They're just mothers."

"I'm not skinny. That's why my toes don't get cold," Essie declared. "You are kinda skinny though."

"I'm certainly not as thin as Mama," Jolie said.

"Johnny Mundo said you were sort of skinny."

"The boy who lived on the corner in Helena?"

"Yeah. I heard him say that Jolie Bowers was skinny in all the right places, and then he said you weren't skinny in all the right places, too. What do you think he meant by that?"

Jolie tried to remember which one was Johnny Mundo. "I'm not sure what he meant, but if he were here right now, I'd slap him. I don't think he should be talking about me that way."

"Jolie, all the boys talk about your looks."

"They do not."

"Yes, they do."

"Did you ever hear Tanner Wells talk about my looks?"

"No."

"Well?"

"I bet he thinks about them."

"Enough of that!" Jolie pointed up. "What do you think is crawling across our ceiling?"

"A grasshopper."

"Let's get him down because I don't want him to drop onto our bed in the middle of the night," Jolie said.

"Eweeee!" Essie pulled a pillow over her face.

Jolie stood up on the mattress and tried to balance herself. "Hold my legs steady, Essie. There he goes."

"How do they hang onto the ceiling upside down?"

"I have no idea. I need to move over toward the window."

"What're you going to do if you catch him?"

"Take him outside and turn him loose."

"I think we need a different roof," Essie commented.

Jolie put her hand on her sister's shoulder. "Oh, I forgot to tell Mama about those cedar shingles up at Carter Canyon."

"You think we might get a different roof?"

"Maybe." Jolie leaned toward the corner of the ceiling. "Got him!"

"In your hand?"

"Yes."

"Did you squish him?" Essie asked.

"Of course not."

"Is he still wiggling?"

"Yes. Help me down."

Someone stomped his feet on the rough wooden floor.

"Yes?" Jolie called.

Gibs shoved his head inside the open doorway that separated the small backroom. "You got a visitor on horseback. He's waitin' out in the yard," he shouted and then sprinted back outside.

"Oh . . . my," Jolie murmured.

"Who is it?" Essie asked.

"It must be Leppy Verdue."

"He wants the envelope!"

Jolie tried to peer out the window. "Yes, but I'm not going out there like this. I do not entertain men barefooted."

"Never?" Essie pressed.

Jolie shook her head. "Never."

"Do you ever entertain gentlemen with a grasshopper in your hand?"

"Never."

"Can I take the envelope out to Leppy?" Essie asked.

"Yes, you may."

"Jolie, if you throw Leppy away, can I have him?"

"I'm not throwing him away. And, no, you can't have him. You're only twelve."

"I won't be twelve forever."

"Go on. Take him the envelope."

Jolie pulled the thick brown envelope out from under the new mattress and handed it to Essie, who sprinted out of the room.

Jolie sat on the edge of the bed. *I can't put on my shoes with a grasshopper in my hand. This is quite bizarre. I'm sitting here waiting for a man to leave so I can go outside and turn a grasshopper loose. It would be funny if it wasn't me. Lord, You must laugh when You see the situations we get into at times.*

She heard voices out in the yard but could not discern what they were saying.

Some of us are more bizarre than others.

Essie tramped back into the room, carrying the brown paper envelope.

"You didn't give the envelope to Leppy?"

"It wasn't Leppy."

"Who was it?"

"Tanner."

"Tanner!" Jolie jumped up. "What's he doing here?"

"He came to see you, he said. He wanted to apologize for how he acted in the store. He closed up and rode all the way out to see you."

"Tell him I'll be right out when I get my shoes on."

"He left."

"What do you mean, he left?"

"I told him you never entertain men when you're barefooted."

"What?" Jolie moaned.

"That's what you said."

"This is absurd!"

Jolie scurried out of the house, holding her skirt up to her ankles with her left hand and the squirming grasshopper in her right. The dirt felt hot, yet soft against her bare feet. She saw Lawson and Gibs stop seeding to watch her run. Essie stood in the doorway.

A tall, broad-shouldered man rode his brown horse north up their rutted drive.

Jolie ran after him. *I can't believe I'm doing this. Lord, what am I doing?*

The man kicked the horse's flanks, and the animal broke into a trot.

Jolie stopped running. She waved her clenched fist in the air. *Oh, no you don't, Mr. Wells. You're not running away from me.*

She felt something sticky crunch in her hand. When she opened her fingers, the lifeless grasshopper dropped to the dirt next to a disc of dried mud that had been pressed hard by a hoof, cut out like a big mud cookie. Jolie scooped it up and flung it toward the departing rider. Like a well-aimed snowball in January, the packed mud slammed into the man's back. He spun the horse around.

"What did you do?" he shouted.

"Tanner Wells, you came over here to see me. Here I am; so don't you dare go home. You come back here and talk to me."

Tanner grinned as he slid off the saddle. He pulled off his hat and led the brown horse back toward her. "Are you goin' to clobber me again?"

She waited for him to approach. "No. I'm sorry. I just didn't know how to get your attention."

"Then we're friends?"

"Yes, of course."

"You wouldn't mind shakin' hands on that, would you?"

"Shaking hands? Eh, you really don't want to shake my hand right now," she warned.

"Why not?"

"Trust me."

"I don't mind a little mud."

"I do. I'm sorry I tossed the clod at you. I couldn't run any farther barefoot."

"You were runnin' after me?"

"Well, don't . . . I wasn't . . . It's not that . . ."

"Then what?"

"That's all in the past. Let's just shake hands," she stated.

He reached out and took her hand. "You can tell a lot about people by the way they shake hands," he added.

He pulled his hand back, stared at it for a moment, and then brushed it clean. "Eh, usually, that is."

When Jolie turned back toward the house, Tanner walked alongside her, leading the big brown horse. She spotted her father and mother in the field. They had stopped plowing and were watching her. Lawson and Gibs stood at the woodshed and traced her every step. Essie perched at the doorway and shook her head.

Jolie pulled her long cotton gown over her head and turned down the light. She scooted in under the white sheet and studied the flickering shadows on the ceiling as the soft light faded to dark.

"Are you awake, Essie?" she whispered.

"Yes."

"It's been quite a day."

"And quite an evening."

Jolie reached on top of the covers and took Essie's hand. "It was nice to have company for supper."

"I wish Leppy and Chug had stayed."

"I suppose they wanted to get on their way."

"I think they wanted to see you," Essie remarked.

"I was busy."

"Going for a walk at twilight with Tanner doesn't seem like being busy."

"It was nice. I think sunrise and sunset are my favorite moments in western Nebraska."

"Leppy visited with me for a long time," Essie told her.

"What did you talk about?"

"He said the story about him pulling down a whole town was a lie. They only pulled down one building, the bank that the mayor owned. But they didn't run the cattle over it. He didn't want to hurt the cows."

"I don't suppose it made him too popular in Placid City."

"He said the mayor threatened to have him arrested, and so he left Colorado. I guess that mayor posted a reward on Leppy, and there are some lawmen and bounty hunters looking for him." Essie scooted over and put her head against Jolie's shoulder. "What did you and Tanner talk about?"

"Oh, everything from the weather to the gun business to school and how many children to have after we get married."

Essie sat straight up. "What?"

"Be quiet over there," Gibs hollered. "There are men tryin' to sleep."

"Men?" Jolie whispered.

Essie scrunched down next to her. "What do you mean, you talked about children?"

"I was just testing to see if you were truly awake."

"You didn't really talk about getting married and children, did you?"

"Of course not. It was our first real visit."

"I didn't talk to Leppy about getting married either," Essie whispered.

"That's good, since Daddy wouldn't let you get married for another five years."

"There was a girl in Montana who got married when she was fourteen."

"You certainly talk about marriage a lot for a twelve-year-old."

"You brought the subject up."

"Maybe we should go to sleep," Jolie replied.

"The mattress feels good."

"It's dreamy."

"G'night, Jolie Lorita."

"G'night, Estelle Cinnia."

"Are you two done jawin'?" Gibs huffed from beyond the quilt wall.

Jolie lay still on her back. *Now, Lord, I would rather not have a grasshopper fall on the bed tonight. And let me wake up in the morning without my back hurting. Thank You for a very good day—a confusing day but a good day.*

Essie put her lips up to Jolie's ear. "What was that noise?"

Jolie faced her sister. "It's just Mama giggling under the covers."

"She has a nice giggle . . . for a mother."

"Go to sleep, li'l sis."

"I'm tired."

Jolie folded her arms across her chest and hugged herself. *A very nice evening, Lord. He's so sweet to me. I feel so peaceful. I wonder why that is? We hardly know each other. Yet sometimes, like when we were talking about schools and houses, well, it was as if we had known each other a long, long time.*

Jolie licked her lips and could feel her smile pull up the corners of her mouth.

"Essie, are you still awake?"

"Hmmmmm."

"Do you like Tanner?"

"Hmmmmmm."

"He's very nice, isn't he?"

"Hmmmmmm."

"And strong. He's as strong as Daddy—maybe stronger."

"Hmmmmmm."

"He used to blacksmith a lot."

"Hmmmmmm."

"Not that it matters. And he's very handsome. Don't you agree?"

"Hmmmmmm."

"He doesn't know it yet, but I'm going to marry him. I just know it."

There was no reply.

Jolie nudged her sister and spoke louder: "I said, I'm going to marry Tanner. Did you hear me?"

"We all heard you!" Gibs muttered. "I wish you'd hurry up and marry him so we can get some sleep."

"Who's getting married?" Matthew shouted from the bed in the front room.

"Jolie," Gibs hollered.

Lissa's voice sang out, "Are you going to marry Tanner Wells, dear?"

I can't believe this. We need a bigger house. "Yes, Mama, I am."

"That's nice, honey. I thought so the minute I first laid eyes on him. Now go to sleep. We have a busy day tomorrow."

Jolie thought she could hear her mother giggling again.

With a red bandanna around his neck, Francis the calf followed Essie across the yard as she toted two empty glass fruit jars.

Jolie was sweeping the front porch. "Guess how many grasshoppers I swept out of the house."

Essie stared down at the broom. "Six?"

"Thirteen."

"I guess it's grasshopper season." Essie rubbed Francis's head.

"I really hope it's over soon."

"Do you think Mama and Gibs are in Scottsbluff by now?"

Jolie studied the sun. "I reckon. But I don't know how far it is to Carter Canyon from there."

"Daddy said he thought it was in the Wildcat Hills."

"Mama didn't think they'd come home tonight. I don't suppose it would be that easy, or others would have done it." Jolie stared out across the field. "How's the corn planting coming?"

"Lawson does a good job. Daddy says he has never seen such straight rows."

"That's amazing since Daddy couldn't plow a straight row if he had to."

"Jolie, I think Mama is better than Daddy at almost everything. She drives a team better. She plows straighter. She can even saw a board better."

"Yes, and she can bake a peach pie better. What's your point?" Jolie challenged.

"You bake better pies than Mama."

"That's because I have more opportunities. Daddy can write nicer than Mama. He can discuss more topics. He can meet new people better. He can dance a jig better. He can cut hair better than Mama. And Daddy can sing. Oh, how he can sing."

Essie straightened the bandanna around the calf's neck. "Daddy can shoot straighter than Mama, but Gibs can outshoot them both. And Daddy is really, really good at making ice cream."

"We all have things we can do well."

"What am I good at, Jolie?"

"Essie, there's no one who can talk to animals like you can. Even Mama said so."

"Mama told me once that she could only speak horse. I think I'm pretty good with horse, pig, and cow, but I'm really good at dog, cat, calf, and raccoon," Essie declared.

"Can you speak grasshopper?"

"No! But if I could, I would say, 'Go away!'"

"Oh, look!" Jolie pointed across the vacant homestead to the north. "I think a sagebrush just up and ran away."

"Chester? Really? I'll—I'll . . ."

"I was teasing. What would you have done?"

"Oh. He's not really there?"

"No, of course not."

"In that case, I would have allowed the Lord to change my heart." Essie faked a silly grin.

"Hmmmmmmm."

Essie scratched her neck and peered north. "Someone *is* coming."

"A wagon?" Jolie asked.

"Maybe Mama is coming back."

"No, there isn't a cloud of dust."

"Doesn't it seem strange that we get so many visitors back here?"

"You wait here and greet them," Jolie instructed. "I'll put the teakettle back on the stove."

"Should I go get Daddy and Lawson out of the cornfield?"

"Not until we find out who it is."

Jolie had lined up four cups, saucers, honey, and a tin of crackers on the table by the time the wagon rolled into the yard.

"It's the Vockerys," Essie called out.

Jolie walked out to the wagon. Her pale yellow apron covered most of the front of her blue calico dress. "Welcome. It's nice to see you again."

"We were on our way to town and thought we'd stop by," Mabel Vockery explained.

Jolie brushed back her curly bangs. "Mama and Gibs have gone to Carter Canyon for a load of cedar shingles. She'll be so disappointed to miss you again."

Mrs. Vockery rolled her eyes at the thin man sitting next to her. "My Ernie has promised us a cedar roof for three years."

"As soon as we get a good corn crop, Mama," Mr. Vockery said. "Cain't afford to buy shingles on a homestead."

"We can't afford to buy them either. Mama is hauling several loads for Mr. Mendez, and he promised her a load of shingles for pay," Jolie explained.

"Besides, Stranger and Pilgrim need to work," Essie added.

Mrs. Vockery glanced over at her husband.

"Our wagon and team ain't sturdy enough for Carter Canyon. Besides, there ain't nothin' wrong with a sod roof," he insisted.

"As long as it isn't rainin', and the mud doesn't drip in the stew," she retorted.

"The main problem we've had is grasshoppers," Jolie said. "Do you have many?"

"It usually ain't too bad. Old-timers say there was a time when they filled the sky," Mr. Vockery answered. "Is that your daddy out there?"

"Yes, he and my brother Lawson are planting corn."

"Our corn is already up," Mr. Vockery declared.

Jolie felt her shoulders stiffen. She folded her arms and tried to relax. "I know we're quite late, but we have to try to make a cash crop anyway."

Mr. Vockery pulled off his hat. "Do you think he'd mind a visit?"

"Daddy has never been too busy to visit." Jolie turned to Mrs. Vockery and the four girls. Three were dressed in bright blue gingham, the fourth in faded green cotton. "Mrs. Vockery, I have tea and crackers waiting on the table. All you girls are invited."

April, May, and June climbed down behind their mother. Mary leaped off the back of the wagon. "Have you got a pig?" she shouted.

"Yes," Essie said. "His name is Mudball, and he can be quite naughty."

"Really? Can I see him?"

"Sure."

"What's your calf's name?"

"This is Francis," Essie told her. "He follows me everywhere."

Mary patted Francis on the head. "Don't you have a dog?"

"No."

"Do you want one?"

"Oh, yes, but I have to ask Mama."

Mary pointed to Jolie. "Ask her."

"That isn't my mama. That's my sister!"

"Oh, yeah, I forgot."

While Essie and Mary ran to the barn, Jolie led Mrs. Vockery and the other girls to the house where they sat on benches around the homemade table. Jolie served tea and passed honey and crackers.

"My, your place looks quite tidy," Mrs. Vockery observed.

"Thank you. We've added a few things since you were here last."

Mrs. Vockery scrutinized the bed in the corner of the front room. "You have a mattress. Ernest is so tired of our straw bed. How we wish there was a furniture store that sold on credit. Everyone seems to think that homesteaders are a poor risk. They treat us as if we were penniless vagrants instead of penniless farmers."

Jolie felt her face grow warm as she sipped her tea. "I suppose that will change when we all make our farms pay." *I don't dare mention that Mr. Mendez let me sign for these. Of course, that was Mother's doing.*

May Vockery unfastened her dusty straw hat. "Do you know who's living in the DeMarco place?"

"Yes. Their name is Wells. I think they might take it over for Mrs. DeMarco. You heard about Alfonso?"

"Oh, yes," Mrs. Vockery mumbled through a bite of cracker. "Quite a shame."

"What's the oldest Wells boy's name?" May asked.

Jolie's gray-green eyes widened. "Did you meet the Wells family?"

"I just saw them from a distance." May grinned.

"May wants to sport around with their oldest."

Mabel Vockery banged down her teacup. "April Ann!"

"Well, she does, Mama!" June echoed.

"I don't want my daughters talking like that," Mabel snapped.

Jolie studied May Vockery. She was thin-faced, flat-chested, and plain, but her blue eyes sparkled with life. "May, how old was the boy you saw?"

"He was about Lawson's age," April butted in. "Perhaps I should take Daddy and the others some tea and crackers."

"No, the men are busy in the field."

"The oldest Wells son is twenty and is a gunsmith in Scottsbluff. You must have seen Theo or Greg."

"There's two of them?" June grinned.

"Theo is the one with dark hair. He's a year older than Greg. Actually they have a younger brother they call Bullet. But he's rather . . . eh, active. You probably didn't see him," Jolie reported.

"Was he the one hiding in the barrel?" Mrs. Vockery asked.

"I'm sure it was."

The front door was open, and Jolie heard footsteps on the porch. "Mornin', all."

Jolie saw April's eyes light up. "Lawson, I believe you know everyone."

He yanked off his hat. "I reckon I do. Hello, Miss April."

She dropped her chin to her chest. "Hi, Lawson."

"Can I do something for you?" Jolie asked.

"Eh, Daddy and Mr. Vockery are visitin' about corn, and so I came to get a couple jars of water."

"I just sent you both a drink," Jolie reminded him.

"I figured maybe Mr. Vockery was thirsty, too."

"That's very considerate of you."

"Thank you." He blushed.

Jolie retrieved the jars from the counter. "Perhaps you could take out some honey and crackers, too."

"I reckon I could use some help," he said.

April leapt up. "I'll help you."

"Put on your hat, young lady," Mrs. Vockery ordered. "You know, I told Mrs. Skipmode that girls here must be sure and wear a hat or bonnet, or they will look like a piece of burnt toast. Why, when I was their age . . ."

Jolie watched April skip out of the room at Lawson's side. *Lord, I have never before seen Lawson even look at a girl. Do my eyes sparkle like that when I look at Tanner? I suppose I know the answer to that. But it's so grand to see Lawson happy. He's such a hard-working, serious boy.*

" . . . as, of course, I know you are, too . . . and that's why we need to have the meeting."

May squirmed on the bench. "Mama, can I go to the privy?"

"Certainly, but wear your hat."

"Now what with families movin' in left and right . . ."

"Mama, can I go with May?" June asked.

"You both have to go?"

"It's a rather old privy. It might be better if they went together," Jolie suggested.

"Wear your bonnets and don't stay too long in the sun."

June turned toward Jolie and mouthed the words "thank you" as she bolted toward the door.

"Hmmmm," Mrs. Vockery pondered, "now where was I?"

"You mentioned that there will be more than twenty-five students."

Mama says Lawson is just like a young Grandpa Pritchett. He will be a success at anything he tries, and Mama says I'm identical to Grandma. I hope so, especially with her faith and graciousness. But I hope I can relax more than Grandma does.

" . . . and then who should I bump into but Mrs. Cnvoski. Well,

I suppose you know what she was wearing. Oh, you never met the Cnvoskis? Quite an experience, let me tell you. The first time we met was in Gering at the drugstore. She marched right up and demanded . . ."

Grandma Pritchett worries about the President, about Lake Michigan rising, about her sage garden in the windowsill, about her cats, and especially about Grandpa tracking snow into the great room. But, oh, my, how Grandma can pray. When we visited them last time, we lined up in the hall after dark and put our ears to her bedroom door just to hear her pray for us.

"Would you pass the crackers and honey, dear?"

Jolie handed the china plate to Mrs. Vockery.

"We were goin' to raise bees. We bought two hives from a man in Omaha. He shipped them out on the train. Quite a feat, you know. The railroad claimed they would never ship bees again. Two days after we took the hives to the farm, the bees all flew off. Just like that—they were gone. Oh, my, I do like honey. Did you hear about the time Blondie Dantee got stung right on her . . ."

Lord, I remember Shelbee Lewis in Helena always moaning about her strict Christian family, but I'm very proud of mine. I'm lucky to have grandparents and parents with such an unwavering faith. I suppose living in a two-room dirt house doesn't look like much to others, but I don't mind. At least, not yet.

" . . . which is precisely what I told him in the first place. I wonder why it is a banker never listens to a woman? Why, I have a good mind to start my own bank. All I need is $50,000 capital. Hah! Is that ever a fine shinley! Me with $50,000 for a bank. I might as well wish for Solomon's temple. Have you met Mr. Solomon, the jeweler? He has some fine pieces. Next time he's out this direction, I'll send him by. He'll stay for supper as long as you aren't having pork. He's one of those, you know . . ."

Jolie's head began to sag.

"Not that it makes any difference in the world to me. Why, my very best friend when I was young was Helda—"

"Mrs. Vockery, would you like some fresh air?" Jolie interrupted.

"Are you getting sick?"

"No. It's just that I've been cooped up in this sod house all day, and I thought I'd like to get outside. Shall we take a walk?"

"A walk? Oh, my . . . why, yes, of course. You do look peaked. Are you eating all right, dear? We mustn't forget our hats. You know how dreadful that sun can be."

Jolie stood at the door to wave at the Vockerys as they rolled out the narrow drive.

Essie and Francis plodded up next to her. "Did you know that Mary Vockery can ride a pig?"

"Did she ride Mudball?"

"No, he was very rude. But she even knows how to ride steers. She once rode their bull all the way to Bayard and back."

"She's a talented girl."

"She's a tomboy—that's what she is."

"Is that okay with you?"

"Sure, I like it. Next to her I seem kind of nobby—like you."

"I am not nobby," Jolie insisted. "Look at this dress. There's nothing nobby or fancy about it."

"You mean, besides the lace at the hem, cuffs, and collar, the ribbon on the bustle, and the velvet chevrons?"

"Yes, besides all that."

"I meant you're nobby on the inside, anyway. Did you see Lawson and April?"

"I believe they found each other quite compatible."

Essie giggled. "Is that what you call it?"

"Call what?"

"What they were doing behind the shed."

"Were you spying on them?"

"Me and Mary did."

"And just what were they doing?"

Essie closed her eyes and puckered her lips. "Finding each other quite compatible, I reckon."

Jolie had ham, white beans, and gravy ready when Mr. Bowers and Lawson tramped to the house about dark. She handed her father a bar of lye soap and ushered him over to the basin.

"You worked hard today, Daddy."

"I would have gotten more done except for that visit."

"What did you and Mr. Vockery talk about?"

"The Young Farmers' Alliance and schoolteaching. Mostly school."

"Are they still planning to start a school here?"

"Yes. They have a building to use. Some man named Shinley donated it. Vockery says that with a little work it can be made usable."

"Do they have a teacher yet?"

"He keeps thinking Mama or I should teach. Can't see how we could do that and run a homestead."

"Perhaps if the two of you worked at it together, one of you would always be free for the farm. Besides, they don't want you to teach during the summer crops, do they?"

"Can you imagine your mother ever being trapped inside a schoolroom?"

"No. She would hate it. So you told Mr. Vockery no?"

"I told him we'd ponder it. I certainly wanted to talk to you first."

"Me, Daddy?"

"Jolie, darlin', you would make a wonderful teacher."

"I'm only seventeen."

"You're almost eighteen. That's old enough."

"I've never even gone to college."

"Darlin', you're ten steps ahead of everyone else. You always have been. That's all that would be necessary."

She slipped her arm into her father's. "But I have a job—takin' care of my family."

"Jolie Lorita, we have to learn to get along without you doin' so much. This is a good way to learn. You'd still be with us most of the time." He patted her fingers.

"Are you trying to kick me out, Daddy?"

"Darlin', darlin', darlin' . . . I'm tryin' to toughen the rest of us up. 'Cause someday you'll have your own family to take care of, and we need to know we can survive without you."

"Mama is a very good cook, you know."

"I sort of remember. It's faint in my memory. When did you start doin' all the cookin'?"

"When I was nine or ten, I guess. I begged Mama for years before that."

"Jolie, I'm not trying to decide what your future should be, but this would be a good opportunity. Mr. Vockery wants to start the school in September. He can't even talk it up until he has a teacher lined up for sure. He suggests that if none of us wants the job permanently, we take it temporarily while they continue to search for a teacher."

"So it might only be temporary?"

"That's what he implied."

"Can I pray about it for a while, Daddy?"

"I'd be disappointed if you didn't."

Jolie paced around the front room. "What would we do for books and supplies?"

"Mr. Vockery said we'd have to raid all the homes and borrow as many books and slates as we could find."

"How about furniture?"

"Everyone can pitch in and make some desks."

"And I could make curtains and go early and stoke the fire and sweep up . . . but we'd need maps, charts, a dictionary, and pencils and paper. I wonder if we could insist that students bring their own paper and pencils?"

Jolie was still thinking about teaching in a one-room schoolhouse as she washed dishes in the basin in the front room. An exhausted Lawson Bowers had scrubbed his face and gone to bed. Mr. Bowers sat at the table with the lantern and read a battered copy of the *Rocky*

Mountain News. The front door was open, and Essie reclined on the step.

"What are you doing, Estelle Cinnia?" Jolie called out.

"Me and Francis are catchin' grasshoppers."

"Why?"

"To feed to Mudball."

"Does he like to eat grasshoppers?"

"That's what we aim to find out."

"How many do you have?"

"Five."

"That's not a very large meal for a pig."

"It's just a snack."

Jolie wiped her hands and walked to the doorway. "I don't think this house has enough circulation. It's stuffy inside tonight."

"It's stuffy out here, too. I think it's gettin' cloudy."

"If it rains, we'll need to put the rubber tarps back on the roof," Jolie remarked.

"Someone's coming," Essie called out.

"It isn't a wagon. Come on, little sis, back into the house."

Nine

Matthew Bowers stood in the doorway of the sod house when a rider trotted into the yard. "Evenin'."

The man dismounted and walked his horse to the front of the house. "Is this the Bowers place?" The man's voice was deep, commanding.

"I'm Matthew Bowers."

"I didn't figure anyone would buy the Avery claim."

Mr. Bowers blocked the doorway. "It seems that many have purchased it. Avery was an ambitious salesman."

"So I heard." The man dropped the reins and let his horse stand. "Mr. Bowers, I'm Sheriff Riley."

Matthew Bowers smiled and thrust out his hand. "Gibson told us all about you. It seems he applied for a position with your office on our first day in town."

"That's your boy?"

"Yes. He's on a chore with Mrs. Bowers at Carter Canyon at the moment. He'll regret missing you."

"He knows more about sheriff work than nine out of ten deputies I hire."

"He'll be pleased to hear that. What can I do for you?"

The sheriff looped his thumbs in his vest pockets. "There's been a shootin' in town. I reckon I need to talk to Miss Bowers. I was told you have a daughter who's quite the head-turner."

"Sheriff Riley, I'm fortunate to have two beautiful daughters."

Jolie glanced at Essie and winked.

"Is one of them of courtin' age?"

"Yes, but I'd certainly like to know what this is all about."

"Jeremiah Cain, a clerk at Saddler's Grocery, was shot in the back this afternoon."

Jolie grabbed her chest and tried to breathe deeply.

"He's in too bad a shape to talk yet," Sheriff Riley continued, "but Luke McKay said he witnessed a fight between Cain and a couple of drifters last week. The same pair were in town this afternoon. One is named Leppy Verdue. Luke said your daughter might just fill me in a little on their conflict."

Mr. Bowers turned to the girls behind him. "Jolie, did you hear all of that?"

"Yes, Daddy. We heard."

"Do you want to talk to the sheriff?"

"Certainly." She came to the doorway. "You're welcome to come in, Sheriff, although it might be more pleasant out here. It's stuffy inside. May I bring you a cup of coffee?"

"I'd appreciate it, Miss Bowers."

"Did you have any supper? I have a few things left."

"No, miss. I won't put you out for supper."

"But I insist. I have no intention of scrapping good food. I'll bring you out a plate. Daddy, take a lantern out, and you men sit on the bench. There just might be a breeze."

The sheriff pulled off his hat. His gray hair caught what light there was. "If you insist. That would be neighborly."

Jolie retreated to the counter, and Essie scooted up beside her. "Does he think Leppy shot Jeremiah Cain in the back?"

"I suppose so."

"Do you think he did that?"

"No." Jolie spooned potatoes onto the tin plate.

"Neither do I. How come you're feedin' the sheriff?"

"Because he's hungry. Now how about you going to milk the cow?"

"You already milked her," Essie protested.

"But we drank the milk, and the rest is in the butter churn. Perhaps you can get enough for the sheriff. Besides, you always enjoy visiting with Margaret."

"But all she ever wants to talk about is grass and hay." Essie grabbed the milk pail and skipped out into the yard, carrying the smallest lantern. A bandanna-clad calf appeared from the shadows and tagged along after her.

Jolie handed the plate of food to the sheriff and returned with coffee for both men.

"Miss Bowers," the sheriff mumbled between bites, "did you witness a fist fight between Jeremiah Cain and Leppy Verdue?"

"Yes, I did. It was a short fight. Only a couple of blows were thrown."

The sheriff wiped his mouth on the back of his hand. "Why were they fightin'?"

"Because they're both childish, stubborn, prideful men."

Sheriff Riley nodded. "Then I take it they was fightin' over you?"

"That's what they claimed, but I wanted no part of it."

"How did the fight end?" The sheriff smacked his lips.

"I broke it up."

"Now just how did a purdy little thing like you do that?"

She stepped closer to the sheriff. "I grabbed Leppy's gun and threatened to send them to the eternal judgment seat if they didn't stop."

He aimed his fork at her. "And they believed you?"

"I guess so." Jolie yanked the sheriff's gun from his holster and pointed it at him. "They stopped fighting."

He didn't blink an eye but kept eating. "I jist might hire this whole family as deputies. Is that the last time you saw either one of them?"

Jolie shoved the sheriff's Colt .44 back into his holster. "No, I was in town a couple days ago. I saw them both on that day."

"Did they get in a fight then?"

"Not that I know of."

"What was the occasion for your meeting them?"

Jolie felt her neck stiffen. "I didn't say there was an occasion. I was in town shopping. They happened to be in the places where I went. I spoke to them. That's all."

Essie tramped back into sight and paused to listen.

"What about the situation down at the livery? Did Leppy save you from a runaway team?"

"He most certainly did not."

"Jolie stopped the team. He jumped off his horse and landed in the street," Essie explained. "He didn't get hurt. I looked him over real close."

The sheriff swiped half a biscuit across the plate. "What happened next?"

"We came home."

"And you haven't seen either Leppy Verdue or Jeremiah Cain since that day?"

"No, I haven't."

"I have," Essie informed him.

"What do you mean, you have?" the sheriff asked.

"Leppy came out here to see Jolie, but she let me talk to him instead."

"That was nice of her."

"I gave him the envelope."

"What envelope?" the sheriff asked.

"The one Jolie was holdin' for Leppy. Maxwell Dix and Shakey Torrington left it with her."

"Why did Dix and Torrington leave an envelope with her to give to Leppy Verdue?"

Essie swung the milk pail back and forth. "'Cause they thought Leppy was her beau, I guess."

"Is he?" the sheriff pressed.

"No! She's sweet on Tanner Wells."

"Essie!" Jolie scowled.

"It's true."

"Sheriff, if you're through talking to my sister about me, may I say something?"

The sheriff took a big bite of potato and nodded his head.

"I don't believe Leppy Verdue is the type of man to shoot someone in the back."

"But he is the type to jump into a fight."

"Yes, but he's very proud. I'm sure he believes he could whip Jeremiah Cain straight up. It seems to me the only person a proud man would shoot in the back would be one he knew could beat him face to face. And Leppy was not afraid of Jeremiah Cain."

"And if there isn't a purdy girl around to impress, why fight at all?" Matthew Bowers asked.

"Leppy has a very nice smile," Essie remarked. "Would you like some fresh milk, Sheriff?"

"Nope. Thanks, but I never drink the stuff."

Essie frowned at Jolie and then tramped into the house.

The sheriff picked at his teeth. "The fact is, someone shot the clerk in the back. I'd like to know who."

Mr. Bowers leaned back and drank his coffee. "Did they steal anything from the store?"

"Doesn't seem to be anything missing. There was money still in the cash box. But the owner, George Saddler, is still takin' inventory."

"Doesn't make too much sense to shoot a clerk and then not steal anything. Perhaps Jeremiah Cain will shed more light on the situation when he comes to," Mr. Bowers suggested.

"If he comes to," the sheriff replied as he twisted on his long mustache.

"It's that serious?" Mr. Bowers inquired.

"I ain't never seen a good back wound when a man is shot up close like that. But he's alive—so that's good."

"I'll be praying for his recovery," Jolie said.

"I'm sure he needs it."

"How about you, Sheriff Riley? Can I pray for you?"

Mr. Bowers reached out and took her hand. "Darlin', don't put the sheriff on the spot like that."

"Nonsense, Bowers. There ain't a sheriff alive that wouldn't take all the prayers on his behalf he can get."

Right after noon the next day, Lissa and Gibs Bowers rolled into the yard in a fog of dust and a sprinkle of grasshoppers. Essie and Jolie sprinted out to the yard to greet them.

"Hi, Mama. Are these our cedar shingles?" Essie asked.

Lissa Bowers stood up and flipped her braid back over her shoulder. "Yes, they are. It's quite a big load, isn't it?"

Gibs shoved his .22 rifle on the wagon seat and hopped down. "We hauled two loads yesterday. They said no one ever made two trips in one day before."

"I was in a hurry to get home." Mrs. Bowers climbed down and began to unharness Pilgrim and Stranger.

"I almost shot me a big ol' buck, but he was too far away," Gibs reported.

"With a .22?" Essie asked.

"Like I said, he was too far away."

Jolie pulled a torn burlap sack from the stone wall of the corral to wipe down the lathered horses. "Mama, Lawson has been doing some of the plowing."

Lissa glanced out at the field.

"Daddy says he plows almost as straight as you," Essie remarked.

"Did you stop in Scottsbluff?" Jolie inquired.

"Just at Mr. Mendez's house to unload the shingles."

"Did you hear anything about Jeremiah Cain's condition?"

"I heard there was a shooting."

Essie grabbed Stranger's head and rubbed noses with the big horse. "The sheriff came to talk to Jolie 'cause he thinks Leppy and Chug had something to do with it. But I just know they didn't."

"I trust that was a mistake. Mr. Mendez mentioned a considerable sum of money missing."

Jolie felt her mouth drop. "Last night Sheriff Riley said there was no money taken from the cash box."

"Perhaps they found out different."

"It wasn't Leppy," Essie insisted. "He had money enough to buy things when Jolie and I saw him."

"What was he buying?"

Essie hung her head. "Eh, a new revolver."

"When was the shootin'?" Gibs asked.

"Yesterday afternoon," Jolie replied.

"We saw Leppy and Chug in Carter Canyon early this mornin'," Gibs said.

"What were they doing?" Jolie asked.

"They said they were hunting."

"If they were hungry and wanted food, why didn't they just buy some dinner in Gering or Scottsbluff?" Essie grilled him.

"Maybe they didn't have the money."

"If they didn't have any money, that proves they didn't rob Jeremiah Cain."

"But it don't prove they didn't shoot him," Gibs countered.

"Maybe they weren't really hunting," Lissa suggested.

"You mean, they might lie to Gibs?" Essie probed.

Lissa hung the harness on the side of the barn. "Darlin', if a person just robbed a store, the chances are he wouldn't worry about lying."

"Leppy didn't shoot him. And if they were hungry, you—you—you should have invited them to our house. They could come here, and we'd feed them," Essie said.

Jolie, Gibs, and Mrs. Bowers stared at her.

Essie blushed. "We don't mind feeding the hungry, do we? I just know Leppy didn't shoot anyone."

"Are you sweet on a driftin' cowboy?" Lissa asked.

"Maybe. He's nice to me, Mama."

"But you're only twelve."

"I won't be twelve forever. Besides, Daddy said he has two beautiful daughters."

"Everyone knows that. But you have plenty of time before you have to make such big decisions."

"If I have to choose someday between Chester and Leppy, I'll choose Leppy."

"Let's see how mature you really are," Mrs. Bowers said. "Right now you can help unload the shingles."

Essie grimaced. "There are lots of grasshoppers in them."

"There are lots of grasshoppers everywhere," Lissa reminded her.

By evening weighted mosquito netting hung over the open front door to allow air to circulate and keep grasshoppers out.

Lissa Bowers stood at the doorway with a cup of coffee. The dying sun reflected off a distant Chimney Rock. "If we get any more grasshoppers, it will feel like the plagues of Egypt."

"Mr. Vockery said they last five days and then disappear," Essie remarked.

"Did he tell you what day this is?"

"Eh, no, this could be day one 'cause there seem to be ten times more of them since yesterday."

"Someone's coming," Essie hollered. "I can hear a horse."

"I don't hear . . ." Mr. Bowers slipped past his wife and out into the yard. "Yes, you're right. It looks like young Mr. Wells."

Jolie dried her hands on her apron and scurried out beside her father.

"Mr. Theo Wells." Matthew Bowers grinned.

"Daddy, that's Gregory!"

The young man pulled up in front of them. "Evenin', Miss Jolie, Mr. Bowers." He yanked off his hat and slapped a grasshopper from the brim.

"Evenin', Gregory." Jolie curtsied.

"Did you ever see so many grasshoppers?" he asked.

"No, I haven't," she replied.

"Do you folks have any chickens?"

Lissa took another sip from her coffee cup. "Not yet. Why?"

"Mama stuck ours in a crate so they wouldn't eat any more grasshoppers. She was afraid the meat would taste funny or that they might explode."

"Is that why you came over?" Mrs. Bowers pressed.

"No. I'm lookin' for Bullet. Did he come over here today?"

"We haven't seen him," Essie answered.

Gregory leaned across the saddle horn. "He didn't make it back by supper. That's usually a sign that he's stuck somewhere."

"Did you ride across the gulch?" Mr. Bowers asked.

"Yes, sir. I didn't see any trace of him."

Essie tramped out next to her sister. "Was he still dressed up like a sagebrush?"

Gregory stood up in the stirrups and gazed off toward the river. "Nope, but he did take one of Mama's sheets."

"A sheet?" Essie said. "What for?"

Gregory Wells tugged at the tight collar button on his white shirt. "Only Bullet knows the answer to that."

"Can you come in and sit a spell?" Mrs. Bowers invited.

"No, ma'am, I need to keep lookin', but I'd surely like to come back another time."

"You're always welcome," Mr. Bowers said.

Jolie stepped over by the dark brown horse. "Would you like us to look around the place for him?"

"I'd appreciate it. I'm goin' to ride back to the tracks. He might be home by now."

Matthew pulled off his spectacles and rubbed the bridge of his nose. "If we find him, we'll deliver him to you."

"Thanks, Mr. Bowers. You could just bring him by on your way to the school meeting."

Mr. Bowers pulled his watch from his vest pocket. "Oh, yes, I almost forgot."

"I reckon you'll be there, Miss Jolie." Gregory smiled.

She tugged on her earlobe. "I hadn't planned to attend."

"Tanner said you'll be there 'cause they're goin' to hire you as the teacher. Me and Theo is thinkin' about attendin'."

"Jolie's goin' to be the teacher?" Essie exclaimed.

"I'm sure there's someone else who wants the job," Jolie said.

"Most are too busy with their homesteads, and city folks don't want to come out here in the winter," Gregory related.

"Are your parents goin' to the meeting?" Mrs. Bowers asked.

"If they can find Bullet in time. If not, they said they'd send Tanner."

"Tanner's home?" Jolie asked.

"Yep."

"I've been plantin' all day, and Lissa had two strenuous days of driving the wagon. Perhaps Jolie Lorita should go and represent the Bowers family. Could you do that?" Mr. Bowers asked.

"By myself?"

"I'll go with you," Essie offered.

"But, Daddy, what if they do want to hire me?"

"You decide what you want to do."

"On my own?"

"No. I expect you'd better ask the Lord what He thinks."

"What do you and Mama think I ought to do?"

"You're mature enough to make decisions about your future," he replied.

"Whatever you decide will be fine with us," Mrs. Bowers added.

"What about me, Daddy?" Essie said. "Am I mature enough to make decisions about my future?"

"No, not yet."

Essie wrinkled her nose. "I didn't think so."

Gregory turned his horse toward the drive. "I'll tell Tanner you're goin' to the meetin'." He kicked the horse's flanks and galloped north along the narrow trail back to Telegraph Road.

"The boys and I will sweep around the buildings and make sure

Bullet isn't hiding here," Matthew said. They marched off toward the corrals.

"I'll hitch the DeMarco team and wagon for you," Lissa told her daughter.

"Can't I drive Stranger and Pilgrim?" Jolie asked.

"They might be a little tired from hauling all that cedar."

"Then they should be about right. Please, Mama."

"Okay, I'll hitch them to the DeMarco wagon. That way, they'll think it's a treat."

Jolie and Essie ducked behind the mosquito netting at the front door.

"Are you really going to be the teacher?" Essie asked.

"I think that was all talk."

"What if they actually ask you?"

"That depends on the financial remuneration and the road conditions between here and the school in the winter."

"Oh, you would get paid, wouldn't you?"

"That's usually the case for teachers." Jolie traipsed to the back-room. Her boot heels knocked against the wooden floor.

"But you're always teaching me things, and I never have to pay for it."

"And I'll continue teaching you, no matter what this meeting decides. That's the privilege of being the big sister."

"What's the privilege of being the little sister?" Essie scooted over to the girls' side of the room and flopped back on the bed.

Jolie picked up her oak hand mirror and studied her curly bangs. "You don't have to cook, sew, wash, or clean the house very often."

"And what else?"

"You get to giggle any time you want."

Essie sat up. "What do you mean?"

"I'm supposed to act mature. I'm not supposed to giggle very much."

"Mama giggles," Essie declared.

"Yes, well, Lissa Bowers is a very unconventional lady."

"And she's different from all the other ladies."

Jolie stared at her sister. "Sometimes I wonder if you're teasing me."

Essie giggled. "Would teasing you about big words be conventional or unconventional?"

"I'm going to change dresses." Jolie laid the mirror on a crate that served as a small table.

"Can I wear the one I have on?"

"Certainly, but you'll need to wear shoes."

"Are my shoes over there?" Essie asked.

"I don't see them. Maybe they're under the bed."

Essie dropped to her knees and peered under the rough wood bed frame. "Nope. There's nothin' under here but the crate of Grandma Pritchett's linens and that old rolled-up sheet."

Jolie froze in place. "What old sheet?"

Essie wandered back to the front room. "Here they are! I found them."

Jolie didn't move. "There's an old sheet under our bed?"

"Next to Grandma's crate."

"Essie, would you bring me the broom?"

"I thought we needed to get ready to go to the school meeting."

"Yes, but we have to clear out the grasshoppers first."

Essie meandered back carrying the broom. "Here. But I don't see any grasshoppers. The mosquito net is keeping them out of the house."

"There is just one very large one."

"Really? Where?" Essie asked.

Jolie held her finger to her lips. She slowly slid the broom handle under the bed. "Right . . . about . . . here!" She gave a quick, hard jab, which was followed by a scream from under the bed.

Essie yelled.

A sheet-draped figure rolled under the blanket wall to the boys' side of the room.

"Stop him!" Jolie yelled.

"Who is it?" Essie screamed.

"Bullet Wells."

He tossed aside the sheet and sprinted toward the open front door. He hit the mosquito netting head-on, ripped it from the door-jamb, and sprawled on the front porch. Essie pounced on top of his chest. Jolie trapped his flailing legs.

Bullet hollered.

By the time Jolie and Essie drove Stranger and Pilgrim out of the yard, Mr. Bowers and Bullet Wells were riding across the gully toward the DeMarco homestead.

"I wouldn't want to be Chester when his daddy hears what he did," Essie remarked.

"I wouldn't want to be him right now. Rolled up in a sheet, tied up, and thrown across a saddle isn't a very comfortable way to travel," Jolie said.

"I'm never, never, never goin' to get ready for bed until I've searched every inch of our room," Essie declared.

"Daddy says Bullet needs our prayers."

Essie brushed down her dress. "Mama says he needs a good whipping."

"They're probably both right. Hang on, sis. I'll let these boys stretch their tired legs."

Jolie wrapped one lead line around her right wrist and the second around her left wrist and braced her boots against the floorboard of the wagon. "Are you ready?"

Essie clutched her straw hat with her right hand and grabbed the iron railing with her left. "Yes!" she shouted.

Jolie slapped the lines. The horses bolted north along the rutted drive.

"This little wagon bounces more than the big one," Essie called out.

Jolie threw her shoulders toward the back of the wagon and

yanked the lead lines. When her full weight tightened the lines, Stranger and Pilgrim settled into a mild trot.

"This is nicer." Essie dropped her hands to her lap.

"I love these two big, old horses. They have such incredible power."

"And poop. Did you see what Lawson has to shovel out of the barn?"

"There are times when it's nice to have brothers."

They continued at a trot until the railroad tracks came into view.

"Someone's waiting out at the road." Essie pointed north. "I think it's Tanner Wells."

Jolie glanced over at her sister. "Do I look all right?"

"You're just as pretty as you can be."

"Which means nothing."

"That's what Daddy always tell me," Essie replied. "I ask him, 'Am I as purdy as Jolie?' and he says, 'Darlin', you're just as purdy as you can be.'"

They pulled up to the corner where a man waited on horseback. Jolie yanked on the lead lines. The wagon slowed to a quick stop.

"Hi, Tanner!" Essie called out.

"Evenin', Miss Essie." He tipped his hat. "Evenin', Miss Jolie."

"Good evening, Tanner," Jolie replied.

He rode his horse beside the wagon as Jolie urged the team forward.

"Are we late for the meeting?" he asked. "You were in quite a hurry coming up the drive."

Jolie studied his blue eyes. "This is the slowest speed these two old boys will go." *Oh, Mama, you told me some boy's smile would melt me in my boots, but I always thought you were exaggerating . . . until now.*

"We found Chester," Essie called out.

Tanner pushed back his hat. "Where was he this time?"

"Under our bed," Essie announced. "Daddy is takin' him home hogtied."

Tanner rubbed his temples. "Mama will die of shame."

"I don't want to talk about it," Jolie announced. "Did you come out from town this afternoon?"

"Yep."

"Did you hear how Mr. Jeremiah Cain is doing? I heard he got shot."

"I heard he regained consciousness. Dr. Fix says she thinks he'll pull through."

Jolie kept the lead lines tight. "That's wonderful. Did he say who it was that shot him?"

"He said it was Leppy Verdue."

"No!" Essie wailed. "Leppy wouldn't do that. I just know he wouldn't."

"You and him close?" Tanner asked.

Essie held her chin up high. "Yes, we are."

Tanner raised his eyebrows at Jolie.

"Essie has visited with Leppy several times," she explained.

"He didn't seem like a back-shooter to me," Tanner said. "Of course, he didn't seem like one to run off with a waitress either."

"What do you mean?" Essie demanded.

"Bailey Wagner, whom I believe you both met in the back of the gun shop, works at the cafe next door and disappeared about the same time as Leppy. She told Maxine Walters at the dress shop that she was goin' to Cheyenne to marry Leppy Verdue."

"She can't do that," Essie wailed. "He doesn't even like her."

Tanner stared east along the railroad tracks. "No one around town knew anything about it. Come to find out, Bailey and Jeremiah Cain were a couple until a week or so ago. Now folks are saying she just set him up to be robbed."

"So there was a robbery?" Jolie questioned.

"Yeah, the cashbox was untouched, but there were funds in another box. Not even Mr. Saddler knew about it until today. Seems that Jeremiah has been splitting up the receipts. He said he was doin' it for safety—that it wasn't safe to have them all in one place."

"Didn't Leppy have some funds to buy that new Colt?" Jolie asked.

"He said he was expecting a boost in income any day now."

"Robbing a store is quite a boost, all right," Jolie commented.

"But he didn't need money," Essie wailed. "Why would he take it?"

"How do you know he didn't need the money?" Jolie demanded.

Essie's hand went over her mouth.

"Estelle!"

"He had $1,632 in that brown envelope."

"Whoa, I could buy the whole gun shop, less inventory, for that," Tanner declared.

"Essie, you had no business peeking at someone else's mail."

"It wasn't real mail. It didn't have a stamp or nothin', and I fought it for a long, long time. Honest, I did, Jolie. But then one day I couldn't help myself. There are some things you know in your bones that you just got to do. May the Lord forgive me."

"Don't be frettin' over it, Essie. You could have done worse things," Tanner consoled her. "But it doesn't make much sense for a rich man to rob a store."

"And it doesn't make any sense for a waitress to run off with an outlaw and tell everyone which way they're going. What kind of woman would do that?" Jolie pondered. "I can't figure her out."

"I don't think I have anyone in this county figured out yet." Tanner looked straight at Jolie.

"Maybe the trouble is that everyone is so new," Jolie replied.

"Just like our horses—we're all strangers and pilgrims," Essie called out.

"Essie is right. No one really knows anyone yet."

"Which gives some a fresh start," Tanner added.

"And others a shield for bad behavior."

They trotted up a rise. At the top they could see through the twilight for several miles.

"There's the schoolhouse," Tanner called out.

"Where?" Essie asked.

"The building with the lantern at the gate."

"Is it sod?"

"Yes, but it has a tin roof."

Jolie began to wrap the lead lines tight around her wrists.

"What're you doin'?" Essie whispered.

"Hold onto your hat and the railing," Jolie murmured. She jammed her heels into the floorboard.

"But what about the teacher's job? They might not want you to drive fast horses," Essie whispered.

"There're some things you know in your bones that you just got to do. May the Lord forgive me."

Essie nodded.

"Mr. Wells," Jolie called out, "can we race you to the schoolhouse?"

"Are you kidding?"

"You don't know me very well, Tanner Wells. I don't joke about racing horses."

"You can't race a wagon against a man on horseback. You can't possibly win."

Essie giggled. "You shouldn't have said that."

"Mr. Wells, do you accept the challenge?"

"This is crazy," he hollered.

"I'll take that for a yes." Jolie raised the lines high and slapped them on the horses' rumps.

Matthew and Lissa sat on the edge of the bed/divan in the front room. Lawson leaned over a copy of the *Young Farmers' Alliance Journal*. Gibs had his Winchester 1890 taken down, both parts lying in his lap. Essie peered behind the mosquito net at the moon's reflection on the yard to count grasshoppers that clung to the other side of the netting.

Jolie paced the room in front of the kerosene lamp. "They offered me $45 a month to begin, and it would go to $50 after a three-month probation."

"How many students did they project?" her mother asked.

"They said they have eighteen right now. That includes Essie and Gibs."

"Not me?" Lawson asked.

"I didn't want to guarantee that without asking you first."

"Is, uh . . ."

"Yes, April Vockery is going to attend. As are May, June, and Mary," Jolie said.

"Maybe after the crops are in, I could go," Lawson said.

"Chester Wells is going to be there. I can't believe it," Essie fumed.

Lissa combed out her long, wavy brown hair. "Yes. He'll be a challenge."

"What happens if there's a big influx of students before September?" Mr. Bowers asked.

"I told them that room would hold no more than twenty-five. If there were more, I would have to have a bigger room and some help. They agreed to that."

"What about supplies?" Lissa added.

"They said they'll petition the county for books and supplies, but that might be difficult."

Lissa handed the comb to her husband. "Did you decide on an opening day?"

"Around the 20th of September, but we'll wait and see how the harvest goes."

Matthew Bowers began to comb his wife's hair. "For how many months do they want to hire you?"

"They suggested a six-month school year, but I said that a six-month vacation from school would impair the retentive ability of the students. So that's up for negotiation."

Lissa glanced back at her husband. "I believe they chose the right person for a teacher."

He nodded. "How about the schoolhouse, darlin'? Will it work for you?"

"The parents will do repairs as needed and provide wood or coal for the stove. The rest is up to me."

"I take it you accepted the offer?" Mrs. Bowers quizzed.

"I told them I wanted to pray about it."

Matthew handed the comb back to his wife. "That's good, darlin'."

"How did Mr. Tanner Wells take all of this?" Lissa tossed the comb down and ran her fingers through her hair.

"He was pouting at first," Essie blurted out.

"No, he wasn't," Jolie corrected.

"Yes, he was. Jolie raced him to the school, and Stranger and Pilgrim beat his black horse."

"Oh, my." Lissa Bowers grinned. "That would tend to make a man sulk."

"But by the end of the evening, he was very cordial," Essie announced.

"How cordial was very cordial?" Lawson asked.

"She whispered in his ear," Essie replied.

"I did not."

"Yes, you did. I saw you walk around behind the wagon and whisper in his ear."

"I was not whispering."

Essie jammed her hands on her hips. "What were you doing then?"

"I was kissing his cheek."

"You kissed him?" Gibs blurted out. The butt stock of the .22 crashed to the floor.

"And he kissed my cheek."

"Why?" Gibs asked.

"Because he was congratulating me on being hired."

"Do you know him well enough to let him kiss you on the cheek?" Matthew Bowers smiled.

"Yes, Daddy. I believe I do."

He turned to his wife. "What do you think, Mama?"

"I think that the Lord surely led us to Nebraska just so Jolie Lorita could meet Tanner Wells."

"You really think so, Mama?" Jolie probed.

"It sounds like a very good reason to me."

"Did you know that there are fourteen grasshoppers stuck to the netting?" Essie declared. "Do you think they're attracted to the light like other bugs?"

"That's a good question for the schoolteacher," Mr. Bowers suggested. "What do you think, Jolie?"

"I believe that would be a very good experiment, class. Let's turn out the lights and go to bed. Then in the morning when it's light outside and dark inside, we can count the grasshoppers on the netting and see if there's a notable change in number."

"Splendid idea," Lissa agreed. "You get ready for bed. But first I'm goin' to check on the animals. I could use some help."

"I'll help you, Mama," Lawson offered.

She cleared her throat and glared at Matthew. "I said, I could use some help."

Mr. Bowers stood up and grinned. "Can I be of assistance to you, my dear?"

"How kind of you." Lissa tugged him to the doorway.

Essie and Jolie meandered back to their room. Essie dropped to her knees to look under the bed.

"Are we safe?" Jolie asked.

"For now. Daddy said Chester got a whipping."

"I trust he learned never to do that again."

"Jolie, did you see the way Mama's eyes danced when she looked at Daddy?"

"She's so crazy about him."

"I like that. Mama never changes. Other mothers get older and do things different, but Mama is just the same."

"Essie, sometimes she acts like she's twenty."

"And sometimes you act thirty."

"Did I act thirty with Tanner?" Jolie quizzed.

"No, but you did at the school meeting."

"Essie, tell me the truth. Did my eyes dance when I was with Tanner?"

"Yes, but I think it's okay."

"Why?"

"Because his eyes were dancing, too."

Jolie had the breakfast dishes washed and dried before her mother drove the wagon to the front yard.

"Are you ready, Essie?" Jolie called out.

"Yes. I can't believe they're letting you and me go to town by ourselves."

"I need to find out about the lending library in Gering. They'll be a good resource for the school, and while I'm there, I'll sign some papers at the courthouse for teaching school."

"Oh, I thought we were going to town to stop by the gun shop."

"Of course we are, but we need to check on Jeremiah, too."

"And convince him that Leppy Verdue didn't shoot him."

"Somebody did it, little sis."

"Jolie, if we found out who shot Jeremiah, then they would have to stop chasing Leppy."

"Come on," Jolie called out from the doorway. "Mama's got Stranger and Pilgrim prancing in the yard."

Essie scooted out the door ahead of her. "Are we goin' to race to town?"

"What do you think?"

Mrs. Bowers handed the lead lines to Jolie.

"I think I'd better tie my hat down tight."

Jeremiah Cain was stretched out on his stomach on a narrow bed in a room above the grocery store. There were no windows, but a tiny lantern gave off a dim light.

Jolie knocked on the half-open door. "Jeremiah, are you awake?"

"Jolie?"

"May we come in?"

"There's a bench under that quilt. Drag it over and sit down. If I have anything uncovered, cover me up, please."

Jolie bit her lip. "You're all covered. We can't stay long."

Jeremiah turned to the wall, his back toward Jolie and Essie. "I was hopin' you'd come, Jolie."

"Why?"

"I wanted to talk to you."

"What about?"

He struggled to turn his head around to Essie.

"Do you want me to leave?" she gulped.

His reply was soft. "Do you mind?"

"I think my sister should stay."

"I need to talk personal, Jolie Bowers."

"I'll wait downstairs at the candy counter," Essie offered.

"No, you wait in the hall with the door open," Jolie instructed.

"How come?"

"Because schoolteachers must conduct themselves properly."

"Are you going to teach school?" Jeremiah asked.

"Yes, if all goes well."

Essie stared at a shadowy shelf. "Jeremiah, can I read one of your books while I'm in the hall?"

"Yeah."

"Can I read *Ambush at Rattlesnake Pass?*"

He closed his eyes. "Stuart Brannon goes up against a whole outlaw army. But don't cry over the opening scene."

"It's only a book," Essie mumbled.

Jolie scooted the bench closer. "What did you need to talk to me about, Jeremiah?"

His voice was soft. "A man gets to thinkin' about important things when he's worried about dyin'."

"But you aren't dying, are you?"

"Doc says I could be fine as long as I don't fester and swell. But when I first got shot, I didn't know that. I thought about some things I'd like to tell folks and was afraid I wouldn't get a chance."

"Like what?"

"I wanted to tell my mama that I love her one more time."

"Where is your mother, Jeremiah?"

"Denver."

"Can I write to her for you?"

"Doc Fix already did that. She surely is a fine lady."

"And which others did you want to talk to?"

"I wanted to tell Mr. Saddler that I'm sorry I wasn't a better store clerk."

"It's not your fault that you got shot in the back."

"No matter whose fault it is, store money got taken."

"Who else did you want to talk to?"

"To you, Jolie."

"What about, Jeremiah? We don't know each other very well."

"No, but that don't mean I don't think about you."

"That's very sweet of you to say."

"Oh, no!" Essie moaned from the hall.

Jolie turned around. "What's the matter?"

"His horse got shot and killed on the first page! What kind of book is this?" she complained.

"Keep readin'. It gets better," Jeremiah called out.

"Please continue," Jolie urged him.

"Where was I?"

"Jolie just said, 'Jeremiah, that's very sweet of you to say,'" Essie hollered.

"Estelle Cinnia!"

"I'm reading, I'm reading."

Jolie leaned nearer to the injured man.

"I don't reckon you realize how much you changed my world," he said.

"I don't know how you can say that."

"You're the reason I got shot."

"Jeremiah Cain, don't you go making me feel guilty. If you and Leppy were arguing over me, it's your own fool fault. I begged you both not to fight."

"It's a long story, Jolie. But I know you're Tanner Wells's girl now."

"How do you know that?"

"You are, aren't you?"

"Yes, she is!" Essie called out.

"Yeah, I kind of figured I didn't have a chance."

"But I've only been in town a couple of weeks. The future is not settled."

"She's goin' to marry Tanner Wells someday!"

"Estelle Cinnia, you go down and wait for me in the store."

"What about being proper?"

"I assure you, I'll be proper."

"What about Jeremiah?"

"He's bedridden."

"Can I buy a piece of candy?" Essie called out.

"Do you have any money?"

"Two pennies."

"Then, yes, you may."

"Thank you, Mother."

Jolie waited until she heard footsteps fade toward the stairs.

"Now, Mr. Jeremiah Cain, why did you say it was my fault that Leppy Verdue shot you?"

Jeremiah propped himself up on his elbows. "I said it was your fault I got shot, but I didn't say it was Leppy who shot me."

Ten

Jolie held the palms of her hands against her cheeks. "You mean, Leppy didn't shoot you?"

"Please listen to me, Jolie." He lay back down and seemed to be staring at the floor. "'Cause I'm feelin' mighty low. For almost twenty-four hours I've been lyin' here wishin' I had died. I made some dumb decisions, and I don't want to make any more."

"You aren't making any sense to me."

"Do you know Bailey Wagner?"

"I met her once. I understand she took off with Leppy."

"That story was just to throw 'em off her trail."

Jolie rested her elbows on her knees. "I'm totally confused."

"Me and her used to be thick, if you catch my drift."

"She used to be your girlfriend?" Jolie quizzed.

"I suppose that's what some might call it. We was livin' in the same cabin in Lake City, Colorado."

"Oh, that kind of thick."

"She moved out and came to Scottsbluff when the railroad opened up this place. I moved soon after. Shoot, I missed her, Miss Jolie."

"But things weren't the same here?"

"We didn't live together. She said I was just a clerk and would always be a clerk."

Jolie sat up. There was no circulation in the room. "There's no sin in that." She wiped her handkerchief across her forehead.

"It didn't fill her stocking, if you know what I mean. But I kept hoping. Last spring she came up with a plan for me to make more money and buy us a place up in Deadwood."

"An illegal plan?" Jolie asked.

His reply was soft. "Yep. She figured I could just skim some of the profits off here at the store. A little here, lost inventory there—it can all add up, especially in a new town with people comin' and goin' and merchandise comin' in ever' day. It's been too hectic to keep ever'thing straight."

"Like charging for blackberries when a person buys prunes?"

"Yeah, but that was an honest mistake."

"So you've been holding back on Mr. Saddler?"

"I didn't want to do it at first. But it went so smooth, and nobody seemed to notice. I kept the extra in a locked box. That way if it was called for, I could produce it."

"But it wasn't missed?"

"Nope. And I got to justifyin' it. Figured if nobody missed it, then it wasn't hurtin' anyone. So I jist let it ride."

"And then Bailey pressed the issue?"

Jeremiah propped himself up on his elbows again. "Yep. I just wasn't her type. It took you to convince me of that."

"How did I do that?"

"Miss Jolie, from the first day I met you, I was realizin' that you're my type. I don't mean just you, but your whole family—the hard-workin' homesteader type. That's who I am. That's what my family was like. I didn't figure I had too much chance with you, but I wanted to cast my lot with your type. I guess that's what steamed me about Leppy sniffin' after you. I didn't figure he was your type."

"And you decided to protect me?"

"I know. It's all crazy now."

"So Bailey Wagner decided it was time to cash in the money and go to Deadwood?"

"I found out she didn't want a place in Deadwood after all."

"What did she want?" Jolie probed.

"Tanner Wells."

"What?"

"She had her eyes set on him as soon as they met last week. But when she figured out she couldn't compete with the likes of you, she was ready to cash in the chips and pull out."

"And wanted you to come along?"

"I guess I was second choice."

"And you refused?"

"I wouldn't give her the money."

"So she shot you in the back."

"Yeah. Don't that beat all?"

Jolie fanned herself with her straw hat. "Why did you tell the sheriff it was Leppy?"

"Luke and Raymond were tellin' the sheriff about the fight, and the sheriff asked if it was Leppy. I was protectin' myself, Miss Jolie. I didn't want to admit skimmin' the store. Besides, I wanted to get at Leppy Verdue. I know it was wrong, and that's why I lie here in this hot, dark, stuffy room wantin' to die. But when I woke up today and realized I wasn't goin' to die, well, I needed to talk to you."

"Jeremiah, what do you want me to do?"

"Go talk to the sheriff for me. You think they'll throw me in prison?"

"I don't know. You . . . you didn't take the money yourself, and you kept it in the store. I just don't know. If the money is retrieved, perhaps Mr. Saddler will forgive you. I don't think you'll have a job though."

"Will you forgive me?" he murmured.

Jolie sat straight up. "Of course I will. So will the Lord if you confess it to Him."

"I already done that, Miss Jolie. Like I said, you folks is my kind of people. That's the way I was raised, too. Will you pray for me, Miss Jolie?"

"Of course I will, but right now I need to go find the sheriff."

"To turn me in?"

"To tell him to quit chasing Leppy Verdue before someone else gets shot."

Jolie scurried down the stairs and across the store. Essie trotted along beside her.

"What did you find out?" Essie asked.

"Leppy didn't shoot him."

"See? Didn't I tell you that?"

"Yes, and now we have to tell the sheriff."

"Who did shoot him, Jolie?"

"It's a long story."

"Does that mean you won't tell me?"

"It means we'd better find the sheriff before your Leppy gets hurt."

Essie grinned from ear to ear. "My Leppy! I like that."

"Don't tell him I ever said that."

"Oh, no. That's just between you and me. And don't tell Daddy 'cause he still thinks I'm a little girl."

Both girls were jogging when they reached the gun shop.

"You ladies look like you're in a hurry," Tanner greeted them.

"You have to help us," Jolie panted.

He scooted around the counter and stood by her. "What is it?"

"The sheriff went after Leppy Verdue because he thought Leppy shot Jeremiah, but it was Bailey Wagner who shot him. Now if we don't stop them, either Leppy or the sheriff will get hurt."

"Bailey shot him? She and Leppy were in it together?" he asked.

"No, Leppy had nothing to do with it," Jolie replied. "It was Bailey Wagner and Jeremiah Cain who were in cahoots, but Jeremiah backed out."

"She just got steamed and plugged him!" Essie blurted out.

Tanner stared down at Estelle Cinnia Bowers. "This sounds like something out of a penny-press novel. What am I supposed to do?"

"I think someone has to go into Carter Canyon to tell the sheriff so he will quit chasin' Leppy. And someone has to go after Bailey

Wagner and get that money back she took from the store. Maybe Jeremiah won't have to go to jail if the money is returned."

"Lookin' after your men is a full-time job," he maintained.

"They aren't her men. You're her man, Tanner," Essie declared.

"Estelle Cinnia!"

"It's true."

"It's only true if the man allows it to happen."

Essie turned to Tanner. "Do you allow it to happen?"

"On one condition," he said.

Jolie frowned. "A condition?"

"Yep. If I'm your man, you have to be my girl."

Jolie rubbed her chin. "All right, I agree."

"Don't kiss," Essie squealed.

"What?" Tanner said.

Essie stepped between them. "I said, don't kiss and all that stuff. We don't have time. We need to go find Leppy before the sheriff shoots him."

"We're not going to kiss," Jolie declared.

"We aren't?"

"I knew it. I knew it!" Essie stepped back, closed her eyes, and bit her tongue. "Are you through yet?"

Tanner took Jolie's hand and kissed it with a loud smack.

Essie's eyes shot open.

Tanner laughed. "So you *are* lookin'."

"I couldn't help myself." Essie rolled her brown eyes. "But it doesn't look like I missed much."

"You two go after the sheriff. I think I know where to find Bailey," Tanner instructed.

"Where?" Jolie asked.

"She has access to a cabin up on Spottedhorse Creek."

"How do you know that?"

"She, eh, kept leavin' me notes in my dinner, sayin' to, eh . . . you know . . . meet her up at that cabin."

"Did you?" Essie asked.

"Of course not, but I reckon I ought to close the shop and ride up there and take a look."

"We'll go look for her. You find the sheriff," Jolie suggested.

"You don't know her state of mind. When a gal like that latches on to something, she can get desperate. You could get yourself into a lot of trouble up there."

"So could you, Tanner Wells," Jolie insisted.

Tanner blushed and cleared his throat. "What I meant was, she's got a gun, and she'll use it again. She proved she don't mind shootin' someone in the back." He paused. "I reckon we should wait and let the sheriff handle the matter with Bailey. I'll get a horse and ride up to Carter Canyon."

"We can all go in the wagon. I have Pilgrim and Stranger."

"One man horseback is faster."

"I think I proved that idea wrong when we raced to the schoolhouse."

"That was a short distance. Carter Canyon is up in the Wildcat Hills. It's not a short distance. . . . Oh, Jolie, I forgot. . . . I need someone to tend the store. Captain Richardson is comin' in this afternoon for those four Winchester '73 carbines I repaired. If I miss him, he won't be to town for another month. I need the money. Mrs. DeMarco is sellin' the folks her place, but they don't have any cash."

"I'll run the store for you if you hurry and make sure Leppy doesn't get hurt. But I know very little about guns."

Essie pointed to a shotgun in the case. "Jolie shot a man in Helena once."

"Estelle!" Jolie scowled.

"I hadn't heard about that. She's a good shot?" Tanner asked.

"Don't know about that. She had a scattergun and hit him in the—"

"Estelle Cinnia!" Jolie barked.

"Yep, that's where she hit him, right in the Estelle."

Tanner hung his shop apron on a nail and grabbed his hat. "I'll be back as quick as I can." He trotted down the boardwalk toward the livery.

"Tanner surely is tall, isn't he?" Essie declared.

"He's six feet, three inches."

"That's taller than Leppy and Jeremiah. He's even taller than Daddy."

"He has strong arms, too," Jolie added.

"How do you know that?"

"I can just tell. Can't you?"

"Nope. All I can see is a shirt. Of course, if he were to hug me, then I could tell. Did he hug you?"

"We're not going to discuss my private life."

"Why not?" Essie pressed.

Jolie surveyed the twenty-by-forty-foot room with its twelve-foot ceiling. "We have a gun shop to run."

"We don't have any customers."

"Then we will do some cleaning. The floor is gritty. The windows could use a good washing, and there's clutter everywhere. This is no way to run a business."

"There are dead grasshoppers in the windowsill," Essie reported.

"Let's look for a broom and feather duster."

They searched through the back of the room lined with work counters, tools, and half-finished gun repairs.

"Just look at these workbenches. There are parts scattered every-where. As soon as we clean the rest of the room, we'll get these parts organized," Jolie fussed.

"I don't know why we can't just sit out front and talk about you and Tanner," Essie grumbled.

There were no windows in the backroom. It was dark and musty.

"Are we goin' to clean this room, too?" Essie asked.

"If we have time."

"Jolie, how come every place we go, you have to clean and organize?"

Jolie picked a shirt up off the floor. "That's nonsense."

"You organized all the stick candy at the store."

"I was waiting for my order to be crated." Jolie held the shirt to her nose and sniffed.

"Here's the broom. What does the shirt smell like?"

"Tanner." Jolie folded the shirt and set it on top of a dresser covered with books. "Do you see a feather duster?"

"Nope. I don't think one has ever been used in this room. I'll just use this rag instead." Essie stared it. "I think it's a rag. Maybe it's a shirt, too."

"What does it smell like?" Jolie asked.

"Like dust. Does this room really smell like Tanner?"

"Yes, it does. Can't you smell it?"

"I just smell sweat and dust. Kind of like a barn."

"Try hard. Don't you smell that special scent?"

"Just your perfume."

"I'm not wearing perfume."

"Then it must be me. Daddy says I'm a sweetie!"

Within half an hour, they had swept the floor, banished the grasshoppers, and dusted the glass cases full of rifles, carbines, muskets, and revolvers. Jolie balanced on a chair out on the boardwalk to wash the large display window.

Essie held the old oak chair steady. "This is embarrassing."

The glass squeaked as Jolie circled the rag across the large pane. "What's embarrassing about being clean and neat?"

"People are staring at us."

"What people?"

"All those boys over there."

Jolie glanced over her shoulder. "You mean those two barefoot boys your age with coveralls?"

"And a dog," Essie added.

"The dog is staring at us?"

"Yes, and I don't like it."

"What do you think we should do?"

"We could stick out our tongues."

"Hmmm. Do you think that would make them quit staring at us?"

"It would make me feel better."

"Okay, I'll count to five, and we'll turn and stick out our tongues."

Essie's brown eyes widened. "Really?"

"That's what you want, don't you?"

"Oh, yes! You're a really fun sister no matter what Gibs says."

"Mmmm. Just what does Gibson Hunter Bowers say about me?"

"He says you would make someone a good mother, but he's not the one."

"He does? And what does Lawson Pritchett Bowers say?"

"He says if he finds a girl that's half as hardworking as you, he'll marry her on the spot."

"Ah hah, now I find out what you all think."

"Are we going to stick out our tongues?" Essie asked.

"Are they still there?"

"I think so, but I don't want to turn around and look."

"As soon as the wagons roll by, I'll count to five."

"Do we turn around on five or stick out our tongues on five?" Essie asked.

"Turn around on four and stick out our tongues on five."

"Okay!"

"One."

"What if they're gone?"

"Two."

"What if there's someone else standing there?"

"Three."

"Is that a carriage driving up?"

"Four!" Jolie spun around in the chair.

"Five!"

Both girls stuck out their tongues—at the passengers in the wagon now parked in the middle of the street.

"Oh!" Jolie shouted.

"Hi, Mama!" Essie ran out into the street. "Hi, Gibs!"

"What are my charming daughters up to?" Lissa probed. "Is this just a family greeting, or are you harassing any who pass by?"

"We were sticking out our tongues at those boys over there," Essie explained.

"I don't see any boys," Gibs said.

"They were right over there next to the dog. I guess they're gone."

Jolie climbed off the chair. "Mother, we were just playing a little game."

"Have you hired out to clean windows?"

"Oh, no, we're doin' it for free," Essie confessed.

Lissa pulled her braid around and let it drift down the front of her dress. "Mr. Tanner Wells must be quite persuasive."

"He's not here. We're just watching the store for him," Jolie explained.

"You're runnin' a gun shop?" Gibs asked.

"More like caretaking actually."

"Wow! Can I help? After I retire from being a sheriff, I'd like to have a gun shop."

"What're you doing in town, Mama?"

"I came to help a friend of yours—both of yours."

"Who?" Essie asked. "I hope it isn't Chester."

"I'll tell you in a minute. Let me park this rig."

"I can park it," Gibs offered.

"I suppose you can. These DeMarco horses are a bit tame." She handed the lines to Gibs and hopped out of the wagon.

They entered the store. "I thought Daddy needed these horses to plow with," Jolie remarked.

"The plow got bent on a big, old river rock. Lawson is heating the plow to pound it back straight. Daddy and your friend are digging out the rock."

"Which friend?"

Lissa gathered her daughters. "Leppy Verdue is at the homestead."

Essie clutched her fingers. "What's he doin' there?"

"He's trying to figure out why the sheriff is chasing him," Mrs. Bowers said.

"He didn't do it, Mama. Jeremiah Cain told me that Bailey Wagner shot him."

Lissa Bowers plucked a revolver off the counter, cocked the hammer one click, and spun the chamber with her thumb. "Who's Bailey Wagner?"

"It's a long story. That's why Tanner went after the sheriff—to tell him it wasn't Leppy."

"Where is this Bailey Wagner?" Mrs. Bowers asked.

"Tanner said she probably went to a cabin up on Spottedhorse Creek."

"He knows this woman?" Lissa quizzed.

"Yes, but he didn't run off with her," Essie explained.

Lissa pursed her lips. "I'm glad to hear that. Well, Jolie Lorita, what do we do now?"

"I think Leppy should stay at our place until the sheriff is contacted. But I should stay here because Tanner will probably bring the sheriff back, and I will need to explain everything."

Mrs. Bowers glanced at Gibs. "I suppose that means we turn around and go back to the homestead."

"Can I go with you, Mama?" Essie asked.

"And desert your sister?"

"Let me stay with Jolie," Gibs begged. "I can run a gun shop."

"Hmmmm." Lissa studied her eldest daughter. "You live a very complicated life. Do you know that?"

"I don't try to, Mama."

"I know, darlin'. Some are destined to be in the middle of every controversy." She brushed Jolie's auburn hair off her forehead. "Now I'm goin' to leave you the boring team of horses and take Pilgrim and Stranger home with me. If you're late getting back, I'll have to cook supper for company. I hope I remember how."

"I was going to make the leftover ham into a soup. There are white beans soaking, a big onion, and two turnips."

"I just might use your menu."

"If you get back in time, you could use those green apples for a pie. They are getting mealy anyway."

Mrs. Bowers tossed her braid to her back. "Jolie, I can't make pie crust like you can."

Jolie chewed on her lip. Then her hands flew up. "You could serve baked apples with raisins and molasses."

Lissa shook her head. "Jolie, Jolie, Jolie . . . do you ever stop cooking and cleaning and planning?"

"Do you think it's obsessive?"

"If that's how the Lord made you, then keep doing it. Anything else would betray your own heart. But don't ever, ever be that way because you think Daddy or I need you to. Don't be a slave to anything but God's will, darlin'."

Jolie brushed her hair back over her ears. "I like doing these things, Mama. They make me feel useful and important."

"That you are." Lissa marched toward the door. "Now, Mr. Gibson Hunter Bowers, look after your big sis . . . and mind her."

He squeezed one eye shut and tried to peer through the eyepiece of a long-range vernier peep sight. "How can I look after her and mind her at the same time?" he muttered.

"You're a very resourceful young man. I'm sure you can do it."

"He's only fourteen," Essie protested. "He's not a man yet."

"He's a young man," Lissa Bowers insisted. "And just as handsome as his father."

Gibs stuck out his tongue at Essie.

"I presume this tongue thing is inherited from your father's side of the family," Lissa remarked. "I will expect you home around dark."

"What if Tanner isn't back by then?" Jolie asked.

"Close the store and leave him a note. I will not have my daughter sleeping in a gun shop."

"There's a bedroom in the back," Essie told her.

"Home around dark." Mrs. Bowers wrapped her arm around Essie. "Come on, young lady. We're going to buy some more citronella candles. Mrs. Wells says they keep the grasshoppers out of the house."

"But they stink."

"Yes, we'll have to ponder that."

Gibs led the way back inside the store. "Did you have many customers?"

"We haven't had any customers."

"Then you ain't doin' all that good at the store business."

Jolie opened a glass case and straightened the butt stocks of the rifles. "I don't think it's my role to attract customers."

"There're some leanin' against the front window," Gibs reported. "I reckon you attracted them."

Jolie spun around and saw three men wearing big felt hats and grins. One had on a dusty suit and tie. The other two wore leather vests over their cotton shirts.

"I'll just see about that!" Jolie stormed out to the sidewalk. All three men yanked off their hats.

"Howdy, ma'am," said the one in the suit. "We're new in town. Is this here your gun shop?"

"I'm watching it for a friend. Are you customers, or are you just going to dirty up my clean windows?"

"Eh . . . well . . . I could use a box of bullets. You got any .45-.75s for my Winchester '76?"

"I could use a tang screw," one of the other men declared.

"Have you got a blade insert for my front sight? I knocked it off when I was fixin' the barn door. I've had to use a filed dime," the tall one explained.

"Eh . . . actually . . ."

"Yep, we got them all," Gibs announced as he scooted up beside her. "You want the short tang filler screw or the long one?"

"The short one," the man said.

"We got Rocky Mountain sights, but we don't sell the inserts separate. You have to buy the whole sight," Gibs explained.

"Will you install it?"

"Yep." He turned to the other man. "You want a box or a case of .45-.75s? We get them by the wooden case, you know."

"Say, is this the fella that owns the store?" the tallest of the drovers teased.

"Nah, I'm just Jolie's brother."

"Miss Jolie, that's a sweet name," the tall cowboy said. "I named a mare Joliemae one time."

"Come on in. Now if you boys will excuse me, I need to straighten up a little in the storeroom. Gibs will take care of you."

All three marched into the store. "Eh, would it offend you if we offered to buy you supper tonight?"

"And this little gunsmith is welcome, too, of course," a second one added.

"No, it doesn't offend me, but I must decline." She retrieved the broom.

"You ain't married, are you?" the tallest asked.

"No, but her beau owns the gun shop," Gibs reported.

The one with dark hair laughed. "Say, Mr. Gibs, do you have any other sisters?"

"Yep." Gibs opened a glass case and pulled out a small green box of cartridges. "One."

"Is she a heart-stopper, too?"

"Sort of, but she's only twelve." He strolled over to a small cigar box on the counter. "Here's a bunch of Rocky Mountain front sights. Take your pick."

"Is anyone chasin' that youngest sister of yours?" the blond-headed one teased.

Gibs glanced at Jolie. "Bullet Wells has chased her."

"Hmmm, Bullet Wells . . . where have I heard that name?" dusty suit pondered.

"Ain't he the one that stopped that train on the trestle at Canyon City?"

Jolie laughed. "No, this Bullet is only . . . Actually it could be the same one who stopped a train. You take good care of them, Gibs."

Gibs scooted next to his sister. "I can't believe you're lettin' me do this."

She squeezed his hand. "You see, I don't always boss you around, Gibson Bowers."

Jolie lit a kerosene lamp hanging in the middle of the dark, musty backroom. It cast a dull glow. A beam of light cracked along the sill of the backdoor.

He didn't even close the door all the way. No wonder so much dirt blows in. Lord, someday I'd like to try living in a place that didn't have blowing dirt. I've never been to such a place, but Mama says there are whole towns in the East where you only have to dust the house a couple times a week.

Jolie opened the backdoor and stared out at the empty alley. The air was slightly cooler. She took a deep breath. When she turned back, she saw dust particles hanging in the air. She picked up a dirty gray shirt off the floor near the backdoor, shoved aside a half-built leather holster, and spread the shirt on the round table. Then she folded the shirt slowly. Jolie brushed off a blonde hair and glanced around the empty room. She could hear Gibs talking to the men out in the store.

She pulled the shirt to her face and buried her nose in it. *I like the way he smells, Lord. Is that strange?*

She stacked the shirt on an empty shelf near the quilt-tossed cot.

This is the messiest bed I've ever seen in my life. I thought Gibs was bad, but this looks like a battlefield.

She pulled at the first rumpled quilt.

Now, Lord, there's nothing sinful about making a man's bed. Housekeepers do it for rich people all the time. Just keep me from impure thoughts.

Jolie yanked back the thick quilt and gasped. She stared at a fully clothed blonde woman.

Bailey was either sleeping or dead.

Jolie was too stunned to tell.

Then the blonde sat straight up, a brass-framed pistol in her hand.

"I—I don't know what you've doing here," Jolie stammered.

"I know what I'm doing here. I don't know what you're doing here. Isn't it funny that we keep meeting in Tanner's bedroom."

"I'm . . . I'm cleaning."

"Oh, you're playing chore girl today. That's nice." She stood only inches from Jolie. "Where's Tanner? I need to talk to him."

Jolie didn't budge. "Bailey, where do you think he is?"

Bailey Wagner glanced back at the crumpled covers. "He's sure not in bed."

Jolie looked away.

"Oh, did that offend you?"

"It just embarrassed me. I thought you'd be on your way to Deadwood."

"I need to talk to Tanner."

"What about?"

"I don't have to explain myself to you. Go get Tanner," Bailey growled.

Jolie stared at the woman's blue eyes. *Lord, she isn't nearly as confident as she wants to sound.* Jolie's voice was low, barely audible. "Bailey, are you going to shoot me in the back like you did Jeremiah?"

The woman's shoulders slumped. She began to rock back and forth. There was a long pause.

Jolie never took her eyes off Bailey Wagner. *Lord, I don't know all she has gone through, but it hasn't been easy. Those eyes are way too old for a girl her age. I bet she isn't much older than I am. She's pointing a gun at me, and I'm not scared. But I don't know why.*

Finally the blonde spoke in halting words. "Did . . . Jeremiah . . . die?"

Jolie shook her head. "No."

"Will he pull through?"

"The doctor thinks so."

The gun now dangled at her side, pointing at the floor. "Praise the Lord for that."

"What did you say?"

Bailey wiped the sleeve of her green cotton dress across her forehead. "I said, thank the Lord that Jeremiah didn't die."

Jolie raised her eyebrows. "You shot a man in the back, and now you thank the Lord he didn't die?"

"Who else should I thank? I've just spent twenty-four hours praying that Jeremiah would live. So I don't see any problem in thanking God. Are you laughing at me?"

"It just seems ironic, Bailey. If you hadn't shot him, you wouldn't have needed to pray. I guess I don't understand."

"I don't always understand my actions either. Tell me, Jolie Bowers, do you understand everything you do?"

Jolie folded her arms. "No, I certainly don't. I sometimes embarrass myself with my foolishness, but I, eh . . ."

"You've never shot anyone?"

"I shot buckshot at someone once."

"So you've gotten so angry that you lost control."

"I was in complete control," Jolie replied.

Bailey looked down at the gun in her hand. "I wasn't yesterday. I have no rational explanation for shooting him. Do you know what I did after I shot him?"

"Rode up to the cabin at Spottedhorse Creek?" Jolie questioned.

"So you know about the cabin. I suppose Tanner told you. No, I rode as far as Tub Springs and started to vomit. I was so sure I had killed him."

"I guess I would feel the same way."

"But you're surprised a woman like me would feel that?"

"I didn't say that. I know that compared to many, I've lived a very confined life."

"Yeah, so have I," Bailey replied. "I spent six months in the Colorado State Women's Prison."

"For what?"

"I stole a dress."

"One dress?"

"A cowboy asked me to a dance, and I only owned one ragged dress. So I stole one. I was sixteen and wanted to go to the dance so bad. Unfortunately, the store owner was at the dance, and he filed charges when I wouldn't, eh, . . . accommodate him. His brother was the judge, and they decided to teach everyone a lesson by using me as an example. Now prison is a confined life. It shows on my face, don't it?"

"Oh, I don't know about that."

Bailey stepped closer, the gun still hanging at her side. "It shows."

"It just looks like you've had to work hard."

"Yeah, it shows. Just like your virtue shows on your face."

"Bailey, I'm sorry about the prison term for stealing a dress, but if you're repentant, the Lord will forgive. You could start a new life."

"I tried that," Bailey said. "It didn't work."

"What do you mean, you tried that?"

"I left Jeremiah and moved to Nebraska to start over. But the only job I could get barely keeps me alive. And every man thinks me no more than a dance hall girl."

"But why did you scheme with Jeremiah to steal the store money?"

"How is a woman like me going to get a fresh start without money?"

Jolie held out her hand. "I'm sure if you work hard and—"

"I work twelve-hour shifts." Bailey rejected the outstretched hand. "Have you ever worked twelve-hour shifts?"

Jolie let her hand drop to her side. "I cook, clean, and wash for my whole family. I've done it since I was ten or eleven."

"But you haven't worked—"

"I'm seventeen years old—almost eighteen. Bailey, some nights I can't stand up straight when I go to bed. Can you imagine how my shoulders will look ten years from now? Sometimes I lie awake with pain like a knife blade in the base of my back, and tears dribble on my pillowcase."

Bailey's voice lowered. "Then you *do* know what it's like."

"But I have absolutely no one to tell except Mama and Daddy. They would never let me continue if they knew I was in pain."

"Why don't you tell them?"

"Because taking care of my family is who I am. That's what I do. It gives me a place and purpose every day. I need it. They need me. I really like being needed. Do you know what I mean?"

Bailey brushed tears back from her eyes and reached her hand out. "I'm happy for you, Jolie Bowers. Life isn't that simple for me. Only in my dreams. But I reckon my dreams aren't all that much different than yours."

Jolie held onto her hand. "What are your dreams, Bailey?"

"I'd like to move someplace where no one knows my past. Marry a nice man who loves me and is hard-working. Settle down, buy a house, and raise a family. Make a difference in someone's life. Doesn't that sum it up?"

"Yes."

"But you see, the difference between your dream and mine is that you know yours will come true, and I don't have a chance in the world at mine."

A boy's voice broke into their concentration. "Jolie, who are you talking to?"

She and Bailey turned to see Gibs standing in the doorway. "This is Bailey Wagner."

"Are you all right, sis?" Gibs questioned. "She's got a gun in her hand."

"This is a gun shop, isn't it?"

"But . . . but ain't she the one that shot—"

"Gibs, Bailey and I are visiting. Go clean some guns or something."

"Visiting about what?"

"It's girl-talk."

"But she has a gun, Jolie! Ain't you afraid?"

"You carry that .22 of yours almost all day long. I'm not afraid of you."

She heard the front door of the store open. "Is that the sheriff?"

Gibs looked back over his shoulder. "No, it's Captain Richardson."

"Settle up with him on the '73 carbines that Tanner repaired," Jolie instructed.

"Tanner's not here?" Bailey asked.

"No, but he'll be back."

"Then can you do me a favor?"

"Perhaps," Jolie said.

"Can you take the money back to the store? It's all there except three dollars."

"You spent some?"

"I had to buy myself a new dress. I told you the other was ruined."

"Yes. I'll take it back. What will you do, Bailey?"

"Go somewhere."

Jolie continued to hold her hand. "Where?"

"I'll manage. Jolie, I don't want to go back to prison."

"How will you eat? Where will you stay?"

Bailey tossed the gun on the bed and retrieved a cigar box. "A woman like me can survive. Here are the funds."

"No woman can survive in your situation unless she gives up what she doesn't want to give up. Why don't you come home with me until we can figure something out?"

"You don't know what you're saying. I'm wanted for attempted murder and theft," Bailey protested.

Jolie stood shoulder to shoulder with the blonde. "What if I can talk Jeremiah out of filing charges against you?"

"Why would he do that?"

"I don't know. Let me try."

"I've got to go."

Jolie squeezed her hand. "Please stay with us."

Bailey clutched tight. "When I woke up and saw you hovering over the bed, I was sure I was goin' to shoot you."

"I'm glad you didn't."

"So am I. But I need to hide out for a while. There's a lot I need to ponder. I'll come back to the gun shop after you talk to the sheriff and Jeremiah Cain."

"You be sure and come back. I want to talk to you."

"I will."

"Don't let me down, Bailey Wagner."

She jammed the cigar box into Jolie's hand and slipped out the backdoor.

Lord, sometimes my life is like a dream, like I'm just watching it unfold. Things happen so fast I don't have time to find Your leading. But maybe You lead me anyway. I trust I'm doing this right.

With the cigar box under her arm, Jolie strolled back into the gun shop.

"Guess what, Jolie? Captain Richardson paid me with three cash dollars." Gibs held up the coins. "Put that with what the drovers bought, and I pulled in five dollars. What should I do with it?"

"Give three to me, and put the rest in Tanner's box with a note that I owe him three dollars."

"What're you goin' to buy?"

"A new dress."

"Really?"

"It's already been bought, sort of. Can you run the store by yourself? I need to talk to Mr. Saddler and Jeremiah Cain."

"Is Bailey Wagner still in the backroom with the Whitneyville .32-caliber brass-frame revolver?"

"No, she left. But the gun is on the bed."

"What did she want?"

"To return something that wasn't hers."

"I'll take care of the store, Jolie."

"If you want something to do, straighten up that shop bench. There are parts scattered everywhere."

"Oh, no, I can't do that. Tanner has the parts exactly where he wants 'em."

"Nonsense. It's a mess."

"Just 'cause it ain't tidy, Jolie, don't make it a mess," Gibs argued.

The sun had dropped so low that the muddy North Platte River had taken on a golden hue when Jolie returned to the gun shop. Tanner Wells paced in front of the case of lever-action rifles.

"Jolie, what's goin' on here?" he demanded.

"Did you find the sheriff?" she asked.

"No." Tanner unfastened the top button on his shirt. "I ran across a shingle camp, and they said the sheriff picked up Leppy Verdue's trail east and headed that way two hours before I got there. Jolie, I'm a gunsmith—not a tracker. I don't know which tracks is which. So I came back hopin' the sheriff would end up in town."

Jolie folded her hands. "I know exactly where the sheriff is going."

"Where?"

"To our homestead. Because that's where Leppy Verdue is."

"You sent me to Carter Canyon knowin' he was at your house?"

"I didn't know it then. Mama and Gibs came to town to tell me. I had no way of letting you know."

"What do we do now?"

"We've got to get back to the homestead."

"What about Bailey? Shouldn't one of us go after her?"

"Yes, I suppose so."

"I could ride up to Spottedhorse Creek now," Tanner offered.

"No," Jolie replied. "Gibs will fetch her."

"What?"

"Gibs, go tell Bailey she can come out now."

"I thought she left."

"She's in the backroom. Didn't you smell her perfume when she came in?"

"Is she coming home with us?"

"Yes."

"Why?"

"Because I invited her."

While Gibs scurried to the backroom, Jolie sidled up to Tanner. "Could you ride out with us to the homestead? You could spend the night at your folks'. I'm worried about the sheriff and Leppy going at it."

"I reckon. Let me fetch a scattergun and lock up the store."

"I'll drive the team over to the stairway beside the grocery store. Meet us there. I'll need you to help Jeremiah Cain into the wagon," Jolie instructed.

Tanner shook his head. "You're takin' him to your house, too?"

"Yes. We must hurry before there's a gunfight at our house."

"We won't be that fast. We ain't got Stranger and Pilgrim," Gibs reminded her.

Jolie watched as Bailey Wagner strolled up to them. "Gibson, we're all strangers and pilgrims."

Eleven

Jeremiah Cain lay on his stomach on blanket-covered hay in the back of the wagon next to Bailey Wagner. Gibs sat with his back against the sideboard, his .22 lying across his lap. Jolie held the lead lines while Tanner Wells tied his black horse to the back of the wagon and climbed up beside her.

"Are you goin' to let me drive?" he asked.

"No, I am not. I'm quite capable of driving this team."

"Jolie Bowers, I'm sure you're capable of doin' anything you and the Lord make up your mind to, but I would appreciate the opportunity of driving you home since it's something I've not yet experienced."

A wide grin broke across Jolie's face. "If you're going to be that sweet about it . . ." She handed him the reins.

Tanner slapped the lines, and the rig creaked out into the street. Jolie glanced over her shoulder. She could see Bailey and Jeremiah talking but didn't hear their words.

When they reached the eastern edge of Scottsbluff, Tanner leaned down toward her ear. She pinched her lips together and waited for a kiss.

There wasn't any.

"Now, Jolie Bowers, are you goin' to tell me what's goin' on?"

She let out a long, deep sigh. "Bailey returned all the money to Mr. Saddler. He was happy because he didn't even know how much he was missing. It's sort of a windfall."

"Of his own money."

"Yes, and Jeremiah said he would not have Bailey arrested if . . ."

Tanner glanced back at Bailey and Jeremiah and then leaned even closer. "If what?" he whispered.

The wagon hit a bump. Jolie's ear jostled against his lips.

"You did that on purpose," he laughed.

"I beg your pardon!"

"I wonder what will happen if we hit a bigger bump?"

I'll be more subtle—that's what. "Tanner, are you implying that I have to resort to trickery to secure your attention?"

"If what?" he said.

"What do you mean, 'If what?'"

"Finish your statement about Jeremiah." Tanner nodded to the back of the wagon. "He won't have her arrested if what?"

"Oh, that 'if what.'"

"Are there other 'if whats'?"

"You have so much to learn, Mr. Wells."

"And you're goin' to teach me?"

"I consider it one of my goals in life."

"It will take that long?" he laughed.

"Oh, yes. On that I'm quite confident. However, with the matter at hand, Jeremiah said if he had a place to recover, he would not have her arrested. Mr. Saddler wouldn't let him stay in that room above the grocery store. Besides, it was a dark place with stale air, much like a certain backroom in a gun shop."

"So you offered to take him in?"

"Until other arrangements could be made."

"And Bailey?"

"She needs a safe place until this whole legal matter gets solved. We still don't know what the sheriff and the judge will say."

"So you invited her, too?"

"Of course. She needs a friend."

"I was thinkin' the same thing."

She jabbed an elbow into his side. "No, you weren't."

He slipped his free hand into hers. "Jolie Bowers, is your life always this complicated?"

"Whatever do you mean? There's nothin' complicated about helping friends."

Tanner shook his head. "That's what I thought."

"It's all just temporary." She laced her fingers in his.

"That's what the generals in Washington said about the firing on Ft. Sumter."

"You're very dramatic, Tanner Wells."

"No, you're dramatic. I'm boring."

"Nonsense."

"No, I'm boring, and I like it that way. How long have you been in Nebraska, Jolie?"

"Twelve days and six hours."

"And you have succeeded in getting all of western Nebraska to spin around you."

"That's preposterous."

"Now I realize why you want to teach. A room with thirty boisterous kids will seem like a quiet respite to you—just a meditative vacation."

"I do look forward to it."

"I know you do."

"What do you look forward to, Tanner Wells?"

"Besides preventing bloodshed at the Bowers homestead this afternoon?"

"Oh, yes. I pray nothing has happened yet."

"I look forward to a time when Jolie Bowers and I can actually be alone."

"You mean with absolutely no one around?"

"No one for miles. Not a man, not a woman, not a sibling, not a barking dog—nothing," he said.

"How about grasshoppers?"

"No grasshoppers."

"Hah!" she laughed. "Now you *are* dreaming, Tanner Wells."

He leaned his shoulder into hers. "You want to dream with me?"

"Yes, I would." She laid her head on his shoulder and bounced along in rhythm to the jostling wagon. "If we were alone, what would you want to do, Tanner?" she whispered.

There was a long pause. "Smooch," he said.

"On the lips?"

"I ain't much for kissin' foreheads."

"Now, Tanner Wells, you have really given me something to dream about."

"I reckon you got my world spinnin' around you, too, Jolie Lorita Bowers."

"I'm impressed. You memorized my middle name."

"Jolie, I've memorized a whole lot more than your name. I memorized your dancin' gray-green eyes, your sunshine smile, the way you bounce when you . . ."

Jolie sat straight up but continued to clutch his arm. "You're going to make me blush."

"A little blush looks good with auburn hair."

"We ain't goin' that fast," Gibs hollered from behind them.

Jolie turned around. "What?"

"So fast that you need to hold on to Tanner's arm like that."

"We most certainly are!" She clutched Tanner's arm even tighter.

They pulled over at the DeMarco homestead. There was no one in sight, but Jolie could see Mr. Wells and the boys hoeing in the corn-field. A grasshopper lit on her skirt, and she brushed it off.

"Bullet, tell Mama I'll be comin' home after a while. I'll spend the night out here," Tanner called out.

Jolie looked around and saw no one in the yard. "Where is he?"

"In the trough."

"It's full of water."

"See that reed? He's hiding under the water and breathing through the reed."

"Can he hear you?"

A soaking-wet, shirtless Bullet Wells raised his head and shoulders out of the water. "I heard you," he hollered.

Tanner slapped the lead lines. They drove on down Telegraph Road.

"That's one way to wash your duckings," Jolie remarked.

"I don't reckon he was wearin' trousers," Tanner replied.

"Oh!" She blushed. "Bullet is quite a free spirit, isn't he?"

"That's about the nicest thing anyone ever called him. He hasn't been bothering you or Essie again, has he?"

The wagon hit a pothole. Tanner's arm slipped around her waist to steady her. "Not that I know of," she murmured.

When they made the turn south toward the river, the road turned into two ruts.

"Stop a minute," Jolie said.

Tanner reined up.

Jolie turned to the back of the wagon. "Jeremiah, do you feel strong enough to peek over the sideboard?"

Bailey helped prop him up on his elbow. "I reckon. Why?"

"Do you see this piece of ground?" Jolie asked.

"Ain't nothing but yucca and sage," he mumbled.

"And some old plowed ground," Bailey added.

"I heard Daddy say it's an abandoned claim. It will become available on January 2."

Jeremiah continued to survey the land. "Why are you telling me this?"

"An ambitious person could camp out in front of the land office on January 1, and when they open the door the next day, he could file on this place."

He slumped back down. "Me—a homesteader?"

"Why not?" Jolie replied. "You said us homesteaders were your kind."

"It would take a lot of work," he protested.

Jolie looked him in the eyes. "You're a hard worker."

"It don't have no house, does it?"

"I heard you can build a sod house for $12," Tanner told him.

Jeremiah shook his head. "I ain't got no sod plow."

"We have one at our place," Gibs said. "Lawson said it looked kind of dull."

"I can sharpen it," Tanner offered.

"I ain't got $12 or even a filin' fee."

"It's not January," Jolie said. "Once you heal up, perhaps there will be some harvest work."

"I think it's a nice location," Bailey observed.

Jeremiah raised back up and spied out the land. "How come?"

Bailey pulled off her straw hat and fanned herself. "Because you can see both Chimney Rock and Scott's Bluff from here." She plucked a grasshopper off Jeremiah's blanket and dropped it over the back of the wagon.

Jeremiah slouched back down, his head on her lap. "I ain't feelin' like plowin' right at the moment."

"Will you ponder on it?" Jolie challenged.

"Yes, we will," Bailey blurted out. Then she put her hand over her mouth. "I mean, you will ponder it, won't you?"

Jeremiah craned his neck to peer at Bailey. "I reckon I will."

When they pulled into the Bowerses' yard, the sinking sun cast long shadows. Two rapid gunshots rang out. Tanner stopped the wagon near the door of the sod house.

Gibs stood up in the back of the wagon and pumped his .22. "What's goin' on?"

Essie ran out of the house with Lawson behind her.

"You have to stop it, Jolie. The sheriff's over at the barn and is trying to kill Leppy," Essie shouted.

"They're both shootin'," Lawson added. "Leppy's in the barn. The sheriff's behind the woodpile."

Jolie stood and steadied herself by holding on to Tanner's shoulder. "Did you tell the sheriff that Leppy didn't shoot Jeremiah?"

"The sheriff said he wanted to take Leppy in anyway just to check out the story," Lawson reported.

Jolie glanced around the yard. "Where's Mama and Daddy?"

"The Vockerys' bull is bogged down in the river. They took Stranger and Pilgrim over to pull him out."

"And you didn't go with them?" Jolie asked Lawson.

"Leppy was here by then but not the sheriff. They made me stay with little sis. They said I had to chaperon her. Don't that beat all?"

"He didn't have to stay," Essie declared.

Another gunshot exploded.

"You have to stop them," Essie pleaded.

Jolie glanced at the back of the wagon. "Gibs, you get down and stay here."

"Where're you going?" he asked.

"To stop the shooting, of course." She sat down next to Tanner.

"But I ain't afraid. I've got my gun."

"Gibs, I know you aren't afraid, but which side are you on? Will you shoot at Leppy or at the sheriff?"

He climbed down out of the wagon. "Which side are you on, Jolie?"

"Both . . . and neither." Another gunshot caused her to stare at the gun smoke wafting from the barn.

"What about us?" Bailey called out.

"Hide down in the wagon for a minute," Jolie commanded. "Tanner, give me the lead lines."

"Do you know what you're doin'?" he asked.

She grabbed the lines from his hand. "Since when is that a prerequisite for my actions?"

"What's my role? Shall I grab the scattergun?"

"To be another witness. Leave the gun under the seat." She glanced back. "Are you two ready?"

Bailey Wagner lay down beside Jeremiah. "I reckon."

Jolie sat up. "Tanner, are you any good at stopping bullets from hitting me?"

"I can stop one. After that I'm not sure."

"I was joking," she said.

"I wasn't," he said.

Jolie slapped the lead lines and drove the team between the woodpile and the small barn.

"What in blazes are you doin'?" the sheriff shouted.

"Preventing you from getting hurt," Jolie answered.

The sheriff scooted to the end of the woodpile. "Don't let him get away."

"Where's he going to go?" Jolie hollered. "Sheriff, Leppy didn't shoot Jeremiah Cain."

"But how do I know that for sure?"

Jeremiah poked his head above the wagon bed. "'Cause I'm telling you he didn't. I lied to save my own hide, Sheriff."

"Cain? Well, I'll be!" The sheriff stood and shuffled closer to the wagon. "Who did shoot you?"

Bailey sat up. "I did."

"Miss Wagner?" the sheriff mumbled. "Is that true, Cain?"

"Yes, it is."

"I need to arrest Verdue anyway because he stole the money."

"No, he didn't," Bailey replied. "I stole the money."

The sheriff stepped to the back of the wagon. "Do you have the money on you?"

"No, I returned it to Mr. Saddler," Jolie declared.

"Wait a minute," the sheriff said. "If Leppy Verdue didn't steal the funds, where did he get the money he has on him?"

Jolie faced the barn. "I believe it came from a cattle sale."

"Is that right, Leppy?" the sheriff shouted.

Leppy Verdue stepped to the barn door but kept his revolver in his hand. "That's what I've been trying to tell you."

"Then I ought to arrest Miss Wagner," Sheriff Riley said.

"I ain't pressing charges," Cain declared.

"She shot you in the back, left you for dead, and you ain't pressin' charges?" the sheriff bellowed.

"No, because I helped steal the money," Jeremiah admitted.

The sheriff pulled off his felt hat and ran his fingers through his gray hair. "Then I'll arrest you both."

"But it's all been given back to Mr. Saddler," Jolie reminded him.

"And I suppose he don't want to press charges?" the sheriff mumbled.

"He's considering what to do," Jolie answered.

The sheriff holstered his gun and waved his hands. "This is a mess. I don't even know who to arrest."

Jolie patted the sheriff's shoulder. "I'd suggest you go back to town and talk to Mr. Saddler. Jeremiah and Bailey are staying with us until it's settled."

"What about Verdue?" the sheriff asked. "I hear he's wanted down in Colorado."

Jolie glanced at the cowboy by the barn. "He can stay here, too."

Lawson, Gibs, and Essie trotted up to the wagon.

"This is crazy," the sheriff said.

"This is ordinary for Jolie Lorita Bowers," Tanner replied.

The sheriff pointed to the two in the back of the wagon. "But you hardly know them. You're taking in complete strangers."

"Sheriff Riley," Jolie said, "just because we're all pilgrims and strangers doesn't mean we have to remain such."

"What're your parents goin' to say?" the sheriff asked.

"Jolie's in charge of the house," Lawson told him.

"Is Leppy really going to stay with us?" Essie giggled.

Jolie turned on her sister. "Yes, and you're going to be tied to my apron."

The sheriff jammed on his hat. "I rode up here figurin' someone was goin' to die today and trustin' the Lord it wouldn't be me. Now it seems like a picnic." He turned to Leppy. "Verdue, you give me your word that you're goin' to stay out here until I clear you?"

Leppy holstered his gun and strolled up to the sheriff. "You got my word, Sheriff." He held out his hand.

Sheriff Riley paused. "I don't shake hands with someone who was just tryin' to kill me."

"I wasn't tryin' to kill you."

"You were shootin' at me. What do you call that?"

"Tryin' to keep myself from bein' shot," Leppy replied.

"I'm riding out of here, Verdue, but I'll be back as soon as I gab with the judge."

"I'll be here."

The sheriff reached out and shook Leppy Verdue's hand. "This is crazy. This whole family is crazy. Homesteaders ain't got common sense."

The sheriff mounted his horse and rode north along the rutted trail.

"You did it, Jolie. You stopped a gunfight," Gibs hollered. "Did you see that, Tanner? Jolie stopped 'em cold."

"I saw it."

Jolie glanced around. "That was the easy part."

"What's the hard part?" Essie asked.

"Finding space in a two-room house for three houseguests."

"One of whom is crippled up," Jeremiah Cain added.

"How're you goin' to find room for us?" Bailey asked.

Jolie climbed off the wagon. "Lawson, you put up the horses. Gibs, take Leppy and Tanner to the woodpile and find a few more of those railroad ties. Drag them and the crosscut saw around to the front yard. We'll need more furniture. Bailey, you stay with Jeremiah and keep the grasshoppers off him. They seem to be thicker this evening. We'll get him inside as soon as we have a place for him. Essie, you come with me. We need to get started on a big supper. There are potatoes, carrots, and turnips to chop." Jolie stared at the setting sun on the western horizon. "I don't suppose I have time to make a pie."

After dark seven people were huddled in the front room/bedroom/kitchen/dining room when Stranger and Pilgrim thundered into the yard.

"It's Mama and Daddy!" Essie called out.

Lawson grabbed the smaller lantern and fought his way through the mosquito netting at the door. "I'll put up the team."

"My, the house looks different," Lissa greeted them.

Matthew crowded in behind her. "We're only gone a couple hours, and you open up a cafe?"

"Daddy, I'm just practicing Christian hospitality," Jolie explained.

"Darlin', you're very good at it. Jolie's friends are always welcome for supper," Mr. Bowers said.

Lissa pulled off her hat and scooted toward the stove. "It looks like we have more furniture."

"They aren't just staying for supper. Jolie invited them to move in," Essie announced.

Jolie turned to her mother and father. "This is Bailey Wagner. I think you know Leppy Verdue. And Jeremiah Cain took a bullet in the back. So he's in that new bunk. Would you like an explanation?"

"No," Matthew Bowers said. "What I'd like is supper."

"No?" Bailey replied. "You have three houseguests, and you don't even want to know why?"

Matthew slipped his arm around Jolie's shoulder. "I trust my daughter's judgment."

"I ain't never heard of folks like you," Jeremiah marveled.

"Well," Lissa explained, "we talked with Tanner Wells out on Telegraph Road. He told us the entire story."

"About me shootin' Jeremiah and ever'thing?" Bailey asked.

"That much we know," Matthew Bowers acknowledged. "But I really do trust my daughter. You're all welcome."

Lissa studied the gravy in the big pot on the stove. "Are those potatoes or turnips?"

"Both," Jolie replied. "Plus some carrots and pork."

"I presume these are for Daddy and me."

Leppy jumped up from the bench. "I'm all through, Mrs. Bowers. Take my place."

Jolie dished up a plate for her mother.

"I can stand," Mrs. Bowers replied.

"Not in your own house, ma'am." Leppy grinned. "Besides, little sis said she had a book to read me. We'll sit over here by the lantern."

"What're you going to read to Mr. Verdue?" Lissa asked.

"The Bible," Essie replied.

"That'll take you ten years," Gibs hooted.

"I know." Essie smiled.

Matthew sat down at the table next to his wife. Jolie handed him a plate full of white-sauce stew and a piece of bread. "You know, I don't remember two sets of bunk beds in the living room."

Jolie grabbed the coffeepot. "Daddy, let me warm your coffee. Tanner and Leppy built us some bunks, and we've turned this into the boys' room for now."

"Yes, and handy, too. I imagine you can stand on the table and crawl right into that bunk."

"I know it's kind of crowded," Jolie acknowledged. "I believe we should cut sod and build on a lean-to room. What do you think, Daddy?"

He loosened his tie and dipped the bread in the white gravy. "I reckon we'll wait until mornin'."

Mrs. Bowers broke off a tiny piece of bread and nibbled on it. "I presume your father and I still have a place to sleep?"

"Your bed is in the back where the boys' bunks were," Jolie explained.

"That makes it a bit snug in the backroom."

"There isn't much floor to sweep," Jolie said.

"Bailey is going to sleep with me and Jolie," Essie called out from the corner. "They said I could sleep in the middle."

"Well, lucky you." Mrs. Bowers stared across the room. "How are you, Mr. Cain? I'm surprised you could travel this far."

Jeremiah propped up his head. "I reckon I don't feel any worse than in town, and out here I have plenty of folks lookin' in on me."

"Some of whom seem to be lookin' more than others," Gibs added.

Bailey blushed. "I do feel quite guilty about shooting Jeremiah."

"I imagine you do," Mrs. Bowers said.

"I was really mad at him at the time."

"I'll remember that." Matthew Bowers smiled and held up his coffee cup.

Lawson wandered back into the living room. "I got the horses put up, Mama. It smells like sulfur out there. Do you reckon it will rain?"

Mrs. Bowers stood. "Maybe we should put the rubber tarps on the roof just in case."

Mr. Bowers tugged her back down. "Not until after we eat."

Matthew had just finished the second cup of coffee when a rig pulled into the darkened front yard. "Ho, in the house!"

Mr. Bowers stepped out on the porch. Jolie, Lawson, Gibs, and Essie stood in the doorway.

"Yes, sir, what can I do for you?" Mr. Bowers called out.

"Sorry to bother you, friend, but we just got here from Kansas and are looking for our place," a man implored. "I think we got turned around in the dark."

"The children are quite weary, and it's about to rain," a woman explained. "We have a cabin on our homestead if we could only find it."

"What place are you lookin' for?" Mr. Bowers asked.

"The Avery place," the man declared. "Have you heard of it?"

Jolie grabbed Essie's shoulder. "Get the other sack of potatoes. Lawson, I'll need an armful of firewood for the cookstove. Gibs, you clean off the table. Bailey, I'll need you to wash these dishes while I cook. Leppy, you grind some coffee beans. Daddy, go out and invite them in for supper."

A smile flooded Lissa's face. "I'll go put away their horses. Jolie

Lorita, do you think we have room for all of them to sleep in the house?"

"We can put some on the floor on pallets, and one or two can sleep on the table, plus if we push the benches together, another can go there."

Bailey gathered up the dishes. "How can you do this for strangers?"

"How can we not?" Jolie replied. "After all, we were all strangers once."

"That condition," Leppy Verdue remarked, "only lasts until ten minutes after you meet Jolie Bowers. After that you're part of the family."

Essie poked Leppy in the ribs. "There are other ways to become part of this family."

Leppy handed her the Bible. "Tell me that again when we finish the book of Revelation." Leppy grinned.

For a list of other books

by this author

write:

Stephen Bly

Winchester, Idaho 83555

or check out his website:

www.blybooks.com